# "Brand of the Werewolf"
# and
# "Fear Cay"

# DOC SAVAGE

REG. U S PAT. OFF.

## by Lester Dent
## writing as Kenneth Robeson

### with new historical essays
### by Will Murray

Published by Sanctum Productions for
## NOSTALGIA VENTURES, INC.
P.O. Box 231183; Encinitas, CA 92023-1183

This Nostalgia Ventures edition is an unabridged republication of the text and illustrations of two stories from *Doc Savage Magazine,* as originally published by Street & Smith Publications, Inc., N.Y.: *Brand of the Werewolf* from the January 1934 issue, and *Fear Cay* from the September 1934 issue. This is a work of its time. Consequently, the text is reprinted intact in its original historical form, including occasional out-of-date ethnic and cultural stereotyping. Typographical errors have been tacitly corrected in this edition.

ISBN: 1-932806-86-5    13 Digit: 978-1-932806-86-1

First printing: January 2008

Series editor: Anthony Tollin
P.O. Box 761474
San Antonio, TX 78245-1474
sanctumotr@earthlink.net

Consulting editor: Will Murray

Copy editor: Joseph Wrzos

Proofreader: Carl Gafford

Cover restoration: Michael Piper

The editors gratefully acknowledge the contributions of Bob Chapman of Graphitti Designs, Tom Stephens and Tom Roberts in the preparation of this volume, and William T. Stolz of the Western Historical Manuscript Collection of the University of Missouri at Columbia for research assistance with the Lester Dent Collection.

Nostalgia Ventures, Inc.
P.O. Box 231183; Encinitas, CA 92023-1183

Visit Doc Savage at www.nostalgiatown.com and www.shadowsanctum.com

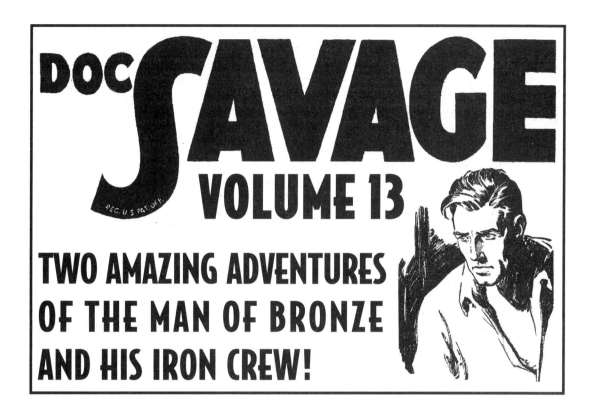

# DOC SAVAGE VOLUME 13

REG. U S PAT. OFF.

## TWO AMAZING ADVENTURES OF THE MAN OF BRONZE AND HIS IRON CREW!

### *Thrilling Tales and Features*

**Cover paintings by Walter M. Baumhofer
Interior illustrations by Paul Orban**

*In the weird surroundings of the North, Doc Savage and his scrappy pals face the crew of skeletons and the*

# Brand of the Werewolf

## Complete Book-length Novel by

## KENNETH ROBESON

### Chapter I
### THE STRANGE MESSAGE

IT was a little way station on the transcontinental railroad in western Canada. Only one man worked there. He had what railroaders call an "OS" job. About all he had to do was "OS" trains—telegraph the dispatcher that they were passing his point.

Usually, nothing much ever happened around there.

Just now, however, the telegrapher looked as if things were happening—big things. His manner was as excited as that of a small boy about to see the circus.

The thing which had flustered him was a telegram that he had just copied. It was addressed to a passenger on the fast express train which was due to arrive soon.

The operator interrupted his routine work frequently to stare at the name of the individual to whom the message was going. He scratched his head.

"If that man is the fellow I think he is—" He finished his remark with a low whistle of amazement.

Some minutes later, the brass pounder gave a start as if he had just thought of something. He got up hastily and went to a row of shelves in the rear of the room. These held magazines. Due to the loneliness of his post, the operator was a heavy reader.

He picked out and thumbed through several magazines which made a practice of publishing stories of famous men. The cover design of one of these consisted of a large bronze-colored question mark. Printed across this were the words:

THE MAN OF MYSTERY
(Story on page 9)

The telegrapher opened the magazine to page nine. The story was what writers call a "fact article." Every word was supposed to be the truth. More large black type asked:

WHO IS PROBABLY THE MOST AMAZING
OF LIVING MEN?

The telegraph operator had read this story before. But now he started to peruse it again. He was interrupted.

A train whistled in the distance, and soon its approaching roar was soon audible.

It was the fast passenger. Smoke and steam rolling, air brakes shrieking, the engine and string of coaches came to a halt. A regular stop for water was made here.

Wilkie came in. Wilkie was the conductor. He had a large head, and an extraordinarily prominent stomach. He looked like a pleasant little goblin in a uniform.

"Hyah, brass mauler!" he greeted cheerfully.

With a dramatic gesture, the operator passed over the telegram.

"Message for one of the passengers, eh?" said Wilkie, and started to stuff the missive in a pocket

"Wait a minute!" ejaculated the telegrapher. "Look who that's for!"

Wilkie eyed the name on the telegram.

"For the love of Mike!" he exclaimed.

"I KNEW you'd heard of him," the operator said triumphantly.

Wilkie absently removed the uniform cap from his enormous head. "Do you reckon this is the same man?"

"I'm betting it is," said the telegrapher. "He's taking a vacation—him and the five men who help him. He has a relative up in the woods along the coast. He's paying a visit there."

"How do you know that?" Wilkie demanded.

The operator grinned. "It's kinda lonesome here, and I kill time by listening to the messages that go back and forth over the wires. I heard the message he sent, saying he was coming with his five friends."

Wilkie hesitated, then read the message. As an employee of the company, he probably had a right to do this.

"Whew!" he exclaimed. "If that chap was a relative of mine, I wouldn't send him a telegram like this!"

"Me either!" the operator replied. He secured the magazine which he had started to read. "Say, did you see the article in here about that fellow?"

Wilkie glanced at the magazine. "Nope. I'd like to read it, too."

"Take it." The operator passed the magazine over. "It's sure worth reading. It tells some of the things he and his five men have done. I tell you, Wilkie, a lot of the things are hard to believe. This fellow must be a superman!"

"Them writers sometimes exaggerate," Wilkie said.

"Not in this magazine," the telegrapher assured him. "It's got a reputation of sticking close to the truth."

The engine whistle moaned out. Echoes came slamming back from the timbered hills.

"That's the ol' highball!" Wilkie wheeled. "Thanks for the magazine. Be seeing you, brass pounder."

The train was moving. With a smoothness that came of long practice, Wilkie swung aboard. He headed for the cars which held drawing-rooms. He walked the swaying aisles with the proficiency of a sailor on a rolling deck of a storm-tossed ship.

Opening the magazine at page nine, he stared at the article. The first paragraph gripped him. Absorbed in his reading, he nearly fell over a suitcase which some traveler had left protruding into the aisle.

"What a man!" Wilkie ejaculated.

The traveler who owned the suitcase, mistakenly thinking the remark was directed at himself, looked indignant.

Wilkie reached the drawing-rooms, and found the porter. "I'm hunting for this man," he said, and showed the name on the telegram.

"Yassah!" gulped the porter. "Golly me! Dat's de stranges'-lookin' man Ah evah saw!"

"What's strange about him?"

"Man, he am de bigges' fella yo' evah laid yo' eyes on!" The porter gazed ecstatically ceiling-ward. "When he looks at yo', yo' jus' kinda turns inside out. Ah seed him with his shirt off, takin' some kinda exercises. Ah nevah seed such muscles befo'. Dey was like big ropes tied around him."

Wilkie nodded. He had come on duty at the last division point, and had not seen all the passengers. "In the observation car, eh? And I'll know him when I see him?"

"Yo' cain't miss him! He's a great big bronze man!"

Wilkie headed for the observation car.

BACK in the tiny way station, the telegraph sounder was clicking noisily. The operator sat down at his typewriter to receive.

He copied the incoming message number, the office of origin, and the address. The missive was destined for a passenger on another train.

The telegrapher reached over to his key and "broke."

"Wrong number," he transmitted.

Telegrams were numbered in consecutive order. This was to prevent a telegrapher sending one "into the air"—transmitting a message which was not received at the other end.

"It's the right number," the man at the distant key tapped.

"You're shy a number," explained the station wireman. "You sent me a message half an hour ago."

"The last message we sent you was four hours ago," rattled the sounder.

The telegrapher shook his head in bewilderment. Getting out his carbon copy of the message which he had given to Wilkie, he "traced" it to the distant man—outlining its contents.

"We sent no such message," he was informed.

"I received it," the station operator clicked back. "There's something strange about this. Do you think the wires were tapped?"

"Search me."

The telegrapher sat and pondered. He reached a decision. Grasping the key, he transmitted: "I'm going to wire ahead to the next station, and let Wilkie know what happened."

"Why go to all that trouble?" the distant operator demanded.

"Because both Wilkie and I thought the contents of that message were strange. We both remarked that it was an unusual communication for this man to receive."

"What do you know about the business of the man the message was going to?"

"I've read of the fellow," tapped the station operator. "I'll tell you about him later. He's worth hearing about. But I'm going to wire Wilkie now."

He began to maul out the call letters of a station at which Wilkie's train would soon arrive.

The station door opened furtively behind him. It made no noise. Two men crept in. They were clad in grease spattered coveralls. Both had handkerchiefs tied over their faces, and both carried revolvers.

The telegrapher, absorbed in calling, did not hear them. It was doubtful if he ever knew of their presence.

One of the marauders jammed his revolver to the operator's temple, and pulled the trigger. The report of the shot was deafening.

The operator tumbled from his chair. He had died instantly.

Reaching over, the murderer grasped the telegraph key.

"Never mind that stuff about another message," he transmitted. "I was mistaken."

"That lonesome place must be driving you nuts," chided the distant telegrapher, thinking he was still talking to the station man.

The killer gave an ugly laugh. He grabbed the key again.

"Nuts, nuts! Ha, ha, ha!" he transmitted erratically. "King George couldn't be crazy. Ha, ha! I'm King George—"

For several minutes he sent crazily, in the manner of a demented man. Then he carefully wiped the fingerprints off the murder revolver and placed it in the fingers of the lifeless station telegrapher.

"That fixes it up," he told his companion. "They'll think he went mad and committed suicide. Nobody can trace my gun. The numbers are filed off."

"I don't like this!" gulped the fellow's companion.

"We hadda keep 'em from findin' out we tapped the wire and sent that message, didn't we? C'mon! Let's blow!"

The pair departed. Some time later, a somber black monoplane lifted them from a level bit of grassland which lay about three miles from the tiny station.

The plane moaned off in the eye of the evening sun. It was following the railroad westward, as if in pursuit of the passenger train.

WILKIE, the conductor, stood stock-still in the observation car and stared. The colored porter's words, and what he had read of the article in the magazine, had prepared him to a degree for what he was seeing. Yet the personage before him was even more remarkable than he had expected.

Had Wilkie not known better, he would have sworn the individual was a statue sculptured from solid bronze. The effect of the metallic figure was amazing.

The man's unusually high forehead, the muscular and strong mouth, the lean and corded cheeks, denoted a rare power of character. The bronze hair was a shade darker than the bronze skin. It lay straight and smooth.

Only by comparing the bronze man's size to that of the observation car chair in which he sat, were his gigantic proportions evident. The bulk of his great frame was lost in its perfect symmetry. No part of the man seemed overdeveloped.

Wilkie snapped himself out of his trance and advanced.

"Doc Savage?" he asked.

The bronze man glanced up.

Wilkie suddenly realized the most striking thing about the fellow was his eyes. They were like pools of flake gold glistening in the afternoon sunlight that reflected through the train windows. Their gaze possessed an almost hypnotic quality, a strange ability to literally convey the owner's desires with their glance.

Undeniably, here was an amazing man.

"Doc Savage," he said. "That is right."

The man's voice impressed Wilkie as being very much in keeping with his appearance. It was vibrant with controlled power.

"A wire came for you at the last station," said Wilkie, and handed over the message. It was the first time in years that Wilkie had been awed in the presence of anybody.

"Thank you," said Doc Savage.

Wilkie found himself retreating, although he had intended to hang around and strike up a conversation with this remarkable man. The tone of those two words had impelled him to depart. At the same time, he found himself feeling very friendly toward the metallic giant.

It was eerie, the things the bronze man's voice could do.

Wilkie was almost out of the observation car when another weird thing happened. An uncanny sound reached his ears.

He came to an abrupt stop. His face was blank. Absently, he felt of his ears. The sound was so curious that he half suspected it might be a product of his imagination. The note seemed to be coming from no particular spot, but from everywhere.

It was low, mellow, and trilling, that sound—like the song of some strange feathered denizen of the jungle, or the sound of a wind crawling through a leafless wilderness. It ran up and down the musical scale, having no tune, yet melodious. Then it ended.

Wilkie did not feel awed by the sound. Rather, there was something inspiring about it.

As he went on, Wilkie felt as if he had just taken a drink of fine old liquor. The trilling sound had that kind of an effect.

## Chapter II
## THE TRAIN WEREWOLF

THE sound Wilkie had heard was part of Doc Savage. It was a small, unconscious thing which he did in moments of intense concentration, or when he was surprised. Often when Doc made the sound, he was unaware of doing so.

Reading the text of the telegram had caused the tiny, weird note to come into being.

Leaving his chair, Doc strode for the observation platform on the rear of the coach.

There were other passengers. These were amazed by the bronze man's appearance—so much so that they forgot their manners and frankly stared.

A stout, elderly man with a slightly swarthy face gazed at the bronze giant's hands. Enormous, supple tendons showed those hands contained incredible strength. The hands seemed to mesmerize the swarthy man.

A ravishingly pretty dark-haired girl sat beside the elderly man. Her eyes were large and limpid, and her lips a most inviting rosebud. She looked very fresh and crisp, so impeccable, in fact, that it was obvious she had not been on the train long. Even the neatest of individuals soon show the effects of traveling.

These two were clearly father and daughter.

The attractive young woman seemed intrigued, not by the bronze man's undeniable physical strength, but by the fact that he was one of the handsomest fellows she had ever seen.

Doc Savage went on, seeming not to notice the pair.

Frowning, the elderly man dropped a hand on his daughter's arm.

"*Quita alla!*" he ejaculated severely in Spanish. "For shame! You were smiling at that man, Cere."

The enchanting Cere colored in confusion. She had smiled, although she had not meant to.

"*Eso es espantoso!*" she laughed. "It is dreadful! Thank goodness, he did not see me. He would have thought me very forward."

"*Si, si,*" her parent agreed disapprovingly.

Father and daughter were staring after the receding bronze man when a low voice sounded at their side.

A man had joined them silently. This individual was tall and slenderly athletic. His face was more than handsome. It was pretty. It was almost a girl's face. His age was somewhere around thirty-five. He had hard eyes.

"I trust you are retaining your courage, señorita," he said fawningly. He bowed to her father. "You also, Señor Corto Oveja."

"You need have no fear of our nerve, El Rabanos," said Cere in excellent English. "Instead of discussing our troubles, we were remarking on the striking qualities of the bronze man who just passed. Do you happen to know his name?"

The girl-faced El Rabanos leaned close to breathe: "Not so loud, Señorita!"

A close observer could have noted that the pretty Señorita had suddenly begun turning pale. "You mean—"

"The bronze man is Doc Savage," said El Rabanos.

Señor Corto Oveja came up rigid in his chair. "So that is the man—the fiend who is to kill us! *Dios mio!*"

"*Si, si!*" muttered El Rabanos. "We must watch this Doc Savage. From him, our very lives are in danger."

"And his appearance made such a good impression," Cere murmured forlornly.

DOC SAVAGE, unaware of the bombshell his passage had exploded, stepped out on the observation platform.

One man rode there. The outstanding thing about this fellow was his gigantic hands. Each of these was composed of more than a quart of bone and gristle, sheathed in hide that resembled rusted sheet iron. The man was very big—over six feet, and weighing fully two hundred and fifty pounds—but the size of his hands made the rest of him seem dwarfed.

He had a long, Puritanical face, which bore an expression of great gloom. He looked like a man on his way to a funeral.

"Have a look, Renny," said Doc Savage, and extended the telegram.

The big-fisted man was Colonel John Renwick, known in many parts of the globe for his accomplishments as an engineer. Also, he was noted for a playful habit of knocking panels out of doors with his incredible fists. With either fist, he boasted, he could vanquish the stoutest wooden door.

Renny's funeral-going expression was the one he habitually wore when at peace with the world.

Renny was one of a group of five singular men who were Doc Savage's helpers.

The telegram was addressed to Doc Savage, care of the train, and read:

JUST RECEIVED YOUR WIRE ADVISING YOU ARE PAYING ME A VISIT STOP WISH TO INFORM YOU I HAVE NO USE FOR REST OF SAVAGE FAMILY STOP DO NOT WISH YOUR COMPANY STOP WOULD BE DELIGHTED TO HAVE YOU STAY AWAY
                                    ALEX SAVAGE

Renny had a pet expression which he used on all occasions calling for vehemence. He employed it now.

"Holy cow!" he exploded.

"Those are something near my own sentiments," Doc Savage agreed.

"Dang it!" Renny's voice was something like the roaring of an angry animal in a cave. "What if he don't want our company? The crowd of us weren't going to drop in and sponge off him! We were going to do some fishing and hunting, and merely pay him a visit as a courtesy. If he don't want us, we won't bother him. But I'll be blasted if that will keep us from our vacation!"

"Alex Savage owns a large stretch of land along the coast," Doc pointed out. "It has the reputation of being the best spot in Canada for hunting and fishing."

Renny groaned thunderously. "A fine gesture of welcome! Say, Doc, don't this Alex Savage know you?"

"Not personally," Doc replied. "He is an uncle. I have never met either him or his daughter."

"Daughter?"

"An only child, I understand. Her name is Patricia. Age about eighteen."

Renny tapped his huge fists together. This made a sound remindful of two flint boulders colliding with each other.

"If your uncle and cousin don't want us, Doc, I reckon we'll go somewhere else," he said gloomily. "Where's the map? I'll try to find another place where there's good fishing."

"Better postpone that, Renny," Doc said dryly.

"Huh?"

"There's something very suspicious about this message," Doc Savage informed him.

PUZZLED and wondering, big-fisted Renny followed his giant bronze chief back through the observation car. Renny's relation to Doc Savage was unusual. He willingly carried out Doc's smallest order. Yet Renny received not one penny of salary.

Renny, in fact, was considerably more than a millionaire in his own right. His skill as an engineer had made into a fortune. He had, in a sense, retired—retired to follow the trail of what he liked above all else, adventure. Peril and excitement were the spice of his life.

Peril, excitement, and adventure were the bonds which cemented him to Doc Savage. Doc seemed always to walk amid these things. Each minute of his life was one of danger.

For Doc Savage had a strange purpose in life, a creed to which his existence was dedicated. That creed was to go here and there, to the far corners of the earth, helping those in need of help, punishing those who needed punishment.

Doc had been trained for this purpose from the cradle.

The other four aides of the bronze man, like Renny, were bound to him by a love of adventure. And, like Renny, they were masters of some profession.

One was an electrical wizard, one a world-renowned chemist, another a great geologist and archaeologist, and the fourth, one of the most astute lawyers Harvard had ever turned out.

Trouble-busting was the life purpose of Doc and his five aides. Their exploits had pushed their fame to the ends of the earth. Doc, mighty man of bronze, was by way of becoming a legend—a specter of terror where evildoers were concerned.

Doc Savage entered his drawing-room, Renny at his heels. The room was stacked with bags and many metal boxes equipped with carrying straps.

Doc opened one of the boxes. A compact radio transmitter and receiver came to light. Corded fingers moving with deftness, Doc manipulated the controls. The set was fitted with a "bug"—a mechanical key for rapid transmission.

"What station are you callin', Doc?" Renny queried.

"There is a Royal Canadian Mounted Police station in the railroad town nearest Alex Savage's home," Doc explained. "I'm trying to raise them."

Renny heard this without batting an eye. That Doc should know there was a Mounted station at the town, and have the call letters at his fingertips, did not impress Renny as anything out of the ordinary. Doc Savage had a fabulous fund of information of all kinds.

Doc contacted the Mounted station, and made known his identity.

"At your service, Mr. Savage," was the reply to this.

Renny heard this come from the earphones. He was not surprised. This was not the only great police system which cooperated fully with Doc Savage.

"I received a telegram which pretends to have been sent from your town by Alex Savage," Doc transmitted. "Will you check up and see if it was sent, please?"

There followed fully five minutes of silence, while the distant Mounted operator made inquiries.

"No such message was sent from here," came back the report.

Doc wirelessed his thanks, then replaced the radio set in its case.

"You've got one guess about that telegram," he told Renny.

"It was a fake!" Renny thumped. "But, Doc, what in blazes made you suspicious?"

"The message was addressed care of this train," Doc explained. "Our earlier message to Alex Savage said nothing about what train we would be on."

DOC Savage, Renny lumbering at his side, now sought out Wilkie, the conductor.

Wilkie was absorbed in the magazine which held the feature story about Doc Savage.

"How soon will we reach a point from which I can send a telegram?" Doc inquired.

Wilkie swallowed twice before he could answer. What he had been reading had tended to increase his awe of this bronze man.

"We pass a little station in a few minutes," he replied. "We don't stop, but I can clip it to an order hoop, and get it to the telegrapher as we go past."

"Good!"

Doc proceeded to write out a message. It was addressed to Alex Savage:

SOMETHING STRANGE GOING ON STOP DID YOU GET MY TELEGRAM ADVISING THAT MYSELF AND FIVE FRIENDS PLANNING SPEND FISHING AND HUNTING VACATION YOUR VICINITY STOP DID YOU WIRE US NOT TO COME STOP PLEASE ADVISE IMMEDIATELY
    DOC SAVAGE

Folding this, Doc gave it to the conductor.

"I don't know what it will cost," Wilkie said.

"This should more than cover it." Doc passed over a large Canadian five dollar bill. "Keep the change for your trouble."

"I couldn't do that," Wilkie said hastily. "I'll deadhead the message for you, Mr. Savage. It won't cost a thing."

Wilkie was outdoing himself to please the bronze man.

Doc seemed faintly puzzled for a moment. Then he caught sight of the magazine article which Wilkie had been reading. His inscrutable, metallic features did not change, but after a moment he indicated the periodical.

"The chap who wrote that had a lot of imagination," he said dryly.

Doc and Renny turned away from the admiring conductor. They almost bumped into two swarthy men and a beautiful, dark-haired girl. These were Señor Corto Oveja, his daughter Cere, and the girl-faced El Rabanos.

The three looked steadily away from Doc and Renny. They had been standing there eavesdropping as Doc gave Wilkie his message. But they did not want the bronze giant to know that.

Doc and Renny went on up the car.

"A peach!" Renny breathed when they were in the next car.

"What?" said Doc.

"The girl with those two swarthy men," Renny murmured. "Holy cow! Was she a looker!"

"You mean the three who were spying on us as we gave the conductor that message?" Doc queried softly.

Renny gulped: "They were spying on us?"

"They were."

Señor Corto Oveja, Cere, and El Rabanos would have been surprised, had they overheard this statement. They had not imagined they had been discovered. They did not know that few things happening around Doc escaped his attention.

RENNY scowled and banged his knuckles together. "What do you make of this, Doc?"

"Somebody wants to keep us away from Alex Savage's place, and the beautiful Señorita and her two dark complexioned companions are very interested in us," Doc summarized.

"But what's at the bottom of it?"

"Trouble!"

"You're tellin' me?' Renny grimaced. "But what's at the bottom of it?"

"I neglected to bring my crystal ball," Doc said dryly.

Renny grinned. Somebody, incredulous at the eerie precision with which Doc could read the meaning of mysterious events, and deduct what was to come, had once declared the bronze man was a mystic, able to see the future in a crystal ball. The truth was that Doc's foresight came from a brain that operated with crystal clarity.

"The rest of the gang will want to know about this," Renny suggested.

Renny was referring to the other four members of Doc's little group. These gentlemen were playing a game of chess in another drawing-room.

"A good idea," Doc agreed. "We'll tell them."

Doc and Renny went to a drawing-room door. Doc's hand, drifting toward the knob, came to a rigid stop.

"Look!" He pointed at the door.

The panel bore a weirdly shaped smudge. Faintly imprinted, discernible only after a close glance, the thing was more than a foot high, and about half as wide.

Renny stepped around so that he got a better view with the light on it

"Holy cowl" he gasped. "The thing is shaped like a wolf head, Doc—a wolf with hideous, humanlike features!"

Doc nodded slowly. His bronze lineaments, his strange golden eyes, had not changed expression.

"Werewolf," he said.

"What?" Renny was puzzled. "There ain't no such critter. It's just a legend of these Canadian trappers and natives."

"A legend of human beings who, thirsting for the blood of their fellow men, turn into wolves that they may satisfy their vampire lust," Doc said quietly. "Most unsavory creatures, even for ghost stories."

Renny hesitated, then stroked a finger through the design on the door. His enormous digit left a clean path in its wake.

"Just dust!" he muttered. "But it's strange it'd settle there in that kind of a shape."

Doc tried the door. It resisted. He showed no surprise. "Locked," he said.

"Blazes! Something's wrong!" Without hesitating, Renny blocked one huge hand into a fist. He swung it.

The door panel was of metal, but it gave as if it were a kicked tin can. With a loud crack, the lock broke. The panel jumped open.

Doc and Renny shouldered in.

Four men lay sprawled about a table. Their positions were grotesque; they lay exactly as they had fallen from their chairs.

The men were Doc Savage's four aides.

*"They're dead!"* Renny walled.

At that instant, a small depot flashed by the speeding train. It was the station at which Wilkie planned to drop Doc Savage's telegram.

Wilkie got rid of the message successfully, and before the train was out of sight, he saw the station telegrapher, carrying the missive, enter his office.

## Chapter III
## WARNING OF THE WEREWOLF

THE window of the drawing-room in which the four rigid forms lay, was closed tightly. Lunging to it, Doc wrenched up the sliding sash. The noise of the train wheels came in through the window like the moaning of a mechanical monster.

Big-fisted Renny, after his one wailing cry that the four men were dead, went into action. He sank beside one of the prone forms.

The individual over whom Renny stooped was a startling figure. He hardly exceeded five feet in height, yet outweighed Renny's own tremendous bulk fully ten pounds. Nearly as wide as he was tall, he had arms inches longer than his legs. His face was incredibly homely. The fellow would pass as first cousin to a gorilla.

This was "Monk." As Lieutenant Colonel Andrew Blodgett Mayfair, his accomplishments in the field of experimental chemistry were known to both hemispheres.

"Holy cow!" Renny yelled. "They're not dead!"

Doc Savage replied nothing. He made a round of the drawing-room, sensitive nostrils testing the air. His weird, flake-pool golden eyes roved about.

He examined the doorlock, the key. The latter was in place from the inside. Obviously, the drawing-room had been locked from the interior.

Doc picked up the nearest of his four inert friends. This man was extremely tall, and as thin as a skeleton. His coat draped on his shoulders as on a coat hanger. Spectacles were still in place on his nose. These were peculiar, in that the left lens was extraordinarily thick.

This man was "Johnny"—William Harper Littlejohn. The proudest possession of a famous Eastern museum was an archaeological exhibit of the ancient Mayan civilization which Johnny had contributed. Mining engineers consulted textbooks which he had written on geology.

Johnny had lost use of his left eye in the War. Needing a magnifying glass in his business, he carried one in the left side of his spectacles for convenience.

Doc Savage hurried into the corridor. Within a few minutes he was back, carrying a medical case.

He began administering restoratives.

"Pulse very slow in all four of them," he announced to Renny. "Respiration only perceptible when you hold a mirror in front of their lips. They're about all in."

"Ain't a mark on 'em!" Renny rumbled.

"So I notice," Doc agreed.

"But what happened to them?"

"Something very mysterious," Doc said grimly. "Let's snap them out of it and see if they can shed light on what has occurred."

STRANGELY enough, it was the most unhealthy-looking fellow in the group who was first to revive. To all appearances, this man was easily the weakling of the crowd. He was undersized, slender, only fairly set up, with a none too healthy complexion. He had pale hair and pale eyes. He looked as if he might have lived most of his life in a dark and moldy cellar.

This was "Long Tom" Roberts. Long Tom—he was occasionally known as Major Thomas J. Roberts—was an electrical expert. "A wizard of the juice!"—men of his own profession declared.

Long Tom frowned blankly at the table, on which a chessboard stood. Then he peered at his three motionless fellows.

"What kind of a game are those guys playing?" he demanded weakly.

"Game, hell!" Renny boomed. "Listen, Long Tom, we busted in here and found you four birds all spread out. What happened?"

Long Tom considered. "I don't know."

"You don't—" Renny waved his huge hand. "Come on! Snap out of it!"

"We went to sleep," Long Tom groaned. "We just felt drowsy all of a sudden, then went to sleep."

"You have no idea what caused it?" Doc questioned.

"Nope."

Doc continued his resuscitation efforts on the other men.

"Ham" was the second individual to awaken. Ham was famed for two things: he was one of the cleverest lawyers Harvard had ever turned out, and he was a snappy dresser. Tailors often followed Brigadier General Theodore Marley Brooks down the street, to see clothes being worn as they should be worn. He was a slender man, quick moving, and a fast thinker.

It chanced that, as Ham's eyes opened, the first figure he saw was homely, gorillalike Monk.

"I can't be in heaven!" he grinned feebly.

Renny snorted. Ham was always making some wisecrack at Monk's expense. To listen to the sharp-tongued lawyer, one would think nothing would have given him more delight than to see Monk burned at the stake.

This peeve of Ham's dated back to the Great War—to an event which had earned him his nickname. Thinking to have fun, Ham had taught Monk some French words which were highly insulting, telling him they were the proper expressions with which to flatter a Frenchman. Monk had addressed the words to a French general, and landed in the guardhouse.

But very shortly after Monk's release, Ham was haled up on a charge of stealing hams. He was convicted; somebody had planted the evidence. Ham was mortally certain Monk had framed him. But to this day, he had not been able to prove it.

"What happened to you guys?" Renny asked.

Ham acquired a bewildered expression. He moved about weakly until his hands found a black cane. This cane appeared innocent-looking. Actually, housed in its slender length was a razor-sharp sword. The tip of this blade was daubed with a chemical, a touch of which, in a wound, would produce instant unconsciousness. Ham was rarely seen without his sword cane.

"He don't know what happened to him!" Renny boomed, interpreting Ham's befuddled expression.

Johnny, the archaeologist and geologist, and the homely Monk now opened their eyes. Johnny promptly felt for his glasses which had the magnifying lens, just as Ham had groped for his sword cane.

Both men admitted they had not the slightest idea of what had happened. While playing chess, they had simply gone to sleep.

Monk had a small, childlike voice that was surprisingly mild for one of his apish build.

"Well, what about the head of the werewolf on the door outside?" Doc asked them.

PUZZLED wonderment stamped the faces of the four men. Doc knew they had no knowledge of the weird design on the door.

"A werewolf!" Monk muttered.

"I just called it that," Doc told him. "It is the head of a wolf, with a grotesquely human face."

Bracing himself on his sword cane, Ham sought to sit erect. He gave it up and fell back dizzily.

"Golly, I feel washed up!" he groaned.

"Ain't that too bad!" Monk jeered faintly.

Ham ignored the insult. "I can't imagine what is behind it, Doc. We were just sitting here—"

His eyes protruded. His hands grasped his sword cane wrathfully.

Under the bed, an unearthly squealing and grunting suddenly arose.

"Habeas Corpus!" Monk yelled weakly, but joyfully.

A pig staggered from under the bed. The porker family probably never produced a more grotesque specimen than this one. The pig had legs as long as those of a dog, and ears that rivaled airplane wings.

"Ow-w-w!" Ham groaned.

Habeas Corpus was the present great misery of Ham's existence. Monk had bought the pig on a recent expedition to Arabia, paying the equivalent of four cents in American money as purchase price for him.

Monk's story was that Habeas Corpus' former owner, an Arab, had sold the pig because he had been making a nuisance of himself by catching hyenas and dragging their carcasses up to the house. It was possible that either Monk or the Arab had exaggerated.

The homely Monk was greatly attached to Habeas Corpus, probably because the presence of the pig enraged Ham.

"The door was locked on the inside, and you had the windows closed?" Doc inquired.

"That's right," Ham replied.

"The pig seemed to have been laid out, the same as you fellows," Doc said dryly. "It's all very mystifying. This isn't the first queer thing that's happened, either."

Ham blinked. "What do you mean?"

Doc told them about the telegram incident

"Do you think the fake telegram and what happened to us has a connection?" Ham demanded.

"Can't say," Doc replied.

Doc went to a hand bag and opened it. The piece of baggage held several weapons which resembled overgrown automatic pistols. They were fitted with curled magazines.

These were machine guns of Doc's own invention. The weapons were tiny, compared to the destruction they could wreak. They fired so rapidly that their roar was like the note of a gigantic bull-fiddle. Magazines were charged with what big-game hunters call "mercy bullets"—slugs which produce unconsciousness instead of death.

Doc distributed the rapid-firers to the four weakened victims of the mystery attack.

"Keep a sharp lookout!" he warned.

Renny demanded: "What are you gonna do, Doc?"

"You and I are going to talk to the three persons who were eavesdropping when I gave the conductor the telegram," Doc told him.

Trailed by Renny, Doc glided out into the corridor.

THE two men had not progressed far when they encountered Wilkie.

"I'd like to get some information about two dark-complexioned men on the train," Doc told the conductor.

Wilkie scratched his large head. "There are a number of dark men aboard, I notice."

At this, Renny shot a sharp glance at Doc. The bronze man's features told nothing.

"The two I am interested in were in the company of a very pretty girl," Doc explained.

"Oh, them!" grinned Wilkie. "They got on at the division point where I went on duty. That was two stops back."

"Know their names?"

"No. Passengers don't usually give a conductor their names."

"Have you noticed anything queer about their actions?" Doc persisted.

Wilkie scratched his large head again. "Nothing, except that they seem to be moving around a lot."

"These swarthy men—did they get on at the same time?"

Wilkie nodded. "Yes. At the division point."

Doc and Renny left the goblinlike little conductor.

"This thing is beginning to shape up like a mess of first-class trouble," Renny said thoughtfully.

Doc said nothing. He sought and found a porter.

The porter directed him to a drawing-room which had been reserved by the three individuals whom Doc wished to see.

Doc found the door and knocked. Silence answered. He rippled his knuckles on the panel again. Then he tried the knob. The door was locked.

Doc called the porter. "You're sure they're in here?"

"Yas, suh," said the porter. "Dey went in about five minutes ago. Two of 'em did, anyhow—dat pretty gal and her pap! Don't know if dat man with de gal face is in dere or not."

Renny held up a huge fist and gave Doc an inquiring look.

"I guess we'll go in," Doc told him.

Renny drew back to slam his fist against the panel. Then he lurched. The train had slackened speed abruptly. Renny had to grasp the doorknob to maintain his balance.

"Guess we're pulling into a station," he rumbled.

*Bang!* went his big fist against the door. The sheet metal bulged, but held. Renny swung again terrifically. It seemed a miracle that his fist was not smashed to a pulp.

The train had slowed rapidly; it was now crawling.

Renny's next punch exploded the door open. He plunged across the threshold, then brought up quickly, his jaw asag.

"Holy cow!" he gulped.

Señor Corto Oveja and his attractive daughter were draped across the drawing-room bed. They lay perfectly still. Black leather straps were drawn so tightly around their necks as to be almost buried in the flesh!

## Chapter IV
## DEAD MAN

"THE window!" ejaculated rock-fisted Renny. "It's open!"

"Take a look!" Doc rapped. "Whoever did this may have jumped out as the train slowed down."

Doc was already bending over the two forms on the bed. The garroting straps were strong, yet they broke under Doc's sinewy fingers like cardboard strips.

The girl's wrist in one hand, the man's in the other, Doc explored for pulse.

Both were still alive; pulse was strong, respiration firm.

"This didn't happen more than a few moments ago," Doc told Renny. "The would-be killers must have escaped through the window."

Renny, his head thrust outside, boomed: "I don't see anybody!"

"They had time to duck."

"Yeah," Renny agreed. He lifted his gaze skyward. "Holy cow! That thing is almost an omen!"

"What is?"

"An airplane flying overhead!" Renny rumbled. "The thing is black—looks kinda like a buzzard."

Doc stepped to the window and studied the plane. His sharp eye noted something Renny had missed.

"That plane has no identification numeral!" he said sharply.

Renny made a silent whistle. "In view of what's happening on this train, that's more than passing strange, eh? Police on lawful business usually have identification numbers."

Like a somber vulture, the black monoplane dipped off to the westward, and was soon lost to sight.

Doc twisted a faucet at the washbowl, caught cold water in a palm, carried it over and dashed it on the faces of Señor Corto Oveja and his daughter. He waited expectantly, but they did not stir.

"They should be coming out of it!" Doc said in a vaguely puzzled tone.

He tested pulse and respiration. Then, for the briefest moment, the bronze man's weird trilling note was audible. It trailed softly up and down the musical scale, and abruptly was gone.

Turning to Renny, Doc said: "It looks as if, in addition to being choked, they got a dose of the same thing our four friends got—that weird unconsciousness."

Renny was staring fixedly at the door. There was an expression of bewilderment on his long, puritanical face.

"Yeah," he mumbled. "Look, Doc!"

His huge hand indicated the inner side of the door panel which he had damaged.

The sheet metal bore an eerie smudge. It had the likeness of a wolf head—a wolf with horribly human features.

"I saw it earlier," Doc explained.

"You did!" Renny gulped. He had not seen Doc show any surprise, whenever it was that he had made the discovery.

"That same mark was on the other door," Doc Savage said. He stepped close to the hideous smear. His eyes measured it "It's exactly the same size, too."

Renny nodded. He could not tell, himself, that this mark was the same size as the other. He knew Doc Savage could judge the relative sizes within fractions of an inch.

"Two men have been accompanying this girl about," Renny rumbled. "I wonder where the other one is."

With a rather unpleasant jerk, the train got into motion.

"We'll revive this man and the girl," Doc declared. "Then we'll hunt the other one."

"Yeah!" Renny boomed. "We'll get that gink!"

Outside in the passage, a man yelled shrilly. "Help! Help! They're going to kill me!"

RENNY and Doc bounded to the door. They expected to see a murder scene—or at least a fight. They got a shock.

The swarthy, girl-faced man stood in the corridor. He leveled an arm at Doc and Renny.

"You heard them!" he bellowed. "They said they would *get* me. *Sabe!* That means they plan to kill me!"

Wilkie, the conductor, stood just behind the girl-faced man. Wilkie looked flabbergasted.

"Now, now, mister," Wilkie said soothingly. "There's some mistake here."

"It is no mistake!" wailed the dark man. "Look quickly! They must have killed my friends, Señor and Señorita Oveja!"

Wilkie advanced. He mumbled apologetically to Doc: "I sure don't know what this is all about."

The swarthy man yelled: "I know what it's all about, señor! This bronze man is trying to kill my friends and myself."

He came to the door and looked in. *"Eo es terrible!* It is terrible! What did I tell you? They are murderers!"

Renny made big square blocks of his fists. "You'd better dry up, girl-face!"

At this point, Señor Corto Oveja and his daughter showed signs of reviving. Doc splashed more water on them. They stirred about, and finally opened their eyes.

Señor Oveja pointed weakly at Doc.

"Seize that caballero!" he cried feebly. "It was he who attacked us."

Renny was perfectly familiar with Doc's ability to control his emotions. Yet, watching the bronze man now, he had to marvel; Doc showed by not the remotest sign that anything out of the ordinary had occurred.

"You," Doc said, "are mistaken!"

"It is true!" Señor Oveja shrieked weakly.

*"Si, si!"* echoed his pretty daughter. "This man Savage is the one who assaulted us. We became strangely drowsy as we sat here in our room. Before complete unconsciousness overcame us, men entered and began tying straps around our necks. One of them addressed the other as Señor Savage."

"Did he say *Señor* Savage?" Doc asked pointedly.

The girl shut her eyes. Apparently she was thinking. "Yes. He used the word 'señor.'"

Doc glanced at Renny.

The big-fisted engineer was staring at the leather straps which had been around the necks of Señor Oveja and the girl, choking them to death. From the expression on his somber face, he might have been looking at a pair of poisonous serpents.

"I thought you'd notice those straps," Doc told him quietly. "They're carrying-straps from a piece of my luggage."

The man with the womanish face bellowed triumphantly. *"Bueno!* This proves it beyond a shadow of a doubt Savage tried to do murder! Conductor, arrest him!"

Wilkie shifted from one foot to the other. Little bubbles of perspiration stood on his large forehead. He made a bewildered gesture.

"What is your name?" he asked the girl-faced man.

"El Rabanos," the fellow replied.

"What is the motive?" Wilkie demanded. "Why should Doc Savage try to kill you?"

El Rabanos hesitated. A strange expression flickered about his eyes.

"I don't know," he said finally.

Wilkie scowled. "Did you think previously that you were in danger from Doc Savage?"

"Yes," El Rabanos admitted reluctantly.

"For what reason?" Wilkie cracked back.

El Rabanos said angrily: "You arrest this man! Turn him over to the Mounted Police. I'll give them my full story."

Wilkie eyed Doc. "I don't want to arrest you, Mr. Savage, but I may have to. Something strange and horrible is going on around here. I wouldn't be surprised if the death of that poor telegraph operator hasn't got something to do with it."

"What telegraph operator?" Doc queried sharply.

"The fellow who copied the message that I gave you," Wilkie explained.

ONCE more Doc Savage received surprising information without an appreciable show of emotion. Doc was not callous. He simply had his nerves under such control that they behaved as he wished.

"Was the telegrapher murdered?" he queried.

"Not according to a report I got at our last stop," Wilkie replied. "A section worker found the body. He claimed it looked like suicide. But I knew that operator. He wasn't the kind to take his own life."

Doc's hand described a gesture which took in Señor Oveja, his daughter, and El Rabanos.

"I should like very much to hear these three explain why they fear me," he said.

All Doc received was a hateful stare from each of the trio. The girl's look was the least malicious. In fact, her expression portrayed rather plainly that she regretted that this handsome bronze man was an enemy.

"It don't seem like they're gonna talk," Wilkie muttered.

Doc Savage swung over to the door. He closed it so that the rear of the panel was visible, and indicated the smear which resembled a grisly, human-faced wolf.

"Maybe you can explain this!" His powerful voice crashed.

The girl's eyes flew wide as she saw the smudge. She screamed with a sort of exhausted horror. Then she clamped palms over her eyes.

Señor Oveja and El Rabanos reacted almost as sharply. Their eyes protruded; their jaws fell.

"The werewolf!" choked Señor Oveja.

"What does it mean?" Doc questioned.

Pretty Señorita Oveja laughed hysterically. "Why should you be asking me? You know very well what it means!"

"You three are under some misapprehension," Doc told them. "This is all a mystery to me."

*"Que!"* El Rabanos ejaculated sarcastically. "What! Did not your uncle Alex Savage take you into his confidence?"

"So Alex Savage is mixed up in this," Doc said dryly.

"Mixed is a very mild word for it, Señor Savage," El Rabanos sneered.

Ignoring the girl-faced man, Doc Savage turned to Wilkie. "One of the gang who assaulted Señor Oveja and his daughter called the other by the name of *Señor* Savage. Obviously they were trying to frame me. But use of the Spanish word 'Señor' was a slip. I believe you said there were other swarthy-skinned men on this train."

"Right!" exclaimed Wilkie. "I'm going to check up on them right now."

The goblinlike little conductor hurried off.

DOC paid a visit to his four friends who had

been victims of the weird sleep. There was no danger of anyone escaping from the speeding train.

When he entered the drawing-room, Monk and Ham were scowling blackly at each other. This was a good sign. It indicated Monk and Ham were back to their normal quarreling state.

Johnny and Long Tom also seemed fairly chipper.

"The effects of the stuff wear off quickly," said gaunt Johnny, polishing his spectacles which had the magnifying left lens. "What's new, Doc?"

"We're in the thick of a mess," Doc announced.

Instead of looking gloomy or apprehensive at this, all four men grinned. They were a strange bunch. Peril and excitement were the things for which they lived.

Speaking rapidly, Doc told them what had happened when he went to investigate Señor Oveja, the daughter, and El Rabanos.

"They seem to think I'm some kind of a bogy man," he finished.

"Do they really think that, or are they pretending?" questioned apish Monk, scratching the airplane-wing ears of his pig, Habeas Corpus.

"I'm not sure yet," Doc replied.

The train whistle moaned. Its sound was a banshee wail over the noisy progress of the coaches.

Doc glanced through the window. It was only a road crossing for which the train had whistled.

A porter ran past the drawing-room door, crying in a horror-stricken voice: "Lawsy me! Lawsy me!"

Doc collared him. "What is it?" he demanded of the porter.

"It am de conductor, Mistah Wilkie," the colored man moaned.

"What about him?"

"He done been stuck!"

"Show me where he is!" Doc commanded.

Wilkie lay in the washroom of a Pullman car—lay in a wet lake of crimson which had leaked from his own body. He had been knifed numerous times in the chest.

Doc Savage was skilled in many things—but in surgery and medicine above all others. A glance convinced him that Wilkie was dead.

"Anybody see anything?" Doc asked the porter.

"No sah!" said the porter. "Not that Ah knows of."

Doc Savage stood like an image graven in the metal he resembled.

On the washroom door, he had discovered another of the hideous smears—a human-faced wolf. The mark of death!

Standing there, the bronze man was so quiet as to seem without life. An unseen monster of horror and death was slowly wreathing its tentacles about him. Why, he did not know. But it must be something that concerned his uncle, Alex Savage, or his uncle's daughter, Patricia.

Absently, Doc's golden eyes roved to the north and west. In that direction lay the estate of Alex Savage. And there, it was possible, lay also the explanation of the mystery.

## Chapter V
### THE WEREWOLF CRIES

DOC Savage was a man of profound accomplishments. But he was no clairvoyant with a gift of transporting his vision. So he was unaware that mystery and horror also stalked the domain of Alex Savage.

There, too, the werewolf was spreading its uncanny violence.

The estate of Alex Savage was no mere backwoods homestead. It was true that forty years ago Alex Savage had homesteaded it. But now it had grown, until the estate spanned up and down the coast for miles, and reached no little distance inland.

Scattered over other parts of Canada, Alex Savage had wheat ranches, mines, and an industrial plant or two. He was considered a business success.

The estate at the edge of the sea was in the nature of a hunting preserve. Within its bounds was some of the roughest land in Canada. The shore was a ragged stone wall which shot up out of the water. The coast was fanged with reefs and tiny islands.

The estate itself was a collection of pinnacle and canyons, boulders and brush. Alex Savage boasted freely that there were parts of his estate upon which he had never set eyes. Moreover, he claimed there were spots which no one had ever explored. This was possible, since there were places to which none could climb.

In this labyrinth of stone and brush, Alex Savage had erected a log cabin. In it, he spent part of each summer, and all of the hunting seasons. The cabin had several rooms. It was filled with electric lights, electric refrigeration, radio, and even air-conditioning apparatus, although there was seldom need for the latter. The rugs were rich. Anyone who sat in one of the luxurious chairs was in danger of sinking from sight. The place was no backwoodsman's hut.

From the wide veranda of the cabin, an excellent view could be had of the sea. Monster boulders and tall trees towered around the place; thick underbrush made these surroundings almost a jungle. Twilight came to the brush almost an hour before the sun actually set.

The birds usually made a good deal of noise settling for the night.

It was twilight now, but the birds were making no noise. The feathered songsters had been chilled into silence by an eerie sound.

This noise pealed out erratically. At times, there was five minutes of dead silence. Then weird, unearthly cries would shiver out, a babbling volley of them. They had a human quality, those cries. They were tremulous with an incoherent horror.

The bird life could not have been more silent had death been astalk.

The latest outburst of the banshee cries was somewhat more human than before. They sounded very like someone in frightful agony.

Inside the Alex Savage cabin, a feminine voice called sharply: "Boat Face! Haven't you got that rifle fixed yet?"

There was no answer.

"Boat Face!" the girl called again angrily.

There was a moment of silence. Then a squaw shuffled out of the kitchen region. She was very fat, very brown, and wore enough clothes to garb several of her white-skinned sisters. She looked as competent as the Rock of Gibraltar.

"Boat Face, him in kitchen, Miss Patricia," she said calmly. "Him scared out of skin."

"Boat Face won't go out and investigate those cries?" the girl asked.

"Him heap big coward," said the squaw.

THE girl stepped back from a window. She had a wealth of bronze hair—hair very closely akin in hue to that of Doc Savage. She had been watching the brush that circled like a wall.

She was tall; her form was molded along lines that left nothing to be desired. Her features were as perfect as though a magazine-cover artist had designed them.

She wore high-laced boots, breeches, and a serviceable gray shirt.

A cartridge belt was draped about her waist. From it dangled a heavy Frontier Single Action six-shooter—freely admitted by those who know to be one of the most reliable guns ever made. In the crook of her right arm lay a very modern automatic big-game rifle.

"I'll talk to him, Tiny," said the girl.

"O. K., Miss Patricia," said Tiny. "It do no good. That damn half-breed husband of mine plenty afraid."

Tiny was the cook. Boat Face was man-of-all-work around the place. These two were the only servants.

Patricia's heels tapped angrily into the kitchen.

Boat Face was a squarish, copper-colored man, who sat in a corner, holding a rifle. His squaw, Tiny, had called him a breed, but he looked pure Indian. Just what had given him the name of Boat Face was a mystery only an Indian could fathom. His beady black eyes refused sullenly to meet Patricia's gaze.

Patricia started to speak—then held back her words.

The eerie, banshee cries once more babbled from the gloomy brush outside the cabin. They were unmistakably human now, appealing for succor.

Boat Face's ink-black eyes wavered. He took a firmer grasp on a rifle which lay across his knees.

"I no go out," he muttered. "Rifle broke."

Patricia Savage suddenly seized Boat Face's rifle. She examined the mechanism, threw it to her shoulder, and snapped it.

"You're lying!" she cried. "There's nothing wrong with this gun!"

"He heap big piker," grunted Tiny.

Boat Face's eyes rolled nervously.

"That noise—him werewolf," he mumbled.

"Nonsense!" Patricia said sharply. "There is no such animal!"

Boat Face did not seem convinced. "Your pa—if him alive, him no ask me go and see what make that noise."

The words seemed to wash Patricia's rage away. She paled visibly. Even the fingers which held the rifle tensed to whiteness.

"These sounds have something to do with the murder of my father!" she said shrilly

"Me no go outdoors," Boat Face mumbled. "You tie can on me, if you like. Me no go, anyway."

"I won't discharge you," Patricia told him in a weary voice. "After all, I won't ask you to do anything I wouldn't do myself. You can stay here. I'll go out and investigate."

Tiny waddled over to a corner. She came back with a double-barrel shotgun and said stoically: "Me go, too!"

"Thanks, Tiny," Patricia said gratefully. "But you and Boat Face stay here on guard."

Tiny nodded reluctantly. Boat Face looked much relieved.

PATRICIA moved into the cabin's large living room, and drew the shades carefully. Then she indicated one of the uprights which formed a rustic support for the ceiling. This was a log over a foot thick, still covered with natural bark.

"Guard that, especially," she said meaningly.

Tiny and Boat Face showed no surprise—they seemed to comprehend fully what she meant.

Patricia pocketed several extra ammunition clips for her automatic rifle. Then she opened the door and stepped swiftly outside.

Tiny watched her go with evident concern. Boat Face's aboriginal features were inscrutable.

Sunlight still penetrated to the clearing immediately adjacent to the cabin. Gloom lurked in the tangle of rocks and brush beyond. Walking away from the cabin was like leaving a lantern and going into the night.

Patricia walked warily, rifle alert. She kept fingers on safety and trigger. Her ears strained to catch the next outburst of the unearthly cries.

Off to her right, the noise arose. It was low, sinister; a horrible bleating. It persisted only a moment, then whimpered itself into nothingness.

Patricia shivered. She tripped the rifle safety. This time the cry had not sounded so human. Indeed, it seemed to have taken on a repulsive, animal-like quality.

The sound had come from inland. From, perhaps, a hundred yards away—maybe more! The girl could not tell.

She went toward the noise, her pretty face so set it was almost a mask. When she was near the spot from which the sound had seemed to come, she searched for tracks. The terrain was not the sort to show a trail; it was too rocky.

Patricia heard the cries again. They now wailed from a little farther on. She advanced—again she found nothing.

A bit later, the sounds came once more. They had moved on ahead. Patricia shuddered. It seemed the eerie crying thing was trying to decoy her away.

Patricia suddenly gave it up as a bad job. She went back toward the cabin, steps hurried, eyes roving uneasily.

She was baffled, and more than a little terrified, and drew a sigh of relief when the cabin came in sight.

"Tiny! Boat Face!" she called. "It's me!"

She did not want the sullen Boat Face or the competent Tiny taking a shot at her by mistake.

Patricia reached the cabin and shoved the door open. She went in—and jerked to a stop. Her pretty features became blankly startled.

The cabin interior looked as if the proverbial cyclone had hit it.

Patricia's eyes wandered. Then she saw something which caused her to cry out shrilly in horror.

Tiny and Boat Face were brown, unmoving forms on the floor!

STUFFING was ripped from rich chairs. Rugs had been plucked up and flung aside. Drawers had been emptied on the floor. Everywhere signs showed the cabin had been searched wildly.

Patricia ran to the voluminous, copper-hued Tiny, and felt anxiously for pulse.

"They're dead!" she wailed miserably.

Within a moment, however, she realized this was a mistake. There was a heartbeat—very faint.

Getting ice cubes from the electric refrigerator, Patricia Savage rubbed them over the faces of Boat Face and Tiny.

Pulse strengthened slowly under the copper skins.

Confident both servants would recover, Patricia ran through the cabin. Everywhere, there was wild upheaval and destruction. From attic down, the search had missed little. The covered motor of the electric refrigerator was even torn open.

There was no trace of the men—certainly it seemed the work of more than one—who had ransacked the place. They must have come in through the rear door, or an unlocked window.

Something like twenty minutes elapsed before Tiny and Boat Face were revived enough to speak coherently.

"What on earth occurred?" Patricia demanded.

The two servants exchanged blank looks.

"Dunno," Boat Face mumbled. "Me and squaw just go to sleep."

Patricia snapped: "That's ridiculous!"

"Boat Face tell truth," said the ample Tiny, with a roll of jet eyes. "We get heap much sleepy and fall over."

Patricia stared fixedly at the floor near where the two servants had been lying. She had discovered something she had not observed before. The sight of the thing had a striking effect. She stood erect, tense, gripping her rifle.

It was a weird, blackish smudge—more than a foot high and half as wide. The thing had the contour of a wolf's head. The features were grotesquely human.

"It's the werewolf's head again!" Patricia said shrilly. "It's the same mark which we began seeing shortly before my father's death—and which we have seen since!"

Boat Face mumbled. "Werewolf! Indian know them. They devil-man with body of wolf. They prowl in woods and eat plenty hunter and trapper."

"Campfire ghost tales!" Patricia snapped. "There are no such creatures! This particular werewolf is very human, Boat Face. You and Tiny both know what he is after."

Patricia went to the large bark-covered timber which supported the living-room ceiling. It was this timber which she had asked Tiny and Boat Face to guard.

It had not been disturbed, although the search had missed little else.

Patricia pressed certain projections on the bark. A concealed door flew open. She withdrew from within what looked like a solid block of ivory. The white cube was perhaps two inches square.

"They're after this," Patricia said grimly.

### Chapter VI
### SQUARE WHITE DEATH

FOR once, Tiny's aboriginal face lost its stoic indifference. She stared at the ivory cube as if it were a charm which guaranteed the coming of evil events.

**Her small right fist swung with the timing and precision of a trained boxer's.**

"Him bad medicine," she muttered, indicating the snow-white block.

"I cannot understand what significance it has." Patricia turned the cube slowly in her slender fingers. "It seems solid—there is no hollow sound when it is tapped."

"You know where your dad get him?" Tiny asked.

"Father found it under a ledge about two miles from here, years ago," Patricia replied. "It lay amid a cluster of human skeletons. The skeletons looked as if they had been there for centuries. No one knew anything about them."

"Sure!" said Tiny. "That how he find it. That alone enough make it bring bad luck."

Patricia eyed the white cube thoughtfully.

"Dad never dreamed the thing was of any value," she said. "Three weeks ago, he found a prowler searching this cabin. The fellow escaped. A little later, dad received a mysterious demand for the cube. He refused to turn it over."

"Better if him give it up," muttered Boat Face.

Patricia nodded miserably. "Maybe. We began finding those mysterious werewolf marks around the place. We got other demands for the cube. Then we found dad dead. The doctors called it heart failure."

"They make blood bubble," said Tiny. She nodded elaborately. "Your pa, him murdered."

"I think so, too, Tiny," Patricia said jerkily.

"You bet!" The squaw nodded again. "Him die

from same thing that almost get me and Boat Face a minute ago."

"You mean the thing that made you unconscious?"

Again Tiny nodded. "You bet."

"But what was it?" Patricia pondered.

"We go to sleep," said Tiny, as if that explained everything.

Nor did Patricia come any nearer a solution of the mystery, although she asked many questions, and finally went outside and searched the immediate neighborhood.

The rocky earth bore no footprints. That meant nothing, however. The marauders could easily have avoided leaving tracks.

The weird banshee crying had not come from the gloomy brush since Patricia had returned to the cabin. The blush of dusk still spread over the sea.

Unexpectedly, a long, doleful sound moaned out, causing echoes to bang against the cliffs. The noise was greatly different from the earliest banshee cries, yet Patricia started violently.

The sound repeated itself a moment later. She knew, then, what it was.

"The trader's launch!" she exclaimed. "They're letting us know that they have some mail."

SO rugged was this region in which the Savage cabin lay, that no automobile could penetrate. A stout wagon could get through, but only with difficulty. To come and go, either a speed boat or a seaplane was the most feasible conveyance. A rustic boathouse on the beach held a fast launch.

Mail was delivered to the Savage hunting lodge in an ingenious fashion. A trader who lived up the coast made regular daily trips to the settlement. His route was past the Savage place.

A few hundred feet from shore, there was a floating buoy box. In this, the trader was accustomed to leave the Savage mail.

The estate had no other communication with the outside world. During his sojourns there, Alex Savage had always made it a point not to be disturbed. The place was his refuge from business worries.

Patricia secured binoculars, and focused them on the trader's boat. There was light enough for her to make it out distinctly.

She saw the trader place at least one piece of mail in the box. Then his boat went on.

"Get the launch!" Patricia commanded Boat Face. "I'm going to keep my eyes on the mail box until we get out to it. That's another mysterious thing that has happened. Our mail has been disappearing!"

Boat Face was slow about complying with the order; he seemed reluctant to leave the cabin. Only

when Tiny shouted angrily, "You big bum! You do what Miss Pat say!" did he shuffle off toward the boat.

It was fully five minutes before the breed got the launch out of the boathouse and alongside the little wharf in front of the cabin.

During this time, Patricia had not removed her binoculars from the inspection of the buoy.

"I'm betting nobody got that mail this time!" she declared.

She kept her glasses fixed on the box as Boat Face guided the launch out. At no time had she seen anything suspicious.

The floating mail box was an ordinary buoy with a container countersunk in the top. It turned and bobbed with the waves, being anchored by a light chain to a heavy concrete weight.

Capturing the box with the aid of a boat hook, Patricia opened it.

The container was empty!

"But this is impossible!" Patricia exclaimed incredulously. "I saw mail put in it. I've watched it since. Every instant!"

"Werewolf!" mumbled Boat Face, and shrugged beefy shoulders.

Patricia examined the buoy box. The mail container had no lock, since thieves were scarce in this region. However, a wave could not possibly have tossed the mail out.

Patricia had Boat Face run the launch in a big circle. She could not find a thing to shed light on the mystery.

Her face was somewhat white as the launch swerved shoreward.

"I CAN'T understand it," Patricia said grimly.

"Werewolf!" muttered Boat Face. "Him heap bad customer."

The girl ignored the redskin's prognostications. She leveled her binoculars inquiringly at the shore line. The cliffs were cracked here and there by canyons, scratched by watercourses. Huge boulders were piled at the foot of the cliffs. Some of these were fully as large as city apartment houses.

"I don't see a thing," she said.

"Werewolf, him can disappear," said Boat Face.

"You say 'werewolf' to me again, and I'm going to have Tiny work out on you!" snapped Patricia.

Boat Face subsided uneasily. Boat Face was something rare in the brotherhood of red men—a henpecked husband. Most bucks make their squaws walk a chalk line, but not Boat Face. On occasion, the lethargic Tiny would shed her stoical air long enough to give Boat Face what metropolitan cops call a "good shellacking." The implement which Tiny used was the same as that employed by her paleface sisters, a rolling pin.

"Did you ever hear of Doc Savage?" Patricia asked suddenly.

"Me no hear of him," said Boat Face, flinching as if he had felt his squaw's rolling pin.

"He's a cousin of mine," said Patricia. "He lives in the United States. I understand he does remarkable things."

"What kind of things?" asked Boat Face.

"He gets people out of trouble."

"Unh!" Boat Face grunted expressively. "How him make money out of business like that?"

"He doesn't do it for money, if what I've heard is true," Patricia announced. "He goes all over the world and helps others, and doesn't charge them anything. He just does it for the excitement."

"Sound like him crazy," Boat Face offered.

Patricia frowned at the servant

"You're getting a bit insolent lately, Boat Face!" she said pointedly.

"You t'ink so, eh?" Boat Face asked indifferently.

"I don't think—I know!" the girl snapped.

"Me not care what damn gal t'inks!" said Boat Face, plainly sneering.

Bronze-haired Patricia sprang suddenly to her feet. She shot forward like a metallic tigress. Her small right fist swung with the timing and precision of a trained boxer's.

Boat Face saw it coming. He tried to dodge, was a fraction too late. *Pop!* Patricia's knuckles caught him in the right eye.

The blow had snap and power. Boat Face's arm flailed, he wavered off balance, then toppled overboard.

Patricia ran to the rudder as the launch left the floundering brave behind. She turned the craft back, came alongside, and, with her boat hook, hauled Boat Face over the gunwale.

"You apologize for swearing at me," she gritted, "or I'll knock you overboard again!"

Boat Face squirmed. He was a greatly embarrassed redskin. If this ever got out, the other Indians would laugh him out of Canada. He had not dreamed Miss Patricia was such a hellcat.

"Me sorry!" he muttered.

"Starting right now, you are going to jump quick when I give you an order!" Patricia informed him.

"Yes'm," said Boat Face meekly.

"The first thing you are going to do in the morning is to take the launch down the coast to the nearest telegraph office, and send a telegram," Patricia advised.

"Who telegram go to?"

"To Doc Savage," Patricia said grimly. "I need his help!"

IN preparing for the night, the cabin windows and doors were locked. This done, it seemed impossible that anyone could enter without creating an alarm. Patricia did not think it necessary for the two servants and herself to stand guard.

Night came, a tidal wave of gloom that poured in from the eastward. Darkness crawled down the canyons like predatory black monsters stalking the sun.

Boat Face had quarters in a small room at the rear of the cabin. His ample mate occupied the same cubicle.

Tiny was a substantial squaw. It was doubtful if anything would ever excite her enough to spoil her sleep. She began to snore with astonishing promptness soon after she had retired.

Boat Face had been careful to remain awake. He knew how soundly his squaw slept. After Tiny had snored a half dozen times, Boat Face eased silently out of his small room and crept to the door of the chamber occupied by Patricia Savage. He listened intently, an ear mashed to the wooden panel.

Regular breathing assured him Patricia was asleep.

Careful to make no noise, Boat Face sidled to the bark-covered pillar in the living room. Fumbling until he located the secret catch, he pressed it. The concealed door in the timber flew soundlessly open.

"Heap good!" Boat Face breathed. "Still here. Me use him for bait to croak um damn werewolf! Yah—Boat Face not as dumb as ever'body seem t'ink around here."

Patricia had replaced the ivory cube.

Boat Face withdrew the white block. He fingered it, hefted it. An evil grin warped his swarthy face. He swiped a greedy tongue over his lips.

He seemed to indulge in deep thought for a time. Then he returned the cube to its hiding place, and closed the cleverly constructed door. After this, he let himself out into the night.

His first stop was at the boathouse. There, he carefully unscrewed the plug in the gasoline storage barrel, and let the fluid gurgle out. Then he emptied the launch tank.

"Nobody go from here to send telegram for Doc Savage," he chuckled. "Not right away soon, anyhow. Now, me go fix trap!"

Quitting the boathouse, he faded into the brush. The night swallowed him.

Boat Face was gone nearly an hour. When he appeared again in the vicinity of the cabin, his manner was equally furtive as before. He felt of his clothing, and made a disgusted face. He was soaked with water to the armpits.

"Trap, him all O.K.," he chuckled. Then he stood in the murk near the cabin, pondering.

"Damn squaw will want to know how me get wet," he muttered once. "Me no tell—she use rolling pin."

As if to banish that possibility, Boat Face started to remove his wet clothing. The process was hardly underway, however, when a low hissing came out of the gloom. It was faint, and had apparently originated some distance away.

Boat Face's manner showed that he had heard this hiss before, and that it had a definite meaning. He fastened the buttons he had loosened, then crept off in the gloom, toward the source of the hiss.

His objective proved to be a clump of spruce two hundred yards distant. These trees narrowly missed growing as thick as hair. Boat Face came to a stop near the dense covert.

"What you want?" he called in a low, grouchy tone.

Out of the sepia of spruce came harsh words: "Have you found where the ivory cube is hidden?"

Boat Face stood in sullen silence. Apparently he was giving the matter thought.

"Me know!" he said finally.

"For crying out loud!" snarled the man in the thicket. "Why didn't you let me know! Had you found it before we searched the cabin this evening?"

Boat Face seemed to give this some thought, too.

"No!" he lied.

"Well, go bring me the block," the unseen man directed.

"Me get five hundred dollars!" Boat Face reminded.

"O.K! O.K!" snarled the other. "Get the ivory cube. I've got your mazuma for you. Five hundred good Canadian dollars."

Boat Face shuffled off.

THE wily redskin servant succeeded in entering the cabin without arousing anybody. He went directly to the hiding place in the rustic ceiling support and got the ivory cube. Then, easing out doors again, carrying the ivory block, he shuffled for the spruce-thicket rendezvous.

Before Boat Face had covered many yards, however, he came to a stop. His tongue traveled greedily over his thick lips. He scratched the end of his hook nose, fingering the white cube.

"Ugh!" he grunted. "Five hundred dollar not enough! Him worth a million. Them guys bad actors. But me got way to fix um."

He nodded profoundly over this bit of logic.

"Me make feller pay more," he decided.

Boat Face turned at right angles toward the beech. He had never moved more soundlessly. The wilderness of boulders along the edge of the little bay swallowed his slinking form.

There was silence then, except for the calling of a night bird somewhere and the suck of small waves at rock crevices. Several times, there were splashings; these were such as might be made by leaping fish. A breeze shuffled leaves together, making noise like mice running on paper.

Like a red-skinned ghost, Boat Face materialized in the vicinity of the spruce thicket.

"How!" he called.

"You got the cube?" asked the harsh voice of the unseen man.

"Me got him," Boat Face admitted.

"Cough up, then. I've got the five hundred you were to get for delivering it."

"Five hundred not enough," pronounced Boat Face.

The man in the thicket cursed softly. "So you're a welsher, eh?"

"Welsher—what him?" asked Boat Face.

"It's a guy who makes an agreement and don't go through with it," the other gritted.

"Me want ten thousand dollars," Boat Face announced.

A choking sound came out of the spruce. "So Jesse James has put on feathers!"

"Me no like funny guys," Boat Face said sullenly. "Ten thousand dollars! Put up or shut up!"

"Now listen, Indian!" the other argued angrily. "We played square with you. We even took you into our confidence and told you what the ivory block is, and why we wanted it. And now you're welshing!"

"Put up or shut up!" Boat Face insisted.

The unseen man was briefly silent.

"Shut up it is!" he said abruptly.

There was a sharp swishing sound—a note that was half a whistle. It was followed by a dull thud which resembled a rock falling into mud.

Boat Face pitched soundlessly backward. The hilt of a knife protruded from his chest over the heart, and he gave only a few weak squirmings while he died.

The killer crawled from the spruce thicket at once. He kept on hands and knees, making him seem sinister, more spiderlike than human. He had a handkerchief bound over his face, mask fashion.

"Shut up, it was!" he snarled at the lifeless Boat Face. "A shut-up for you!"

With eager fingers he searched for the ivory cube. Searched again! He fell to cursing in a low, guttural voice which had suddenly betrayed a trace of foreign accent.

Then he cursed aloud.

The ivory cube was not in Boat Face's clothing.

SOME minutes later, a curious conclave took place in a deep canyon far up on the mountain side. The meeting was held on the water-worn stone bottom of the canyon. Stygian realms never produced a more intense darkness than that which gorged the scene of the conference.

Several men were present. Not one of them could see his fellows in the ebony void.

"I made a hell of a bad move!" announced the man who had thrown the knife that brought death to Boat Face. "I should have searched him before I croaked him."

"You are telling us!" snarled another voice.

"How was I to know he didn't have the ivory cube?" the killer defended.

"The milk is spilled, hombres. Why cry?" said a man with a marked Spanish accent.

"That's an idea!" agreed the slayer. "The redskin probably didn't have the cube at all. My guess is that the girl still has it. We'll soon get it from her!"

"Si, si! But what if the Señorita Savage does not know where it is?"

"She knows. Her old man would tell her."

"Possibly. And it is possible, too, that we made a mistake in disposing of the Señor Alex Savage in such haste."

"He caught me talkin' to that redskin, didn't he?" snarled Boat Face's slayer. "It looked like my best move to put him out of the way and let the redskin get the cube."

"Si, si!" agreed the other amiably. "You are not being criticized, my friend. Our chief may not like this, however. But we will consider other matters. You got the letter from the buoy box?"

The query was addressed to another member of the sinister gathering.

"Sure," replied the man who had been spoken to. "It wasn't a letter, though. It was a telegram."

The man now thumbed on a flashlight. The brilliant beam, splattering at his feet, disclosed a contrivance which vaguely resembled a gas mask. This was a self-contained diving lung.

The diving lung held the explanation of how the man had gotten the letter from the buoy box without being seen by Patricia Savage. He had merely weighted himself, marched to the float underwater, climbed the mooring line, and reached into the box. In the poor light of dusk, Patricia had not seen his hand enter the container.

The man extracted a telegram from a pocket. "This is it."

A gnarled brown hand whipped out and snatched both the telegram and the man's flashlight. The telegram was exposed under the beam.

"Que lastima!" exploded the man who had seized the message. "What a pity! This is from Doc Savage to his uncle, whom he evidently does not know is dead. But it asks if the esteemed uncle got the telegram in which the Señor Doc Savage said he was coming for a visit."

"They did not!" chuckled a man. "We secured that message as we did this one."

"It is evident that Señor Doc Savage suspects something is wrong," said the one who had read the telegram. "That is bad."

Someone laughed fiercely.

"The boss will take care of that!"

"Si, si!" agreed the man with the telegram. "He is very ingenious, that maestro of ours. He will thoroughly dispose of this Doc Savage."

A few minutes later, the sinister gathering dispersed.

## Chapter VII
## STRANGE ATTACKERS

THE train was still driving its way westward, excitement and tragedy hovering over it.

Girl-faced El Rabanos waved his arms and screamed: "This man Savage is the murderer!"

Renny shook fists that were larger than brickbats, rumbling: "Say that again, sissy-faced squirt, and I'll hit you so hard you'll turn into a grease spot!"

Monk's pig, Habeas Corpus, squealed violently.

Señor Corto Oveja glared and shrilled: "I, too, think Señor Savage is the murderer."

Pretty Señorita Oveja put hands over her mouth to crowd back sobs. She made no accusations either way.

The train was in a general uproar—it had been thus for more than two hours.

The dead form of Wilkie, the conductor, was still sprawled in its crimson puddle on the Pullman washroom floor. His murderer was as yet uncaught.

With the noisy violence of Latin temperaments, Señor Oveja and El Rabanos had shouted the length of the train that Doc Savage was the killer. They were still shouting insistently. The very noisiness of their assertion was producing an effect.

"This man Savage suggested the mission on which the conductor was killed!" El Rabanos repeated for probably the dozenth time.

"That mission was ridiculous in the first place!" snapped Señor Oveja. "It was to summon and question all Spanish people on this train."

"I notice there's a lot of them," Renny said pointedly.

"You have heard their story!" El Rabanos snapped. "They are going to a convention of a Spanish society being held on the Pacific coast."

This was true. On the train were about a dozen individuals of Spanish ancestry. Without exception, they declared they were going to the meeting of the society. The news butcher on the train had found a story in one of his papers which proved there actually was such a meeting scheduled.

Doc was not under arrest. But that was simply because there happened to be no officers on the train.

The most unpleasant of recent developments, from Doc's standpoint, was the work of Señor

Oveja. The señor had dispatched a telegram to the Mounted Police at the train's next stop, asking that officers be on hand to arrest Doc. This was a through train. It had not paused since the discovery of Wilkie's body. Señor Oveja had dropped his message at a small depot as the train had flashed past it.

Renny sidled close to Doc.

"This is beginning to look bad!" he said in a low voice. "There is not the slightest clue to show who murdered Wilkie."

Girl-faced El Rabanos sprang forward, shouting. "These men should not be allowed to talk together! They may plot an escape!"

Doc Savage shrugged wearily and sat down.

"Would you mind bringing a glass of water, Renny?" he asked.

"Glad to!" said Renny.

There was a long glass cylinder mounted in a corner of the coach. This held paper cups which dropped out when one inserted a penny. Renny ignored these. He wandered off to the regions of the diner.

After a bit, Renny was back, carrying a plain glass beaker, brimful of cold water.

Doc drank the water. Holding the empty glass in both hands, he toyed with it as he addressed entrancingly pretty Señorita Oveja.

"I wonder if you would do me a favor?" he asked.

"What?" the young woman inquired shortly.

"Tell me why you think I am your enemy."

El Rabanos put in wrathfully: "That is information which we shall give to the Mounted Police!"

"Would I like to smear that face of yours!" Renny thundered at El Rabanos.

"Here," Doc said, and handed Renny the glass.

Renny took the beaker. There was a strange expression on his long, puritanical face.

Renny departed as if he were returning the water glass to where he had gotten it.

Seemingly with no particular purpose in mind, gaunt Johnny and pale Long Tom sauntered off together.

Twirling his sword cane, Ham was next to leave the group. The pig Habeas Corpus under an arm, Monk trailed after the dapper lawyer. Ham was inviting Monk to quit following him around as they passed out of hearing.

"We should keep an eye on those men!" El Rabanos declared.

"Fat chance they've got of getting off the train!" somebody told him. "We're hitting all of sixty miles an hour."

Doc Savage went to a writing desk and selected a book of telegram blanks. He addressed a message to the Mounted Police at the metropolis where the train next stopped.

ADVISE YOU HAVE STATION AND VICINITY BRILLIANTLY LIGHTED WHEN OUR TRAIN ARRIVES STOP ALSO HAVE ENOUGH TROOPERS ON HAND TO SEE THAT NO ONE ESCAPES STOP CONFIDENT SOMETHING CRIMINAL UNDERFOOT.
    DOC SAVAGE

Doc tied the telegram in his handkerchief, first weighting it with two silver dollars. Then he opened the window. He did this in plain view, not wishing to have somebody get excited and take a shot at him. He consulted his watch, then waited. He had studied the timetable earlier, and knew they were due to pass through a small town in a few moments.

The train whistle moaned. A pinpoint eye of light opened in the distance. This approached with a rush. It was the illuminated window of a railway station. The little depot looked like a match box in the headlight glare.

Standing in front of the station was a man who wore a green eyeshade, and had black dust protectors over his shirt sleeves. The accouterments stamped him as the telegraph operator.

Doc threw his message as the train hooted past. Considering the terrific speed, his aim was uncanny. The handkerchief, the telegram inside, all but bounced into the operator's hands.

In the act of closing the window, Doc noted something from the corner of an eye.

Señor Oveja was bending over the desk where the telegram had been written. He hastily sauntered away from the desk when he saw Doc observing him.

Doc gave no sign of having noticed. He knew what Señor Oveja was doing at the desk. There had been a sheet of carbon paper in the pad upon which Doc had written his message. Señor Oveja had read this carbon copy of Doc's wire.

It was possible the señor imagined he had done a neat bit of detecting. As a matter of fact, Doc had left the carbon copy deliberately uncovered, and had been careful that the señor saw it. Doc wanted to see what Señor Oveja's reaction would be. He learned little. The señor kept his thoughts well concealed.

THROUGHOUT the next half hour, Doc Savage remained within sight of the writing desk. He wanted to observe any others who might seek to get a look at the carbon copy.

No one else went near the desk.

The train charged recklessly through the night, swooping across bridges with a thunderous moan, and panting noisily over grades.

Some sage once wrote that the presence of death makes people silent. He should have been on that train. He would have heard more conversation than at a chamber-of-commerce luncheon. In smokers, diners, Pullmans, day coaches, discussion waged. A number of uninformed persons had never heard of Doc Savage. These were speedily enlightened by their neighbors.

One man spoke steadily for five minutes, reciting the remarkable ability of Doc Savage, and the things he had accomplished. He finished with: "This man Savage is a person of mystery. Not much is known about him."

"Oh, yeah!" snorted his listener. "A mystery, eh? And you just told me more about him than you can tell me about the Prince of Wales."

"What I mean is—Savage don't parade his feats around in public," the other explained. "He don't brag. For instance, take his five helpers. There's an engineer, a chemist, a lawyer, a geologist, and an electrical expert. What do you know about them?"

"I have heard this: in their respective lines, they are among the most learned men in the world," was the reply.

"That's right," declared the first man. "Yet Doc Savage is a greater expert in these lines—engineering, chemistry, law, archaeology, and electricity—than his aides, and he's just as proficient in many other lines. They say he is, beyond a doubt in the least, the greatest living surgeon."

"Sounds like a fairy tale."

"Sure it does!" agreed the other. "Just the same, I don't think this bronze man murdered the conductor, and I'd hate to be the fellow who did. Savage will get him, sure."

Heedless of this discussion, and many others along similar lines, Doc Savage returned to his drawing-room. Hardly had he entered when his sharp eyes noted something amiss. A folded newspaper reposed in the wastebasket. He had not placed it there.

His movements unhurried, the bronze man locked the drawing-room door. Then he went to the basket and investigated.

The newspaper was one published in the large town they had passed through some hours before—the division point where unfortunate Wilkie had gone on duty. It was at this town that Señor and Señorita Oveja and El Rabanos had boarded the train.

The newspaper was folded so as to enwrap a knife. The long blade of this was still smeared with gore.

Doc's practiced eye measured the width of the blade. He decided it would exactly fit the wound which had caused Wilkie's death.

Opening one of his many hand bags stacked in the compartment, Doc drew out a powerful magnifying glass. He used it on the knife hilt. Fingerprints had been wiped off.

Doc opened the window and threw the knife out into the night, far from the plunging train.

GLANCING at his watch, Doc saw they would soon reach the next stop—within thirteen minutes, to be exact.

Precisely nine minutes later, the holocaust broke.

From beneath the train came a sudden scream of steel on steel! It was like the wail of a demented monster. The cars rocked in sickening fashion!

Doc Savage plunged the length of the drawing-room, but brought up lightly against the bulkhead.

In the coaches, passengers were hurled against seats. Parcels and suitcases fell off the overhead racks. In the diners, dishes hit the floors as if tossed by invisible scoop shovels. In the mail cars, clerks brought up in tangles with their sacks.

Doc Savage unlocked the drawing-room door, wrenched it open, and whipped out. The steely screeching underfoot died slowly; the train was coming to an unbelievably quick stop.

Doc leaned from a window. With a final squeal of brakes, the train became entirely stationary.

It was no mean feat of agility which Doc performed now. He managed to stand erect outside on the narrow ledge of the train window. One of his hands stretched up, groped, and found a projection on the roof. The practiced swing of a gymnast put him atop the coach.

From this vantage point he could see, as far as darkness permitted, what was occurring. Somewhat more than a quarter of a mile ahead of the rest of the train, the locomotive was just coming to a standstill. In some manner the engine had become detached. No doubt the air brakes were adjusted to stop the coaches instantly in such an emergency.

Doc Savage ran forward along coach tops. It was his guess that some one, possibly traveling over the tops of the coaches as he was doing, had severed the connection between the engine and cars. Doc hoped to glimpse the malefactor.

At the forward end of the train, Doc dropped to the side of the tracks and conducted a brief examination. There was a film of grease and dust on the connecting mechanism. This was smudged where a hand had grasped it.

From his pocket, Doc produced a small flashlight. It gave an intense white beam, no thicker than a pencil. Whoever had caused the locomotive to separate from the train, had worn gloves. There were no fingerprints.

The engine was backing slowly to rejoin its lost string of coaches.

With an ease that would have amazed an onlooker, Doc regained the top of the train. He ran rearward. He was taking no chances. It seemed he had violent enemies on the train. They might chance a shot at him.

Swinging down, he reentered his drawing-room. No one was there. Plucking a hand bag out of his luggage heap, Doc opened it.

He lifted out a metal contraption which resembled a pocket-size magic lantern. The lens of this was almost black. Doc turned a switch on the side of the contraption. Apparently, nothing happened.

Then Doc went to a shelf over the washbowl and picked up a large water glass. The glass had not been on the shelf when he departed. It was the same beaker in which Renny had brought Doc the drink of water.

Doc held the glass in front of the lens of the thing that looked like a magic lantern. What happened was startling.

To the naked eye there was nothing unusual about the glass. Certainly no writing was visible. But the instant Doc held the beaker before the magic lantern, written letters sprang out in a dazzling, electric blue. The writing at the top was in a script so perfect that it might have been done by an engraver. It was Doc's own handwriting. It read:

All five of you shadow Señor Oveja, his daughter and El Rabanos.

Below this was another communication, done in a more scrawling hand. This one read:

The three of them prepared to leave the train just before it stopped, Doc. It looks suspicious, although they might have intended to get off at the next station. Señor Oveja is wearing a big white panama hat that you can't mistake. We're trailing them.

There was no more. Doc dropped the glass and crushed it to fragments under a heel. Then he switched off the lantern contrivance, pocketed it, and stepped out in the corridor.

Moving swiftly, he began a search of the train.

DOC Savage did many things which to the layman were puzzling and sometimes inexplicable. Always he had a reason for what he did. His method of communicating with his friends by leaving writing on glass—writing quite invisible to the naked eye—was something to amaze one unfamiliar with the bronze giant.

When Doc had asked for water, the big-fisted Renny had understood that what his bronze chief wanted was a tablet on which to write some orders.

The writing was done with a bit of strange chalk. Its markings were almost undetectable—until exposed to ultraviolet light. Then it would fluoresce, showing in blue. The lantern contrivance Doc had used was an ultraviolet projector.

Passengers stood in aisles in the coaches, feeling tenderly of spots which had been bruised when the train stopped so suddenly. A few had clambered out and stood beside the track. Not many had done this. There is something which makes the average man reluctant to leave his train when it stops, a subtle fear that he will get left behind when the train starts again.

Doc Savage walked all the way to the baggage cars, and back again to the observation coach. His giant stature, the remarkable bronze hue of his skin, drew much attention. Passengers stared. Without exception, they had heard the gossip concerning this giant man with the golden eyes.

Everyone knew the bronze man had been accused of stabbing Wilkie to death. But no one showed an inclination to stop Doc. The metallic giant did not look like a safe fellow to meddle with.

Doc reflected that events must have occurred swiftly while he was forward making his unsuccessful hunt for whoever had separated the engine from the train.

Nowhere on the train could be seen Señor Corto Oveja, his attractive daughter, or the girl-faced El Rabanos. They had vanished.

From the group of swarthy passengers who claimed they were en route to the meeting of a Spanish society, four were missing.

Doc's five men were also not to be found. Even the pig, Habeas Corpus, was gone.

Doc came out on the observation platform at the conclusion of his search. He noted a man with a red lantern standing some distance down the track. That would be a flagman sent back to guard against a rear-end collision.

From forward came a low crash. This traveled the length of the train, like a rock bouncing downstairs. The locomotive had hooked on. The whistle blared. The man with the lantern came running back. The train was preparing to go on.

Doc Savage vaulted over the observation platform rail, landing lightly on cinders and gravel. The brakeman, running with his head down, did not see Doc Savage. The passengers who had stepped off the train were too busy climbing back on to notice the departure of the bronze man.

The locomotive whistled again, then began to chug mightily and spew steam. The train moved, slowly at first, but gathering speed. The tail lights went past. They looked like little eyes on a monster snake which was crawling backwards. The serpent monster lost itself and its roaring in the distance.

The blacker gloom in the lee of a large rock seemed to detach itself and scud along the track. Doc Savage had become a soundless phantom. From a coat pocket, he drew the rather bulky black metal box which was his ultraviolet lantern. He switched this on and played its invisible beam before him.

Shortly a tiny, arrow-shaped mark sprang out in dazzling, electric blue. It was drawn on top of a rock with the chalk which Doc and his men employed to exchange secret communications.

Doc glided in the direction which the arrow indicated. Two rods, and he found a second pointer.

From a pocket, Doc extracted his small flashlight. His men—trailing their enemies, no doubt—had left these arrows to indicate the direction they had taken. Doc intended to inspect the track, and find just how many individuals his friends were following. He thumbed the flash on.

To his left, a machine gun opened up! It's deadly cackle was like the sound of a gigantic cricket!

Doc Savage seemed to melt down before the hideous gobble of noise and the moaning stream of jacketed lead.

### Chapter VIII
### THE MAN IN THE WHITE HAT

THE stuttering of the rapid-firer ended as abruptly as it had started. The last few empty cartridges to jump from the ejector mechanism tinkled brassily on the rocks. There was no sound after that, but the mad flight of a rabbit which had been frightened out of its wits by the sudden uproar. Eventually, that noise also died away.

*"Bueno!"* hissed a voice. "That, amigos, settles our troubles!"

*"Si, si!"* a low whisper agreed.

Men advanced. From the sound of their movements, there were four of them. They strode warily.

*"Un fosforo!"* commanded one. "A match!"

There was a tiny clatter of safety matches in a box. The box scraped open. But no match was lighted.

One of the marauders screeched! The sound was awful—as if invisible hands had seized his heart and were tearing it out. The ghastly peal trailed off in a sob—a sob like water pouring through a pipe.

The other three skulkers were brave enough. They leaped to assist their companion.

*"Que hay?"* yelled one. "What is the matter?"

He found out soon enough. Something seized his left arm—something which crushed flesh against bone with an awful pressure. The arm went numb with pain. It had no more feeling than a thick cord attached to his body. And by that cord the man was abruptly lifted and flung far to one side.

As he slammed down in brush and rocks, the man was quite sure that it could not have been a human hand which had seized him. It must have been some hulking colossus of the night.

He was wrong.

The other two men became aware of the truth, for their groping hands and striking fists encountered a form unmistakably human.

*"En verdad!"* choked one. "Indeed! It is the bronze hombre! Our lead missed him!"

The four men, seeing Doc sink as their shots roared, naturally supposed he was done for. Not knowing the blinding speed with which the bronze giant moved, they had been too optimistic.

Doc had been warned in advance by a faint click as a machine-gun safety was released, and had dropped in time to get clear. But some rapid-firer slugs had come so close that his ears still rang with their whine.

One of the would-be killers tried to use his machine gun. The weapon muttered deafeningly! The bullets dug up a cloud of dust.

Doc seized the gun, pulled, and got its hideous gobbling stilled before it could do any damage.

Then came a new development. Somewhere nearby, running feet sounded. Reinforcements arriving!

Doc listened, wondering if they were his own men.

They were not. A guttural ejaculation in Spanish told him that.

Flashlight beams—blinding funnels of white—jumped from the hands of the newcomers. The glare illuminated Doc.

One of the new arrivals fired a revolver. Had Doc not pitched violently to one side, that bullet would have ended his career. It was well aimed.

DOC Savage had, for much of his life, walked in the shadow of peril and sudden death. Many men had sought to end his existence by violent means. To kill in defense of his own life, frequently seemed imperative. Yet Doc never did that.

The bronze man's enemies by no means went unscathed. They frequently perished—but always in traps of their own setting. Doc did not take life with his own hands.

Doc still held the machine gun which he had seized. He could have fired upon the approaching gunmen. His chances of downing them were excellent, for there seemed to be only two. But because of the darkness, he knew he would have to kill rather than merely wound.

Flinging aside in a leap that was of almost incredible length, Doc temporarily evaded the white funnels of the flashlights. Doubling low, he raced from the vicinity.

The surrounding terrain was level. Boulders and brush were both small, and would conceal a man only if he lay prone and perfectly still. Doc was forced to race fifty yards before he found adequate cover.

Twice, in that distance, flashlights found him and guns cackled noisily. One bullet cut his coat across the shoulders, but did not open his bronze skin. This was excellent shooting, since Doc was traveling at great speed.

He ducked into the shelter of a boulder, and waited.

The newcomers smashed out more random bullets. They made no effort at pursuit; instead, they helped the four they had rescued to stand erect.

The whole party retreated at a wild run.

Doc promptly set out after them. He deemed it wise to go slowly, for they blasted frequent bullets in his direction. At first, because it would be very dangerous, he made no effort to overhaul the group. Once they reached rough going, he intended to whip close to them.

He suddenly quickened his pace. The rusty squeak of barbed wire against staples had told him the men were mounting a fence.

An automobile engine burst into noisy life! Headlights came on. The car rocketed away.

There was a road beyond the fence, very dusty, but wide and well graded. Doc stood in it and watched the receding car. The taillight bulb had been extinguished, so he could not read the license number.

A flight of bullets came up the road from the receding auto, and Doc hastily quitted the thoroughfare.

Going back to the scene of the fight, he dabbed his flashlight beam about. Tracks were numerous. Doc's practiced eye measured these for possible future reference. He gathered up several empty machine-gun and revolver cartridges.

Beside a studded bush, he found his chief clew. This was an extremely white Panama hat, wide of brim and high of crown. Inside the sweatband of the hat, printed in gold lettering, was a name:

OVEJA

Thanks to the darkness, Doc had not glimpsed the features of any of his attackers. The first four had been sprawled on the ground when the two rescuers appeared with their flashlights. Had they been on their feet, Doc might have glimpsed their faces.

Doc recalled the message in invisible chalk which one of his five men had left on the water glass. It had stated that Señor Oveja had donned a large white Panama. And who had read Doc's wire asking the Mounted Police to surround the train on arrival? Oveja, of course.

Switching on his ultraviolet lantern, Doc resumed what he had been doing when the attack came—following the arrow markers left by his men. The indicators jumped out in unearthly blue flame at frequent intervals. The route angled away from the railroad tracks and mounted a hill.

Beyond the hill, lights were arrayed like white-hot beads strung on taut wires.

THE spots of iridescence were street lamps of the town which the train had been nearing when it had stopped so suddenly. It was not a large metropolis—only a few thousand in population.

Doc Savage followed the luminous arrows down the slope. They turned, paralleling the railroad. When the trail dropped into a small gulley, he used his flashlight, which gave a light as bright as burning magnesium.

The sandy gulch floor was pocked with tracks. To an individual of average perception, they would have looked pretty much alike. An experienced tracker might have known, from the depth of the prints, that two of the men making the tracks were very heavy, and that one was a woman.

Doc Savage, however, read the prints like a chart. He picked out the tracks of his five men—he knew their every peculiarity, from the fact that Monk and Renny, the giants, made deep, big prints, to the straight, military preciseness of Ham's walk, with the little irregularity when the lawyer twiddled his sword cane.

When he had the five segregated, three sets remained. These had been walked over by Doc's aides, so he knew his friends were trailing the three persons. Two of the quarry were men, the other a woman. Her prints were high-heeled and very feminine.

Near the edge of town, the trail turned abruptly and began to circle the settlement.

Doc studied the town, judging its size from the street lights. In small villages, telegrams were usually handled from the railway station. This borough looked large enough to have an office uptown.

Deserting the trail, Doc entered a street and ran along it. His pace would have taxed a proficient sprinter, but, even after he had traversed several blocks, the bronze man's breathing had not quickened appreciably. His mighty muscles were conditioned by regular exercise until they seemed to show no more fatigue than the metal of a machine.

The telegraph office was nested in the front of a brick hotel. It was brilliantly lighted, and relays were cheeping on the instrument table.

On duty was an exceedingly tall and freckled young man, whose hair stood up like the coiffure of a Fiji Islander.

"I want information about certain telegrams which may have come here tonight," Doc told him.

"That is against the rules!" the young man replied promptly.

Doc brought a wallet out. This held numerous cards. He selected one particular pasteboard from the collection in that wallet.

"Does this make it any different?" he asked, and exhibited the card.

The young man looked, then whistled softly. "I'll say it does!"

The card was signed by the highest official of the company, and informed all employees that Doc Savage was to receive every assistance possible, no matter of what nature, or what the possible consequences.

GOING behind the counter, Doc sorted through carbon copies of messages received that evening. He found his own communication, addressed to the local Mounted Police. There was also a wire signed by Señor Corto Oveja, asking the Mounties to arrest Doc as soon as the train arrived.

The prize, however, was one signed simply, "John Smith." It was addressed to "Sam Smith." Doc eyed the body of the message. At first glance the thing seemed unintelligible. The stuff sounded like bad poetry.

THE HORSE OF IRON HE SAW THE CITY FLEAS AWAY DID RUN AND THAT VERY SWIFTLY STOP MAN OH MAN WAS THE GAS BUGGY HANDY

Doc read the doggerel again. Its meaning became clear. It was simply a message from John Smith to Sam Smith, advising that the train would be deserted at the edge of town, and that an automobile should be on hand. The Smith names were probably fakes.

"Remember the fellow who received this?" Doc asked.

"Yep!" said the operator eagerly. "There was two of them. They came in and asked if there was a message for Sam Smith. I remembered them because of the funny way that message sounded."

"Describe them," Doc requested.

"Both were short and dark-skinned. They wore greasy coveralls. I saw an aviator's helmet sticking from the hip pocket of each man."

"Fliers! And strangers in town, eh?"

"Yes, sir!" The telegrapher was beginning to look awed. "Gee whiz! Say, I just happened to think that I've heard of you. Aren't you the Doc Savage the newspapers carry stories about—the fellow they call the 'Man of Mystery?' Aren't you the man who just got back from Arabia, where you took a submarine and followed an underground river under the desert? And at the end of the river you found—"

"I'll use your wires," Doc told the frizzle-haired operator. He had not changed expression, but he was a bit embarrassed. Hero worship got Doc's goat—when he was the subject of admiration.

He examined the "John Smith" telegram. It had been sent from a small way station on the railroad some fifty miles back.

Doc opened the telegraph key. A moment later, he was in communication with the station from which the message had been sent. He described the missive in which he was interested.

"It was thrown off the fast train," reported the distant telegrapher. "But I didn't get a look at the party who threw it."

"Was it handwritten?" Doc queried over the wire.

"It was printed," the other replied.

Doc closed the key and stood up. Since the message was printed, there was no chance of tracing the author by his handwriting.

The freckled, frizzle-haired young man stared at Doc in open-mouthed amazement. He had been listening to the wire talk. He had just heard some of the fastest and most perfect hand-sent Morse to which he had ever listened. It had been as rapid as if sent with a fast automatic key, a "bug." The freckled young man had not believed such a thing possible.

LEAVING the telegraph office and its stunned manager, Doc resumed the luminous-arrow trail left by his friends. He had sprinted the entire distance from the telegraph office. He continued running as he followed the trail.

Around the fringe of the settlement, his course led.

A prowling dog, sighting the bronze man, began to growl fiercely.

"Cut it out, old fellow," Doc called.

The calm friendliness of the mighty man's tone had a marked effect upon the dog. It exchanged tail-wagging for growling. Doc was forced to toss a rock near the dog to keep the suddenly friendly animal from following him. This was another example of the remarkable things his great voice could do.

Unexpectedly, Doc came upon Monk. The homely chemist was sprawled flat on the ground. The pig, Habeas Corpus, lay comfortably beside him.

"Hands up!" Monk growled. "Grab a cloud!" He had failed to recognize Doc.

"Bite him, pig!" Doc ordered dryly.

Habeas Corpus promptly stood up and bit furiously at Monk. Monk dodged. Much to the homely chemist's disgust, somebody had recently taught his pet pig the trick of biting the nearest human when told to do so. Monk was usually the victim of these nips. He suspected the dapper Ham had taught the pig the trick.

"Where is the rest of the gang?" asked Doc.

Monk waved a furry arm in the gloom. "They're watching that joint over there."

Doc peered into the night. He made out a building which resembled a gigantic, square hatbox. "An airplane hangar!"

"Sure," said Monk. "There's a little flying field over there. Señor Oveja, the girl, and El Rabanos are in the hangar."

"You're sure Señor Oveja is there?" Doc asked quickly.

"You bet! We've been right on their heels since they left the train. He couldn't have slipped away."

"Señor Oveja has been wearing his white Panama hat?" Doc queried.

Monk's voice was very small in the murk. "He tossed that aside before he left the train."

"What made him do it?"

"Don't know for sure," Monk said. "It looked like El Rabanos pointed out that the white hat would show up plain in the dark."

Doc informed Monk of the attack which had come as he followed the trail.

"The first four men to jump me might have been off the train," he declared. "From what I learned at the telegraph office, the other two were obviously fliers, waiting near by in a car."

Monk grunted softly. "Renny said he saw a black monoplane that seemed to be following our train. That was just before dark."

"It might have been carrying the two who got the telegram at this town," Doc admitted.

"This thing is sure a mess," Monk muttered. "It shapes up like this: Señor Oveja, his daughter, and El Rabanos are after you. Another gang is after them, and also you."

"And the motivation behind the whole thing is a deep, black mystery," Doc agreed. "Let's collar the three in the hangar, here, and see what we can dig out of them."

AS if touched off by the decision, a hollow roaring burst from the airplane hangar.

"Blazes!" Monk barked. "They've started up a plane!" He raced for the hangar.

The pig, Habeas Corpus, bounced after him, squealing and grunting with each jump.

Doc joined Monk in the race. Both heard metal doors on the hangar rasp open. A plane jumped out of the structure. Its exhaust stack was a fiery mouth that slavered sparks! Its roar was like cannonading!

Except for one thing, Doc and his men might have seized the plane's occupants. It was doubtful if those in the craft knew of the presence of their pursuers. Had the wind been coming from straight ahead, they would undoubtedly have stopped in front of the hangar to warm the engine, before taking off. But the wind was in the opposite direction; it was necessary to taxi across the field before taking the air. The pilot decided to warm his engine while doing that.

Away the ship went. It rolled too swiftly even for Doc's fleet running. Landing lights jutted fans of incandescence from the wing tips of the airplane.

Reaching the far edge of the tarmac, the plane taxied around and took off. It was a large yellow biplane, with a cabin for six.

## Chapter IX
### THE IVORY-CUBE TRAIL

DOC Savage's other men came pounding through the night. Big-fisted Renny was leading.

"Five of us!" Renny boomed disgustedly. "And we let 'em get away!"

"Six of us!" Doc corrected.

"We could have shot 'em down, of course," rumbled Renny. "But the girl was aboard the plane."

The sky was like an overturned bowl of black cotton. Into it, the moaning yellow biplane crawled.

"Let's see if there's another plane in the hangar," Doc rapped.

They raced back for the black box of a hangar. Reaching it, Doc cast his flash beam into the structure.

"There's a crate!" Renny thundered. "No! Two of 'em!"

The planes were small. One was a monoplane, the other an open cockpit. Neither accommodated more than two passengers.

Renny ran to the biplane. It looked the speedier. He latched out the choke, then bounded around in front to spin the prop. But his huge hands only dropped listlessly from the metal blade. He glared at the engine itself.

"Holy cow!" he muttered. "They've got us stumped!"

Doc came around and inspected the plane engine.

"They did it very simply, too," he said dryly. "They just smashed all the spark plugs. There's no need of replacing them. The other plane will be gone before we can get in the air."

Doc had been moving as he spoke. His last word came from near the door.

The other five hastily followed. The bronze man's rapid movements showed he had a plan.

"What's up?" Monk demanded.

"Let's see how fast you are on those bow legs of yours!" Doc suggested.

Heading for town, Doc set a pace which he judged was about the fastest speed the others could travel. It was not slow; they were all adept at running.

Monk, short gorilla legs going like pistons, brought up the rear. At his heels trailed Habeas Corpus. The pig could run like a dog. But, as before, the porker was squealing with every jump.

"Cut that out, or I'll kick you loose from your appetite!" Monk advised the homely shoat.

Habeas Corpus at once stopped squealing.

"That pig has brains, I'm telling you!" Monk shouted.

"That's more than can be said for the guy who owns him!" Ham replied nastily.

The purpose of their pell-mell progress was still a mystery to Doc's five men. They exchanged puzzled looks when Doc entered town and went straight to the telegraph office.

"Do you know the surrounding country?" Doc asked the frizzle-haired operator.

The young man replied: "I've hunted over most of it."

"Mountainous and timbered, isn't it?"

"You bet!"

"I want you to point out all fields which are level enough to land an airplane on," Doc told him. "Don't count the local airport, unless there's more than one."

The young man seized a pencil which dangled from the counter by a chain, planked a telegraph blank on the counter, and drew a map. His movements were rapid.

"There's only three level places near town," he explained. "One is about a mile north. The other two are at least five miles out. There's only one local airport. You said not to count it, so I'm not."

Doc Savage nodded at Monk and Ham. "You two pals go to the field farthest out. The other three of you take the next one. I'll go to the nearest."

"We're after that black monoplane!" Renny rumbled, suddenly enlightened.

"Right!" Doc agreed. "Grab taxicabs for the trips!"

DOC and his men separated in front of the telegraph office. All but Doc went hunting taxicabs.

Deciding not to bother himself with a cab, Doc headed northward through town. The distance to the field was only a mile. Chances were that he would lose time hunting a hack.

The little metropolis was quiet. Every other street light had been extinguished to conserve electricity. Very few houses were illuminated.

Overhead, the clouds abruptly parted and let moonlight spill down. After the earlier darkness, the moon rays seemed as brilliant as sunlight. Trees along the thoroughfare were scrawny, probably because of the cold winters here in Canada. The shrubs and the houses cast moon shadows.

Dwellings became scattered, then abruptly ceased. Doc crossed a washboard of small black hills. Gullies gaped here and there, as if the skin of the earth had cracked. The road was narrow, graded only in spots. Bridges were crude spans of logs, earth-covered. Apparently the road saw little travel.

Indeed, according to the telegrapher's map, the road terminated shortly beyond the field which was Doc's destination. It was a lane leading to a ranch home.

Doc kept on it, his long strides eating up distance. Soon the road dipped. Two hundred yards ahead in the moonlight, Doc distinguished a gate; beyond that was a patch of level meadow.

A black raven of a monoplane stood at the meadow's edge, some distance from the gate.

Without slackening his pace, Doc came up on his toes, making less noise, thus. He could see no one in or near the black plane, but he was taking no chances.

Small hills reared beyond the meadows. Suddenly the tops of these became weirdly white. It was as if an invisible hand had spilled thin snow upon them.

Then Doc discarded all caution, put on more speed. For he knew what the whiteness meant. A car was coming up the road behind him, and its headlights had bleached the hill.

He heard the engine mumble. The machine was coming fast. Doc had hoped to reach the ebony monoplane; but that, he saw now, was impossible.

The neighborhood was unpleasantly bare of vegetation which might furnish shelter. A mowing machine stood near the gate. Its moon shadow made a spidery hump of gloom.

Doc took shelter behind the mowing machine.

The automobile clattered up. Tire treads squealing and throwing dust, it stopped at the gate. The car was a sedan, very shiny with good care, but a model some three years old. It had all the marks of a car hired from a rental agency.

The sedan was jammed with men. In the glare of the moonlight Doc could count six men. All were swarthy complexioned.

Four of them had been on the passenger train. The other two, attired in greasy coveralls, were obviously the aviators who had called at the telegraph office.

A man clambered from the rear of the car and walked ahead to open the gate.

DOC Savage usually wore a vest of pliable leather under his outer clothing. This vest had numerous pockets, and these held ingenious devices—apparatus with which Doc Savage could cope with almost any emergency. The vest now reposed in his baggage, wherever that might now be. Doc was headed for a vacation, and had not been wearing the vest. He was empty-handed.

There was no doubt but that these six men were armed. Under such conditions, the course of safety was to remain undercover.

Doc quitted the shelter of the mowing machine,

and glided up to the car. He had little expectation of reaching the sedan unobserved. Nor did he.

*"Ver!"* cried one of the gang. "See! The bronze devil!"

The men in the machine seemed to go through a convulsion as they grabbed for weapons. The driver let the clutch out; the car went forward like a thing kicked.

Doc had anticipated that the sedan would spring into motion. He had reasoned that by the time it reached the gate, it would be going too swiftly for the man there to spring aboard.

His logic was right—and wrong. The man at the gate was caught off guard. Moreover, he must have been a nervous individual. As the uproar burst forth, he gave one long leap—in the wrong direction! He was directly in the path of the car!

The sedan hit him, and bore him down as if he were a weed. For a moment after he disappeared, ugly crunchings and crackings came from under the machine. The sounds were those of monster jaws munching. When the unlucky man appeared again—behind the rear bumper—he was shapeless.

Inside the car, guns began a hollow coughing. The windows were up; holes appeared in them. The car pushed its radiator snout through the gate with a roar of splintering wood!

Ducking and weaving, Doc Savage ran after the machine until he reached the gate. The post on which the gate was swung was large, and offered more adequate shelter against bullets than the mowing machine. Doc ducked behind it and made himself as thin as possible.

The car was headed for the plane. It traveled too swiftly for those in it to do accurate shooting. Probably twenty shots were fired. Only two of them hit Doc's post. The rest made short, sharp sounds which were strangely remindful of shrilly barking prairie dogs.

In the road, the man who had been run over was moaning and groaning feebly.

The sedan careened to a stop near the black plane. Using revolvers, four of the men fired steadily in Doc's direction. The other two worked at getting the plane motor started.

Taking a chance, Doc dashed to the man who had been run over. The fellow had carried a revolver—he must have had it in his hand when the car hit him, for the weapon was buried in the dust nearby. One of the tires had passed squarely over it.

Doc sought to pick the gun up. But the cylinder fell out. It was a cheap firearm, and the metal pin on which the cylinder turned had been snapped by the weight of the car.

Dropping the useless weapon, Doc whipped back to the post. The dangerous foray had been executed with his best speed, so swiftly that his foes had hardly perceived his move.

The plane engine caught with a *bang! bang!* and a moan. The four swarthy gunmen ceased shooting and piled into the craft. The ship began to scud, its tail lifting.

Without time for his engine to warm up, the pilot pulled off. It was his lucky day. The engine kept turning, and the black bat of a craft clubbed its way up into the moonlight.

LEVELING off in the air, the black plane headed westward.

Doc Savage watched it only long enough to make certain of the direction it was taking. Then he swung over and knelt beside the man who had gone under the sedan.

Life remained in the fellow; he was still moaning.

Doc grasped the man. To a bystander, the bronze man's manner might have seemed rough. But Doc knew what he was doing; he possessed a fund of surgical lore which was probably unequaled.

He straightened the victim out until he was more the shape of a human being. Then, using his flashlight, Doc examined him. An X-ray would have helped; but he learned the important thing without it.

This man could not live long.

"Not a chance, fellow!" Doc told him. There was no use keeping it from him.

*"Como dice?"* The man's query was a wispy, tortured whisper. "What did you say?"

His hearing must have been damaged.

Instead of repeating the statement, Doc Savage put a question: "What's behind all this, hombre?"

The man's eyes only stared glassily. It was as if he had not heard.

"What are you fellows after?" Doc asked, his voice even louder.

The man's eyes seemed as crystal balls fixed in his head. Nothing came past his lips but labored, painful breathing.

"Who is your boss?" Doc persisted.

*"Voy a casa!"* said the man. "I am going home."

He was delirious. Strands were breaking in the already thin life thread which suspended him over the Infinite Abyss.

Doc Savage, seeking to draw something of value from the delirium, leaned close and shouted loudly: "Señor Corto Oveja!"

"Oveja!" gurgled the dying man. "Oveja—fool—easily tricked."

"Tricked by whom?" Doc shouted.

This query brought no response.

With the tips of sinewy, practiced fingers, Doc touched the various nerve centers in the broken body. His vast knowledge enabled him to alleviate pain in this fashion. Although even his surgical skill could not save this man's life, he might prolong the flow of information, such as it was.

"Ivory cube!" gulped the dying man.

"What?" Doc yelled.

"All square, and of ivory!" the fellow moaned in Spanish. "Must get it—worth many million pesos!"

Doc continued his dulling pressure on the nerve centers. It was probable that the man did not even know be was being spoken to. Whatever information that came would be incoherent and by chance.

*"Rico hombres!"* came the agonized whisper. "Rich men? Rich men it will make us! Skeletons under a rock—the ivory cube was gone! The galleon with the crew of skeletons, we cannot find it!"

Doc's bronze features remained composed, but he was about as near bursting with impatience as he ever got. The mutterings of this man only deepened the mystery.

The dying man said loudly and clearly: "Señor Oveja and his daughter are fools, and easily deceived. Alex Savage—"

And then the man died.

"BUT what did he mean?" Monk demanded. "An ivory cube—a galleon with a skeleton crew—skeletons under a ledge—and a lot of pesos! What a hash of information to try to make something out of!"

Doc Savage had assembled his five men, and they stood together in the darkness at the edge of town. It was well past midnight.

"Figuring it out is a swell job for Monk!" dapper Ham said in a jeering voice.

"What do you mean?" Monk asked innocently.

"Trying to dope it out would drive an ordinary man half-witted," Ham assured him politely. "You're safe."

"Meanin' I'm half simple, huh?" Monk growled pleasantly. He addressed his pig. "Habeas, this shyster don't like you and me. Whatcha say to that?"

"T' hell with 'im!" said the pig—at least it sounded as if the pig had replied.

Ham dropped his sword cane and jumped a foot in the air. "For crying out loud!"

"Don't he look funny!" questioned the voice which seemed to come from the pig.

Ham caught on, then. He grabbed his sword cane, straightened, and made a pass at Monk.

Only by a frenzied leap did Monk escape. He retreated to safety, carrying his pet shoat.

"I didn't know Monk was a ventriloquist!" chuckled Long Tom, the electrical wizard. "He must have just picked it up!"

A pitiful groan escaped Ham.

Doc Savage had delayed his recital while the horseplay progressed. Their escapades rarely got so perilous but that Monk and Ham could have no spats. This was only Monk's latest scheme to insult the sartorially perfect Ham.

"Much of what the dying man said was incoherent," Doc resumed. "But two fragments of the information were fairly significant."

Johnny, the skinny archaeologist, took off his spectacles which had the magnifying left lens.

"Which were they?"

"The reference to money," Doc explained. "Once he mentioned a hundred million pesos! That must be the motivation—the loot the gang is after."

"A hundred million pesos!" Monk gasped from the adjacent darkness.

"It may not be that much," Doc pointed out. "The fellow was delirious. He may have spoken the first large figure that came to his wandering mind."

"The dying man tipped us to one thing we had already guessed," mumbled the big-fisted Renny. "Señor Oveja, the guy with the peach of a daughter, is being tricked."

"We're making headway!" said the sharp-tongued Ham. "Now, will someone kindly explain what was meant by an ivory cube, and skeletons under ledges and in boats?"

No one had an answer to that.

"We may see some action before we get it cleared up," Doc said dryly. "Let's set sail, brothers!"

"Where to?" Ham questioned.

"To see about our baggage," Doc told him.

Their luggage, they discovered, after a bit of reconnoitering, was locked in the freight room at the local depot. The night station agent not only refused to turn it over, but when he learned Doc's identity, ran for a Mounted Policeman. It seemed the agent had been advised that Doc was wanted for questioning in connection with the death of the conductor, Wilkie.

Doc glided to the locked freight room the instant the agent was out of sight. He had no implement other than the thin blade of a pocket knife, which Monk produced. But he got the lock on the freight-room door open in a bit less than a minute.

By the time the station agent returned with a Mounted Policeman, Doc and his men had lost themselves in the night, carrying their various pieces of luggage with them.

Ordinarily, Doc coöperated freely with the police, but just now he did not care to be delayed. These Mounted Police were thoroughgoing; they might jail him, despite his influence.

"Where are we going?" asked Ham, trying to balance both his sword cane and his luggage in his arms.

"To the place where this trouble seems to be coming from," Doc told him. "Alex Savage's estate!"

## Chapter X
## CABIN OF MURDER

"ALL I can say is that we picked *some* spot for a vacation!" Ham wailed loudly and mournfully.

The time was somewhat past noon, the following day. The spot was in the neighborhood of Alex Savage's cabin.

"I've been in a lot of tropical jungles!" Ham continued dolefully. "But they were boulevards compared to this!"

Ham was a man who entertained little liking for getting close to nature. He heartily disapproved of all rough going. This was not because he could not stand hardship—Ham could take it. What Ham did dislike, though, was seeing his costly, well-tailored clothes torn off his back. Clothes were Ham's passion. He would forego anything—except possibly a fight—to remain sartorially perfect

His present garments were rapidly beckoning rags. His spirits were sinking accordingly. Ham had donned a nifty woodsman's outfit before starting on this hike. His Park Avenue tailor had told him it was the proper thing when he purchased it. Ham had known better at the time, but had failed to resist the well-tailored lines of the outfit.

"Doc, where's a camera?" Monk demanded loudly. "I want Ham's picture as he looks now! The newspapers would go for it!"

Ham glared indignantly.

The business of reaching Alex Savage's woodland retreat they had found to be no small task. Doc had searched for an airplane, but the only craft available had been an old two-seater biplane. Locating the owner shortly after dawn, Doc bought the decrepit ship outright.

By dint of howling and groaning like a dying thing, the old crate had proved it could take three of them off the ground at once.

Lack of landing fields near Alex Savage's cabin had been another obstacle. To complicate things, a thick fog had been sweeping in from the sea. It had taken three hours of flying to even locate Alex Savage's cabin. Once he had found it, Doc could discern no sign of life about the place.

Doc had been forced to land something like ten miles from the cabin, directly inland. Four trips had been necessary to carry his friends and their load of baggage.

Now, they had been fighting their way through the wilderness for some hours.

"Holy cow!" Renny boomed. "Do you reckon they ever got your telegrams into this country, Doc?"

"I understand the mail is brought up the coast by boat," Doc told him. "Telegrams would probably come in the same way."

"If we only had Doc's big plane!" Ham groaned.

The ship to which Ham referred was Doc's enormous speed plane, a bus capable of descending on land or water. This craft now reposed in Doc's hidden hangar on the Hudson River in New York City. With it, a landing on the little bay in front of Alex Savage's cabin would have been a simple matter.

Doc had not used the plane to fly to Canada simply because he wished to get away from speed and bustle during his vacation.

For some time they had been following a small river. This stream flowed at a terrific pace, a great flat, moaning green serpent which shook white spray off its back at frequent intervals.

The river, Doc had determined from the air, emptied into the tiny bay on the shores of which Alex Savage's large cabin stood.

"Look!" Doc said abruptly. He leveled an arm.

Fog was crawling through the brush like lazy smoke; the vapor lay like a gray mold on the sky, stifling sunbeams and making the day almost twilight. In the creamy illumination, the object which Doc indicated was barely discernible.

It was a fresh grave, marked by a cross.

AS they drew nearer, it became apparent that the cross was ponderous, reaching above Doc's shoulders. It was of wood, roughly hewn.

"The grave is only a few days old," Long Tom offered.

They all walked around to get a look at the inscription on the cross, burned into it on a place where the wood had been chiseled flat.

ALEX SAVAGE

"My uncle!" Doc said sharply.

Silence wrapped the little group for some minutes. Their faces were grim. Discovery of the grave had been a shower of cold water on their spirits.

That Alex Savage was blood kin to their bronze chief, accounted for part of the gloom settling on the group. Ordinarily, they were inclined to sail grandly through all sorts of perils, taking the occurrence of a death as an unpleasant thing which was part of the game.

But this was different. For a little while, as they stood there, adventure seemed somewhat to lose its tang.

"Do you suppose—" Homely Monk made a vague gesture. "I wonder if the death was natural?"

No one replied.

"He had a daughter, Patricia Savage," Doc said at last.

The sartorially inclined Ham seemed to have forgotten both his ragged garments and his good-natured enemy, Monk.

"Let's move!" he muttered. "Graves always get my goat!"

They left their depressing find. The grave was on a level shelf of ground. The gray fog hung all around like water-logged curtains. Doc surmised that the spot overlooked the sea, for the way soon dipped sharply downward, and they could hear the mushy splashing of waves.

They scrambled over rocks, shouldered through brush. Behind them, the river moaned, but they eventually left that sound behind.

The fog, growing more dense, swirled about the men like the clammy tentacles of some fabulous colossus. No birds sounded in the trees. There was

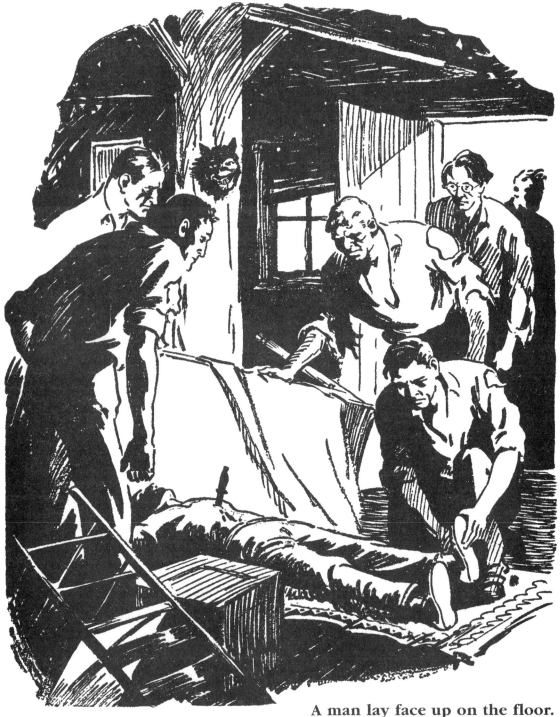

**A man lay face up on the floor. A length of staghorn stuck upright from his chest—the hilt of a knife!**

no perceptible wind, but waves continued to make low splashings in the distance. The splashes came at regular intervals, and no doubt were the result of a ground swell. In the thick fog, these sounds might have been the shuffling steps of some spectral wanderer.

"I don't care a lot for this place!" Monk announced.

"We're getting near the cabin," Doc said.

Monk glanced up sharply. He wondered how Doc had learned that. He decided the bronze man had recognized landmarks.

The truth was that Doc's sensitive nostrils had caught certain faint odors—scents which the others had missed. Doc's olfactory organs were of almost animal keenness, for training them was a part of the daily exercise routine which he took unfailingly.

The vague odor which he had detected was mainly that of gasoline. Also, there were certain flower scents alien to the region, which probably came from a woman's dressing room. Too, there was the faint odor of wood smoke. The smoke tang was old—not such as would come from a blazing fire.

Within the next hundred yards, the cabin came in sight. The sumptuous nature of the rustic establishment created a sensation.

"Holy cow!" Renny ejaculated. "This is quite a place!"

Doc said sharply: "There's nobody here!"

Again the bronze man was voicing what his amazing senses had told him. His ears, sharp beyond those of an ordinary human, had detected no stirrings of life.

The front door of the cabin gaping open, they went in.

A man lay face up on the floor. A length of staghorn stuck upright from his chest—the hilt of a knife!

GLIDING across the floor, Doc Savage studied the dead man.

"An Indian!" he said.

Then he made a brief examination. "A half-breed, I should have said. He died, as near as can be told, about the time we were having all our troubles on the train."

Doc indicated the wrinkled condition of the dead man's lower garments. "The fellow got soaked to the armpits just before his death. His clothes show plainly that they dried on his motionless body. That means they were wet when he was killed, and dried later."

Doc removed the beaded moccasins from the corpse. There was more than a spoonful of bright, clean sand in each slipper.

To the trousers on the corpse was sticking smears of an amber-colored, sticky gum. There was more gum on the lifeless fingers.

To the gum on the trousers clung bits of bark; and to the gum on the hands stuck, not only bark, but tiny feathers and lint.

If the gum and the stuff clinging to it informed him of anything, Doc Savage did not remark on the fact at the moment.

Long Tom, the electrical wizard, looking slightly more unhealthy and pale than usual, asked: "Who is he?"

Doc shook his head in a slow negative. He walked through the other rooms. Everywhere there was evidence of a thorough search—furniture ripped apart, bedding torn and scattered, rugs jerked up. The stuffed, snarling head of a bearskin rug had been chopped open.

"The cabin was searched twice," Doc announced after his scrutiny.

"Twice!" exclaimed skeleton-thin Johnny, puzzled. "How do you figure that?"

Moving into the kitchen, Doc indicated a smear on the floor. It resembled molasses which had been spilled, and had become as hard as glass. An overturned can nearby showed where the stuff had come from. This can bore a varnish label.

"Look at the label," Doc advised. "Notice how long it requires for that varnish to dry."

After he had looked, the dapper Ham said: "Twelve hours."

"Exactly. It is now perfectly dry, but it was spilled during the search. That means the hunt occurred at least twelve hours ago."

Doc went into a bedroom. A gasoline lantern lay on the floor. Its fuel-reservoir base had been split open. The floor about the wreck of the lamp was wet with gasoline.

"You fellows know how fast gasoline evaporates," Doc said. "That gas was spilled less than an hour ago. The second search was more thorough. They even split open the lantern base."

Johnny adjusted his spectacles which had the magnifier lens.

"I've been noticing things, too," he announced. "The breed lying dead in the front room is a servant. I noticed clothes which would fit him. These were in a small room in the rear—obviously a servant's room. There were woman's garments in the room, too. That means he had a wife."

"She's a very large woman, too," Doc agreed. "Her clothes were big. She's an Indian, judging by the bright colors she affects. Apparently she and her husband were the only servants on the place."

"What about the daughter, Patricia?" Renny rumbled.

DOC did not reply immediately. He roved into a bedroom where feminine garments littered the floor. He ended his wandering at a wastebasket which had been overturned, and which had held—

among other trash—rumpled cleaning tissues. These were the paper napkins young women use to remove facial creams.

Picking up one of these tissues, Doc crushed it between his sensitive, metal-hard fingers.

"It was used this morning," he said. "That means the young woman was present that recently."

"But where is she now?" Renny boomed. "And where is the fat servant?"

Renny was asking questions as if he thought his bronze chief had been present at whatever had happened here in the cabin. Renny knew from past experiences that Doc could come upon a scene such as this, and, because of his weird ability to read vague clews, get a story which came uncannily near being the truth.

"I'll show you," Doc said, thereby proving Renny had not been too optimistic.

Doc beckoned the group outdoors. He pointed to tracks in the soft earth. It had evidently rained at dawn, or shortly afterward. And distinguishable in the dirt were footprints of three men and two women. One of the women had worn moccasins, the other low-heeled, hobnailed boots.

"The two women have been kidnaped," Doc said bluntly.

The five aides swapped blank glances. How Doc could look at a set of footprints and tell there had been a kidnaping was beyond their deepest understanding.

Pointing, Doc said: "Notice the tracks show where one of the men shoved the girl—shoved her hard. It was no playful push. He would hardly have done that if the girl was going with them willingly."

Renny waved acknowledgment with his big hands. "You win, Doc."

"The kidnapers were our friends who escaped in the black monoplane," Doc continued.

The five men were fairly accustomed to this sort of thing—Doc's habit of plucking gems of information out of thin air. They had seen him do miracles on more than one occasion. But they could not help looking a bit stunned.

"Holy cow!" Renny rumbled. "I don't see how you can tell that, Doc."

"These tracks were made by the same men who attacked me when I started to follow the trail of luminous arrows from the train," Doc replied. "Those men were members of the gang who escaped in the plane."

He dropped to a knee and inspected the footprints more thoroughly. Then he reiterated: "I am sure of it! Not only the size, but certain worn patches on the soles exactly coincide."

"O. K., O. K.," Renny muttered. "All we need to know now is where the two women prisoners are being held."

"That will take some trailing," Doc replied.

The trail following was an easy matter for a few yards. Then, in the center of a great litter of rocks, the prints vanished. Nowhere could they be seen.

"They began leaping from rock to rock," Doc decided. "They can't do that forever. We'll circle."

SCATTERING, Doc and his men ranged the vicinity. They did not spread so widely but that they could hear each other call, however.

Shortly, Long Tom cried loudly: "Come over here, you guys! I ain't got the trail, but I've got something else!"

The unhealthy-looking electrical wizard was standing near a dense thicket of spruce. At his feet, brownish stains colored the rank woods grass.

"Blood!" he exclaimed dramatically.

"Thoroughly dried," Doc agreed after a close scrutiny. "Part of it was washed away by the rain last night."

The bronze man swung slowly around the spot, eyes on the ground. Several times, he stopped and parted the grass.

The rain had washed away signs, leaving few that could be read. To eyes less than superbly trained, the stretch of forest presented absolutely no clew. Penetrating the spruce thicket, Doc spent some time in it.

He came out of the spruce and said: "In there was where the breed was murdered."

"Yeah?" Monk grunted.

"Maybe I should have said, *from* in there was where he was murdered. The knife must have been thrown. Signs show the breed came out here to meet someone. Evidently, whoever he was meeting got him with a knife thrown from the thicket."

"Any chance of trailin' the killer?" Renny demanded.

"No. The fellow was careful to follow rocky ground coming and going. The rain last night wiped out what few tracks he did make."

Monk had been inspecting the rain-faded prints around the bloodstain. Laboriously, he was finding the tracks which Doc had discovered almost at a glance.

"The two women evidently found the slain Indian," the homely chemist declared. "They carried him to the cabin. Here're the tracks. One set was made by boots, the other by moccasins."

Monk glanced over his shoulder. He wanted to see if Doc would verify the deduction. Monk started. His eyes flew wide.

Doc Savage was nowhere about!

Doc's five friends showed no excitement over the bronze man's disappearance. Doc had a disconcerting habit of vanishing on certain occasions. Doc had merely glided into the brush, of course, but his going had been so silent as to seem spectral.

By the time his absence was noticed, Doc had covered scores of yards. He traveled swiftly until he was a full quarter of a mile from the cabin. Then he swung in a wide circle.

The bronze man seemed to undergo a strange change. He became animal-like in his searching for the trail. He utilized not only his eyes, but his sense of smell as well. Much of the time, he traveled on all fours. Occasionally, when desiring to move swiftly, or to clear a tangle of brush which no man could have penetrated without infinite labor, he sprang upward and swung along, with the prodigious agility of a monkey, from one tree limb to another.

IT was a tangle of spider webs which finally showed Doc the trail.

The webs had been torn from their anchorage by some passing body, and hung dangling. A few yards from that point, Doc found a footprint. It was small; unmistakably feminine. He did not touch it, did not span its proportions with his fingers. But he knew it was the footprint of the girl who had been seized from the cabin.

It was somewhat uncanny, the ability, which Doc had acquired by long practice, to judge size by eye alone. Like Doc's other unusual accomplishments, there was nothing supernatural about this. It was an accomplishment perfected by his remarkable routine of exercises.

This routine occupied two hours daily, and in it was a process where he cast small white balls on the ground repeatedly, calculating just how far apart they had fallen. Careful measurements verified his judgment.

Doc followed the trail. It was not easy. The kidnapers had taken pains to conceal their path. They trod rocky ground wherever possible. They entered a small stream, followed it fully two hundred yards; here, water had washed away the tracks.

At one point—an eddy where the water was stagnant—Doc found a faint haze of mud still suspended. It had been stirred up by the passing of his quarry. This proved they were not far ahead.

Going became more difficult. The trail mounted sheer slopes, dived into rocky gulches. Stony boulders and ledges were steadily underfoot. The stuff would not retain footprints.

The wild western country produces certain individuals who are known as "sign readers." These are expert trackers, and are employed to trail thieves, find lost livestock, and kindred other jobs. So expert do these men become that they can look at a stretch of ground and see a clear trail where another man can distinguish nothing.

Had a sign reader been watching Doc Savage now, he would have been driven to conclude himself a veritable amateur. For it was in actuality no trail at all which Doc followed. The stony earth retained no prints.

Doc ranged back and forth, his strange golden eyes photographing everything in his mind's eye. He discerned certain bugs and small lizards loitering about the rocks. In other places, these were not in evidence. It was plain they had been frightened to cover.

They were such vague clews as this which guided the bronze giant.

The noise of the river became audible. The kidnapers seemed to be heading straight for the rushing torrent. The noise of the river was like that made by a large tree being shaken by some gigantic hand.

Wadded masses of fog crawled through the rocks like enormous, gray phantom cats. In spots underfoot, little puddles of water stood, the result of the rain of the night before.

Doc found where one of the party he was following had stepped into a pool, and left a plain trail for some distance. The boot tracks were small—those of the girl. A bit farther on, Doc began finding small colored glass beads, of the sort used in decorating Indian moccasins.

Both women seemed to be doing their bit to advertise the trail.

THE roaring of the river became louder. It might have been a noisy beast drawing near. The sound had lost its likeness to a tree being shaken. It was ugly and throbbing, and full of sobs and gurgles. It had a quality of ugly savagery. It caused the very eardrums, against which it battered, to ache.

Then Doc came to a canyon. It was perhaps a hundred feet deep. He could not see the opposite walls, nor the bottom. He had to climb down to see how deep it was.

Upstream a few rods, there was a high waterfall. This was making the roaring that hurt the ears.

The trail which Doc was following ended at the water's edge. The waterfall made a vast thunder in the canyon, and it was shattered into spray by its plunge over the precipice. From the noisy inferno, mist arose like smoke from a burning house. It mingled with the fog; it darkened the sun. Its wetness drooled on the surrounding rocks until they ran rills of water, as if it were raining.

Doc lifted his gaze. Overhead, the mist clouds collided and merged and tumbled like fighting things.

For perhaps a minute he stared upward. Then he lowered his eyes. The river was all foam. Waves snapped twice the height of his head. Their tops spat foam like ravenous jaws.

Here and there a rock jutted from the stream bed. So swift was the flood that air spaces were left behind these rocks, which reached far down toward the stream bed.

By peering closely, Doc could discern the tracks of those he was following. The party had waded directly out into the boiling waters.

This was puzzling. No human being could wade the current; no boat could exist in it.

Doc glanced upward again. The mist that lathered the air overhead seemed to fascinate him. He watched it go through convulsions for a bit. Then he clambered up the canyon side.

The walls were not exactly sheer, but they were steep enough that no loose rocks clung in mid-air. Fifty feet, Doc climbed—seventy-five. He was still in the clouds of spray. The stuff dashed against his face.

Pausing, he aligned himself with the tracks which had disappeared into the stream. He was a little to the right. He corrected his position. Then he looked upward.

Very low, yet penetrating the cataclysmic roar of the waterfall with seeming ease, came a tiny trilling note—the sound that was characteristic of Doc Savage. The fantastic note seemed hardly to come into being, then it was gone again. Doc himself showed no sign of being aware that he had made it.

The bronze man was studying what he had found. It was simply a rope tied securely to a tree. The rope stretched across the canyon.

DOC had expected something like this. It was the only thing that explained the tracks which had entered the stream. Some kind of a sling was pulled back and forth on this aerial cableway, he believed. The sling must hang low enough to enable those in the water to grasp it. The ingenious thing about this crossing device was that the cable stretched where it was completely hidden by clouds of mist and spray from the waterfall.

Doc grasped the cable and tested it. Then he leaped high in the air and landed, perfectly balanced on his feet, on the cable. He did not go hand over hand across the ropes, as another man might have done. He ran atop it, in the fashion of a tightrope walker.

Spray had made the rope very slippery. More treacherous footing would have been difficult to imagine. Doc seemed to give it no more consideration than he would have given a sidewalk. He carried no balancing rod—without which few tightrope walkers venture to perform—yet his balance was perfectly maintained.

The rope sagged in the middle, making the crossing more dangerous. Below, waves darted up like green-snouted, repellent lizards of titanic size. A fall meant certain death.

The rope curved sharply upward. Doc tilted far forward to maintain his balance, and his feet slipped repeatedly on the spray-wet fiber. These slippings, which would have raised the hair of a spectator, seemed to affect Doc's nerve not at all. He appeared to be as immune from fear as the metal he resembled.

A tree appeared in the misty void. To it was secured the rope end. Doc discerned a rude basket of sticks, pulleys, and ropes lying nearby. It was a makeshift car for the cableway over the canyon.

Doc was almost on the point of leaping from the rope to solid ground when a man appeared beside the tree. He was squat, swarthy, and wore greasy coveralls. He had a rifle stock jammed against his shoulder.

The rifle coughed a tongue of flame which actually blackened the coat fabric over Doc's heart. The bullet made a tiny, ragged hole in the patch of powder-burned cloth.

## Chapter XI
### THE VANISHED BOX

DOC Savage's shoe soles seemed to acquire roller bearings. His giant form skittered back down the sloping wire.

He was bent nearly double now—he had folded into that position an instant after the rifleman fired. His movements were strangely grotesque. He slouched forward and seized the rope, his arms and legs whipping wildly! Doc seemed to be trying to retain his grip on the rope.

The swarthy rifleman leaned far out to peer through the mist.

*"Bueno!"* he hissed. "My bullets hit his heart!"

The man jacked a fresh cartridge into his rifle, planted the weapon against his shoulder, and aimed deliberately.

He could barely make out Doc's figure. It was a feverishly contorting, bronze-hued smear in the dripping gray abyss. The bronze man's movements reminded the rifleman of a squirrel that had been shot, and was attempting frantically to cling to its limb. Even as the man peered over his rifle sights, the metallic figure fell away from the overhanging cable.

Spray which boiled up from the water swallowed Doc's falling body.

*"Bueno!"* hissed the swarthy man again. He lowered his rifle. "He did not need a second shot."

The rifleman did not take the death of the bronze man for granted, however. He scrambled down the steep wall of the canyon to the water. There, washed by spray which the mad waters flung up, he explored.

He was positive Doc Savage had fallen into the river where it was roughest and running most violently, and equally sure Doc could not have escaped, even had he not been shot through the heart.

The man climbed back up the canyon wall and left the vicinity. He seemed none too familiar with the region. His progress was a series of careful sallies from one landmark to another. He stood near a tree, which had an extra large trunk, until he located a pair of large boulders which looked familiar. His next lap was to a brier thicket.

The fellow was plainly no woodsman, and he was taking no chances on getting lost.

He did not have far to go, soon entering a large grove of trees. There was a clearing in the center of the grove.

Four tents were pegged out in the clearing. The canvas was painted a green hue which camouflaged perfectly with the leaves overhead.

At the edge of the clearing stood an enormous, brushy-looking mound of green. This had a somewhat artificial look. However, only close examination would have revealed that the mound was made of freshly cut green boughs.

The boughs were stacked over a black monoplane, concealing it thoroughly. It would be almost impossible for an aviator flying over it to detect the presence of the black ship.

Several men sprang to meet the bridge guard. They had rifles in their hands; revolvers were belted about their midriffs.

*"Mulo cabeza!"* gritted a man. "Mule head! You were left to guard the rope over the river!"

"Keep your shirts on, caballeros!" chuckled the rifleman. "What do you think I have just done?"

"Deserted your post!" somebody growled.

"No, amigo! I was standing at the rope end with my rifle ready, when the bronze man tried to cross. I shot him in the heart! He fell into the river!"

*"Bueno!"* chortled the other, suddenly delighted. "Good! Did he fall where the water ran swiftest?"

"He fell where no man could swim, amigo."

MORE men stumbled out of the green tents. They crowded around the man who was the self-admitted killer of Doc Savage. They were prepared to make a hero of the fellow.

"You are quite a caballero!" declared a man. "Many others have tried to kill this bronze wizard and failed. I once heard a rumor that he was gifted with everlasting life—that he could not be killed."

"Where did you hear that rumor, señor?" demanded a listener.

"In our native Spain, amigos."

*"Tue?"* ejaculated the other. "What? Has the fame of Doc Savage penetrated to our native land?"

*"Si, si!"* That bronze man was known to many lands."

*"Was* is correct, señors," chuckled another fellow.

The late bridge guard swelled with pride. He flashed white teeth in an expansive grin, and stuck out his chest like a pouter pigeon.

"It is possible I shall draw a bonus when our boss hears of this, eh señors?" he queried.

"We must find the ivory cube before anybody draws a bonus!" one of the others reminded.

"Have you not yet learned where the white block is?" snapped the guard.

"What do you think we are—magicians?" snarled one of the group. "We have not had time to question the señorita—fittingly."

"The fat one—the squaw—she is what the Yankees call a bat from hell!" a man offered. He felt tenderly of an ear. From the upper end of the ear, a semicircular segment had been bitten. "Like a dog, the squaw snapped at me! Before I could dodge, she was spitting out a piece of my ear!"

Somebody unkindly laughed.

Five of these men were the fellows who had escaped in the black monoplane. The others—there were seven more—were somewhat incrusted with grease and dirt, an indication they had been encamped here in the wilderness for some time. The only clean, well-kept thing about them was their guns. These were spotless, freshly oiled, and carried in open holsters.

"What do we do next?" questioned a man.

"We will let our chief know that I have killed Doc Savage," said the rifleman who had guarded the rope bridge.

"Have you forgotten, my friend?" somebody chided him, "that we have strict orders never to go to our chief. He always comes to us."

"The chief, señors, should know what I have done," insisted the man. "It was no small feat! Here is how I did it!"

The man now proceeded to describe a terrific fight at one end of the rope bridge. Many blows had been exchanged; bullets had flown, and knives had flashed—to hear him tell it.

The fellow was an accomplished liar. Out of his imagination, he conjured an amazing battle; before he had finished talking, he had not only slain Doc Savage, but had first bested the bronze giant in a physical contest.

"And that is how it happened, hombres!" The tale spinner wiped perspiration from his forehead. The sweat had been brought out by the very fierceness of the combat which he had just described. "Truly, it was the great fight of my life."

"You are *mucho hombre!"* a listener agreed, tongue in his cheek. "If you could now lead us to the galleon with the crew of skeletons, you would indeed be a hero."

*"Si, si,"* agreed the world's champion liar. "The galleon of skeletons! We will find it, amigo! But the ivory cube comes first!"

THE words caused the men to exchange glances. An ugly determination rode each face. Here was a question on which they all seemed to be of the same mind.

"A man should go and guard the river crossing," some one suggested.

"Not me, señor!" snapped the man who had lately been at the post. "I have done my guardings for this day."

This struck the others as being a reasonable statement. So another man was dispatched to take a position at the rope over the river.

"Now to question the Señorita Savage," the leader announced.

They moved in a body to one of the green tents.

"Come out, Señorita Savage!" commanded the leader.

There was no response from the tent.

"Come, señorita" the man directed, more sharply.

Once more, nothing happened.

The man stooped and looked in. He emitted a surprised yell. He dived into the tent like a terrier after a rat. There was noise as he jumped about, and two blankets flew outdoors.

"Es no posible!" the man screeched. "It is not possible! Señorita Savage is gone!"

Had the men suddenly discovered that they were standing over a lighted charge of dynamite, they could not have scattered more quickly. In a wild wave, they spread around the tent. At the rear wall, one fellow found a stake loose.

"Here is where she escaped!" he cried.

"En verda!" sneered the former bridge guard. "Indeed! So this is the way you hombres keep track of your prisoners!"

"Your own big mouth is to blame, caballero!" someone advised him angrily. "While you were talking so loud and fast, telling us what you did to this man Savage, she escaped!"

"Scatter, hombres!" shouted the man who seemed to possess some semblance of authority. "Look everywhere for her! She cannot have gone far."

Like a pack of hounds which had lost a trail, the men dispersed. Some dashed madly into the woods; others peered in brush clumps. There was plenty of shrubbery, for the gang had not troubled to clear the camp site.

Some of the men probed about the camp. One of these went to the green tent which held the squaw, Tiny. A single glance inside sufficed to show that the squaw's legs were still bound securely. The man started to back out.

"Wait!" grunted Tiny. "You want know what way white gal go?"

"Si, si, Señorita!" said the man. "Yes, yes!"

"Cut um loose," said Tiny. "Me tell um."

"Si!" exclaimed the man delightedly. He sprang inside.

He was hardly in the tent when a slender, sinewy brown arm enwrapped his throat from behind. This caused his mouth to fly wide open. Another brown hand promptly stuffed a wadded handkerchief between the gaping jaws.

PATRICIA Savage had been crouching to one side of the tent door while Tiny enticed their victim inside.

During the excitement which had attended the arrival of the killer, Patricia had managed to free herself and crawl into the tent which sheltered the squaw.

Her escape had been discovered at an inopportune moment. Given a few seconds more, and Patricia would have been gone, along with Tiny.

Tiny reared up to help subdue the man. She gave a wrench, and the rope fell off her wrists. A kick, and her ankles were free. The ropes had merely been arranged to look like they were tied. That was Patricia's idea.

The man was probably not more than twenty-five, and quite husky. He had a neck like a young bull. He was more than a match for nine out of ten run-of-the-street men.

Patricia, however, had taken him by surprise. Moreover, she was a young lady who combined good looks with a well-developed muscle. She not only kept the man from yelling an alarm, but she had his wind completely shut off.

The man kicked, struck backward. Not for nothing had Patricia taken fencing lessons in a finishing school. She evaded his blows easily. The man grabbed her attractive bronze hair and gave it a tremendous yank.

Tiny went into action. Stooping, she seemed to pick something off the floor and plant it forcibly on the man's chin. It was a beautiful haymaker.

The man stopped struggling as suddenly as if he had been shot through the brain.

"Me learn that practicing on Boat Face," Tiny muttered. A moment after she had spoken, Tiny seemed to remember that Boat Face was dead. Her lower lip quivered, and tremendous sobs shook her enormous bosom.

Patricia eyed their unconscious victim, then appraised the squaw's size.

"I'll have to put on his clothes and walk out of camp," she said. "If they would fit you, I'd let you go, Tiny. But you're too darn big. When I get out of camp, I'll make a fuss. I'll yell or something. When they rush to investigate, you beat it."

"O. K.," said Tiny.

The man had a gun. Patricia took that; then she yanked off the man's shirt. After this, she turned her back.

When she wheeled around again, Tiny had the fellow's pants and shoes, and had spread a blanket over his sleeping form.

Patricia now donned the garments. She picked up the man's hat, looked at the greasy interior, grimaced, scrubbed it vigorously with her elbow, and put it on. She stuffed her bronze hair under it.

"How do I look?" she asked Tiny.

Tiny leaned over and popped their prisoner on the jaw with a fist. He had shown signs of reviving. "You look all right, Miss Pat."

Patricia calmly walked out of the tent and strolled for the woods. If any of her enemies discovered her, there was a good chance that they would start shooting. They were of a race notoriously quick on the trigger.

No one, fortunately, saw through her disguise. When she reached the first trees, Patricia resisted an impulse to run. The woods were full of maddened searchers.

PATRICIA had not covered two rods when she saw a human hunter. He was prowling around, peering this way and that. It chanced that he was the same individual who had been guarding the bridge.

Patricia, peering out of her tent while making her escape, had seen this man. She had heard him bragging of the murder he had committed. The name of the murder victim had been a shock.

It was Patricia's first knowledge that her famous cousin, Doc Savage, was in the vicinity.

The young woman was at a loss to explain why Doc was in this part of Canada. She did not know it, but she had not received the bronze man's messages advising her of his northern vacation.

Patricia had intended to send to Doc for help. But that morning, she had found both the storage barrel and the launch tanks empty of gasoline. This had prevented her from going to send a telegram. She was relieved that no gesture of hers had drawn Doc to his death.

However, Patricia was horrified to think that Doc had perished. She was also filled with a consuming rage against his killer.

Patricia was no butterfly who blossomed forth only at social functions. That did not mean she was a wallflower when confronted with the glittering pomp of society. But at the same time, she was a two-fisted young woman who could go out and do things.

Glaring at the self-admitted murderer of Doc Savage, she made a decision. She concluded to seize the fellow and turn him over to the nearest Mounted Policeman.

Stepping behind a tree, Patricia drew her gun—the weapon she had taken from the man she had overpowered. She examined it; the thing was loaded. She waited purposefully.

Patricia could hear her victim approaching. He had been headed in this direction when she first saw him. She believed his course would take him within arm's length of the tree behind which she stood. In this, she was not wrong.

The man rounded the tree. He was looking in another direction, so his back was half turned. He did not see Patricia.

Reaching out, Patricia jammed the barrel of her gun against the nape of the man's neck.

The man gave one horror-stricken scream and fell over in a dead faint.

Patricia was thunderstruck. She would have maintained that it was beyond the most nervous of women to faint at the mere touch of cold metal on the back of a neck. But what Patricia had no means of knowing was that this man was highly wrought up.

For the last half hour, the fellow had been seeing Doc Savage in his mind's eye. Especially did he remember the metallic quality which was Doc's chief characteristic.

When cold metal touched his neck, his reaction was that Doc's frosty ghost had seized him. So he fainted.

"Darn it!" snapped Patricia, and began running deeper into the woods.

By yelling before he had keeled over, the man had upset her plans. The howl had spread the alarm.

"*Que hay!*" shouted a man from somewhere. "What is the matter?"

Patricia hoped he would be a long time finding out. She put on more speed, and began to have a faint hope that she would make it. If she did, her plan would have worked out to a nicety. The alarm would be exactly what was needed to give Tiny her chance to escape.

Patricia was too optimistic, however. A man hurled himself from behind a tree into her path. His gun was in its holster. With bare hands, he sought to seize the fleeing girl.

The fact that the man was not using his gun saved his life. Instead of shooting him, as he no doubt deserved, Patricia made a pass at his head with her revolver barrel.

*Clank!* went the gun on the fellow's skull. He fell at her feet.

Thinking he was unconscious, Patricia started to step over him. But the man grasped her by the ankles and tripped her.

Too late, Patricia sought to shoot him—through a leg. They scuffled for a moment. Then Patricia lost her revolver.

That marked the finish. In a moment, more swarthy men came rushing through the timber to the aid of their comrade. Seizing Patricia, they bound her hand and foot. Then they carried her back to camp.

THE first thing Patricia saw in camp was the voluminous Tiny. The squaw lay on the ground in an attitude of slumber.

"What have you done to her?" Patricia shrieked.

A man tapped his rifle barrel expressively and said: "I kees her weeth thees, señorita."

Patricia gripped her upper lip between firm white teeth, and said nothing. She was worried and angry enough to burst into tears. She felt certain she would not get another such opportunity to escape.

"What do you want with me?" she demanded of the men.

"We have told you that, señorita!" one said.

"The ivory cube?" Patricia asked bitterly.

"Si, señorita. The ivory cube is right. We want it."

"It'll be a long old day before you get it!" Patricia retorted angrily.

The man shrugged his shoulders and made expressive hand-spreading gestures.

"Quien sabe?" he smiled coldly. "But why are you so determined not to give it to us?"

"I'll never turn the cube over to my father's murderers!" Patricia rapped.

The young woman's captor looked hurt at this. His face assumed an injured expression. He shrugged several times.

"But, señorita," he said mournfully, "you do us mucho wrong to think that."

Patricia sniffed indignantly.

"Of course, I have no proof," she said. "You could claim the werewolf did it."

The man gave a pronounced shiver. He rolled his eyes skyward. He crossed himself.

"Heaven forbid!" he muttered. "The werewolf, señorita—has he bothered you also?"

Patricia eyed the man narrowly. She could not for the life of her tell whether he was putting on an act for her benefit, or telling the truth.

"Oh, don't try to kid me!" she said finally.

"We are not kidding anybody, señorita. We know nothing of this murder. But we do know you have a certain ivory cube. It is imperative that we have it. We are going to get it."

"Why do you want it?" Patricia countered

"That, señorita, is our own affair!"

"I examined the block," Patricia said wonderingly. "There is no inscription of any kind on it. It seems perfectly solid—it does not ring hollow when you tap it. Of what possible value can a plain ivory block be to you?"

"So you do have the block!" her captor exclaimed triumphantly.

Patricia bit her lips. The cat had been in the bag without her knowing it, and she had let it out.

Her captor waved his arms in excitement. He shouted loudly to his fellows: "You hear, amigos? She has the block! We have but to make her tell where it is!"

THE swarthy men gathered about. Eyeing them, Patricia decided they were about as evil-looking a collection as she had ever seen. Any one of them would have drawn a second look from a policeman. She did not like the fierce greed on their ugly faces.

The men began to make cruel suggestions.

"A knife on her pretty face!" proposed one. "That will make her talk!"

"Si, si," agreed another. "But a red-hot iron is better."

"Why not work on the squaw?" asked one man. "I think the Señorita Savage is a young woman who will talk to save her servant."

At this point, the man who had fainted when he felt Patricia's cold gun against the back of his neck, regained consciousness. He glanced about in a dazed fashion, keeping silent until he found out what was going on.

"What happened to you?" somebody asked him.

"She struck me over the head!" replied the wily liar. "But, at great risk to my life, I managed to yell the alarm!"

A man ran up. He carried a small portable gasoline stove of the type woodsmen sometimes use—usually tenderfoot woodsmen who have trouble building fires.

He pumped up the pressure tank on the stove, and applied a lighted match. The stove began to roar softly, and give out an intensely hot blue flame.

The man placed the stove near Tiny. Then he prepared to grasp the squaw's feet and hold them over the blue flame.

He had almost forced the feet into the flame when there was a loud crash. The gasoline stove lost much of its shape, and jumped end over end. It had been hit by a large rock, flung with terrific force.

The swarthy men whirled.

They saw a sight which, to a man, they carried in their memories to their day of death.

## Chapter XII
### THE HAND THAT BECKONED

HAD an elephant walked out in that clearing in the Canadian woods, consternation could hardly have been greater. Certainly, the shock would have been less.

The late bridge guard shrieked loudly, spun around, and fled! His wild terror would have been comical, had it not been so harshly real. The man was stricken with horror.

He had seen a ghost coming across the clearing. A ghost of the bronze giant he had sent into the torrent below the waterfall! More appalling, this ghost was not moving with the stately walk usually attributed to its kind. The thing was coming with a speed which in itself seemed beyond human ability.

A towering bronze Nemesis, Doc Savage bore down on the swarthy man.

Doc's escape had been managed quite simply. He now wore the remarkable vest of many pockets which held his assortment of apparatus. This was lined with a metallic mail which would stop even a big-game rifle slug.

In one of the vest pockets was a long, slender, very strong silk cord. To the end of this was fixed a grappling hook.

Doc had simply hooked the grapple over the rope spanning the river, then lowered himself until he hung concealed in the clouds of spray boiling above the water. It chanced that the wait was almost his undoing, however. In the terrific roar of the falls, he had not heard his enemy descending the canyon side. Luckily, Doc had seen the other first.

Doc had climbed back up his silk cord to the cable, and swung hand-over-hand to terra firma.

The bronze man had followed his assailant to camp, and had been lurking nearby ever since. Unfortunately, he had not been in a position to help Patricia with her escape. Her flight had been opposite Doc's place of concealment.

Doc had demolished the gasoline stove with the thrown rock.

What now transpired happened with the violence of exploding dynamite and the rapidity of an electrical phenomena.

Patricia Savage had often wondered what her famous cousin looked like. She had read of some of his feats. She had heard tales of him. But she had never met Doc, and she had doubted his being the man he was said to be.

Watching Doc in action, Patricia concluded he was all he was rumored to be, and then some. Discounting the fellow who had fled, there were eleven men in the clearing. All were fair physical specimens. Moreover, they were armed.

One man sprang forward, leveled his revolver at Doc's chest, and pulled the trigger repeatedly. The range was short. He could hardly miss. It was possible to count the ragged holes which his bullets caused to appear magically in the bronze man's coat front.

Doc did not waver. The slugs might have been beans pelted at a rhino. He came on like a juggernaut of metal.

The gunman finished shooting, and threw his revolver wildly at Doc.

The bronze man dodged. The way he did this was in itself reason for popeyed surprise. The gun seemed to pass through flesh and bone, so swiftly did he weave his head aside and back.

"I shoot him six times!" shrieked the one who had thrown the gun. "He should be dead!"

The seeming impossibility of what they had just witnessed held the others spellbound. The fractional moment during which they stood and stared proved disastrous.

The mighty bronze man drove a hand inside his clothing, brought out a small metal egg of an object. He flung it.

The metal lump dropped among the swarthy men with a loud report!

Without exception, the men clapped hands over their eyes. They began to yell in terror. They could see nothing—the world had suddenly gone jet black!

They were either too stupid or too surprised to realize they were now standing in a smoke cloud—a great wad of inky blackness which had spread with lightning suddenness from the metal egg.

PATRICIA SAVAGE was only slightly less surprised than her captors. She was lifted and borne rapidly through the black cloud. With such uncanny ease was she carried that Patricia was slow to realize human hands were bearing her.

She could not see a thing in the almost blue-black void, but she knew it must be the gigantic bronze man who was bearing her.

Patricia was carried out of the smoke. The day, dim and vaporous as it was, seemed almost brilliant after the sooty pall out of which they had come.

The young woman discovered her eyes had not been affected by the dense smoke. They did not smart.

She was lying across the bronze man's mighty shoulders, she discovered.

Patricia looked down and gave a violent start. Under one arm, as easily as another man would carry a sack of groceries, Doc had tucked Tiny. The squaw weighed well over two hundred pounds.

Doc Savage whipped across the clearing, his great speed seemingly impeded not at all by his burdens. Patricia found it hard to believe. This metallic giant had the strength of a dozen men!

Reaching the edge of the clearing, Doc planted the two women on their feet.

"Run!" he said, and pointed in the direction of the rope spanning the river gorge.

Patricia began: "If you need any help—"

"Do what I say!" Doc said sharply.

Patricia looked slightly indignant, but began running.

Turning to the right, Doc veered around the clearing edge. His progress was swift, but he also zigzagged from side to side, keeping behind brush and trees as much as possible.

None of the swarthy men had come from the black cloud as yet. This was probably because the somber pall had spread until it was more than a hundred feet across. The smoke boiled like a dark foam.

One of the men finally staggered into view. He stood staring stupidly at the fog-packed sky, as if it were something he had never expected to see again.

Suddenly, he understood the nature of what he had thought to be a weird blindness. Drawing his revolver, he fired it rapidly into the air.

"This way, hombres!" he screeched. "We have been tricked!"

IN his excitement, the man failed to observe a bronze apparition which streaked under the pile of green boughs that covered the black monoplane.

The instant he was concealed under the brush, Doc glanced back to see if he had been observed. Apparently he was unseen.

He was under the right wing of the plane. Doc crawled to the big radial motor, and his deft fingers explored its innards.

Doc's familiarity with airplane motors was as profound as his other lines of knowledge. He had, in fact, designed a motor which was in use on a large air line in the United States. This was not public knowledge, it being popularly supposed that the motor was the work of an elderly and kindly inventor whom Doc had befriended. Nor did any one but the inventor, who was also the manufacturer, know that the design for the motor had saved the old gentleman's business.

The motor of this black plane was fitted with two carburetors. Doc removed both, his corded fingers loosening the fastener nuts after a little straining. Fortunately, they were not tight.

Doc buried both carburetors under the plane, carefully replacing the dirt so that the hiding place would not be noticed.

Peering through the fur of brush which camouflaged the ship, Doc saw the swarthy men. They were in a group, and heading for the opposite side of the clearing. A moment later, veering behind the immense wad of inky smoke, they were lost to view.

Doc Savage promptly deserted the plane. Entering the timber, he circled widely.

Patricia and Tiny had been running with all the speed they could muster. Patricia gave a start of surprise when Doc Savage materialized like a phantom beside her.

"One of those men shot right at you!" she gasped wonderingly. "I saw the bullets hit! Why didn't they harm you?"

"Bullet-proof vest!" Doc explained cryptically.

Many things were puzzling Patricia. Speaking as she ran, she sought to get them straightened out.

"You are Doc Savage, aren't you?" she asked.

"Right," Doc admitted.

"How does it happen you are here?"

"Better save the breath for running," Doc told her.

Patricia gasped with faint indignation. The fact that her father was a fairly wealthy man had not exactly spoiled her, but she was not accustomed to being told what to do in such short fashion.

"But," she snapped, "I want to know what—"

"There're lots of things we both want to know!" Doc told her. "We can save them until we get clear."

Patricia seemed about to express an opinion contrary to this. But a loud, fierce shout from behind caused her to change her mind.

"Buenos!" was the cry. "Here is the trail!"

"Darn it!" cried Patricia, and saved her breath for running.

THEY reached the rope which spanned the gorge below the falls. The canyon was like a great cauldron in which water boiled thunderously and poured up frost-cold steam.

Patricia glanced over the brink and shuddered.

"I was never so scared in my life as I was when they hauled me over in this thing," she declared, indicating the rickety cage which could be pulled across the rope.

Doc was somewhat at a loss to know why the swarthy men had spanned the river in this fashion. He put a question to clear that up.

"I presume there is no other point nearby where the river can be crossed?" he asked.

"Not for miles in either direction," Patricia replied.

She peered over the brink once more, and watched bucketfulls of spray being flung higher than the canyon walls by the force of the torrent.

Patricia had been under a great strain for the last few hours. The thought of crossing this ominous chasm was the last straw. Her grip on her nerves slipped.

She clapped her hands tightly to her eyes and shrieked: "I won't go over! I can't!"

Doc reached for her. There was no time to be lost.

Patricia struck at him hysterically, shrieked again.

The young woman realized what she was doing, and was not at all proud of her performance. Nevertheless, she could not help it. She had a bad case of what is generally called the jitters.

She felt herself seized. One of the bronze man's hands glided past her cheek and pressed a certain spot near the cranial nerve center. There was a slight tingling sensation, and Patricia suddenly found herself powerless to move a muscle. It was weird.

She was tossed lightly across Doc's shoulders. Then the mighty bronze man seemed to leap outward, straight into the cauldron below the falls. However, his feet landed on the rope, and he came to a perfect balance. He glided along the hemp strands.

During any one of the dozen seconds which followed, Patricia would have died cheerfully. It was the most ghastly interval of her existence. She had admired the work of circus performers in the big top—trapeze and tight-wire artists who did amazing things. But she had never seen a feat which equaled this bronze man's seemingly unconcerned defiance of death.

Patricia was placed safely on her feet on the opposite side. Doc's bronze fingers found nerve centers again. The young woman recovered use of her limbs magically.

Patricia knew enough of human anatomy to comprehend some of the enormous skill which lay in Doc Savage's fingers. She crouched on the edge of the cliff, dazed. She was frankly ashamed of herself.

Doc Savage crossed back over the chasm, running lightly on the rope.

Tiny was waiting there. She gazed into the chasm and shuddered.

"Wait!" she grunted uneasily. "Me take um chance—stay on this side."

The voluminous Tiny never was exactly sure what happened after that. The bronze hands pressed her head. She became helpless. Then she, also, was borne out over the thundering abyss.

Doc seemed to handle the squaw's weight as easily as he had managed Patricia's.

Safely across, he loosened the pulley from the anchor tree, and let the rope fall back into the torrent. This blocked pursuit.

Patricia had said that, for several miles, there was no other way of crossing the violent little river.

DOC SAVAGE'S five men greeted their chief noisily when he appeared. They were no little impressed by the exquisite beauty of Patricia Savage.

"Look at that bronze hair!" Monk breathed ecstatically in an aside. "Say, she might almost be Doc's sister!"

"She's a knockout for looks!" agreed the debonair Ham, forgetting himself so much as to agree with Monk.

"Back to the cabin," Doc directed. "We've got some talking to do."

Doc had encountered his aides some distance from the cabin. They retraced their steps to the structure.

Out of courtesy to the young woman, Doc unfolded his part of the story first. He began with the fake telegram on the train, and omitted few details.

"To sum up," he finished, "the whole thing is pretty baffling. The gang who just kidnaped you seem to be after an ivory block. And in some fashion, they must have learned we were coming here on a visit."

"They probably learned that by robbing the mail box," Patricia Savage suggested.

"That would explain it," Doc agreed. "They attacked me on the train in an effort to prevent me coming here. Then there's Señor Corto Oveja, his daughter, and El Rabanos. They headed in this direction, although we have seen no signs of them being around here."

"What part do they play?" Patricia asked.

"That's more mystery," Doc told her. "They were attacked on the train. They laid it onto me. And their assailants left one of those werewolf marks."

Patricia shuddered violently. "The werewolf marks! I have found several of them around this cabin."

"We saw one on the cabin floor," Doc admitted.

"Yes. That one appeared when I found Boat Face and Tiny afflicted with that weird sleep."

Doc and his men exchanged glances. They had by no means forgotten their own experience with the weird slumber. But what the fantastic affliction was, they had not yet learned.

"When did this all start?" Doc asked Patricia.

"Some weeks ago. My father found a prowler in our cabin. The fellow fled. A little later, a mysterious voice called from the woods and demanded that dad hand over the ivory cube. Dad refused—"

"What ivory cube?" Doc interjected.

"One father found on a rock ledge near here," Patricia replied. "Several human skeletons lay around the little block. It was years ago when he found it."

Speaking rapidly, the young woman told of the repeated demands for the ivory trinket.

"Then my father was found—dead!" she finished jerkily. "Doctors said his heart had gone back on him. I think he was murdered—a victim of that fantastic sleep."

Doc Savage indicated the lifeless figure of Boat Face. "When did that happen?"

"Last night, sometime," Patricia said slowly. "Tiny and I found his body this morning, just before the rain. We carried it to the cabin. A few minutes later, those swarthy men came and seized us. They took us by surprise."

"You haven't the slightest idea why the ivory cube is in demand?" Doc questioned pointedly.

"No."

"Let's have a look at it."

"Of course!" Patricia went to the bark-sheathed pillar which supported the living-room ceiling. She pressed a concealed catch, and the door flew open.

She shoved a hand confidently inside, and

groped around. Then she bent over and stared into the recess.

"It's gone!" she gasped.

"DID Boat Face know where the cube was hidden?" Doc asked. His remarkable voice was smoothly unexcited, and told nothing.

"Yes," Patricia admitted.

"And he could have removed it without your knowing it?"

Patricia hesitated. As yet, she had no knowledge of the half-breed's duplicity.

"He could have," she admitted. "But I would rather think he did not take it. No doubt he heard a prowler, went to investigate, and was knifed."

"Boat Face—him no good!" said Tiny, with scant consideration for her dead husband. "Him no mean. Him just weak. And him foxy."

"Boat Face was killed at a secret meeting," Doc declared.

"How do you know?" Patricia asked.

"There were tracks."

"I didn't see any tracks!"

"They were there," Doc assured her. "I'm sorry, Pat, but Boat Face seems to have been a crook."

Patricia nodded slowly. She felt an agreeable tingling. Doc Savage had called her "Pat." This seemed to indicate that he had accepted her as one of the gang. Patricia was pleased.

"I don't know who took the ivory block," she said. "This thing is getting more involved all the time."

Doc Savage now made a second survey of the cabin and its vicinity. This search was so intense that it made his earlier hunt seem but a careless glance in comparison.

From a pack, which he had carried to this wilderness retreat, he removed what looked like a pair of tiny binoculars mounted in spectacle frames. The lenses of these were extremely powerful, and adjusted for a short distance.

Doc's unaided eyes were keen. But, wearing these eyeglasses, he could cover the ground with microscopic thoroughness.

It was around the boathouse that his scrutiny became most intensive. In addition to the launch, the boathouse contained several canoes. There was also a rack of holding spades, saws, axes, and other tools.

Doc studied one of the spades closely.

"Has this been used recently, Pat?" he asked.

Patricia thought it over before she answered.

"No," she said, "I'm quite sure it hasn't."

Lifting down the canoes one at a time, Doc examined them. Especially did he concentrate on the floor boards. On one of these he found a semicircular scar. When he tried the tip of the spade, it exactly fitted the mark.

Doc laid the spade aside.

Patricia picked it up, examined it. To her astonishment, she found nothing.

"I don't understand!" she said, puzzled.

Johnny came forward hastily, removing his glasses which had the magnifying lens. He let the young lady inspect the spade under magnification.

"Oh!" Patricia ejaculated. "This spade has been used recently to dig in sand! There are tiny scratches which are not a bit rusted."

Inspecting further, Doc found where a canoe had been carried to the water. The canoe had been floated to an out-of-the-way spot under some overhanging brush. There was no reason why it should be used for a regular point of launching. Yet marks in the sand showed that the canoe had arrived and departed numerous times. All of the tracks had been made by Boat Face's moccasins.

Doc noticed that bushes prevented the landing place from being seen from the cabin.

"Boat Face seems to have made numerous excursions!" he announced.

Patricia stared at Tiny. "Did you know about his trips?" The squaw shrugged stoically. "Me sleep sound! Me not hear!"

Doc collected his men before the door of the cabin.

"Let's get organized," he said.

DOC'S five aides brightened visibly at the words. So far, they considered themselves as having been rather useless. At least once in each adventure, Doc usually had occasion to make use of the particular talent which each of his men claimed.

Monk, the chemist, was first to receive orders.

"Got your portable laboratory?" Doc asked him.

The question was hardly necessary. Monk was rarely to be found far from his remarkable outfit of chemicals. This piece of equipment was wonderfully compact, yet Monk could do work with it which called ordinarily for a great outlay of equipment. Monk was something of a Houdini with the test tubes.

"I've got it," he said.

"I want you to go to work on the inside of the cabin," Doc told him. "Analyze and test everything."

Monk did not comprehend fully.

"But what will I look for?" he demanded.

"Anything that might give a clew as to what caused the weird sleep," Doc explained.

"I get you, Doc."

"Renny," Doc said; "think you can find our plane?"

Renny flicked an enormous hand inland. "Sure! I remember the way we came."

"You have a small mapping camera in your luggage, haven't you?"

"A special mapping lens which fits our regular camera," Renny said. "It amounts to the same thing."

"O.K.," Doc told him. "I want aerial photos of the vicinity of this cabin. Cover the region for several miles up and down the coast. Take one set of photos at a height of about five hundred feet. Take the others from a much higher altitude, at least a mile."

"Got you!" boomed Renny.

Patricia's pretty face was frankly incredulous.

She exclaimed, "You can't get pictures in this fog!"

"We use cameras equipped to utilize infra-light," Doc told her. "Haze and fog don't faze these infra-rays."

Renny gathered his equipment together and moved off, a giant of a man who was made to look smaller than he was by the incredible hugeness of his hands.

Doc Savage now addressed Long Tom and Johnny.

"You two fellows will work at the same job, but using different methods," he advised. "Long Tom, I want you to take electric-wave tests that will help to determine the possible presence of oil or deposits of mineral underground. Johnny will prospect outcroppings in search of anything that might be valuable. We, of course, are hunting for whatever this gang is after."

The two men lost no time getting busy. Few living men knew more of the earth's structure than did Johnny; if there were mineral outcroppings, the gaunt geologist with his magnifying-lens spectacles could find them.

The electrical device which Long Tom would use, employed several principles known to scientific oil prospectors and others. Wave impulses, both sonic and electric, were sent into the earth. Their subsequent reaction betrayed any unusual subterranean formation.

"What about me?" Ham demanded.

"You will guard Miss Patricia," Doc said.

The rather handsome Ham grinned widely at this.

Homely Monk, who had overheard, emitted a loud groan. If there was anything Monk hated, it was seeing Ham enjoying himself in the company of an attractive girl.

Disgusted with the latest developments, Monk turned away to conduct his chemical experiments.

### Chapter XIII
### AN OFFER

IT was mid-afternoon of the following day. Things were pretty much at a status quo. Nothing had happened; nothing had been discovered that was of value. And it was still foggy.

Renny was off continuing his mapping, using the old plane. Johnny and Long Tom were still prospecting. They had found nothing the day before.

Monk was dividing his time between scowling at Ham, who was enjoying himself entertaining Patricia, and dabbling with his chemical equipment.

Doc Savage was just completing his exercise routine. He had been at it without pause for two hours. From the cradle, he had never missed a day of this ritual.

They were unlike anything else in the world, those exercises. Doc's father, a great surgeon and adventurer, had started him taking them. They were solely responsible for Doc's amazing physical and mental powers.

He made his muscles pull one against the other, straining until a fine film of perspiration covered his mighty bronze body. He juggled a number of a dozen figures mentally, extracting roots, multiplying, dividing.

In a small case, Doc carried an apparatus which made sound waves of frequencies so high and low that an ordinary ear could not detect them. Through a lifetime of practice, Doc had perfected his hearing to a point where the sounds were audible. He named several score of different odors after a quick olfactory test of small vials racked in the case which held his exercising equipment.

He read pages of Braille printing—the writing for the blind, which consists of tiny upraised dots. He did this as rapidly as another would peruse ordinary type. This attuned his sense of touch.

The whole exercise routine was pushed with an unbounded vigor. Five minutes at the clip would have prostrated an ordinary man—and an ordinary man would have found it impossible to do most of the work.

Monk came outdoors to get a breath of air. The chemical analysis he was conducting at the moment was giving off a most unpleasant odor.

The sight of Ham and Patricia together seemed painful to Monk. He turned his gaze away, letting it rove the brush surrounding the cabin. Suddenly, his little eyes almost popped from their sockets.

Monk emitted a yell! The howl had tremendous volume. It scared birds off their limbs almost a mile away.

"A hand!" Monk bawled.

Ordinarily, Monk's voice was small, weak as a baby's. But it underwent a startling change when he was excited. It became tremendous, bawling, and made even Renny's thunder seem puny by comparison.

As he shouted, Monk pointed with both hands.

The others followed his gesture. They saw—nothing!

"WHAT is it?" Patricia gasped, racing to Monk's side.

"You'll have to get used to him," Ham said, jerking his thumb at Monk. "He's part ape. You can never tell how he'll act."

Ignoring this pleasantly, Monk charged for the clearing edge. He hit the brush like a bull moose. He had, he was mortally certain, seen a hand projecting from the brush. A slender, white hand, it was. It looked like a woman's.

The hand had been visible for only a fractional moment, but Monk was certain it had been there. As he searched through the brush, however, he became less positive. There was no sign of any young woman.

Monk studied the ground. As a woodsman, he was no amateur. But in this tangle of rocks and shrubs, not a track could he discover.

Disgusted, he returned to the cabin.

"Don't get excited at what the missing link does," Ham told the attractive Patricia. "Just look at his monkey face, and you'll understand. There couldn't possibly be good sense behind a mug like that."

"Oh, yeah?" Monk grinned. "Listen, you shyster, where has Doc gone to?"

The men glanced about hastily. Monk's words had prepared them for what they found. Doc Savage was not around.

"He's gone!" Patricia gasped. "What on earth can that mean?"

A grin on his homely face, Monk began: "Well, you see, Doc has a habit of—"

"Shut up!" Ham snapped. "I'm doing guard duty here. Go play with your test tubes!"

Monk rambled off, Habeas Corpus at his heels.

THERE was hardly a mystery about Doc's disappearance. He had simply glided away while the others were watching Monk's wild charge. Once in the brush, he quickened his pace and swung in a wide circle.

Doc had seen the hand which had excited Monk. In fact, the hand had been gesturing at Doc when Monk chanced to glimpse it.

The hand had been feminine, and its owner unquestionably wanted to talk with Doc.

Doc had not gone far when he found a leaf crushed on a rock. A bit farther on, a creeper dangled, torn from its anchorage. There was no breeze here in the undergrowth, yet the creeper swung slowly from side to side. Below it were feminine footprints.

"Señorita Oveja!" Doc called softly.

There was no answer. The swayings of the creeper, however, gradually became shorter and shorter.

"There's no one with me, Miss Oveja," Doc called.

This secured results. Attractive, dark-haired Señorita Oveja appeared in the shrubbery some distance ahead.

"Buenos dias," she greeted. "Good morning. I wanted to talk with you, Señor Savage."

"I recognized your hand," Doc told her.

"Your man—the big, hairy one—frightened me away," Señorita Oveja smiled.

"Monk makes a lot of noise," Doc agreed. "But he wouldn't hurt a fly—unless the fly bit him."

"We have been thinking things over—my father, El Rabanos, and myself," said the girl.

She came closer. Doc noted her olive cheeks were flushed from running.

"You haven't decided you and I may have the same enemies?" Doc asked dryly.

"Then it is that way?" the girl gasped.

"It looks very much like it," Doc admitted. "Our common enemy is a fellow who uses a likeness of a werewolf for his mark."

The beautiful Spanish woman shivered from head to foot. "That is what my father and El Rabanos decided after we talked it over."

"This enemy seems to be after an ivory cube," Doc offered.

Cere started. "You know that, too?"

"Yes," Doc replied. "My cousin, Patricia Savage, has the cube—or did have it."

At this, the Castilian girl showed every evidence of unbounded surprise.

Doc was an expert at reading human character. He was watching her closely. As far as he could tell, her astonishment was genuine. Doc had a suspicion, however, that the man did not live who could read a young woman's mind unfailingly by looking at her pretty face.

"Patricia Savage has it?" gasped Cere.

"Had it," Doc corrected. "The cube seems to have complicated things by disappearing."

"Suppose you tell me—"

"Suppose you tell me," Doc interposed. "We'll start off with: What gave you the idea that I was your enemy?"

The girl said promptly: "More than a week ago, your uncle, Alex Savage, shot at us from the woods, saying he would kill us unless we left the vicinity."

"Did you see Alex Savage at that time?"

"No. Nor did we see him two days ago when he came again and said that he had sent for you, and that you would come and kill us for not leaving the vicinity."

"Alex Savage warned you again two days ago?"

"Yes."

"It was not Alex Savage!" Doc said flatly.

"But he said his name was Alex Savage!"

"Alex Savage has been dead more than a week."

Cere placed a hand over her heart. "In that case we have been terribly mistaken. This other man was a fake!"

"Anyone can be misled," Doc assured her.

"Now, suppose you tell me exactly what is behind all this."

The girl nodded. "You have heard of Sir Henry Morgan?"

"The pirate?"

"That is the one," Cere replied. "In the year 1670 he started across the Isthmus of Panama with twelve hundred men. The Spaniards received warning of his coming. Treasure from the Panama City cathedral, and wealth belonging to merchants, was loaded onto a galleon. This craft fled out to sea, carrying some of the owners of the treasure besides the crew."

"That incident is a matter of history," Doc told her. "The pirate Esquemeling, who was with Morgan at the sacking of Panama, wrote of the galleon in his book. Shortly after he had captured Panama, Morgan heard of this treasure craft. He knew the treasure to be of more value than all else the expedition had secured put together. He seized several Spanish boats, and sent them out in pursuit of the galleon. But they did not find the craft."

"And for a very good reason, Señor Savage," Cere resumed. "Part of the galleon crew had mutinied, murdered the merchants and the others aboard, and seized the treasure."

"There is no historical record of such an occurrence!" Doc told her.

"In a moment I'll explain how I know it is true," Cere retorted. "These men who mutinied and seized the galleon loaded with treasure, were not very intelligent. One of them had heard that there was a water passage around North America. He converted his companions to his belief. They sailed north.

"The journey was long and full of hardship. The coast became bleak, and the climate cold. Finally, it was necessary to anchor in a small bay, careen their boat, and make repairs to the hull. They pulled the galleon up on the sandy floor of a small, canyonlike inlet. Bad luck plagued them. An earthquake caused the gulley side to topple over, burying the boat in a sort of cavern."

The Castilian beauty paused to stare steadily at Doc. "The spot where the boat met disaster was only a few miles from here!"

"How do you know that?" Doc demanded.

Señorita Oveja shrugged. "My story will bring that out, Señor Savage. To get back to what happened hundreds of years ago: not all the crew were on the galleon when it was entombed. About a dozen had camped nearby. They dug a tunnel to the tomb where their fellows lay. That took many days. Their comrades were dead when reached. No doubt, by now, only their skeletons remain.

"The survivors thought to remove the treasure from the boat, but hostile Indians made that impossible. They determined to leave it and travel southward until they found men of their own race. Later, they would come back by sea.

"One of the men was an expert carver of ivory. He took six small flat pieces of ivory and made a relief carving of the vicinity where the boat lay. He fitted these ivory pieces together, carved portions inward, and made a box. This he packed with clay. Due to the cleverness of his construction, and the clay packing, the box seemed solid."

"The ivory cube!" Doc said understandingly.

"Si, si!" Cere assured him. "Even when opened and spread flat, the relief map inside the box would be apparent only to a close observer."

"Go ahead with your story," Doc directed.

"The men closed up the hole which led to the buried ship," Cere resumed. "They started south. Almost at once, they were attacked. Several were slain, including the one who carried the box. The massacre took place under a rock ledge in this vicinity. Those who escaped had to leave the box behind."

The girl made a somewhat shamefaced gesture. "One of those men who escaped was an ancestor of mine. He left a written account of the incident. It was handed down in our family for centuries."

"This clears the situation a lot," Doc told her, "you and your father came for the treasure, eh?"

"Myself, my father, and El Rabanos," Cere corrected. "El Rabanos is financing us."

"You hoped the ivory block would still be under the ledge where the men were massacred?" Doc questioned.

Cere bobbed her attractive head. "Yes. But we were disappointed, señor. It was gone."

"Then you began searching for the galleon itself?"

"Si, si! But on this rugged coast, that is a hopeless task."

"And then this fake Alex Savage appeared with his lies, eh?"

"Si, si!"

"One thing puzzles me," Doc said.

"Quien sabe?" said the girl. "What is that?"

"How did you happen to be on the train?"

The young woman smiled archly at Doc. Obviously she was captivated by the bronze man's manners and unmistakable character. For the last few minutes she had hardly taken her eyes off him.

Doc realized this, but carefully kept his bronze face expressionless. To Doc, young women were something of a problem. There was no provision in his perilous existence for feminine company. It was necessary for Doc to ignore all eligible girls—for the personal safety of the young things, if for no other reason.

Doc's enemies were legion. They would not hesitate to strike at him through a girl whom they thought he liked.

The prettier the young women were, the harder Doc found it to gently repulse them. The more beautiful the girl, the more stunned she was when the bronze man failed to bow before her charms; and the more vigorous her renewed efforts to ensnare him.

"You have not answered my question," Doc reminded her.

Señorita Cere Oveja colored prettily. "We were on the train to get rid of you, so that you would not give us trouble."

"I trust you didn't contemplate a murder, señorita?" Doc said dryly.

"*Gracias,* no!" the Castilian beauty ejaculated.

DOC SAVAGE nodded slowly. "I can see now why you suspected me," he said. "It was the work of the prowler—the fellow who said he was Alex Savage."

Dark-eyed Cere said eagerly: "He told us he had sent for you to come and take our lives. Naturally, when we got upon the train, we looked upon you as a sort of ogre. We had heard that you were famous for deeds of violence."

"Violence against those who have it coming to them," Doc corrected the pretty señorita.

"My first sight of you brought doubts, Señor Savage," said Cere.

Doc hastily headed her off.

"On the train, someone tried to choke you to death with a leather strap," he said. "Naturally, you thought that was my work."

"*Si, si,*" said Cere. "That is, father and El Rabanos did."

She paused expectantly, as if inviting Doc to ask what her own opinion had been. Doc passed up the opportunity.

"It looked suspicious when you fled the train," he reminded.

"Father and El Rabanos were in terror of you," said the girl. "When the train stopped we decided to flee."

"That brings us down to the present moment, I believe," Doc told her. "Now, what is the purpose of this conversation?"

Cere's entrancing dark eyes dropped.

"Father and El Rabanos are still a little doubtful of you, I regret to say. But they have agreed to talk with you. I wish you would do that."

"You came to persuade me to meet them?"

Señorita Oveja nodded. "*Si! Si!* Please do."

"I shall be delighted to accommodate you."

"*Buenos, señor!*" Cere exclaimed. "You make me so happy!"

Doc looked like a fellow who had taken a big swallow of too-hot coffee. He asked: "Shall I go with you now and meet them?"

"Oh, no!" the young woman said hastily. "We are away from our camp now, searching the coast for the buried galleon. You must meet them tonight. Let us say—shortly after sundown. Come alone."

"Alone?" Doc asked sharply.

"Please! If you bring your men, Father and El Rabanos will be suspicious of you."

Lifting on tiptoe, Cere pointed through the trees. There was a line of cliffs perhaps a quarter of a mile distant. She seemed to be indicating a gap in these. The opening was like a knife slash.

"Our camp is just beyond that," she smiled. "You can come there?"

"Just through the gap in those cliffs," Doc said. "I'll come—and alone, too."

Usually Doc was an extraordinarily quick mover. There were men who claimed the bronze giant could dodge a bullet. This was a rank exaggeration, of course, but it gave an idea of the speed with which Doc could maneuver himself.

Nevertheless, he now got kissed full on the lips—before he could avoid it. The kiss was clinging, and quite ardent. The Señorita Oveja's lips were entirely delicious, Doc decided.

As if appalled by her act, pretty Cere turned and fled. However, she paused before she was out of sight, and looked back.

Doc Savage had vanished.

Cere turned hastily and went on. She did not head for the gap in the cliff beyond which, according to what she had told Doc, her camp lay. Instead, she angled off to the right.

Unexpectedly, her father and El Rabanos appeared before her.

"We were watching, *hija mio!*" Señor Oveja chuckled. "It was excellently done!"

"As the Americans would say," Cere smiled proudly, "he fell for it—hook, line, and sinker."

"THAT bronze caballero is no fool," El Rabanos reminded seriously. "Are you sure that he did not suspect he was being tricked?"

"He was like a lamb in my hands," Cere said loftily.

El Rabanos shrugged. "He will be a lion on our hands, if he suspects, señorita."

"What did you tell him?" Señor Oveja demanded.

"As you say, he is clever," the pretty Castilian girl replied. "I did not trust myself to lie to him, so I told the truth. I told him all about our ancestor, and the galleon of treasure from Panama. He claimed to know none of the story."

"He has a tongue tied in the middle—loose at both ends to tell lies!" Señor Oveja snarled. "It was he who made the attempt on the train to kill us."

Cere looked doubtful. "I am not so sure about that, *padre.*"

The father eyed his daughter severely. He made a tongue clicking sound of disapproval.

"This bronze caballero is very handsome," he said. "A young woman's opinion of such a man is not to be trusted."

Señorita Oveja stamped her foot. "I knew you would say that! But Señor Savage is not to be harmed!"

"Of course he will not be harmed," El Rabanos put in sharply. "We will merely seize him and hold him as a hostage to insure our securing the ivory cube. We will trade the bronze man for the cube."

"I could slit the big hombre's throat!" Señor Oveja growled.

"There must be no violence!" El Rabanos rapped. "I insist on that."

"*Si, si!*" the older man mumbled. "As you wish."

They walked off in the direction of their camp.

The camp was nowhere near the cliff, but nearly a mile to the northward. It nestled in a forest of large boulders near a rather rocky stretch of level ground.

At one end of the comparatively level field stood a plane. It was canted over on one wing. A landing wheel was smashed, and the rocks had damaged the wing tip.

El Rabanos stared at the plane and growled in Spanish: "It is unfortunate that the ship had to hit a rock while I was landing it. We are virtually marooned here in this wilderness."

For shelter, the party had tents. These were small, and of a leaf-green in color.

Cere entered a tent and busied herself improving her appearance. The woods country, she had discovered, was hard on complexions. Moreover, it was difficult for a young woman to be captivating in hobnailed boots, corduroy trousers, and a flannel shirt. This was the garb Cere was wearing, because it was the only raiment which would withstand the rigors of her surroundings.

Señor Oveja and El Rabanos retired to their tents. They were city men, not used to hardship, and each period of exertion called for a corresponding rest.

The woods were quiet. The fog rolled like smoke. It was an altogether dreary day. Faintly, from the distance, came the mushy noise of the waves on the rocky shoreline.

POSSIBLY an hour later, in a gloomy stretch of timber something over a mile from the Oveja's camp, a sinister meeting occurred. It was a convention of evil conducted with a furtive caution. It began with the appearance of eleven men. They were swarthy fellows, and they skulked along as if afraid of being seen. Their visages were anything but pleasant to look on.

These were the men who had kidnaped pretty Patricia Savage.

The ominous little caravan of men progressed to a spot where the timber was particularly dense. They clustered together and waited, making no disturbing sound.

"Cere led Doc Savage into the trap for us," a hollow voice said suddenly.

The portentous words were spoken slowly. This, and the fact that the voice was dull and resonant, gave the impression of an exotic drum beating.

Obviously, it was a disguised voice. The speaker was fifty feet or so to the left. He was thoroughly hidden from the group of men by the trees.

The men showed no surprise at the voice. They had been expecting it. Several peered furtively in the direction from which it had come. It was as if they were trying to get a glimpse of the speaker.

"There is no chance of a mistake?" asked one of the men nervously. "This man Savage has an uncanny way of avoiding traps."

The drumlike voice boomed a hollow laugh. "It was a woman who tricked Savage this time. He was too dizzy to suspect anything. You should have seen how still he stood after she kissed him."

"It was clever—using the woman," a man muttered.

"The beauty of it is that she does not know she is being used," said the concealed voice.

A man began sharply: "But I thought that—"

"Oh, the señorita knows she is drawing him into a trap," said the concealed man. "But she does not know that he is to be killed."

"How will we manage it?" questioned one of the group.

"Look off to your right. Do you see that gap in the line of cliffs?"

There was no need of an answer. The rent in the cliffs was plainly distinguishable through an opening in the trees.

"You will post yourselves just inside that opening," said the unseen voice. "You have your machine guns?"

"*Si,*" one fellow muttered, "we have them."

"Set them up just inside the opening in the cliff," their hidden chief ordered. "When Savage appears, you will turn them on him instantly."

"*Si, si.* It will work."

"That is all. Go! *Vamos!*"

## Chapter XIV
### THE TRAP IN A TRAP

THE time was approximately one hour before sundown. Doc Savage had not yet informed his men of his meeting with Señorita Oveja. Anyway, of the five, only Monk and Ham were around the cabin.

Monk was absorbed in the kitchen. Test tubes, retorts, mixing bowls, and glass containers of chemicals stood about. Once unpacked, Monk's chemical laboratory seemed of considerable size. Monk was making numberless analysis tests.

So far, he had not announced whether he had drawn any conclusions regarding the weird sleep.

The debonair Ham was having a very enjoyable time entertaining Patricia Savage. The young lady had altogether captivated Ham. Not only was she one of the most beautiful specimens of femininity Ham had ever seen, but she was also one of the most intelligent.

Ham and Patricia were occupying a rustic bench in front of the cabin.

"You wouldn't think it," Ham was saying, "but that homely missing link, Monk, has a wife and thirteen children."

"You don't say!" exclaimed Patricia.

Ham nodded solemnly. "Not only that, but the thirteen children are just like their father. You know—they swing from chandeliers and things."

Patricia looked curiously at Ham. The dapper lawyer's expression was sober as a judge's.

Patricia knew something was amiss. With a face just as straight, homely Monk had told her the same story about Ham. Monk's yarn had differed only in that Ham's thirteen children were half-witted.

"You and Mr. Mayfair are very good friends, aren't you?" Patricia asked.

Ham blinked. He so seldom heard Monk called Mr. Mayfair that he had failed to recognize the name.

"Friends!" Ham exclaimed indignantly. He flourished his sword cane. "Nothing would give me more pleasure than to chop the ears off that missing link!"

The pig, Habeas Corpus, wandered into the vicinity. The shoat sat down and eyed Ham. The pig's actions were strangely human. It raised on its rear legs.

"Who is your trampy-looking pal, Miss Pat?" Monk's ventriloquial voice asked through the medium of the pig's jaws.

Ham launched an indignant kick at the shoat. He might as well have tried to kick a mosquito. The pig evaded him easily.

Ham glared about in search of the homely chemist. Monk, however, was not in sight. He must have thrown his voice from concealment.

Patricia was laughing heartily. There was something about the easy fearlessness of these men, and the frequent touches of comedy which relieved their doings that was highly satisfying.

Fifteen minutes later, Monk appeared in the cabin door. His homely face was innocent.

"Doc!" he called.

The bronze man appeared from the direction of the boathouse.

"I can't find a thing to indicate what causes the weird sleep," Monk reported.

NUMEROUS times during the afternoon, a plane had prowled overhead. This ship was traveling back and forth systematically. It seemed to be searching for something. It covered the ground twice.

One hunt was made at a very low altitude—less than five hundred feet. The second search was conducted at a greater height—so high that the roar of the motor was barely audible.

Renny was flying the ship, making an aerial photographic map. An uninitiated person would have sworn that no one could take pictures in the fog. But Renny, utilizing infra-rays, was no doubt securing pictures equal to those which could be obtained by sunlight.

For an interval now, however, the plane had not been in evidence.

Not unexpectedly, Renny came out of the brush and strode toward the cabin. The disappearance of the plane from the skies indicated that he had landed some time ago. Under an arm, he carried a bulky package which held camera and photographs.

Entering the cabin, Renny spread his prints on the table. It was not necessary to lose time developing them. The camera was an ingenious type which printed its pictures as they were taken.

"I got a fair layout of the district," Renny reported.

Patricia Savage came in to inspect the work. She was still a bit skeptical about securing pictures in the fog.

"Why!" she ejaculated, "I never saw clearer photographs!"

"Taking pictures with films and lenses sensitive to infra-rays isn't a new idea," Renny told her. "It was a military secret years ago. And for some time it has been utilized on a commercial scale."

"The pictures are in harsh shades," Ham took up the explanation for Patricia's benefit. "Because of that, photography with infra-light is unsuitable for portrait work. A picture taken with infra-light makes you look ugly as sin—like Monk, for instance."

Monk only grinned at the insult.

With a powerful magnifying glass, Doc went to work on the prints. He arranged them in the order in which they had been taken. This gave him an aerial map of the region.

Johnny and Long Tom were still missing. But the bronze man had hardly begun his examination when they appeared.

Johnny removed his spectacles and polished the magnifier on the left side.

"I have little to report," he said. "Of course, I could make only a sketchy inspection of the vicinity. But there was no sign of a valuable ore outcropping. Nor are the rock formations favorable for it."

Doc Savage eyed Long Tom.

"What did you find?" he asked the electrical wizard.

"Nothing particularly unusual about the underlying rock strata," Long Tom said wryly.

"So you guys both drew a blank!" Ham put in.

"Wait a minute!" Long Tom said. "Let me finish! I found something, all right!"

"What?" Doc demanded.

"A rock ledge," Long Tom replied. "With a bunch of skeletons on it."

"That must be where my father found the ivory cube," Patricia offered.

Doc said: "Let's take a look."

Gathering Renny's aerial photographs together, he stuffed them in a pocket.

THE ledge was well up on the stony face of a mountain. Too, it was more of an elongated pit dug in a wall of stone, than a ledge. A beetling overhang above made the spot almost a cave. To reach the recess, it was necessary to make a laborious and sometimes dangerous climb.

"Until today, my father was probably the only visitor to this spot," Patricia declared.

"I don't wonder," Ham puffed. The climb was wreaking more damage on Ham's clothing.

"This is a swell spot for a goat!" he growled.

The skeletons met their gaze. The bone heaps were white as snow. Cavernous-eyed skulls bore marks hacked by a knife ages ago. These marks explained themselves—the victims had been scalped.

"These are the skeletons of white men," said Johnny, whose knowledge of archaeology made his opinion practically indisputable. "They are well preserved, due to the fact that the overhang of the cliffs kept off the weather. This is really a pocket in the side of the mountain."

Doc Savage glanced at Long Tom. "Did you dig up the sand around these bones, then smooth it out again?"

"No," said Long Tom in a startled voice. He peered at the ground.

The sand had been disturbed. All over the ledge it had been dug up and sifted. Then it had been carefully replaced to give the appearance of having been unmolested.

"You were mistaken," Doc told Patricia. "Your father was not the only visitor to this ledge before today. From the condition of the sand, it seems a search was made about a week ago."

"They were hunting for the ivory cube!" Patricia gasped.

Doc nodded. "Yes—the cube which remained behind with the massacred galleon crew."

Doc became a magnet for astounded looks.

"Huh!" Monk ejaculated. "You must know something that we don't!"

Doc nodded. Then he told them of his meeting with attractive Señorita Oveja. He repeated, exactly as the girl had told it to him, the story of the treasure galleon from Panama, and the crew who had mutinied. He failed to mention the kiss.

"According to the girl's story," he finished, "the galleon is entombed near here. The relief map inside the ivory cube is the clew to its location."

"But where in blazes is the ivory block?" Monk demanded.

TO Monk's query, no answer was forthcoming. Doc Savage, if he had any knowledge on the subject, did not put it into words. The others frankly had not the slightest idea what had become of the troublesome white cube.

Monk peered at the red blur in the fog which marked the position of the sun. It looked like a bonfire on the horizon.

"You say you are to meet the Oveja girl and the two men right after sundown, Doc?"

"Right."

"Then you had better be on your way," Monk said. "It's almost that time."

"Ham, you take Patricia back to the cabin," Doc suggested. "The rest of us had better be, as Monk says, on our way."

For once, Ham looked as if he were not wholly in accord with his job of guarding Patricia. He sensed that he was going to miss some action. Nevertheless, he offered the young lady his arm and guided her away.

"Wait!" Monk called after them. "Miss Pat, would you mind taking Habeas Corpus back with you? The going with us may get kinda tough for the pig."

"Yes, she would!" Ham said indignantly. "She don't want to do it!"

"Why, I'll be glad to," Patricia said contrarily. "I think the pig is very intelligent!"

"Sure he is!" Monk laughed. "Habeas, follow the prettiest girl in the world!"

Habeas Corpus instantly trailed after Patricia and the disgusted Ham.

"The rest of us are going with you, eh?" Monk asked Doc.

"It looks like it."

"But didn't you say you told the girl you would go alone to the meeting place beyond the opening in the cliffs?" Renny put in.

"We're not going to *that* meeting place," Doc replied.

"Huh?" Monk exclaimed.

To explain his change of mind, Doc drew

Renny's aerial photographs from his pocket. He spread them on the smooth sand beside the skeletons, then borrowed gaunt Johnny's spectacles. He used the magnifier which was the left lens.

Beckoning his men close, Doc indicated an irregular whitish line on the map.

"There is the line of cliffs," he said. "And there is the opening which the girl told me to walk through. Look close. Notice anything peculiar?"

"Blazes!" Monk exploded. "That opening is the mouth of a blind canyon. There's no sign of a camp in it."

"Look still closer," Doc suggested.

Monk did so, squinting and making grotesque faces. He let out a surprised gasp.

"Look at this!" he told big-fisted Renny, mild voice suddenly fierce.

"Holy cow!" ejaculated Renny after a glance.

"Well, is it a secret?" snapped Long Tom, who had not yet secured a look.

"There's a gob of machine guns planted around that opening in the cliffs," Monk explained. "Men are crouched beside them. The guys didn't bother to get out of sight when they heard Renny's plane. They didn't dream we could take pictures through this fog."

"It's an ambush!" Long Tom snapped.

"Take the head of the class, son," Monk said dryly.

Ignoring him, Long Tom turned to Doc. "Say, did you suspect this before you saw the aerial photographs?"

Doc was slow to answer. "The young woman's insistence that I come alone was slightly suspicious. I'll confess, though, that my doubts were not strong."

"What do we do now?" queried big-fisted Renny. "Go after the guys with the machine guns?"

"We'll call on Señor and Señorita Oveja and El Rabanos, first," Doc decided.

"But where *is* their camp?"

Doc indicated the aerial photograph. "It shows on here, and is not very far away. You'll notice the plane they flew here is lying in the clearing beside their camp, apparently wrecked."

A grimly silent, purposeful file, Doc and his men clambered down from the ledge which held the macabre collection of skeletons.

THE night had descended with an unexpected abruptness. Surprisingly, with the coming of darkness, the fog had disappeared. Bright stars speckled the sky. A fat, milky bag of a moon leaked its beams.

The night was offering better visibility than the fog-filled day.

An air of expectancy gripped the Señor and Señorita Oveja and El Rabanos, in their camp. They had consumed an evening meal cooked over a gasoline stove which gave forth no smoke.

Pretty Señorita Oveja had cleaned the dishes outdoor fashion, by scouring them with sand, and rinsing them. From the grimaces she made, she apparently did not think much of dish-washing.

"Is it not about time we were going?" she demanded in Spanish.

*"You* are staying here!" her father said calmly.

"But I wish to go!" the young woman retorted.

"No!" the elder Oveja refused firmly.

That settled it as far as Cere was concerned. In her country, young people did not argue with their parents.

"You will not harm the bronze man?" she asked anxiously.

"What happens to Doc Savage is not your affair!" her father snapped. He turned to El Rabanos. "Come, señor, let us be on our way. The meeting time is near."

Señor Oveja went over to get his rifle. It was leaning against a large rock, a rock the size of an automobile.

He reached out for the weapon. Moon shadows darkened the base of the rock like thickly roosting crows.

Señor Oveja suddenly emitted a sound between a whimper and a sob, and fell backward. His body remained perfectly stiff as it tumbled; it retained its rigidity when it hit the sand.

It was as if the señor had turned to stone. The momentum of his fall caused him to rock, like a frame of sticks, from side to side. His arms and legs stuck up with weird stiffness.

*"Padre!"* Cere cried shrilly. "Father!"

Darting forward, the young woman sank beside her parent. She grasped his strangely stiffened arm. The muscles were rigid under her touch. By wrenching, she tried to change the position of one of the arms.

The arm remained at the angle to which she moved it, like the cold limb of a dead man.

"Oh, oh!" wailed Cere. She turned wildly in El Rabanos' direction. She intended to demand his help. But her lips parted and her dark eyes became staring.

El Rabanos had also fallen a victim of the fantastic paralysis. The swarthy, girl-faced man was spread-eagled, as if staked out. His face was turned sidewise, so that moonbeams spilled on it. The features showed no agony—only an unbounded wonder.

"El Rabanos!" Cere cried.

She was close enough to see the man's eyes roll in her direction. It was plain that El Rabanos knew what was going on, but was powerless to move or speak.

WHAT had just happened was the most uncanny occurrence the pretty señorita had ever encountered. She gazed about in terrified bewilderment.

There was not a mark on her father or El Rabanos. There was not a sound from the surrounding shadows to show what had happened.

Suddenly, Cere sought to spring wildly to one side. She moved a trifle too slowly, however.

Bronze hands, floating out of the shadows beside her, trapped her arms. The fingers inclosed like steel bands. The grip, for all of its strength, however, was not tight enough to inflict pain. It was just snug enough to hold the girl tightly.

**Bronze hands trapped her arms.**

Cere gave one violent wrench, then realized the futility of that. She relaxed. She knew that Doc Savage must be responsible for the uncanny happening to her father and El Rabanos.

"What have you done to them?" she demanded.

Doc did not answer. Renny and Monk, two mountainous figures, came up in the murk. Johnny and Long Tom approached from the opposite direction.

Doc released Cere. The young woman instantly started to run. She had taken only her second stride when Doc Savage overhauled her, picked her up, and carried her back. His touch was still impersonally gentle, but the Castillan beauty found herself absolutely helpless against his strength.

Cere did not learn what had happened to her father and El Rabanos. The huge forms of Monk and Renny blocked her view as Doc went to the two strangely paralyzed men.

With an experienced sureness, Doc stroked certain nerve centers. Previous pressure on these had induced a sort of paralysis. Doc's practiced touch relieved this condition.

Use of their limbs did not return instantly to the two men; full recovery required perhaps a minute. During that interval, Doc searched Señor Oveja and El Rabanos. Each had a pair of revolvers belted about his middle. Doc removed those. He also took a knife, which he found in a sheath inside Señor Oveja's shirt.

"What does this mean?" Señor Oveja demanded indignantly.

"It means that you weren't as slick as you thought!" rumbled big-fisted Renny.

Oveja glared. "What do you—"

"We have no time for an argument!" Doc interrupted. "Long Tom, Johnny—you guard the prisoners. Monk, you and Renny come with me."

As he spoke, Doc was already gliding away through the moonlight. Renny and Monk pounded after him.

"Where are we headed for?" Monk demanded.

"For that machine-gun ambush at the cliff," Doc told him.

## Chapter XV
### WHEN TROUBLE DOUBLES

"THEY'RE gone!" Monk exclaimed in his small voice.

"Yeah," Renny rumbled. "You can see that they were around recently, too. Here's a match one of them was chewing on. The end is still wet."

Doc and the two men stood on the edge of the blind canyon which penetrated the line of cliffs. They had approached with the greatest of caution. They were sure the ambushers had not seen or heard them. Yet the gang was gone.

Doc Savage listened intently; training had given his ears a keenness which rivaled that of a jungle creature. But they picked up no sound.

"The gang isn't in the vicinity," he decided aloud.

"But how'd they get tipped off?" Renny growled. "How did—"

He shut his thin lips tightly on the rest.

Two loud reports came snapping through the night! They were sharp. Their echoes bounced back and forth with an uproar that sounded like a fantastic dragon coughing!

Monk, confused by the multitude of echoes, demanded: "Where did the shots come from?"

"From the Oveja camp!" Doc decided.

They listened. But a dead stillness had fallen. There were no more shots.

"We'd better go back!" Doc declared.

The bronze man whipped over the brink of the cliff. Below, the drop was almost sheer. Footholds were few and unpleasantly precarious. Yet, Doc seemed to take no particular pains with his going. His speed seemed unaffected by the peril of a fall.

Monk and Renny, tackling the dangerous descent, found it necessary to lower themselves a few inches at a time. Doc was far ahead of them by the time they reached the bottom.

Coming in view of the camp some time later, Monk and Renny received a surprise. They had expected to find violence. However, there was nothing about the scene to indicate anything desperate had occurred.

Señor and Señorita Oveja and El Rabanos stood in the moonlight. Long Tom and Johnny were near. Doc Savage was to one side.

The pig, Habeas Corpus, was galloping slow circles in the moonlight. The shoat's running gait was more than ever like that of a dog.

Monk stared at his pet. "Where did Habeas come from?"

"It came tearing through the brush," Doc explained. "Thinking it was a prowler, Johnny fired a couple of shots in the air. Those were the shots we heard."

"I'm sure Patricia took him back with her," Monk declared. "Ham must have turned him loose. That's the kind of a trick the shyster would pull. He don't think a whole lot of Habeas Corpus."

"I imagine his opinion of the pig is improving a little," Doc declared.

Monk's jaw fell. "What do you mean, Doc?"

By way of answer, Doc Savage produced his tiny lantern, which threw ultra-violet rays. He switched it on, and played the beam on Habeas Corpus.

Letters in an electric blue flame sprang out on the pig's back. Due to the uncertainty of the bristled surface on which they had been drawn, the letters were large and irregular. Each time the pig moved, they seemed to convulse. The letters spelled two words.

SLEEP—GETTING—

"Holy cow!" Renny muttered. "What's that mean?"

"Ham's idea of a joke!" Monk growled.

Doc Savage set out swiftly in the direction of the cabin.

"I hardly think it's a joke," he called grimly. "Long Tom, you stay here and guard these three prisoners."

The electrical wizard nodded, and turned back to watch Señor and Señorita Oveja and El Rabanos.

The other three men ran in Doc's wake toward the cabin.

THE cabin was silent as a house of death. It might have been a tomb of logs, erected on the shore of the little inlet. There was no night breeze to flutter leaves in the surrounding brush. Small waves were piling sloppily against the shore. Out on the sea, moonbeams glanced in long silver shafts.

Doc Savage was first to approach the cabin. Renny, Monk, and Johnny brought up the rear. They did not want to spoil any sign with their clumsy tramping.

Using his flashlight, which gave a powerful beam, Doc Savage made a quick inspection of the house. If he had expected signs of violence, he was disappointed. The place was in a no more topsy-turvy condition than it had been when he left.

But there was no sign of Patricia, Ham, or the fat Indian servant.

"It's all right for you fellows to come in!" Doc called, after his first cursory inspection.

Monk lumbered in and looked around. "That's funny! I don't see any signs of a fight. And Ham ain't the kind to give up without a scrap."

Instead of answering this directly, Doc Savage indicated a black smear on the wall of a bedroom. This had the shape of a wolf, with an unpleasantly human face.

"The werewolf!" Monk ejaculated.

"Placed there recently—no doubt by the gang who captured our friends," Doc replied. "The presence of the werewolf mark indicates why there was no struggle."

"How do you figure that?" Monk questioned.

"The strange sleep we have not been able to explain," Doc reminded him. "It seems to strike coincident with the appearance of these werewolf marks."

Doc led the way to the kitchen. Fresh food stood on the table. A sandwich lay on a plate. One bite was missing.

"They must've been having a snack to eat when the thing happened," Renny said.

A saucer, holding a large lump of butter, stood on the table. Doc handed this to Monk.

"Analyze it," he said.

"For crying out loud!" Monk grunted. "What for?"

"Search for the presence of the following chemicals," Doc said, and rattled off a half dozen highly technical laboratory terms.

The chemical terminology was unintelligible to Renny and Johnny. Both were well-educated men, but it was doubtful if either could have picked two comprehensible words out of the list.

Monk nodded with perfect understanding, however. Behind Monk's low forehead, there did not seem room for a teaspoonful of brains. But his looks were deceiving. A roster of the three greatest living chemists would certainly have included Monk.

Taking the platter of butter, Monk went into the room where he kept his portable laboratory. He set to work.

Doc Savage peered closely at the kitchen floor, then took his portable ultraviolet lantern out of his pocket, switched it on, and played the invisible beams on the floor.

A puddle of blue fire seemed to spring into being.

Renny dropped to a knee and rubbed an enormous hand through the glowing spot.

"It's the chalk we use to do invisible writing," he said. "Ham must have dropped his piece. It's been stepped on."

"I think we stepped on it while wandering around in here," Doc said. "My opinion is that Ham, Patricia, and the squaw were in here eating when they felt the weird sleep begin to creep over them. Ham managed to scrawl those words on the pig, Habeas Corpus. He dropped the chalk as he passed out."

Outdoors, a voice hailed loudly.

"Ahoy, the cabin!" it cried. "Don't shoot me!"

RENNY and Johnny sprang to a window and looked out. They could see nothing.

Doc's flashlight went out. It made no sound doing so, for the switch was noiseless. The darkness which clamped down was black enough to be solid. Silence lay over the cabin and the surrounding timber. The man who had hailed did not do so again.

"That was Long Tom!" Doc said unexpectedly.

"If it was, his voice was changed!" rumbled big-fisted Renny.

"Something has happened to him, all right," Doc agreed. "But it was his voice."

The bronze man's tone, without seeming to become any louder, suddenly acquired a remarkable carrying quality. It rolled out of the cabin and far away into the brush.

"Come on in, Long Tom!" he said. "What's happened to you?"

There was the sound of shuffling footsteps. Long Tom appeared. The pale-skinned electrical wizard was something of a wreck. He was skinned and bruised, and carried the beginnings of two black eyes.

Long Tom's front teeth were of a large protruding variety. Two of these were missing. The missing teeth had the effect of giving his voice a rather comical, lisping quality. He sounded very much like an irate turkey gobbler.

Monk thrust his head in a door, looked at Long Tom, said: "For cryin' in my sleep! Don't he look funny without them buck teeth!"

"What happened to Señor and Señorita Oveja and El Rabanos," Doc asked Long Tom.

"They took a powder!" gritted the electrical wizard.

"I thought you were guarding them," Renny snorted. A wide grin sat on the big-fisted engineer's usually solemn face. He seemed tickled by the ludicrous appearance which the missing teeth gave the electrical wizard.

"Señor Oveja picked up a rock and whangoed me," Long Tom growled through his missing teeth.

"How'd he catch you off guard?"

The truth, even if it hurt, was the custom of Doc's aides. Long Tom squirmed, felt of the gap where his teeth were missing.

"The darn girl was making eyes at me," he admitted.

Everybody laughed.

"They hit you, then fled?" Doc asked. There was no criticism in his tone.

"Yep," Long Tom admitted. "Señor Oveja followed the rock up with his fists. He walloped me plenty, what I mean! The rock had knocked me too dizzy to dodge."

"Didn't you try to trail 'em?"

"Sure! Kind of a strange thing happened then, Doc. They had not gone far before they managed to get guns. They cut down on me with several shots. I couldn't see 'em. Monkeying around after 'em was useless, with me disarmed."

"Guns!" Renny ejaculated. "But we took their guns when we seized them in their camp."

"Yeah. They must have had other weapons hidden in the brush."

Doc said: "Monk, how about analyzing that butter?"

Monk nodded and returned to his work over the portable chemical laboratory. He had spread his paraphernalia over a large table. Several of the mixing trays were giving off strong-smelling odors.

Going outdoors, Doc searched for tracks. Finding them was a simple matter for his trained eye. In addition to the tracks of Patricia, Ham, and the squaw, there were prints of at least half a dozen other men. The trail did not wander, but headed for the shore.

The procession of footprints crossed a spot where the ground was soft. Doc got down on all fours to make an examination; then he stood up.

"The same gang that we rescued Pat from has seized her again," he said. "I've seen some of those footprints so often they're beginning to look like the tracks of old friends."

The trail terminated near the boathouse. Certain marks in the soft sand might have been made by canoe keels. Doc looked into the boathouse. The canoes which had been stored there were missing.

"They came by land," he said. "But they left by water. That was a wise trick on their part. We haven't a chance of trailing them over water."

At this point, Monk came running from the direction of the cabin. He was excited. He had never looked more like a gorilla than now.

The pig, Habeas Corpus, bounded at his heels, making frantic efforts to keep up.

"I've got it!" Monk shouted. "I've got it!"

"Got what?" Doc demanded.

"The stuff in the butter!" Monk bawled. "You know how butter absorbs the odor of any smelly food you put in the refrigerator with it? Well, when the house was saturated with this stuff, the butter absorbed enough of it for me to find it by making an analysis."

"Listen, you homely missing link!" Renny rumbled. "What have you found?"

"The stuff which caused the mysterious sleep," Monk grinned. "It's an odorless and colorless gas which is poisonous if inhaled long enough."

RENNY, Long Tom, and Johnny were plenty surprised at this development. Doc Savage, however, had expected it. He had already surmised the probable cause of the weird slumber. So closely had he guessed that he had told Monk what chemical components to look for.

"No doubt the stuff was used to kill Alex Savage," Monk said. "To a physician who did not have much experience, and who did not suspect foul play, the effects of the stuff might look like heart failure."

Long Tom grimaced, felt of the gap in his teeth. "I didn't think the stuff was poisonous. You know it didn't kill us on the train."

"That was because you didn't get enough of it," Doc replied. "I thought at first that the attack on the train was made merely to frighten us. Since then, I've learned more of the nature of these fellows. They would as soon kill us as try to scare us.

"Just why such a small quantity of gas was injected into our train compartment is hard to explain. Perhaps the fellow administering the gas was frightened away. The stuff must have been sent into the compartment through the crack at the bottom of the door."

Doc ended his long speech abruptly, and cupped a palm back of an ear. He stood thus for several seconds, perfectly rigid.

"There's a boat coming!" he said. "It sounds like an outboard engine."

A minute passed—two—three. The others began to wonder if Doc could have been mistaken. Then they heard the sound of the boat.

"Probably the kidnapers coming back to make a deal!" Renny boomed.

"The boat is coming straight in from the open sea," Doc decided.

The boat nosed in past the floating mail box. It became distinguishable in the moonlight. It was simply a square-sterned canoe, fitted with an outboard motor.

"Ahoy, Señors!" called a hoarse voice.

"I've got a notion to take a shot at him!" Renny rumbled. "Bet I can hit him!"

"And then they'd bump Ham, Patricia, and the squaw!" Monk grunted. "Don't be a dope!"

Monk was very earnest. Although Monk and Ham seemed continually on the point of flying at each other's throats, and insulted each other with vigor and delight, either would have risked his life for the other. On occasion, each had done so.

"What do you want?" Doc called to the distant men.

"The ivory block, Señor Savage!" the fellow shouted back.

"WE haven't got the block!" Doc told him.

"You cannot deceive us, hombre!" the reply came volleying back. "The Señorita Savage had it. She admitted that fact when she was our prisoner earlier."

"She *thought* she had it," Doc corrected him. "When she looked in the hiding place, the block was gone."

"We are not interested in hearing a smooth story, Señor Savage," said the distant man. "I came to inform you of a fact."

"What fact?"

"Simply, señor, that we now have your six friends in a very safe place."

Several seconds of surprised silence followed these words.

"*Six!*" Renny's big voice rumbled.

"Ham, Patricia, and the squaw—that's only three!" muttered Johnny. He took off his glasses with the magnifying lens, fingered them thoughtfully.

"Did you say six?" Doc called to the boatman.

"*Si, si,*" the fellow shouted back.

"He can only mean one thing," Long Tom said slowly. "I told you that the Ovejas and El Rabanos started shooting at me right after they escaped."

"You were evidently mistaken," Doc told him.

"Sure I was!" Long Tom agreed. "It was this other gang shooting at me. They must have grabbed Señor and Señorita Oveja and El Rabanos."

Renny banged his big fists together. "It beats me!"

"Me, too," Monk agreed. Bewilderment was on his homely face. "I figured Señor Oveja, his daughter, and El Rabanos were in with the other gang. The ambush they fixed for Doc made me think that."

"I figured the same way," said Johnny. "There must have been a contact between the two parties. Otherwise, how did they know of the meeting with Doc?"

"The girl and the two men might have set a snare to capture me," Doc pointed out. "The other gang, hearing of it, could have tried to turn it into a death trap."

"That might be, too," Johnny admitted.

The man in the distant boat had been waiting. His boat had drifted near a large rock which thrust out of the bay; he had wedged the end of a boat hook into a crack in this rock, and was holding his little craft stationary. The rock was a bullet-proof shelter.

"Do you understand me, Señor?" the man yelled. "I have your six friends! They are all safe— so far!"

"Ham, Patricia, and the squaw!" Doc called. "Who are the other three?"

"El Rabanos, Señor Oveja, and his daughter!" came the reply.

"I told you so!" said Long Tom. "When the three got away from me, they jumped from the fryin' pan to the fire. That explains why the machine gunners weren't at the cliff when you arrived. They were watching the Ovejas' camp, and saw us show up there. Then they skipped."

"This seems to indicate the señorita is straight, after all," Monk grunted.

"When she said they were camped behind the cliff, she lied," Johnny reminded him.

"You want to make a swap?" Doc shouted.

"*Si, si, Señor!*" the man in the canoe called hastily, "We will trade our prisoners for the ivory cube."

"I told you we haven't got the ivory cube!" Doc called back.

"You are lying, señor," called the canoeman. "I will return in two hours. If you do not give me the ivory cube, one of the prisoners will be shot, and the body tossed out where it will drift ashore!"

With that, he started the outboard motor, and the square-stern canoe skipped out to sea. Apparently, he had laid down an ultimatum about which there could be no argument.

## Chapter XVI
### INSIDE THE IVORY BLOCK

THE boat had hardly started its seaward retreat when Doc Savage whirled on Long Tom.

"Your electrical ear!" he said. "Get it!"

Long Tom dashed for the cabin.

Just as Monk always carried chemical equipment, so did Long Tom carry a variety of electrical devices. Among these was an apparatus which had been useful on many occasions. This consisted of a compact, highly sensitive parabolic microphone pick-up, together with an amplifier of great power. The thing was no radical departure from the listening devices military men use to spot enemy airplanes. However, it was infinitely more compact.

Long Tom hurriedly assembled the mechanism. The microphone was directional. He pointed it at the receding motor canoe. The outboard engine was no longer audible to the unaided ear.

Long Tom twisted the dial on his amplifier. There was a loudspeaker device. The sound of the retreating canoe poured out with loud volume.

They listened to the noise which the sensitive device picked up. After a while the outboard died suddenly.

Long Tom turned the amplifier on full force. A mosquito flew across the front of the microphone, and sounded like a tri-motored airplane. Then the listener picked up several faint shouts, but they were not understandable.

"Holy cow!" Renny thumped. "They must be holding the prisoners in a boat out at sea!"

"Take flashlights," Doc directed suddenly. "And hunt for birds' nests in pine trees."

"Huh?" Monk grunted, and looked as if he had not understood.

"Birds' nests in pine trees," Doc repeated. "We're not interested in birds' nests in any other kind of trees, though."

"What do we do when we find them?" Monk wanted to know. He was still puzzled.

"Climb up and look in them," Doc said.

"Then what?"

"When you find the right bird's nest, you won't need to be told."

The four men went looking for birds' nests. Each had a dubious and puzzled look on his face. Just why Doc was abruptly interested in nests in pine trees, they had no idea.

Monk cast his light up a tree and spied a telltale knot of twigs, stringy bark, and feathers. He prepared to shin up to the nest.

"Huntin' birds' nests!" he snorted. "I'm glad Ham ain't here to see! Would he hand out razzberries!"

"I wouldn't blame him!" Renny boomed. "Especially since you're looking for nests in pine trees."

"Pine trees—sure!"

"That's a spruce you're starting to climb!" Renny chuckled

"Yeah, it is at that," Monk admitted sheepishly, after taking a second look.

Doc Savage returned to the cabin. He switched on his flashlight, which gave the brilliant beam. From a pocket he drew the aerial photographs which Renny had made. As yet, Doc had not had time to make a complete examination of these photographic prints. He did so now.

On a picture which had been taken something like seven miles up the coast, he found a tiny grayish spot. This might have been a faded, elongated flyspeck. But under a magnifying glass, it became a small schooner.

A tender dangled on a painter behind the schooner—a canoe, fitted with an outboard.

The discovery convinced Doc that it was upon this boat that the prisoners were being held.

The craft was now standing out to sea, of course.

Monk came plunging in from the night.

"I found it, Doc!" he howled.

THE gorillalike giant of a chemist held his prize in both hands. It was a bird's nest—the nest of a very large bird, judging from its size.

"How did you know what to look for, Doc?" Monk questioned.

"Remember the amber-colored, sticky stuff we found on the trousers and on the hands of the murdered Indian?" Doc asked.

"Sure!"

"It was gum off a pine tree."

Monk whistled softly, comprehending. "There was some bark stuck to his trousers, and tiny feathers stuck to his hands."

"Bark off a pine tree and feathers from a bird's nest," Doc agreed.

Monk dived a furry hand into the bird's nest.

"Hocus pocus presto!" he grinned.

He brought out a block of ivory more than two inches square.

Renny and Johnny and Long Tom came up. They stared at the block.

"Boat Face stole it!" Renny thundered. "That's where it went! He hid it in a bird's nest!"

Doc took the block and turned it in his hand. The workmanship was wonderful. The thing looked perfectly solid.

Crooking a finger at Monk, Doc said: "I've got a job for you."

The bronze giant and the homely chemist retired to the room which held Monk's portable laboratory. Two or three minutes elapsed. When Doc reappeared, he was alone. He carried the block in one hand.

On a foundation of books, Doc arranged two flashlights so that they splashed a brilliant glare on the table. He placed the ivory cube in the illumination.

Johnny promptly handed over his glasses with the magnifying left lens. The magnifier disclosed narrow, straight cracks along all four corners of the ivory block. They were too small for the eyes to see unaided.

With his powerful hands, Doc tested the construction of the cube. He was uncertain just how it opened. He tried gentle pressure, without result. He shook it violently, much as one would shake the mercury down in a thermometer. This caused the block to separate into six sections. It had been held together by tiny, ingenious dowel pins.

The core of the cube was a hard, square block of dried mud. Doc inspected this curiously. He turned the mud slowly in his palm. Then, wheeling abruptly, he went into another room.

Boat Face had been buried. His squaw, however, had kept the clothing he had been wearing at the time of his death. Doc selected the trousers and turned the pockets inside out. He had done this on a previous search, but he wanted to make sure.

Several flat leaves, fragments of chewing tobacco, came to light. The tobacco was very black in color.

Doc turned his attention to the mud cube which he had crushed in his palm. There was a leaf of the black tobacco in the mud. Boat Face's chewing tobacco inside the cube!

From Monk's room came brisk tinkling of test tubes and mixing beakers.

Doc's other three aides had been watching the bronze man. Their expressions showed plainly that they were going to ask questions.

But before they could interrogate him, they all heard the mutter of an approaching outboard motor.

DOC Savage whipped outdoors. Three of his men followed him. Monk, however, stayed with the job he was doing.

The sputter of the outboard loudened. A blurred spot appeared out to sea. It soon resolved into the square-sterned canoe. The speedy little craft was crowded with men.

In the gloom, little could be seen of the canoe passengers. Their forms were dark humps. From each hump a slender, black thorn seemed to project. This proved they were not the prisoners—the thorns were rifle barrels.

The outboard stopped, and the canoe coasted behind a rock. The armed passengers used boat hooks to keep themselves sheltered behind the stony hump. One or two could be seen using binoculars. They discerned Doc Savage and his aides.

"Your decision, Señor Savage!" one shouted.

"We have found the block," Doc told him.

"You had it all the time!" the man jeered.

Doc did not argue. "Where are the prisoners?" he called.

"They will be produced when you are ready to make the trade."

"I'm ready now."

The men in the motor canoe held a brief consultation. One of the gun barrels was pointed upward. There was a loud report. Evidently the weapon was a shotgun.

Nothing happened for three or four seconds. Then, high overhead, there was another report and a blinding flash.

"Regular Fourth of July!" said Renny.

"It was a flash rocket, fired as a signal," announced Johnny.

"The prisoners will soon be here," called the man from the outboard canoe.

Nothing more happened for possibly fifteen minutes. Then, far out to sea, the slow throb of a marine engine came into hearing.

Doc listened intently to the engine noise.

"It's a gasoline motor," he decided. "That means there is probably an auxiliary power plant in the schooner."

SHORTLY afterward, using glasses, Doc was able to discern the craft. It was not more than fifty feet long, but had a wide beam and stout lines. The boat was built for service.

Outside the inlet, it swung into the teeth of a light breeze. The auxiliary motor, turning slowly, held it stationary.

"The prisoners are aboard the schooner, señor!" called the man in the motor canoe.

"How do you know that?" Doc countered.

Shouts passed between the canoe and the schooner. Following this, Ham's voice rang strongly from the schooner. Ham had a powerful orators' voice, developed by much courtroom work.

"We're all O.K.!" he shouted. "If they're trying to bargain for our release, Doc, tell 'em to go take a jump at the moon!"

"Are there six of you?" Doc demanded.

"Sure! Señor and Señorita Oveja, and El Rabanos, are prisoners, too!"

Then the spokesman in the canoe interrupted the conversation.

"Will you turn over the ivory cube for their release?" he called to Doc.

Doc lowered his voice so that it could by no chance reach any of the swarthy men.

"Monk!"

"Coming up!" said Monk, also low-voiced.

The homely chemist ambled out of the cabin. His hairy hands swung well below his knees. One paw gripped an object wrapped in a handkerchief.

"All set?" Doc asked.

"Yep. But I was sure pushed for time."

Doc and Monk strode together down to the water's edge. For a moment, they were lost to view in the moonlight as they worked through the brush. They waded out until the lapping waves came somewhat above their knees.

"Come and get it!" Doc called. "But you must release the prisoners!"

"*Si, si!*" called the man in the canoe. "The captives will be turned loose the instant we have the ivory block."

The outboard motor bawled; its propeller threw up a fan of spray. The canoe darted inshore with the speed of a frightened duck.

At a low word from Doc, Monk retreated hastily and got under cover.

The canoe swerved inshore and slackened speed. The boat passed Doc slowly at a distance of thirty feet.

"Throw the cube!" commanded a man. "It had better fall in the canoe, too! We dare not come too close to you. We will free the prisoners when we have it!"

Doc's arm drew back, shot forward. Square and white, the little block sailed through the moonlight. The man in the canoe caught it.

"*Bueno!*" he barked. "Good! Now—this is how we intend to return the prisoners."

As if the exclamation were a signal, every man in the canoe lifted his rifle. The muzzles lipped flame. Gun sounds blended in a ragged roar!

AT the moment when he tossed the white cube, Doc Savage was standing in water above his knees. He was not taken unawares. The first rifle barrel was hardly swaying toward him when he doubled, flopping forward violently into the water. He was completely submerged before the shots crashed.

The perfect physical condition in which Doc kept himself had given him an ability which had saved his life on other occasions. This was the capacity to hold his breath for a seemingly impossible interval!

Actually, the breath-holding did not depend entirely on physical condition. There was a trick to it. Instead of taking as deep a breath as he could, several rapid inhalations were made to charge the lungs with oxygen, and the dive was then made with a normal amount of air in the lungs. Doc had learned this trick from the men who could do it best—South Sea pearl divers.

Keeping close to the sandy bottom, Doc swam underwater. He did not go toward the canoe. Nor did he swim fast enough to raise a betraying ripple.

The water was vibrant with hollow *chunging* noises—rifle shots. The men were driving lead at random, in hopes of making a hit.

As he swam, Doc's hands encountered a rock. He eased around it, still submerged. When the rock was between himself and the canoe, he floated to the surface.

He was in time to hear the first of a series of remarkable sounds.

These noises resembled the moan of a gigantic bull fiddle. They were so loud they hurt the ears. The moans were very short, none lasting more than two seconds. The cove throbbed with their volume.

These sounds were strings of shots, although a human ear could not distinguish between the reports. They came so swiftly as to seem a single shot. The shots were fired by the remarkably compact little machine guns which were Doc's invention.

Doc chanced to look. Being in shadow, he was fairly safe from discovery. The little machine guns were charged with bullets which carried unconsciousness rather than death—mercy bullets.

Three men were down in the canoe. This was not such good shooting, considering that all of Doc's men were good marksmen. Rather, it was evident, they were not trying to capture the gang.

The canoe turned wildly and skittered out toward the bay mouth. A few bullets followed it, fighting wave crests like angry bees. It was noticeable that none of the slugs came close to the canoe, which was now in wild flight.

"It is bad shooting, and this is lucky for us!" squawked a man.

"Those guns!" shivered another. "Never before have I heard anything like them, señors!"

The terrific rate at which the little machine guns fired had produced a near terror. They all showed the effects of it.

The three men who had been hit lay motionless in the bottom of the canoe. As soon as the ugly moans of the machine guns ceased, the three victims were examined.

"*Bueno!*" ejaculated one of the gang. "They are not dead!"

Continuing his inspection, the man gave a grunt of surprise.

"What is this? The bullets seem to have penetrated only skin deep, and then burst!"

Evidently the man had never seen a mercy bullet. He and his fellows were puzzling over the slugs when the canoe reached the schooner. They clambered aboard, after lifting their three motionless companions over the rail.

"Did you get the ivory block?" asked a fellow who seemed to be in charge of the boat.

"We did!" declared one of the group. He pulled the white cube from a pocket, and passed it over.

The other examined it.

FROM the shore, a strange sound drifted. It was a series of guttural, booming words—words which were intelligible to no one on the schooner deck.

It was Doc Savage, shouting in a strange dialect.

The man holding the white block looked at his fellows. "Do any of you understand that language, amigos?" he asked.

There was a general shaking of heads. The tongue in which the shout had been couched was wholly foreign to anything they had ever heard.

Dismissing the shout as unimportant, the men examined the white cube closely. They sought to get it open. Finally, they shook the cube violently. It separated into six sections.

What happened then was strange. The holder of the cube stared stupidly at the segments. Then he leaned over and gazed foolishly down at the deck. And, as if he had found a place to lie down, he toppled forward.

His fall upon the deck produced a loud thump. He lay quite motionless afterward.

## Chapter XVII
### INTO THE EARTH

THE apparent magic which had felled the opener of the box reached swiftly to the other members of the crew. One went down. Another! There was no outcry, no attempt to flee. They simply keeled over.

Each man began snoring softly a few seconds after he had sprawled out.

After perhaps twenty seconds, not a man on the schooner's deck remained upright.

Ham and the other prisoners were below. They had been locked in a small, not too clean cabin. The wrists of each were bound tightly. A long rope had been knotted to the lashings of Ham's wrist, carried to those of pretty Señorita Oveja, and tied, thence to the señorita's father, and the rest of the prisoners.

While men were dropping so mysteriously on deck, the prisoners were doing something that seemed inexplicable.

They were holding their breaths. Señor Oveja's cheeks were puffed with the effort. He seemed about to explode.

With one hand, Ham made slow counting gestures, as if he were measuring the passage of a certain length of time.

Finally, Ham let his breath out in a rush and said: "O. K.! You can start breathing again."

"What was the idea of telling us to hold our breaths, Ham?" Patricia Savage questioned curiously.

"Did you hear Doc shout in that strange language?" Ham asked.

"Yes. I couldn't understand a word of it."

"Probably not a dozen people in the so-called civilized world could understand it," Ham told her. "The language was ancient Mayan. Doc and the rest of us speak it and understand it."

"What did Doc say when he shouted?"

"He said he had some of his anaesthetic gas in the ivory cube," Ham replied. "He said for us to hold our breaths, because the stuff would be released when the cube was opened."

"But why hold our breath?" Patricia queried, puzzled.

"The anaesthetic gas spreads with lightning swiftness," Ham explained. "In less than a minute it dissolves and becomes ineffective. We simply held our breaths until it was dissipated."

Ham now got to his feet. His ankles were not bound, so this was comparatively simple. The others followed his example. Ham headed for the deck. The others had no choice but to follow him. They were tied in a chain by the rope.

Patricia gasped in surprise when she saw the sleeping forms of her late captors.

"The gas got them!" Ham chuckled. "Now, if we can just get this boat headed for shore, we'll be all right."

"Did it work?" Doc called loudly from the beach.

"You tell 'em!" Ham bellowed back. "Like a charm!"

"The engine of the launch won't run," Doc called. "There's no gasoline in the tank. But we'll paddle out and help you get to shore."

"You want to be careful!" Ham called. "The whole gang wasn't on the boat. We've only got about half of them."

"Any idea where the others are?" Doc shouted.

"No!" Ham said. "They're liable to be around somewhere."

Doc made no answer.

Ham, unable to distinguish the bronze man in the moonlight, decided Doc had gone to get the launch.

Patricia glanced uneasily at the swarthy men lying senseless on deck.

"Aren't you afraid they'll revive?" she asked Ham.

"It will take them nearly two hours to wake up," Ham told her. "Doc has been using this anaesthetic gas for a long time. I know exactly how it functions."

Patricia heaved a relieved sigh. "Then we're safe!"

She was too optimistic.

Unexpectedly, from either side of the schooner, rifles banged! The shots echoed back noisily from the cliffs. Bullets chopped savagely at hull and deck house. A slug tore a ragged hole in the furled sail.

THE men doing the shooting were as yet some distance away. Ham, peering hard, could locate them only from the flash of their rifles. They were coming from two directions. Evidently they were shooting at the schooner as a whole; at that distance they could not pick out individual targets.

"It's the rest of the gang!" Ham gritted.

El Rabanos wailed: "Diablos! The devils! They will kill us!"

"Get in the canoe," Ham commanded. "Let me in the stern, where I can start the motor."

Patricia cried: "But the schooner was—"

"No time to get it under way," explained Ham. "Come on, those birds must've been listening. They heard us talking to Doc, and knew something had happened to their pals."

Privately, Ham had no use for canoes. Years ago, one had ducked him when he was togged out in his immaculate clothes. They were tricky things, even when there was plenty of time to get into them.

Getting six excited individuals, all linked together by a rope, into the canoe, proved to be an agonizing job. Twice the canoe rocked sickeningly. Ham groaned and yelled by turns.

The instant he could reach the outboard motor at the stern, he went to work on it. The motor was still hot. That was lucky, for, with his hands bound, he would never have got it started otherwise.

Rifle bullets were still hitting the schooner with loud chugs. Some bit at the water and ricocheted with piercing wails! Others traveled on without touching water or schooner, and spanged noisily among the rocks on the inlet shores.

The outboard motor popped a blue flame through its exhaust ports. It fired again, then began to moan regularly.

Patricia, in the bow, had already thrown off the painter. Ham gave the outboard all the gas it would take. The canoe swerved away from the schooner.

A spatter of lead followed them as they raced for shore.

The riflemen, approaching from two directions, were not yet close enough to shoot accurately, however.

A bullet *spanged* through the thin canvas side of the canoe, just at the waterline. The hole, near the bow, began to let water in.

"I hope lightning doesn't strike twice in the same place," Patricia said, and put a hand over the bullethole to shut out the water.

It was the little supermachine guns in the hands of Doc and the others which insured their reaching shore. The small guns began to emit the amazing bull-fiddle moans.

The bullets, charged with tracer chemical in addition to the sleep-producing potion, raced like red-hot wires through the moonlight. It was probably the sight of the red cords of tracer snapping past their faces that moved the riflemen to stop shooting. Whatever the cause, they fell silent.

Ham ran the canoe against the beach so hard that it skidded up half its length on the sand. He piled out, dragging the others.

The giant form of Doc Savage materialized silently beside them. Doc produced a knife and cut through their bonds.

"Your scheme was swell!" Patricia told Doc.

"Give Monk the credit," Doc replied. "He is the one who made up that fake ivory block. He's a wizard as a chemist, or he couldn't have done it so quickly."

Ham overheard this, and he grimaced. Praise for the homely Monk was a pain to his ears.

The tall, girl-faced El Rabanos came up.

"I wish to apologize for any trouble I may have caused you, Mr. Savage," he said earnestly. "I know now that you are not our enemy."

Señor Oveja approached in time to listen. He emitted a surly growl.

"En verdad!" he snapped. "Indeed! I am by no means convinced that Savage is our friend."

BIG, bronze Doc Savage did not seem particularly interested in what Señor Oveja thought. He turned away.

Girl-faced El Rabanos said in a low voice:

"I am terribly sorry for my friend's actions, Señor Savage."

"Don't worry about it," Doc said wryly.

"But, Señor Savage, it is ungrateful of him, I am sorry to say," El Rabanos insisted. "Those hombres on the schooner were going to kill us! Unquestionably you saved our lives."

Doc said nothing. He kept on walking; he was headed for the cabin.

"We owe you an explanation also," El Rabanos continued in an ingratiating voice. "In case you do not know it, we prevailed upon the Señorita Oveja to deceive you this afternoon."

"I knew it."

"We did not intend to harm you with the trick," El Rabanos said desperately. "We were merely going to seize you. We had the silly idea that we could trade you to your friends for the ivory cube. We had finally decided you must have the cube, but did not know its significance."

Pretty Señorita Oveja overhauled them and joined in the conversation.

"That is the truth, Señor Savage," she added her insistence. "Harm to you was the last thing in our minds."

Doc bowed politely, but said nothing.

A few minutes later, however, when Doc and Monk were together, the homely chemist expressed a private idea.

"Doc," said Monk, "I may be wrong, but I believe there's a connection between our three visitors and that gang out there."

"What makes you think so?"

"The fact that the trap set for you was a death trap."

Doc's strange flake-gold eyes rested intently on the homely chemist. "Who do you suspect, Monk?"

Monk tugged slowly at an ear which resembled

a gristle tuft.

"Señor Oveja," he said.

Doc Savage did not change expression. Neither did he speak further on the subject. Instead, he spread a piece of paper on the table, then he drew an envelope from a pocket, and tore off the corner. From envelope to paper, he poured a tiny heap of clean white sand.

"Where'd that sand come from?" Monk queried curiously.

"From the moccasins of the dead Boat Face," Doc told him, "Guess you were not around when I took it out."

Going to the door, Doc called: "Pat!"

Patricia, alert, and prettier than ever, entered. She gave Monk a gorgeous smile, apparently by way of thanking him for his work in constructing the trick ivory block which had been responsible for their escape.

Monk reacted with the look of a homely cat which had just dined on the canary.

Patricia was by far the prettiest girl Monk had ever seen. He would have liked to stay and talk with her. A glance at Doc, however, showed that the bronze man wanted to be left alone with Patricia.

Monk ambled out, leaving the two together.

Hardly more than a minute later, Patricia reappeared. She looked neither to right nor left, but walked away, along the shore of the inlet.

She was swallowed by the black shadows which gorged the wilderness of brush.

DOC Savage came out of the cabin and moved about in the darkness until he found Long Tom.

"Take your listening device and climb up on top of the cabin," Doc directed the electrical wizard. "Swing the thing in slow circles. Report whatever you hear."

Long Tom hastily complied. The microphone of his contrivance was so sensitive, and the amplifier so powerful, that it would be almost impossible for anyone to approach the cabin without being heard. Long Tom hooked wires together, clicked switches, and thumbed dials. Instead of a loudspeaker for listening, he used a head set. This was more sensitive.

"Hey, Doc!" he called almost at once. "I hear somebody already. It sounds like one person walking."

"Is the person making three sharp rapping sounds at frequent intervals?" Doc asked. "Sounds such as would be made by sticks beaten together?"

Long Tom strained his ears. "Yes."

"Then it's Patricia," Doc told him. "I gave her two pieces of wood, and told her to beat them together three times every few steps. Whenever you hear that, you'll know it's her. If you hear any-

body else, though, fire two shots in the air. That's to warn Patricia to hide herself, or to hurry back."

"What's Patricia doing?" Long Tom asked.

There was no answer from the bronze man. Long Tom looked over the cabin roof. He could see no sign of Doc in the moonlight. He returned to his listening, deciding Patricia's mission would have to be a mystery for the present.

Doc had entered the cabin. On a table, he spread the six sections which had been fitted together to form the ivory block. At first glance, the inner surfaces of these seemed merely carelessly carved. They were a bit rough. However, when a magnifying glass was put on them, the roughness assumed a definite form. It was possible to tell that the block held a cleverly carved relief map of the region around the cabin.

It was necessary to rearrange the parts several times before Doc had them in their proper positions.

"That's it!" Renny said at last. Renny was looking over Doc's shoulder. The big-fisted fellow probably knew as much about maps as any man. It was part of his engineering training.

Doc ran the magnifying glass along the irregular line which indicated the shore on the carving. It was not hard to find the location of the entombed galleon.

The spot was marked by a tiny, exquisitely carved skull. There was no other peculiar mark on the map, which made it almost certain the skull identified the location of the galleon.

"The darn thing isn't over a mile from here!" Renny boomed.

Señor Oveja, his daughter, and El Rabanos had not been parties to the inspection of the insides of the ivory block. Chancing to come into the room now, they observed what had been going on.

"I demand that block!" Señor Oveja said angrily. "It is mine!"

"By what right?" Doc queried.

Señor Oveja sputtered indignantly. "My ancestor—"

"Your ancestor was a thief," Doc said shortly. "The ivory block was admittedly not his property. Nor was the galleon or its contents."

Señor Oveja seemed about to explode. Before he could do that, Doc walked away. The bronze man had the sections of the ivory block in a pocket.

"You fellows drift out in the brush," Doc told Monk in a low voice. "I'll join you a bit later. It'll save trouble with Señor and Señorita Oveja and El Rabanos, if they do not know we are going. We'll leave Long Tom here to watch them. Long Tom has to stay anyway, to protect Patricia with his listening device. He has to give Pat warning if any of our enemies come close, so she can duck."

"We're going to have a look at that galleon?"

Monk guessed in a hushed whisper.

"You have guessed it," Doc told him.

TWENTY minutes later, Ham was hissing peevishly at Monk, "Can't you be quiet, you missing link! You make more fuss than all the rest of us together!"

This was hardly true. Ham had just fallen down, making a considerable racket.

Monk only sniffed. "Why don't you throw that sword cane away, shyster? That's what you're stumbling over."

The dapper Ham had retained his sword cane through the excitement. He had lost it in the cabin when the gang seized him. Upon escaping, his first act had been to find it.

"You tripped me!" Ham growled. "You big accident of nature—"

"Cut out the funnyboning, you culls!" Renny's big voice boomed softly. "The dog-gone galleon should be around here some place!"

The sloppy smack of waves began to reach their ears. Each smack was followed by a long flutter of falling spray. This indicated the shore was a rock wall climbing sheer from the water.

Like mountaineers, the men were carrying a long rope. This was vitally necessary. The way they were traversing was incredibly rough. Deep gashes appeared underfoot with the unexpectedness of crevasses in a glacier.

More than once, they had to lower a man over a lip of stone until he touched bottom. Just as often, they had to remain at the foot of a wall of stone while Doc Savage climbed with the end of the rope, later to haul them up. To Doc's enormous strength, agility, and sense of balance, the canyon walls presented no great obstacles.

Eventually, Doc's men sank on the crest of a small ridge, panting. They rested there. Doc had gone on ahead while they climbed. They presumed he was searching for the spot marked on the map within the ivory cube.

"Here it is, men!" Doc called suddenly.

The men came to life as if lightning had struck nearby. They scrambled down the steep slope toward the spot Doc's voice had come from.

The bronze man stood beside a waist-high pile of evergreen brush. The spot was in a cuplike depression. On all sides, stone walls sloped up steeply.

The gaunt Johnny looked around vacantly. He took off his glasses, put them back on again.

"I don't see anything," he said.

Doc Savage grasped a limb which projected near the bottom of the brush pile. He lifted it, and upset the entire pile.

The brush had covered a hole in the steep slope

of the hill—the mouth of a tunnel. It was perhaps three feet wide, four high.

For a few feet, the tunnel penetrated soft earth. For that distance, it was timbered. The timbers were bright and new. In some spots, twigs still clung to them. Leaves on these were still green.

Beyond the timbering, the tunnel dived into solid rock and sloped sharply downward. Its floor became a series of crude steps.

"This work was done a long, long time ago," said Johnny. If anyone was qualified to judge the age of mankind's handiwork, the gaunt archaeologist was. He could look at a goblet from an Egyptian tomb, and tell what Pharaoh drank out of it.

"But the work at the entrance was very recent," Monk muttered. "It hasn't been done over a week or two, I'll bet."

The steps ended. The tunnel traveled straight ahead for a few feet. It emptied then into what appeared to be a subterranean room.

Doc snapped a long, glaring white beam from his flashlight, and roved it slowly about.

"Holy cow!" breathed Renny in awe-stricken tones.

## Chapter XVIII
## THE SKELETON CREW

THE underground recess was not as large as it had seemed at first. It was, in fact, hardly more than enough to contain the thing it held.

The walls to the right were solid and smooth—once a canyon side. To the left was rock—cracked, distorted slide-in rock, but solid for all of that.

A small rill of water crawled across the sandy floor. It looked like a flow of molten silver.

The galleon had bulked big in front of their eyes. It had been blocked up on rocks for a hull-scraping when disaster had overtaken it. The fact that it had been blocked up had preserved it from dampness to a certain extent. But it was not exactly seaworthy.

Once the galleon might have been a gilded pride of the Spanish Main. No telling what colors had bedecked it. But it was gray now—gray because of a repulsive mold which covered it like a carpet.

To the left of where Doc and his men stood, a skeleton lay on a rock. It lay in a curled position, like a slumbering dog. One of the hands, from which part of the finger bones had dropped, was over a gaping eye socket, as if to keep out the light.

"One of the galleon crew I guess," said Renny. The big engineer's enormous voice was a booming roar which assumed ear-splitting proportions in the cavern confines.

"Use your muffler!" Monk whispered. "You'll shake this place down on us."

Doc Savage turned. His flash beam, like a rod of white flame, impaled each of his men in turn. In their eagerness, all four had followed him into the tunnel.

The flash beam went to the sandy floor. Tracks were there. Fresh tracks! The imprints were those of moccasins!

Doc moved along the side of the galleon, his men trailing him. They passed three more skeletons. Rusty streaks beside the bone assemblies might once have been blunderbusses or swords.

Several piles of rust along the cavern wall hinted at cannons which must have been removed to lighten the galleon for careening.

Reaching out, Doc placed a finger against the hull. With a little pressure, the finger sank for half its length into the mold-covered wood. The galleon was a pile of rot.

Doc came to a halt. Before him in the hull of the galleon, a hole gaped. It was a fresh bole, and at least four feet square. It looked like it had been dug open with a spade.

Doc popped his light into the bole. There were more skeletons—five, six, seven of them, this time. They were gray things, made utterly hideous by the mold which covered them.

It was indeed a macabre argosy, this ship from another age, with its crew of skeletons.

Doc entered. He sank ankle-deep in the spongy timbers. It seemed inevitable that the whole ship would come down about his ears.

Going on, his light picked up objects which bore a marked resemblance to the brass-bound chests which historians write of. He dropped the glittering thread of light into one of these.

"Empty!" Renny thundered. "The treasure is gone!"

DOC Savage stepped swiftly to each of the chests in turn. He worked his way aft through a bulkhead. More of the chests were there. He picked up a small circular piece of metal and a green, glittering object which might have been colored glass—but wasn't.

He carried the articles back and showed them to his men.

"A piece-of-eight, and a small emerald!" Monk muttered. "That indicates there was really a treasure here."

Ham punched angrily at a bulkhead with his sword cane. The cane sank part of its length in the soggy wood.

"It's gone!" he snapped. "Who got it?"

"You noticed those tracks," Doc said. "They were made by feet shod in moccasins."

Ham frowned. "You mean—Boat Face?"

"Boat Face made the tracks," Doc said. "Not only did the Indian have the ivory cube, but he knew its significance. The gang who was after it must have told him what it was. Probably they hired him to get it for them. Then, when he double-crossed them, they killed him."

"It looks like our job now is to find out where Boat Face put the treasure," Renny grumbled.

"Maybe he didn't take it out of here," Monk offered. "After all, this is as good a hiding place as any. Let's look around."

Monk started for the stern. Doc was at his side. They passed through an aperture which had been spaded in a molded bulkhead.

Doc suddenly dropped a hand on Monk's shoulder. Monk's gristled, apish frame weighed in the neighborhood of two hundred and fifty pounds, but Doc's hand brought him up as sharply as if he had been a child.

"Back!" Doc rapped.

"Blazes! What's wrong?" Monk had wheeled, was diving back the way he had come as he asked the question.

Doc Savage made no answer. He was close behind Monk. Just before leaving the compartment, he halted, half turned, and popped his flashlight ahead.

The light disclosed a thin thread as gray as the mold which covered every inch of the ancient galleon. The thread was about six inches above the floor.

Wheeling, Doc followed Monk back to the others. They all stared at him, expecting an explanation. They were all a bit on edge. This place they were in—a grave which covered a hideous ship and its macabre crew of skeletons—had got under their skin somewhat.

Doc did not explain.

"Outside!" he said.

They scrambled into the rock tunnel, mounted the steps, and stumbled out into the night.

The cup-shaped depression into which the tunnel mouth opened was fairly deep. The moon was low in the sky. Its beams did not penetrate to the depression bottom.

"Whe-e-ew!" said Monk. "I'm glad to get out of that place! What went wrong, Doc?"

"Plenty has gone wrong—for you, amigos!" announced a guttural voice.

With that, several flashlights poked white funnels down over the depression rim. Doc and his men were wrapped in a white glare of light.

Squinting against glare, they could see men with guns on all sides of them.

ONE of the encircling gang hastily left his fellows and darted down the side of the depression. His gait down the steep slope was a series of grotesque hops. He came to a stop about halfway down.

"We know all about the gas!" said the guttural voice which had spoken previously. "I mean, Señor

Savage, the gas which does its work while you hold your breath. Do not try to use it. If the man who just came near you drops, we will begin shooting. *Sabe?"*

Monk and Ham exchanged uneasy looks. They had forgotten their animosity. Johnny and Renny stood perfectly still.

Each of Doc's men carried one of the little supermachine guns under his coat. They debated their chances of seizing the guns and making a fight of it. The chances seemed slim.

"Easy does it," Doc said in an expressionless voice. "If we start fireworks, we haven't a chance."

"That is very sensible, hombres," said the voice above. "Each of you will remove his upper garments. Strip to the skin. Roll up your trousers legs to show no weapons are concealed beneath them. Turn your trousers pockets inside out."

The speaker was not one of the ring of gunmen. He stood behind them, hidden from view.

Doc and his four men stripped off coats, shirts, and undershirts. Doc shed his remarkable vest. They rolled up trousers legs, then turned pockets out.

*"Bueno!"* said the masked man. "We can now be sure that they have no weapons left. Go, amigos, and seize them!"

Men came sliding down the side of the depression.

Doc Savage had seen all of the gang on other occasions. They were the kidnapers of Patricia Savage. Doc counted eleven of them. That was the entire gang, except the leader.

Their chief did not appear. He remained above, unseen.

The men carried ropes. They began tying the prisoners. One fellow's rope was of extraordinary length, and it was he who bound Doc Savage.

The ropes were not of hemp, but of braided cotton. They were very strong. The men doing the knotting knew how it should he done.

Apparently, Doc submitted meekly to the binding. But a close observer might have noticed that the cables of muscles on his wrists were even larger than usual. Doc was holding the tendons tense. If he were tied while they were thus, he had merely to relax to get sufficient slack to shake off the binding ropes.

One of the swarthy gang had a canvas bag slung over a shoulder. From this, he drew a bottle-shaped object of shiny metal. The neck was fitted with a valve.

"Now, I will give the hombres the same thing I gave Alex Savage!" growled the man.

From the same sack, which had held the metal flask, the fellow withdrew two fragments of rather floppy rubber. These were carved, rubber-stamp fashion. The carving was that of a wolf with strangely human features. These were obviously the stamps used to leave the weird werewolf marks.

The gold flakes in Doc's eyes seemed to have turned to a tawny frost.

Here was the murderer of Alex Savage!

"No!" called the unseen leader from above. "Not the gas!"

"We can leave them somewhere," muttered the man with the gas flask. "No one can tell but what they died of heart failure."

"No! Not yet!"

Reluctantly, the swarthy man replaced the metal gas bottle in the canvas bag container.

Another dark man drew a knife. He juggled the blade in a way which showed remarkable dexterity. His manner indicated he was the knife-throwing expert of the group, and that he was proud of it.

"Then I will dispose of them as I did Boat Face, amigos," he smirked.

Doc Savage said nothing, made no move. It was a bad sign, the frank way these fellows were speaking of past crimes. It meant that they had little intention of Doc and his men living to bear witness—to tell a jury what they had heard.

"No!" said the concealed chief. "No knife—yet!"

The hidden leader now showed himself. He came skidding down the slope. He was a tall man; little more than that could be seen of him. He wore a mask—a great bandanna handkerchief which covered his head as well as his features.

Doc Savage glanced at Monk.

"Do you know this fellow, Monk?" he asked dryly.

Monk squinted at the masked man. "Nope. Can't recognize 'im.

"Isn't his walk familiar?"

Monk considered, acting as if the individual they were discussing were not present.

"Ain't able to tell, Doc," he said. "You'll have to spill it."

"O. K.," said Doc. "The bird is—"

The masked man snarled. He doubled and scooped up one of the tiny supermachine guns which Doc had been forced to drop. Leveling it, he shot Doc in his unprotected chest.

## Chapter XIX
### THE KILLING DEAD

DOC dropped. The tiny machine gun happened to be latched into single-shot position. That was fortunate. Even though the gun was charged with mercy bullets, at that short range a flood of the slugs would have wrought fatal injury.

As it was, Doc took only one mercy bullet in the chest. The stupefying chemical worked swiftly. Doc was probably asleep before he hit the ground.

Monk and the others stared at their bronze chief. They were dazed. Now that they thought back, this was the first time they could remember having seen Doc entirely helpless.

They themselves, being bound with rope which was beyond their strength to break, were powerless to aid their bronze chief.

*"Bueno!"* said the swarthy man who wielded knives. "Let us give him another bullet—a real bullet!"

The masked man shook his head slowly. "No, amigos! We will delay that. These men may have removed the treasure. If so, we will have to make them lead us to it."

The fellow stepped into the tunnel, his followers crowding eagerly after him. They were hungry for sight of this loot which they had gone to such pains to get.

None troubled to watch the prisoners. They were bound too tightly to escape, it seemed.

The last man vanished into the tunnel.

Monk and the others wrenched at the ropes. They tried to untie each other's bonds with their teeth. The task was not hopeless, but it would take many minutes.

"We'll never make it!" Johnny groaned.

Repeatedly, the men glanced at Doc. They knew the bronze giant was a wizard as an escape artist. These ropes, as vigorously as they had been tied, would hardly hold Doc. But the metallic giant was a victim of the mercy bullet.

Or was he?

The swarthy men had left a flashlight stuck in the side of the depression. The beam of this played directly on Doc. The bronze man's lids seemed to flutter—they *did* flutter!

"Doc!" Renny rumbled softly.

Renny was incredulous. He knew the stupefying power of the mercy bullets; he had not believed a man could recover from their effects in less than thirty minutes.

Hardly ten minutes had elapsed since Doc collapsed. His recovery so soon was a tribute to his fine physical condition.

Doc lay perfectly motionless for a time. When finally he spoke, his voice was unexcited.

"Where did they go?"

"You mean the gang that grabbed us—and the masked big shot?" Monk asked.

"Yes."

"They went into the tunnel."

With a tremendous, convulsive effort, Doc gained his feet. The wound on his chest was small, merely a puncture which hardly oozed crimson.

"They'll be killed—at the galleon!" he rapped. "We may have time to get 'em out before—"

DOC'S words were still banging through the surrounding night, when the earth seemed to heave several inches underfoot.

There was a tremendous, bellowing roar! It seemed to start deep in the earth, and gain and gain in volume. The ground vibrated as if it were about to fall to pieces! Boulders and gravel showered down the depression sides!

Out of the tunnel maw came a dragon-breath spout of crimson fire. A gush of yellow smoke followed it. Then the tunnel seemed to shut itself like a big mouth closing.

The quaking of the earth stopped; the rumbling died. A few rocks galloped the last of the distance down the slope. Then there was silence.

Renny used the exclamation he employed on such occasions.

"Holy cow!" he exploded. "What happened?"

Doc Savage did not answer immediately. Instead, he twisted his arms into various positions. The great muscles that had been tense when he was bound had relaxed now. The rope which had secured him fell away.

He started untying his friends, making explanations as he worked.

"There was a thread stretched across one of the galleon cabins," he said. "It ran to a contact that was barely visible at one side. The contact could have only one purpose—it was connected to an electric detonator for dynamite or gunpowder."

"So that's why you rushed us out of the galleon!" Monk exclaimed.

Doc nodded. "There was a chance of other contacts, better concealed, in other parts of the craft."

"Boat Face's work, huh?" Monk guessed. "But why'd he do it?"

"Boat Face evidently did it," Doc agreed. "He was the only visitor to the place before ourselves; his tracks prove that. He must have known he was mixed up with bad actors. Possibly he set the trap to get rid of them. He might have intended to give them the ivory block so that they would visit the galleon."

Monk stared at the tunnel which had closed like a mouth.

"Boat Face did a great job—for a dead man," he said, "They're all finished—down below."

Doc nodded. "No doubt of it."

Monk swung his gaze back to Doc. "Who was the masked guy, Doc?"

Doc started to answer, but held the words back when he heard a distant cry. The sound was shrilly feminine, cutting through the night. Patricia Savage's voice! She was anxious as to the fate of the men.

"They heard the explosion, and are worrying about us!" Doc decided aloud, instead of answering Monk's question. "We'd better let them know we're safe."

Doc went to meet Patricia. He encountered her within two hundred yards. With the girl were Long Tom, ample Tiny, Señorita Oveja, and Señor Oveja.

Girl-faced El Rabanos was not with them.

Long Tom was excited.

"What happened?" he gulped.

"Where's El Rabanos?" Monk countered.

"Blasted if I know!" Long Tom retorted. "He disappeared, somehow, without me hearing him with the listening device. The only way he could have done it was to creep off at the same time you birds left—following you. Your noise covered his footsteps."

"That explains how the gang found us," Doc told Monk.

Monk emitted a long whistle. "So the guy in the mask was El Rabanos!"

"THE mastermind behind all this violence was El Rabanos," Doc agreed.

*"Eso hace temblar!"* Señor Oveja moaned. "It is shocking! El Rabanos—my best friend! A double-crosser!"

"The same gentleman who ordered his men to throttle you on the train—using my baggage straps," Doc agreed. "Give him credit for a devilish mind! He covered himself by making you think I was an enemy."

"But the treasure!" exclaimed Monk. "Where is it?"

Doc Savage turned to Patricia. "I showed you the sand from Boat Face's moccasins," he said. "You said you knew of a pool in a creek which had that kind of sand in its bottom. You said you remembered wading there. You went to examine it. What did you find?"

"The treasure," Patricia said. "Boat face had carried it out and sunk it. The stuff was in fairly deep water. It was in carrying it out to deep water that Boat Face got the sand in his moccasins."

From a pocket, she produced a thin string of scintillating color. It was a bangle of emeralds strung on gold.

"Here's a sample of the stuff."

Señor Oveja stared at the bauble. He suddenly forgot his grief over his friend's treachery.

"I demand a share, amigos!" he said aggressively. "At least three fourths of the treasure!"

Doc Savage ignored him.

Somewhere behind, there was a low rumbling noise. A great boulder, loosened by the underground explosion, had broken away. The noise was vast, as if the earth were being shaken.

The earth being shaken! That might have been a herald call of what the future held for this remarkable man of bronze and his aids.

*The Man Who Shook The Earth!* He was to be their next foe. A master of ingenuity, of diabolic cunning, of ruthlessness! "The Man Who Shook The Earth" plotted against—not one individual, a city, a State, a nation—he sought to dominate the world!

Mighty man of bronze Doc Savage might be, with powers seemingly without limit—but in "The Man Who Shook The Earth," he would find a foe more vicious and clever than any he had as yet encountered.

Not knowing any of this, Doc Savage strode along in silence.

"What disposition will be made of the treasure," Patricia asked. Then, lest motives be misunderstood, she added: "I don't want any."

"Nobody will get any," Doc said dryly. "Some of it came from the churches of old Panama City. That portion should be easily identified. It will be turned over to the church, its rightful owner."

He considered. "The rest will be used to build public hospitals here in Canada, and to establish a trust fund to keep them operating without charge to patients. That is what we usually do with any money that comes our way."

"Wonder how much the stuff is worth?" Monk pondered.

"Several millions at least," Patricia said. "I know a little of jewels—enough to guess at the value."

Señor Oveja waved his arms excitedly and shrieked: "But what do I get out of it?"

"You," Doc told him, "get the air."

THE END

# INTERMISSION by Will Murray

This Doc Savage volume showcases one of the most popular members of the bronze man's inner circle, and his cousin Pat Savage in her first two historic appearances.

Both *Doc Savage Magazine* editor John Nanovic and Norma Dent agreed that Patricia Savage was the beautiful brainchild of Lester Dent. The scant surviving circumstantial evidence points to him as well.

Just months before writing *Brand of the Werewolf,* Dent had introduced a similar character in his short-lived Lee Nace mystery series then running in *Ten Detective Aces* through 1933. Julia Nace was the cousin of the Missouri-born scientific detective also known as "the Blond Adder." Debuting in "The Diving Dead" *(Ten Detective Aces,* September 1933), she teamed up with Nace to solve the murder of her brother. Julia returned in subsequent adventures as Nace's partner. Spunky and fearless, Julia was the unmistakable prototype for brave bronzed Pat Savage.

PAT

Street & Smith was a very conservative pulp house. They were not big on gratuitous female characters in their stories. According to John Nanovic, "Street & Smith didn't believe in girls."

As Doc Savage ghost Ryerson Johnson once remarked, "It used to fret Les the way they held him to such a tight pattern. With women for instance, you practically had to cut them off at the neck and not bring them back to life again until you got to their knees."

Consequently Lester may have had to lobby for her inclusion.

From a relatively demure debut, Pat evolved into such a high-spirited personality that editor John L. Nanovic once dubbed her "Tarzana." Cut from the same recently emancipated stock (American women only earned the right to vote in 1920) as the Stratemeyer Syndicate's Nancy Drew—who first appeared in 1930—Pat Savage belongs to

that liberated generation of women who came out of the Roaring Twenties determined to conquer a man's world on their own terms.

Pat's trademark single-action Frontier Colt is present from the beginning, but her distinctive golden eyes did not emerge for several episodes. Dent was always careful to say that they were golden, but not the unique flake-gold of her world-famous cousin. Pat was not intended to become a distaff version of Doc Savage.

One of the unsolved mysteries about Pat Savage was her Canadian background. Dent portrays her as a 1930s version of pistol-packing cowgirls like Annie Oakley and Belle Starr, ready and able to unload the contents of her grandfather's.44-40 six-shooter at any and all comers. In fact, she seems quintessentially American in temperament.

No doubt that was Lester Dent's intent. But Street & Smith had equal input into the Doc Savage stories too. It's probably not a coincidence that shortly before *Brand of the Werewolf* appeared, S&S had made arrangements for the magazine to be printed in Canada. The first issue of Doc Savage was reprinted with an August 1933 cover date. *Brand of the Werewolf* was written that summer. It seems probable that General Manager Henry W. Ralston suggested Dent make Pat a resident of British Columbia to appeal to new Doc readers north of the U.S. border.

Pat Savage's second appearance was a fluke. She is not mentioned in the outline to *Fear Cay,* which was published in the September 1934 *Doc Savage Magazine.* Dent kept a notebook of character profiles of the Doc cast, which he revised during that first formative year as he developed his cast. Although he updated it right up to *Brand of the Werewolf,* strangely Pat Savage is not mentioned in its pages. It's as if Lester at first considered her a one-shot character.

A strange story lies behind the composition of

the 19th Doc novel. It was outlined as Doc Savage #14, and abandoned in progress.

As best as the story can be reconstructed, Lester Dent was writing *Fear Cay* in October 1933, turning out fiction as fast as he could under editorial pressure, when he crossed over into the Twilight Zone.

In 1945, Dent recounted the experience matter-of-factly:

> I remember it just as if it were yesterday. I was sitting alone, at my typewriter, writing a boy and girl sequence. Boy and girl meet, and they spat, and they reunite, stuff. I always visualize my characters somewhat, and suddenly I noticed dark hair on the girl's leg. It showed through her sheer hose. I made a mental note that I had better have her shave her leg. Then, I noticed that the hero's shoelaces were tied in a kind of knot that I didn't know how to tie. I had just decided that was curious when the girl and the boy turned and started talking to me. The hero asked me if I had noticed where he had put his hat down, and the girl told me no, she could stand up, when I offered her a chair. They were there; they were real. They were flesh and blood. It took just a moment to realize what had happened, shut that typewriter and get the hell out of there.

While we can't be certain that the story that started Dent hallucinating was in fact *Fear Cay,* it remains the top suspect. Why else would he lay the unfinished manuscript aside for six full months? Mrs. Dent recalled that after the weird experience, Lester had trouble sleeping, and decided to move from Jackson Heights, Long Island, into the city so he could take walks in Central Park whenever "them blasted jitters" as he called then, began acting up.

Dent moved to 101 West 55th Street in November, while writing the nightmarish novel, *The Monsters.* He cut back on all outside writing, concentrating exclusively on Doc Savage. But he continued to struggle with his overwrought nerves.

"He'd wake up at night and start talking to the characters he'd been writing about," Mrs. Dent once revealed. Lester hardly spoke of the incident, except to say once, "Any time your characters start talking to you, it's time to quit."

Dent penned some of his most bizarre Doc novels in the aftermath of this experience, including *The Thousand-Headed Man, The Squeaking Goblin* and scripts for the 1934 Doc Savage radio show. It must have been a strain. In February, he and Norma took a much-needed vacation.

"Six weeks in Florida and I was all right again," Dent commented.

When Dent returned to *Fear Cay* that April, he put his Florida sojourn to good use, and did so again a few months later when he wrote the Everglades adventure, *Red Snow.* But Lester wasn't entirely himself. For he accidentally killed off the same minor villain in twice—once in Chapter VII and again in Chapter XII of *Fear Cay*! Editor John Nanovic failed to catch it.

Pat had not appeared in print when Dent outlined *Fear Cay.* Apparently, by the time Dent felt ready to pick up the pieces of the interrupted adventure, reader reaction had come in on *Brand of the Werewolf,* and a decision was made to bring Pat back for an encore.

Or more than an encore. For immediately after her second guest appearance, Pat moved to Manhattan in the next issue's *Death in Silver,* where she opened up a combination beauty salon and gymnasium, Park Avenue Beautician. It was later renamed Patricia, Incorporated. These two consecutive appearances suggest someone suddenly decided that Pat Savage should become a series semi-regular. Probably this was Lester Dent.

From that time on, Pat was always trying to horn in on Doc's adventures. Ever protective of his only living relative, Doc did his best to keep her from harm. But the willful Pat usually got her way.

It's not clear who actually named Doc's resourceful cousin. But over in Street & Smith's *Bill Barnes,* that hero had a sister named Patricia.

**Pat assists Doc in an interrogation, as visualized in Emery Clarke's cover for *Devil on the Moon.***

So perhaps it was a favorite feminine name of someone high up in the Street & Smith hierarchy.

The look of Pat Savage can be traced to cover artist Walter M. Baumhofer. His wife, Alureda, posed for the bronze-haired adventuress on all of his *Doc Savage* covers.

Dent employed her sparingly. Most of his ghost-writers made frequent use of the character. Except Harold A. Davis. He never wrote Pat into any of his Doc Savage stories, curiously enough.

Pat Savage appeared semi-regularly until near the end of the series, when she narrated *I Died Yesterday* in 1948. It was the only time a Doc Savage cast member told an adventure in the first person.

In that memorable adventure, Pat explained her strong yen for adventure:

> Excitement in any of the three forms it usually takes—danger, suspense or anticipation of violence—undeniably has a stimulating effect on me, and this trait, if it should be called a trait, must be a family inheritance just as much as the six-shooter in my handbag. Doc Savage once told me that it was a blemish that passed along in the Savage blood. He said this unhappily. He also said that he was going to cure me of it, and he said the same thing on other occasions, but never very confidently. Firmly, yes. Angrily, also. But never with much certainty.

About a decade later, when Mort Weisinger was editing the line of Superman comics, he got busy ransacking old issues of *Doc Savage* for commercial concepts. After hijacking Doc's Fortress of Solitude and a few other elements, he realized there might be some super-potential in Pat Savage.

Superman's younger cousin, Supergirl, made her debut in 1959. Can there be any doubt that although Supergirl was a blonde, her true roots are *bronze*?

These two novels possess other distinctions. At 185,000 copies sold, *Brand of the Werewolf* became the best-selling Doc Savage Bantam reprint of them all. It went back to press an unprecedented 16 times. And *Fear Cay* had the distinction of being serialized for *The Adventures of Doc Savage* radio show which aired over National Public Radio in 1985. Robin Riker played Pat.

Both novels have been textually restored for this Nostalgia Ventures edition—although modestly so.

One art restoration graces *Brand of the Werewolf.* Sometimes interior dry-brush illustrations were dropped from a story. Usually these were discarded. But a Paul Orban depiction of the discovery of a murdered body in a cabin deleted from Chapter X was subsequently salvaged as a house ad for *Doc Savage Magazine.* We've carefully restored it to its rightful place. •

Pat as seen on Walter Baumhofer's covers for *The Fantastic Island* and *The Men Who Smiled No More.*

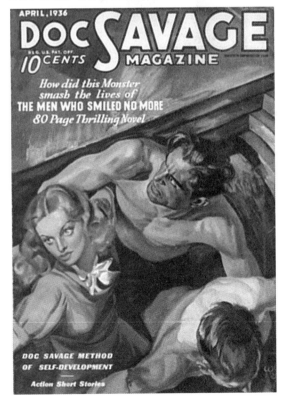

*From the dawn of the ages men have sought and struggled for that which Doc Savage finds on*

# FEAR CAY

*A Book-length Novel*

## By KENNETH ROBESON

### Chapter I
### THE POCKETBOOK GAG

ONE of two pedestrians walking on a New York street turned, pointed at the big bronze man they had just passed, and said earnestly, "I wouldn't trade places with that bird for a million bucks!"

The pedestrian's companion also looked at the bronze man.

"You said it," he agreed. "I wouldn't last a day in *his* shoes, if half of what I've heard is true."

If the bronze man was aware of their attention, he gave no sign. Many persons turned to stare at him; newsboys stopped shouting abruptly when they saw him; but the bronze man merely went on with long, elastic strides.

"He's not often seen in public," someone breathed.

"And no wonder!" another exclaimed. "The newspapers say his enemies have made countless attempts to kill him."

The heads of the tallest individuals on the New York street did not top the bronze man's shoulders. He was a giant. Yet it was only the manner in which he towered above the throng that made him seem as huge as he really was, so symmetrically perfect was his great frame developed.

"They say he can take a piece of building brick

in one hand and squeeze it to dust," offered a man.

Huge cables of sinew enwrapped the bronze man's neck, and enormous thews stood up as hard as bone on the backs of his hands. There was a liquid smoothness about the way they flowed.

Persons who saw the metallic man's eyes made haste in getting out of his path. Not that the eyes were threatening, but there was something about them that compelled. They were like pools of flake-gold, those eyes, and the gold flakes were very fine and always in movement, as if stirred by diminutive, invisible whirlwinds.

Strange eyes! They held power, and the promise of an ability to do weird things.

Two policemen on a corner saluted the bronze giant enthusiastically.

"Hello, Doc Savage," they chorused.

The mighty man who looked as if he were made of metal acknowledged the greeting with a nod and went on. His features were strikingly regular, unusually handsome in an emphatic, muscular way.

More than one attractive young stenographer or clerk felt herself inexplicably moved to attempt a mild flirtation the instant she saw the big bronze fellow. But the amazing giant had a manner of not seeming to see such incidents.

The bronze man came to a section where the sidewalk was almost deserted. He stopped.

On the walk before him lay a small object of leather. Stooping, he picked it up.

The article was a pocketbook of good quality, and its plumpness hinted at a plentiful content. The sinewy cables on the bronze man's hands flowed easily as he opened the purse.

There was a popping sound, such a noise as might have been made by a stubborn cork being pulled from a bottle. Instantly after that, the bronze man dropped the wallet, and it slithered along the sidewalk for a few feet before coming to a rest.

The man's arms became slack, his strikingly handsome head slumped forward, and he began to weave slightly from side to side. Suddenly, as if a master nerve controlling all of the muscles in his mighty frame had been severed, he collapsed upon the street.

NUMEROUS individuals saw the bronze giant drop, but one was nearer than the others. This man was a bulky fellow with an extremely long nose, a round puncture of a mouth, and a skin which was flushed redly, as if the fellow were very warm. One thing particularly outstanding about the man's appearance was the manner in which he always seemed to be perspiring a little.

The man carried a small, plain black leather case.

He ran toward the prone form of Doc Savage, swooping enroute to pick up the pocketbook which the bronze man had been examining an instant before he collapsed. This went into a pocket.

Reaching Doc Savage, the perspiring man sank to a knee. As he placed his black leather case on the sidewalk, it came open—and those curious persons who ran up, saw that it held a doctor's equipment.

"This man has been stricken by heart failure!" the man said loudly, after a brief examination.

A taxicab swerved to the curb and the driver craned his neck. The perspiring man stood erect and beckoned sharply at the hackman.

"Give me a hand!" he shouted. "We've got to rush this big fellow to an emergency hospital to save his life!"

The taxi driver tumbled from his machine, ran over and lent his aid to moving the recumbent Doc Savage. The hackman was burly, but the two of them grunted and strained, so heavy was the giant bronze form they were carrying to the cab.

A cop pounded up, puffing, "Begorra, what's goin' on here?"

"Heart trouble," he was told. "The big bronze fellow had an overworked heart, and it caved on him."

They managed to haul Doc Savage into the cab. The long-nosed man, perspiring somewhat more freely, dashed back, got his bag of instruments, and piled into the taxi.

"Begorra, I'm goin' along," said the cop.

"Is that necessary?" snapped the sweating man.

"This bronze lad be Doc Savage, no less," declared the officer. "The finest ain't half good enough for him, and I'm gonna see that he gets it!"

The cop leaped into the machine.

Behind the wheel, the driver made a pass at the shift lever and the cab lunged forward. The horn blared, pedestrians dived aside, and the cab volleyed down the street.

"Ride your horn and tromp on it!" called the cop.

Tires howled as they took a corner; skyscrapers shoved up close walls that shut out the sunlight, so that the cab pitched through gloom. On the sidewalks not many people could be seen.

The perspiring man dipped a hand into a coat pocket, brought out a heavy blue automatic pistol and lifted it. The policeman was occupied in examining Doc Savage and never saw the gun whip toward his own head.

There was the sound as of a football being kicked hard. The officer let air out of his lungs and slumped, head lolling.

The rear door of the cab opened and the cop toppled out, driven by a lusty shove. Momentum of the car caused him to roll end over end and slam into a parked machine, where he lay, not seriously damaged.

THE hack driver looked around. He had freckles, a loose lower lip and cigarette-stained fingers.

"When that cop piled in I figured we was sunk, Leaking," he chuckled.

"Watch your driving!" growled "Leaking," and dabbed at the perspiration on his forehead.

Leaking now produced the billfold which had lain on the sidewalk. Once he had opened it, there was disclosed a small flat metal phial, the cork of which was yanked when the folding halves of the purse were separated.

"Neat!" the sinister, long-nosed man chuckled. "He never smelled a rat—and when he opened it, the gas in the metal phial got him before he knew what it was all about."

He passed the ingenious wallet forward to the freckled, slack-lipped driver. "Stick this away somewhere."

"Sure." The hackman had been watching his rear-view mirror to make sure there was no pursuit.

The cab swung west and streets became shabby.

A robe hung on the rack in the rear, and Leaking drew this over the slack form of Doc Savage to prevent casual observers from sighting the giant bronze man.

"Sure his nibs is alive?" asked the driver.

"I don't care a hell of a lot," said Leaking. "But he's still breathing."

"Hallet wanted him alive, didn't he?"

"Sure."

"Any idea what that shyster has up his sleeve?"

"No," said Leaking. "Shut up and drive."

"Whose idea was that pocketbook trick?"

"Mine," Leaking snapped. "And will you shut up and drive!"

The cab passed a play street where grimy kids howled, skirted tall gas tanks and a solid vast cube of bricks wherein generators wailed like banshees, and from which high-tension wires stretched in profusion.

Streets became even more decrepit, and the hack ran more swiftly, a carbon knock tinkling under the hood. They were going downtown toward the financial section now, using streets which were almost deserted. The machine slackened speed and turned into more populous streets after a time.

"This is the joint," said Leaking.

The "joint" was a towering skyscraper of white brick, modernistic, impressive, one of scores, all resembling each other closely, which shot up like cold thorns around Wall Street. Between the structure and the one adjacent was a narrow alleyway intended as a freight entrance.

The cab popped into this and dragged its tires to a halt.

The driver alighted and entered the skyscraper. Probably he engaged the attendant on the freight elevator in conversation, for that worthy did not appear to interfere with Leaking as he unloaded Doc Savage's great frame from the hack and, not without some laboring, conveyed the bronze man into the lift.

At the twentieth floor, Leaking unloaded his cargo and employed a large janitors' closet for temporary storage while he returned the freight elevator to the ground level without any one being aware that he had taken it.

Then the man rode up on a passenger lift to the twentieth floor, swabbing at perspiration, waited in the corridor until no one was in sight, then picked Doc Savage up and staggered out of the janitors' closet with him.

Gold-lettered on a frosted glass door was:

N. BECKELL HALLET
ATTORNEY-AT-LAW

Leaking shoved this door open and walked in with his burden. He dumped Doc's great frame in a swivel chair, and the chair squeaked loudly.

Across the office, the solid wooden door of an inner sanctum flew open.

"I knew it!" wailed the man who looked out. "I knew it!"

LEAKING scowled and snapped, "You knew what, Hallet?"

"Knew that Doc Savage would damage you or one of your men seriously," groaned the other.

Leaking's scowl turned into a laugh as he realized that Hallet was not standing where he could see Doc's features and had mistaken the identity of the bronze man.

"Hell!" chuckled Leaking. "This is Doc Savage."

"What?" Hallet gulped incredulously, then advanced gingerly to eye the bronze giant.

Hallet was a fat man with the manners of a bird. He was round and sleek and plump, but there was a mincing daintiness to his movements. His suit was sparrow-colored and added to his birdlike aspect, as did his sharp beak of a nose.

"It is Doc Savage!" Hallet wrung his plump hands.

"Well, you wanted him, didn't you?" Leaking growled.

"Yes, but—" Hallet slumped into a chair, pulled a foaming square of silk handkerchief from his breast pocket and dabbed it at his neck. "How did you do it?"

"Fake pocketbook with a doo-dad in it that threw gas into his face when he opened it," grinned Leaking.

"I never thought you would secure him that easily," Hallet murmured, restoring the handkerchief. "They say this bronze man is incredibly clever. Wrongdoers all over the world fear him."

"Does he look like something to be scared of now?" Leaking jeered.

"His name is synonymous for fear in the far corners of the earth," Hallet went on earnestly. "His life career is helping others out of trouble. They say he has accomplished fabulous things, feats that range from stopping a revolution in an European country to–-"

"In your hat!" laughed Leaking. "He's overrated. Here he is. What do we do now?"

"Tie him up," Hallet said hastily. He minced into the other office and came back with thin, stout, braided cotton rope.

The two men grasped Doc Savage, apparently with the idea of moving him from the chair to the floor, where he could be bound with more facility. But what happened was hardly the thing they anticipated.

There was blinding motion, two slapping sounds. Leaking and Hallet tried to cry out. They made no sound, for a great corded bronze hand had grasped each of them by the throat.

## Chapter II
### THIRTY-STORY DEATH

THE next few seconds offered a study in abject helplessness and an exhibition of incalculable strength. The two seized men at first windmilled their arms, but the awful agony of the grip on their necks seemed to surge like deadening poison through their bodies, and they became limp.

Around Doc Savage's metallic fingers, and between them, the flesh of his victims all but oozed, so terrific was the pressure. The faces of the pair turned purple, eyes ogled and tongues stuck out stiffly.

Doc arose, and the two were limp as rags hanging from his great hands. They quivered a little and that was all.

The bronze man released them, and although neither was fully unconscious, they were too weak to do more than make croaking noises.

A search of their clothing brought the light small sums of money and billfolds containing cards. Leaking's full name seemed to be Manuel Caesar Dicer. Hallet carried a blue army automatic and Leaking the slightly smaller gun with which he had clubbed the cop in the taxicab.

The outer office was fitted with a leather divan. Doc popped the two captives down on this, bound their wrists and ankles securely with the same cord they had intended to use upon him, and fell to eyeing them steadily.

"I want to know what is behind this," he said. "It is going to be very, very unfortunate unless you start talking."

The captives glared, exchanged glances and said nothing. The globules of moisture on Leaking's forehead fattened, broke from their moorings and chased each other downward, forming little rivulets.

"Talk up!" Doc said sharply.

The pair registered discomfort, but held silence. This was something of a feat in itself, for there was a fierceness in the giant bronze man's weird flake-gold eyes.

Doc straightened suddenly, swung around the office once, then went into the inside room. This was fitted with desk, chairs, ice water stand, a large sheet metal clothes locker the color of grass, and shelves holding innumerable law books. Atop a fat legal volume on torts perched a telephone.

Scooping up the instrument, Doc unpronged the receiver and asked for a number. His voice was low, and traffic sounds from the street below the open window kept his words completely from the two in the other chamber.

"Monk?" Doc asked when he got an answer.

"Sure," said a mouselike voice.

Doc Savage now spoke rapidly, but not in English. The tongue he used was not unmusical, composed of liquid gutturals and sharp clackings, but it was doubtful if more than half a dozen people in the so-called civilized world would have understood it. Yet the language was the mother tongue of a race once among the most powerful and cultured—the ancient Mayans of Central America.

His conversation completed, Doc hung up and went back to the prisoners. They had been trying ineffectually to escape, but desisted when they saw him.

"I never saw either of you gentlemen before this afternoon," he said in an ominously calm tone. "Yet you go to great trouble to seize me off the street."

Birdlike Hallet trembled; Leaking perspired; and neither let a word escape.

"Why did you seize me?" Doc asked, his voice vibrating a grim power. "What did you intend to do with me?"

This time, Leaking spoke. "H-how did you get rid of the effects of that gas so quick?"

"The gas never had any effect on me in the first place," Doc said.

"W-what?" Leaking stuttered.

"You underestimate the human powers of observation," Doc assured him dryly. "When you dropped that trick purse, I saw you."

"You picked it up, knowing it was a trick?"

"The picking was done most carefully, if you had noticed," Doc told him. "There were two logical things to suspect—a poisoned needle and gas. To avoid a needle, I did not open the purse in the usual manner of a man who has found one. And to checkmate the gas, I merely held my breath until the breeze blew the vapor away."

"But why—"

"Why pretend to be overcome? Merely to find out what your game was. And now, any more questions?"

Leaking only glared.

"Then perhaps you will relieve my curiosity," Doc suggested. "Why did you seize me?"

Leaking blew sweat off his upper lip and said, "You go to hell!"

VIOLENT action followed Leaking's profane suggestion. Doc Savage lunged, closed metallic hands upon the fellow and lifted him.

Leaking grimaced in agony and opened his mouth wide to cry out. Doc corked a wadded handkerchief into the gaping maw, and Leaking could only squeal through his nose.

Next, Doc gagged plump Hallet.

Leaking was carried helplessly through the door into the inner office. The door was slammed shut.

Hallet, the sparrowlike lawyer, sprawled helpless on the divan and ogled the closed door. He tried to move. His ropes were drawn excruciatingly tight, many of the strands almost buried in the fellow's soft flesh, and the gag distended his mouth to its greatest capacity.

Suddenly his eyes flew wider and his jaw sagged in horror. Out of the inner office were coming awful thuds, smackings and grunts. It was as if a man were being horribly beaten.

"You won't talk, eh?" Doc Savage's grim, powerful voice came through the door.

The sound of more blows followed, together with buzzing sounds that might have been a gagged man crying out in terrible pain.

Hallet tried to scream, but his own gag made his best effort a whining, and he desisted to lay panting through his nostrils, round face draining of color until it had a clay hue. He was the picture of a man scared out of his wits.

Certainly the sounds emanating from the adjacent office were such as to strike horror. Again and again Doc Savage's unusual voice put questions, to which Leaking only whizzed or whined through his nostrils, or, the gag removed, cursed smashingly. The blow thuddings always resumed, more violent than before. And finally there came the climax.

"Well, if you won't talk, out of the window you go!" Doc boomed.

The window rattled up.

Hallet's face was white enough to be written upon with a pencil, for he was visualizing that twenty-story drop to the street, and the hard sidewalk below. Many times he had looked down and visualized what would be the lot of one who fell.

Hallet abruptly tried to scream through his gag. He had heard a scuffling sound, as of a living body pushed over the window sill. A gruesome cry, faintly receding, followed that.

The connecting door leaped open. Doc Savage came through, his weird eyes hot aureate pools, the tendons on his neck standing out like rifle barrels.

Hallet sought to scream again. He had never glimpsed anything which looked quite as terrible as did the bronze giant.

Doc swept Hallet up easily and carried him to the inner office. The window was open, and Doc shoved Hallet half outside.

"Look down!" he directed.

Hallet looked, and shook as if he had taken hold of a charged electric wire.

The crowd on the sidewalk below resembled flies around some dark speck of succulence, while other flies came scudding across the street or climbed out of cars which were stopping. A fly in blue ran for the spot, a police whistle.

Doc wrenched Hallet back. His great voice was a grim crashing.

"They'll be up here to investigate in about two minutes," he said. "You have that long to tell your story."

"I d-don't know anything!" Hallet stuttered when his gag was out.

Doc picked him up helplessly and ran him toward the open window, and the man screeched out in chilling fright, confident the bony hand of death was cupped to receive him down there in the street.

"I'll tell you everything!" he shrilled.

Doc calmly carried him back into the outer office and tossed him on the leather divan.

"Why did you and our—er—unlucky friend, Leaking, attempt to seize me?" the bronze man demanded.

Hallet wet his lips. "We were hired. We were to get ten thousand dollars for grabbing you and holding you where no one could find you for two weeks."

"So someone wants me out of circulation for two weeks, eh?" Doc showed no great surprise at the news; indeed, now that Hallet was talking, the bronze features had settled into a metallic repose. "Who hired you?" he continued.

"I don't know," Hallet muttered.

Doc grasped the man, rumbling, "The window is still open!"

"Fountain of Youth, Inc., hired me!" Hallet shrieked fearfully.

"Who?"

"It was handled in a roundabout way," Hallet mumbled rapidly. "I was approached over the telephone with this proposition to seize you and hold you. The party who called me said there was no need of us ever seeing each other, and it would be better, in fact, if we didn't. The only name I got was Fountain of Youth, Inc."

"Man or woman?"

Hallet squirmed. "I am not positive."

"Don't forget that window!" Doc said meaningly. "You should know whether you talked to a man or a woman over the telephone."

"It was a shrill, unnatural voice," Hallet gulped. "I couldn't tell. Honestly, I couldn't."

"Why did this Fountain of Youth, Inc., want me held?"

"I haven't the slightest idea. I asked that question, of course, but was told that there was no necessity for me knowing."

Doc's strange eyes dwelled upon the frightened lawyer for a moment. "Since you have no information of importance, I shall have to consign you to that window, it seems. Has Fountain of Youth, Inc., got an office?"

"Yes. It is Room 1402, the Queen Tower building."

"What about a telephone?"

"Yes. It is in the Queen Tower office. I had it traced."

"So you tried on your own hook to learn something of this mysterious Fountain of Youth, Inc.?"

Hallet had gotten some of his nerve back and was almost chirping, birdlike, when he spoke. "Do you blame me for trying to get a line on them?"

Doc did not answer, but considered. Although his features showed no expression, there was a certain finality about his manner which indicated that he was sure Hallet had no more information to reveal.

Doc swung into the next office. Hallet could see the bronze man through the open door. Doc went to the big grass-green clothes locker and opened it.

Sight of the object which rolled out caused Hallet to turn very purple in the face.

LEAKING had been in the locker, bound and gagged. He fell out when Doc pulled the door ajar, and his garments made moist squishings, so profusely had he perspired. Leaking was uninjured.

"I thought—I thought—" The words choked Hallet up and he could not finish.

"The power of suggestion," Doc assured him dryly. "A few noises, some words, and you got the idea he had gone out of the window."

"But the body on the street—"

"Ever hear of my five assistants?" Doc asked.

"Y-yes," Hallet mumbled. "But w-what—"

"One of them, Monk by name, played the part of the body in the street," Doc explained shortly. "New Yorkers are curious souls, and they all ran to see what a man could be lying on the sidewalk for.

That naturally made Monk's trick very lifelike. You see, Monk was summoned by telephone."

"Oh!" Hallet swallowed. "I remember I did think I heard you phoning."

Leaking, when the gag was removed from his jaws, swore choice profanity in a low voice that dripped rage. When it was suggested that he tell what he knew, he only snarled.

Of a different caliber was this Leaking. A block of a jaw and ugly eyes showed determination, offering a hint that to get information from him would take application of a more moving third-degree method than had urged Hallet to talk.

"My assistant, Monk, who played the dead man in the street, will be up here shortly," Doc stated. "With him will be another of my group of five aides, Ham. By the way, Ham is a lawyer of no little reputation and may want to take measures to have you, Hallet, barred from practice."

Hallet scowled; Leaking went on profaning in a guttural, hoarse monotone.

The afternoon sun sloped through both offices, throwing shadows into the fear lines on Hallet's face, and glistening on the wetness that filmed Leaking's features.

An elevator door clanked in the corridor outside, then feet tramped the hallway. They approached the office door.

"That will be my two men," Doc said. He walked over and yanked the door ajar.

A man came in, holding a revolver straight out in front of his chest.

"Ain't I the lucky one, Savage!" he gritted. "Get them hands high!"

## Chapter III
### MISTER SANTINI

THE man with the gun was the freckled, loose-lipped taxi driver who had helped Leaking kidnap Doc Savage. The automatic in his cigarette-browned fingers was a large one.

Behind the driver strolled half a dozen other men. They were tough looking after the modern style, too fancy of dress, with a sleek, unnatural manner about them, the manner of men long accustomed to acting either very bad or very innocent. All held weapons.

"Got rid of the hack and was comin' back here with the boys," growled the driver. "We saw some funny stuff downstairs—a guy layin' on the sidewalk. That tipped us off to come up here with our rods ready."

"Watch that Savage!" snarled Hallet from the floor.

"He's covered!" the driver snorted; then, much louder: "Get back! Get back!"

Doc Savage was advancing, apparently heedless of the leveled pistol. The taxi driver jabbed the gun threateningly. It was pointed at Doc's chest.

"I'll plug you," the man blustered.

Sprawled on the divan, Leaking comprehended Doc's intention and tried to yell a warning.

"The guy's probably got a bulletproof vest!" he howled. "Point your rod at his head—"

Too late! Doc leaped. His arms were up clear of the line of fire, and he twisted as he came in.

The gun smacked thunder and the bullet opened a long rip in the bronze man's coat, below the left armpit, then gouged stuffing out of the divan on which Leaking and Hallet sprawled. Doc, by twisting, had caused the slug merely to scrape across his bulletproof vest.

The driver swore, tried to fire again. There was a dull impact. None present were quite sure they saw Doc strike the blow. But the hackman's nose was suddenly a flat, scarlet stringing pulp and he was gagging to keep from swallowing dislodged teeth. He fell down on all fours, concerned exclusively with his own pain.

The other men were not yet inside. Doc banged the door. It had a spring lock and would hold for a time. Swinging into the inner office, he closed and locked that door behind him.

A pistol whooped in the corridor. The bullet, puncturing the door, made a round daisy of splinters, then scooped leaves out of a law book which lay on the reception desk.

"You dopes!" Leaking shrilled. "You'll hit us. Bust the door down!"

Somebody kicked the frosted glass out of the outer door, reached in and turned the spring lock, which was better than breaking the panel down. The six men came inside gingerly, guns darting here and there so that they rather ridiculously resembled movie bad men, except for the killer expressions on their faces.

"The inner office," Hallet grated. "Get him! And tie us loose—I mean, turn us loose!" The excitement twisted his tongue.

Hallet and Leaking were freed by the use of sharp knives. They had to be helped to their feet, so taut had been their bindings.

The inner door resisted kicking. They shouted angrily for Doc to open up, got no response, then lighted on the great idea of picking up the reception desk and hurling it at the door. This knocked the door off its hinges.

The cat-walking across the threshold, guns ready, was repeated. They peered about, bewildered.

"Gone!" Hallet gulped.

LEAKING, mindful of his own incarceration, sidled over and yanked open the grass-colored locker; but it was empty, and he stood cursing, swiping at his moist forehead with first one coat sleeve then the other.

"Was there a rope or somethin' in here that he could've used to slide down to the ground?" he demanded.

"The only rope was the one he used to tie us," Hallet disclaimed.

A man ran over to the window and looked out and down, then drew back, growling, "No sign of 'im!"

Leaking whipped to the window and gave close attention to the nature of the brick walls. They were very smooth, the bricks being set with a minimum of mortar and the mortar not grooved, but smooth and flush with the masonry.

"It'd take a good fly to stick on that wall," Leaking growled.

"I always did hear this Doc Savage wasn't quite human," a man mumbled.

"Shut up!" Leaking told him. "Let's look around. That bronze guy went somewhere."

The telephone rang loudly.

The men started as if something totally unexpected had happened, then looked sheepish, and Hallet went over, his gait more birdlike than usual, to answer the instrument.

The conversation lasted for a long minute, with Hallet saying nothing except "Yes," at intervals. But finally he put in a complete sentence.

"We got Doc Savage, but he escaped," he said.

Explosives came from the receiver, after which Hallet hurriedly explained exactly what had occurred and, judging from the way his neck turned red, took a cursing.

He hung up and stood adjusting a sleeve of his sparrow-colored coat, eyeing his companions the meanwhile.

"That was Fountain of Youth, Inc.," he said. "But it wasn't the same voice that usually calls me. I could tell this one was a man."

"Did this bird give his name?" Leaking demanded.

"He did. Said to call him Santini."

"Santini, eh? Any first handle?"

"None. Just Santini. He said to come to the office of Fountain of Youth, Inc., at once, and if he wasn't there to give us orders, there would be an envelope under the blotter on his desk, with our directions inside."

"Why didn't you tell him to go to hell?" Leaking snarled, and mopped sweat. "This is worth more than we're getting."

"Santini said there would be seven one-thousand-dollar bills in the envelope," Hallet smirked. "I forgot to tell you gentlemen that. The money is by way of a bonus."

Leaking stopped mopping and laughed. "That makes it different. Let's set sail, bozos."

They swung around, apparently having decided to dismiss the problem of Doc Savage's disappearance for the time being, and made for the outer door. But before they reached the aperture, the wrecked panel swung ajar so forcibly that portions of the shattered glass fell out.

A man looked inside the office and said in a tiny, mild voice, "I'm looking for a man named Doc Savage."

The newcomer was a study in evolution. His height barely topped five feet, but he would trip the scales at better than two hundred and sixty pounds. His face was incredibly homely in a pleasant way, and great beams of arms dangled well below his knees.

His eyes were small and bright; big mouth was so large that it looked as if there had been an accident in its making. Exposed portions of his skin were stuck full of hairs which resembled lengths of rusty barbed wire.

Hallet gulped, flopped his arms like wings, swallowed and got words out.

"Monk!" he squawled. "This is Monk, one of Doc Savage's five men! I've seen his picture in the newspapers!"

Pistol snouts leaped in "Monk's" direction. Like an ungainly ape, the hairy fellow bounced back out of sight.

BEHIND Monk in the corridor crouched a slender wasp of a man whose clothing was sartorial perfection, and who carried a black, expensive-looking cane. In leaping back, Monk bounced into this dandified gentleman and almost upset him.

"Drat you!" rapped the nattily clad man. "Watch where you're going!"

"Get outa the way, Ham!" Monk grunted. "There's eight guys in there, most of 'em with guns!"

The two backed hastily down the corridor. Hands dipped into their coats, and from carefully contrived armpit holsters drew strange-looking weapons which perhaps bore more of a resemblance to oversized automatics than anything else. To the firing mechanisms of these were attached curled magazines.

"Any sign of Doc?" "Ham" demanded.

"Nope."

Monk suddenly tightened on the trigger of his strange gun. From the ejector, empty brass cartridges climbed so rapidly that they looked like a brass wire; simultaneously, the weapon emitted an ear-splitting roar.

A man had looked out of Hallet's law office, and the fellow suddenly went limp and fell out into the hallway. His companions grabbed his heels, which

were still in the office, and hauled him out of sight. Voices came out of the office.

"He ain't dead," barked the taxi driver's coarse tone. He evidently referred to Monk's victim. "Looks like the slugs flattened and burst when they got under his skin."

"Mercy bullets!" said Hallet's voice. "They're hulls filled with a chemical which produces unconsciousness. I've read about 'em in the papers."

"Them two guys must be usin' the supermachine pistols that Doc Savage is supposed to have invented," growled Leaking.

After that there was more conversation, but it was pitched so low that the words failed to reach Monk and Ham. The latter two had stopped down the corridor and were exchanging compliments.

"You dumb missing link!" the dapper Ham advised. "You hairy freak! You certainly stirred up something when you walked up and shoved your ugly face through that door."

"I wanted to see if Doc was in there," said the small-voiced Monk. "And if you keep on callin' me names, I'm gonna shove you out where them red-hots can get a shot at you."

The two glared at each other, then, as if each had been nauseated by sight of the other, both spat on the floor.

"Where could Doc have gone?" Ham pondered.

"Suppose you dope it out with that great legal brain of yours," Monk invited.

Out of Hallet's office sailed a metal canister. This *clank-clank-clanked* down the corridor, suddenly went *plop,* and vanished in a wad of vile fumes of its own spewing.

"Tear gas!" Monk howled, his small voice abruptly vast, roaring.

He and Ham dived for the nearest stairway.

THEY stopped one flight down and exchanged black, hateful looks.

"If you had kept that noisy trap shut, we could have heard 'em gettin' ready to throw that crybaby," gritted Monk.

Ham sneered expressively, and his slender-fingered hands tugged at his black cane and it telescoped from a point near the handle, thus disclosing that it was in reality a sword cane with a blade which looked razor-sharp.

"One of these days I'm gonna see if there's a man under that hairy hide," he promised.

"Listen," advised Monk. "There's something going on upstairs."

They strained their ears, catching numerous small sounds that probably were foot scufflings, together with certain grunts and low words. The meaning of these dawned sharply.

"They're takin' the freight elevator down!" Monk howled. He sprinted down the hallway and sloped around a corner, Ham at his heels.

The fact that these two seemed continually on the point of coming to blows appeared to have little effect on their teamwork. They reached the sliding freight elevator door. This naturally could only be opened from inside the shaft.

Ham tapped it with his sword cane. The panel was of steel and sounded solid.

Monk drew back and gave the panel a resounding kick, but with no results.

He reached for Ham's sword cane. "Gimme that tin toothpick."

"No," said Ham. "What do you want to do? I'll do it."

"See if you can loosen the locking device while I shove on the door," Monk directed.

At that point, the cage passed downward with a noisy sigh. This caused the two to redouble their efforts, Ham fishing through the crack between the halves of the door with his sword cane and Monk shoving heavily.

The door came open. Far below, the cage promptly stopped, due to the safety device which cut off the current the instant the door was open.

Monk shoved his nubbin of a head inside, peered down, and snapped back as a bullet climbed squealing in the shaft.

"We got 'em!" he grinned. "They're between floors, and can't do a thing but shoot up through the grilled roof of the cage."

"Look down again and make sure," Ham suggested.

"Yeah—and get shot." Monk hauled out his superfirer pistol, examined the magazine indicator, then leered at Ham. "I'm a great big black cloud and I'm gonna rain on them guys."

"You don't talk like you had good sense," Ham assured him. "But go ahead. It's not a bad idea."

Monk prepared to fire, but instead of doing so, looked over his shoulder and started violently.

Doc Savage stood far enough down the corridor that distance made him seem less of the metallic giant than he was—until his stature chanced to be compared with the nearby office doors.

"Let them go," said the giant bronze man.

Ham and Monk promptly let the sliding doors of the freight elevators swish shut. Then they joined Doc.

DOC SAVAGE had a passenger elevator waiting, and they entered this without delay at the bronze man's gesture. The lift sank, whistling a little.

"Where'd you go, Doc?" Monk demanded.

For answer, the bronze man said no word but simply drew from a pocket a collapsible metal grappling hook, to the shank of which was affixed a slender and very stout silken cord.

"Huh!" Monk grunted.

"Slid from the office window down to the window below, then loosened the grapple by flipping the cord," Doc explained. "Were they puzzled?"

"Plumb stunned, from the sound of it," Monk grinned.

The passenger cage let them out in the lobby. They ran around to the alleylike freight entrance, but a swiftly receding taxi was all that they saw of their quarry.

That the cab carried Hallet and the others, they were sure, due to the heavy way in which the machine was laden and because they saw Hallet's face against the rear window.

Less than a minute later, Doc Savage had secured another hack.

"The Queen Tower building," he directed.

Monk began, "But, Doc—"

"No chance of trailing that gang," Doc explained. "Anyway, I think they will head for the Queen Tower building. The office of Fountain of Youth, Inc., is there."

"What's Fountain of Youth, Inc.?" Monk demanded.

"That is one thing I want to find out," Doc told the homely gorilla of a fellow. "The other puzzle is: why did that gang seize me? Fountain of Youth, Inc., whatever that is, seems to have hired them. But why?"

They mulled over the enigma in silence as their cab jerked and honked its way through downtown New York traffic, but after a few moments, Monk and Ham gave up the problem and fell to glowering at each other.

An onlooker would have sworn they were about to fly at each other's throats. The manner they bore toward each other was deceptive, however, for each would risk his life to preserve the other, and both had done so on occasion.

This was the usual manner of Monk and Ham, for they had a perpetual squabble, one which had started years before and never seemed to slacken. The manner they bore toward each other was deceptive, however, for each would risk his life to preserve the other, and had done so on occasion.

They were no ordinary men, these two sides of Doc Savage. Monk, for all of his apish appearance, was a chemist, whose name was known over most of the world. And Harvard was conceded never to have matriculated a more astute lawyer than Ham. Each had won a fortune in his respective profession.

They received no pay, these five men who were Doc Savage's assistants, nor would they have taken any. Doc himself did not accept financial return for his strange work, for the bronze man was almost fabulously wealthy in his own right, having access, as he did, to the treasure trove of the ancient Mayan nation in Central America.

Doc Savage had but to step into a radio station at a certain hour and broadcast a few words in Mayan; this would be picked up in a valley remote from civilization, in Central America, where dwelt descendants of ancient Maya. A few days later, a burro train of gold would appear mysteriously at the capital of the Central American nation, and the proceeds, not often less then four or five million dollars, would be deposited to Doc's credit in the international bank. Their cab finally groaned to a stop.

"Queen Tower building, gents," said the driver.

THE Queen Tower was one of the newer structures in lower Manhattan, which meant its front was a symphony in black and white and shiny metals. Its lobby was spouting humanity, for the quitting hour of office workers was at hand.

Doc slid out of the cab. Then he seemed to explode, so suddenly was he back in the machine.

A man had stepped from the throng. He presented a startling appearance, due largely to his amazing mustache. This was extremely black, no thicker than a pencil at the base, and each wing was fully three inches long. It resembled a pair of oversize cat whiskers.

The man wore a brilliant red ribbon slantwise across his shirt front, and his afternoon garb was faultless. A pearl-gray derby topped off the ensemble. Even in New York, his appearance commanded attention.

But what interested Doc Savage and his two aides was the flat automatic the stranger was plucking from under the tails of his afternoon coat. The weapon glinted pearl and gold inlay as it came up.

The gun whacked. Two windows fell out of the cab as the bullet passed through.

"Oh, damn me!" shrieked the driver. He spilled out of the front seat and ran down the middle of the street, not looking back.

Doc and his two men got out almost as quickly, hitting the sidewalk on the side opposite the gunman. Monk and Ham had their superfirer pistols out. Doc's hands were empty, for he never carried a firearm, depending rather upon his wits and his scientific devices.

Monk tried to shoot under the cab at the man with the unique mustache. But the fellow was running, jumping high, a poor target. The next instant he popped into the Queen Tower.

"Dang jackrabbit!" Monk grunted.

Doc Savage and his two men reached the Queen Tower entrance together and surged inside.

A wake of howling, excited office workers showed the route their quarry had taken toward the rear. The chase led past the elevators, through a small door, down unfinished stairs and out a rear door, which gave upon an odorous side street.

A heavy, fast coupé was swerving away from the curb. The mustached gunman was at the wheel.

Monk lifted his machine pistol and it moaned. The bullets only flattened against the coupé glass. The homely chemist tried for the tires. He knocked off bits of rubber, but the tires did not go down.

The coupé roiled on, reeled around a distant corner and vanished.

They sought to find a taxi in which to push a pursuit, but the quarry was hopelessly gone before they got a hack lined out on the trail.

"That mug had the coupé waitin' for a get-away," Monk grumbled. "It was some boat. Had bulletproof glass and solid rubber tires."

"Wonder who he was?" Ham pondered.

That question was answered in the lobby of the Queen Tower, for it developed that the proprietor of the lobby cigar stand had not only seen the running gunman, but knew his identity.

"That was Mr. Santini," the proprietor explained.

"And who is Mr. Santini?" Doc queried.

"The president of Fountain of Youth, Inc."

## Chapter IV
## THE UNSEEN MESSAGE

AN elevator let them out on the fourteenth floor of the Queen Tower building and they walked toward a door which bore the legend they were seeking.

FOUNTAIN OF YOUTH, INC.

"Mr. Santini seemed to know us by sight," Monk said grimly, his homely face solemn.

"That doesn't mean anything, you accident of nature," Ham pointed out sharply. "Doc's picture appears often in newspapers and magazines."

"Sure, shyster," Monk sneered. "Nobody but you would think of that."

Doc Savage, studying the door of the office, put in, "The thing which puzzles me most is why these men should be so anxious to get us out of the way."

Doc was listening. His sense of hearing was fabulously keen, due to a scientific device, an apparatus emitting sound waves of a frequency above and below the audible range, with which he attuned his ears for a certain period each day, as a part of a two-hour exercise routine that he had not missed taking each twenty-four hours for many years.

"Seems to be no one inside," he said.

He tried the knob, found the door locked, and employed a small curved metal device which he removed from a pocket. This was an especially designed lock picker and opened the door within a few moments.

The offices beyond—outer reception chamber and two inner rooms—were sumptuous to an extreme, the furniture being of genuine mahogany, the upholstery leather soft and rich, and the carpeting deep and silky. The latest in automatic typewriters, dictaphones, and announcing devices were installed.

Doc Savage made one rapid circuit and ascertained that no one was present, then began a slower and more intensive scrutiny. His strange golden eyes missed little. There were words emblazoned on the door of one of the inner offices.

### Q. SANTINI, PRESIDENT.

In that room, alongside a rich desk, Doc picked up a crumpled envelope to which he gave particular attention, although outwardly it seemed little different from much other wadded paper.

"What's so interesting about that?" Monk wanted to know.

Doc produced a magnifying glass that the homely chemist might discern what the bronze man's highly developed eyes had noticed—the paper was moist, as if crumpled in a perspiring palm.

"One of the fellows who grabbed me was called Leaking, probably because of some strange affliction which makes him perspire a great deal," he explained. "Only a man who sweats freely would have damp palms on a day like this."

The bronze man now gave attention to the desk. In a drawer was a pad of plain white paper, together with a package of envelopes which matched the one he had found on the floor. If there had been a message in the envelope, it was logical to suspect that it might have been written on the pad.

Out of Doc's clothing came a tiny metal device, the principal gadget on which was a small reservoir filled with a liquid the color of coagulated blood. Doc held the paper pad over this and flicked a lever, causing the apparatus to give off a vapor.

After a moment, Doc examined the pad. The vapor had caused it to change color slightly. Vague, but clearly readable, writing had appeared.

"This is the message which was written on the top leaf of the pad," he explained.

Ham fumbled his sword cane and looked bewildered. "But how did you bring it out?"

Doc returned his apparatus to a pocket in a special tool-carrying vest which he wore, a vest cleverly enough padded that its presence was not noticeable to the chance observer.

"The application of iodine vapor to bring out impressions left by a pencil point is not exactly new," he said. "Let's read this."

MONK and Ham came close to read what the paper held. The penmanship was firm, rounded, very readable.

HALLET:
Kel Avery in on eight o'clock plane from

Florida and must be prevented from communicating with Doc Savage. Better grab and hold for me.
SANTINI.

"Oh, oh," Monk grinned. "Now we're getting places."

"Leaking and Hallet and their gang beat us here and got the message," Doc decided.

Then the bronze man continued his search of the office suite of Fountain of Youth, Inc.

"Ain't we gonna do nothin' about this message?" Monk questioned, using a type of grammar that gave little hint that he was one of the most highly educated industrial chemists living.

"It's twenty minutes after five," Doc replied. "That gives us two hours and forty minutes before this Florida plane bearing Kel Avery arrives."

At Doc's words, Ham surreptitiously eyed an expensive wrist watch which he wore. The time was exactly twenty after five, a fact which caused Ham to sheath and unsheath his sword cane thoughtfully, for he knew Doc carried no watch, and there was no clock in sight in the office. To Ham's recollection, they had not passed a clock within half an hour.

Doc's uncanny ability to judge the passage of time was something at which the dapper lawyer had never ceased to marvel.

Doc came to a filing cabinet of metal painted to resemble mahogany, and unearthed cards which held his attention. The cards were large, indexed alphabetically, and each bore a name.

"Look here," the big man of metal suggested.

Monk came over and riffled through the index.

"For the love of mud!" he said, small-voiced. "This looks like a who's who of the town's moneybags."

"An index of the richest men in New York City," Doc agreed, and drew out a second drawer. "And here are other files of wealthy individuals, their names listed by states."

Ham joined them, tucked his sword cane under an arm and inspected the files.

"Every rich man in America," he murmured. Then he pointed at a small silver star which had been pasted on a card. "Wonder what this means?"

Doc's supple fingers traveled back and forth through the cards a few times. He found more silver stars, and gold ones as well.

"You'll notice the cards give not only the man's name and the probable size of his fortune, but also his age and the state of his health. The old and feeble men rate gold stars, while those around fifty are marked with silver stars. The younger and more healthy men are not marked."

Ham twirled his innocent-looking black stick. "Get it, Doc?"

Doc nodded. "I'm afraid I do get it."

"Get what?" Monk demanded.

"I'll explain, hairy stupid," Ham began. "The men marked with gold stars are—"

The phone rang.

DOC SAVAGE swung to the instrument, scooped it up, seemed to hesitate and consider for the briefest of intervals, then spoke. From his lips came an astoundingly exact reproduction of the brisk, birdlike voice of Attorney Hallet. Monk and Ham grinned in appreciation, although they had heard the bronze man's unusual command of voice mimicry exercised on other occasions.

"The office of Fountain of Youth, Inc.," Doc said quietly.

"Kel Avery can be found at 1120 Fish Lane," said a man's voice over the wire.

The voice was surprising. It sounded youthful and as full of bubbling life as a mountain brook, a voice which suggested a rather ridiculous vision of a boy joyfully turning handsprings as he spoke.

Doc Savage began, in Hallet's tones, "But I thought Kel Avery—"

"Was on a plane bound foah New Yawk," said the spontaneous voice. "You are mistaken. Kel Avery is at 1120 Fish Lane."

So exuberant was the voice that the pronounced accent of the South had not been noticeable at first, but as the informant spoke this second time, the twist of speech was more apparent on certain words.

"Who is this?" Doc demanded, impersonating Hallet. "The receiver does not seem to bring your voice clearly enough for me to recognize it."

"You nevah heard mah voice before, Mistah Hallet," said the tone of youth.

"Then who are you? You know my voice."

"You take care of Kel Avery," advised the other. "I'll explain who Ah am later."

The distant receiver went *clank* on its hook. Doc Savage put his own instrument down slowly, eyes on his two men.

"That was the strangest voice," he said. "It sounded indescribably young and joyful, as if it belonged to an irresponsible lad."

"What'd he say?" Monk queried.

"That Kel Avery was at 1120 Fish Lane."

"Fish Lane is out in them Flushing marshes," Monk said slowly. "The district is not so hot."

Ham brandished his sword cane and put in, "But I thought this mysterious Kel Avery was on a plane to arrive from Florida at eight o'clock!"

Instead of commenting, Doc Savage lifted the phone again and requested a number to be found only in private lists which never went beyond the walls of the telephone company offices.

It was the number of Doc's office-laboratory-library on the eighty-sixth floor of the city's most impressive skyscraper.

A gentleman with a scholastic voice and a remarkable command of big words answered. Doc gave him a brief synopsis of what had occurred.

"Tell Renny and Long Tom the yarn, Johnny," the bronze man directed. "Then the three of you head for 1120 Fish Lane. Investigate this Kel Avery report. Monk and Ham and myself will be here for ten or fifteen minutes longer."

"Will you join us later at this piscatorial thoroughfare of Fish Lane?" asked the big-worded "Johnny."

"Right."

"Exactly what is your present whereabouts?"

Doc gave him the address of Fountain of Youth, Inc., then asked "Why?"

It was a rare thing when Johnny laughed, but he laughed now.

"You are going to get a surprise, Doc," he chuckled.

And with that, he hung up.

DOC SAVAGE was thoughtful as he replaced the receiver.

"Johnny does not go in for playful mysteries as a usual thing," he pondered aloud. "I wonder what is on his mind?"

"Maybe his big words finally made him dizzy," Monk grinned.

"More likely his association with you has gotten him down, you hairy mistake," Ham said unkindly.

The pleasantly ugly Monk scowled and registered injury.

"I'm gonna tell Habeas on you," he muttered seriously.

Ham's grip on his sword cane tightened. Habeas Corpus was Monk's pet pig, a big-eared, long-legged shoat which was fully as ridiculous a looking member of the pork family as Monk was of the human race.

Doc went through the file containing the data on America's most wealthy men. One card was dog-eared with thumb marks, as if it had been handled more than the others.

The card bore the name of Thackeray Hutchinson, a banker who was among the wealthiest and whom the United States government had once tried to convict of illegal practices in connection with the failure of a public utilities project. The charge had been defeated by clever lawyers.

Doc got Thackeray Hutchinson on the telephone, then stated that he wished information on Fountain of Youth, Inc.

"Never heard of it!" snapped the pompous banker, and hung up.

"He was lying," said Doc, who was a judge of

voice expression. "We'll investigate him more thoroughly a bit later."

They rode an elevator down to the street. On the sidewalk, they halted and stared.

"Lookit—Habeas!" Monk exploded. "How'd that hog get down here?"

HABEAS CORPUS was galloping toward them, great ears flopping like wings. The shoat, no larger than a small dog, presented such a grotesque picture that pedestrians halted and rubbered.

Ham leveled his sword cane. "What do you know about that!"

He was indicating a long, somber-looking sedan parked at the curb. This machine he had recognized as belonging to Doc Savage; there could be no mistake, for he had ridden in it numerous times and, moreover, it bore the distinctive license plates which the bronze man was permitted to use.

A young woman got out of the sedan.

Habeas Corpus, squealing delightedly, pawed at Monk like a dog.

"Cut that out or I'll kick you out from between your ears!" grunted Monk, who was interested in the girl. Pretty girls always intrigued Monk greatly, and this one was a knockout.

Doc Savage ordinarily did not let his features register much expression, but now he was looking a little astounded.

Doc had a fixed policy which he had adhered to for a long time, and that was to steer clear of feminine entanglements. The life he led was too perilous to permit such, for enemies would not hesitate to strike at him through any young woman upon whom he might permit his affections to dwell. That a young woman should be alighting from his car was entirely surprising.

Then she turned and they saw her face.

"Pat Savage!" Monk howled.

Patricia Savage, tall, exquisitely moulded, had the same remarkable bronze hair as Doc Savage himself. They were cousins, and Doc had last seen her in western Canada, months before, when he and his five aides had gone through some perilous adventures in tracking down a gang who had slain Patricia's father.

Doc went forward eagerly which was something unusual for the bronze man. Ordinarily, he felt uncomfortable in the presence of young women, especially girls as entrancing as Patricia.

But Pat was an exception. Pat was something of a two-fisted scrapper herself, and almost as unique in her way as the big Doc was in his.

"I got tired of the woods," Pat smiled. "Johnny and the others told me I could catch you here if I hurried."

There was no gushing display of affection. She and Doc merely shook hands warmly.

"I brought Habeas along," Pat told Monk laughingly.

Monk took in her smart frock, her chic hat and the slender silk of her ankles.

"Golly, Pat," he said, grinning from one ear to the other, "you sure make these city gals look rusty. Thanks for bringing Habeas. Ham, here, will appreciate that."

Ham scowled at Monk, bowed graciously to Pat.

"Haven't you two settled your quarrel yet?" Pat laughed.

"One of these days I'll lose my temper," Ham said grimly. "Then they'll be hunting for a coffin wide enough to hold that ape."

Doc Savage indicated the car. "We'll talk on the way uptown, Pat, but I'm afraid we'll have to drop you at the office until we get a matter settled."

"A matter?" Pat asked curiously. "Sounds interesting."

"There's a plot afoot," Monk imparted. "Or rather, some other cookies are plotting something."

"I'm going along!" Pat declared firmly. "I've missed all the excitement we had while you fellows were up in my country. To tell the truth, it was in hopes of seeing some action that I came down to visit you."

Doc shook his head. "It's dangerous, or may be."

"Aw, Doc," Monk grumbled. "Pat's regular. What we went through in Canada proves that."

Doc surrendered. "All right."

They entered the sedan, Doc taking the wheel. The machine did not look new or particularly efficient, but the motor came to life under the hood with scarcely a sound, and the quiet power of their departure from the curb indicated costly gears and great power.

"The yearning to hunt trouble must run in the Savage blood," said Pat. "Gentlemen, I yearn for some action."

"Here it is!" Doc rapped abruptly, and stepped heavily on the power brakes.

A taxi had sloughed crosswise of the narrow street. It was the same cab which had been used a bit earlier by Leaking to kidnap Doc.

MEN materialized with sinister abruptness out of the crowds on the sidewalk. Some carried trombone cases, and others long hand bags. They snapped them open. Out came sawed-off rifles, shotguns, a machine gun or two.

Patricia Savage slid off the seat onto the floorboards, opening her chic hand bag as she did so. Out of the bag came an enormous, much-worn single-action six-shooter. The gun had neither trigger nor sights, and a fanning spur had been welded onto the hammer.

Monk and Ham wrenched out superfirer pistols.

"There's that Santini bird!" Monk rapped.

Ham, squinting at the gunmen rushing toward the car, added, "And there's Hallet and Leaking!"

Santini, resplendent in red chest ribbon and cat-whisker mustache, was one of the attackers who depended only on a hand weapon. He held his pearl-and-gold inlaid automatic.

"*Tutto ad un tratto!*" he howled. "All at once! Let them have it!"

The close confines of the street quaked, thundered and echoed with the crash of guns. Fully a dozen men had surrounded the sedan, and all fired simultaneously. Machine gun and automatic pistol ejectors sprayed empty cartridges on the pavement.

It seemed impossible that those in the sedan could live under that storm of powder-driven metal.

## Chapter V
### THE HANGING MAN

FISH Lane was an unpaved rut which ran out into the bog that was the upper end of Flushing Bay. This bog was furred with tall, coarse salt water grass, and along the Lane stood a few shacks of wood, tar paper and tin, most of these structural materials apparently having come from neighboring junk heaps.

A car crawled quietly into Fish Lane, a long, streamlined machine with a fishtail back and pants over the wheels. It stopped.

The man who first alighted from the machine had hands of startling size. Huge and knobby, they eclipsed the other proportions of their owner, who would weigh in excess of two hundred and fifty pounds, and who was gaunt and bony.

Wearing a long, solemn, funereal-going expression, he asked of someone still in the car, "Fish Lane is where Doc said to come, wasn't it, Johnny?"

"Eminently correct, Renny," said Johnny's scholastic voice.

Johnny was a scarecrow of bones, except that the garments hung on his frame were of excellent quality. Nowhere on his skeleton did there seem to be even a normal muscle, far less any surplus flesh. Dangling from his shirt lapel was a monocle on a ribbon.

They were a strange pair, these two. "Renny" was known all over the world for his ability and accomplishments as an engineer, having constructed bridges, dams, power plants, railroads, in many countries.

The bony Johnny was equally famous in his field of archaeology and geology, and he had formerly been the head of the natural science research department of a famous university, an environment which perhaps had given him his love of big words.

Big-fisted Renny's engineer associates knew him as Colonel John Renwick, while scholastic gentlemen knew Johnny as William Harper Littlejohn.

Gaunt Johnny peered into the car and advised, "Alight, Electrophobia."

The man who now got out of the car, stuffing a tangle of wires and delicate electrical apparatus into a door pocket as he did so, looked pale and almost feeble. Alongside the great, big-fisted Renny, he seemed almost an invalid, a fact that was deceptive, however, for the giant Renny would have hesitated about mixing in a fight with the puny looking one, knowing him as he did.

The apparent invalid was Major Thomas J. Roberts, "Long Tom" to his intimates, an electrical wizard extraordinary.

These three were the other members of Doc Savage's group of five remarkable assistants, and each was an expert, a so-called genius, in his line, although in their case as in most others, genius and hard work and protracted study.

Renny pointed with his huge fist. "There's the place where this Kel Avery is supposed to be—1120 Fish Lane."

THE building at 1120 Fish Lane was grayishly shabby and resembled a barred rock hen nested in a tangle of brush. Shingles were scabbing off the roof, tin cans had been split and nailed over knot-holes in the up-and-down plank walls, and sacks and old clothing were wadded in place of missing windowpanes.

The Flushing elevated tracks were not far away and a train passed on it, making much clank and rumble.

"That joint isn't much," Renny rumbled. "We won't need to wait for Doc. Let's take it."

They were all agreed on the idea, and they went forward. Doc's word had been to await his arrival, but they knew the bronze man had made that statement in a general fashion rather than a literal one.

If there had been any apparent need for needing Doc's consummate skill in the present instance, the three would have waited. But to learn whether Kel Avery was in the shack or not seemed but a simple matter.

Doc Savage's five men were not puppets who did the bronze man's bidding. They were men of training, of sharp mentality, and had a habit of going ahead on their own initiative. Sometimes they made mistakes. More often, they did not.

Turning into the ramshackle building, they stepped over a fallen fence and trod a furrow through the brush and weeds where feet had trampled. In one spot they noticed tracks—the prints of long, narrow shoes—embedded in the moist loam.

"Seems to have been only the one guy walking in and out here," rumbled big-fisted Renny.

Another train passed noisily on the nearby elevated.

Gaining the door, the three men knocked; but there was no answer. Gaunt Johnny shifted to a knothole uncovered by tin and pasted his right eye to the aperture. His violent start was plainly visible to both Renny and Long Tom, and he used a pet ejaculation which he saved for occasions of supreme shock.

"I'll be superamalgamated!" he exploded.

Renny and Long Tom reached his side in concerted leaps. They clapped eyes in turn to the knothole, and each tensed. Then Renny bounded back to the door.

There was blurred motion, a crash, and splinters climbed in a cloud around Renny. With one blow, he had sent an enormous fist through the door.

It was a remarkable exhibition of iron ruggedness, but Johnny and Long Tom showed no surprise, for they had seen its equal and had heard Renny's fre-

**The whiskered one dropped down to the floor, white hair flying.**

quent boast that no wooden door was made with a panel so stout that he could not smash through with one swing of the monstrosities which he called fists.

Weakened, the door collapsed. The three men dived inside. They gazed upward the instant they were across the threshold.

"Horrible!" Johnny breathed. "Revolting!"

"Damn bad!" agreed pale Long Tom.

THE trash of years of abandonment lay about the room, and from the rotting floor in one corner had sprouted a few toadstools. Paper had peeled from the walls long ago, while marauding boys had belted glass out of the windows with stones and the glass reposed in shattered fragments over the floor.

The door of a closet hung askew, half closed; from the partition between the shack's two rooms, the door was missing entirely, only hinges that clung like rusty scabs showing that there had been one.

Eyes of the three men remained fixed overhead, where the ceiling lath had long since been torn away to leave the attic naked and exposed to its highest recess, except for the two-by-four timbers to which the laths had been nailed.

They were not calloused men, these five aides of Doc's, although they had walked long in the shadow of violence and peril. They were not beyond being gripped by a scene of horror. They were gripped now.

From the roof peak stretched a rope which was a yard in length and terminated around the neck of a man. The man's feet dangled off one of the two-by-fours a distance of a foot or so.

The hanging man had a white beard which came nearly to his belt, and it covered the front of his chest like the stiff front of a dress shirt. His hair was white and very long, snowy beard and hair lending him a most striking appearance. His face was darkly purple from the throttling effect of the rope.

"Quick!" boomed Renny. "He may be alive!"

Renny and Johnny prepared to lift Long Tom, the lighter of the three, up to loosen the hanging one. Then their hair all but stood on end.

The hands of the man on the rope were crossed. They moved with flashing speed, darting inside his coat. Reappearing, each hand held a blue revolver.

The bearded one squirmed and his feet found a two-by-four cross-piece. He shook his head violently and loosened the rope from his neck.

It all happened in the space of a finger snap, before the three men below could do a thing.

"Bettah keep yoah hands in sight," the stranger advised.

## Chapter VI
### DAN THUNDEN

VERY slowly, so that the white-bearded man with the two blue guns could see each move, Renny

and Johnny lowered Long Tom back to the floor. Then Renny's huge fists knotted and unknotted angrily.

"Take it easy," Long Tom warned. "This guy took us in, what I mean."

The whiskered one dropped down to the floor, white hair flying. There was a weird lightness and agility about his movements. His features were unusual, also. They had the lines of a man of fifty, yet the skin was clear and the eyes had a youthful sparkle.

"Stand still," advised the gunman in a youthful, drawling voice. "I'm going to search yoah pockets."

His bony but agile fingers brought to view, from armpit holsters worn by Doc's three men, a trio of the unique supermachine pistols which were the bronze man's invention. He fumbled these, obviously curious about their mechanism.

Renny thought he saw his chance. He lashed a big hand at the white-bearded one.

The results were choking to Renny. There was a whistling sound, a *bonk!* noise. Renny sat down heavily, eyelids fluttering.

He had been hit between the eyes with one of the blue revolvers and the blow had come so swiftly that he had not even seen it.

Long Tom and Johnny stared. They had just witnessed speed such as they had imagined only one man could possess—Doc Savage.

"Why didn't Santini, Hallet and Leaking come, instead of sendin' you gentlemen?" asked the remarkable white-haired man dryly.

"Are you Kel Avery?" Long Tom demanded.

The other juggled the two blue guns slowly. "Are you tryin' to kid me?"

"Are you Kel Avery?" repeated Long Tom.

The thatch of white hair shook. "No, suh, and you should know that, bein' in Santini's gang."

The electrical wizard frowned, "Wrong, whiskers. We're not working for Santini—"

"Save that guff, suh," snapped the other. "Ah don't believe you can talk fast enough to fool old Dan Thunden."

"Dan Thunden," Long Tom grunted. "That your name?"

Dan Thunden laughed loudly, boyishly. "Just as if Santini hadn't told you."

"I tell you we're not—"

"Shut up!" The blue guns jutted angrily.

Gaunt Johnny put in, calm-voiced, "Would you condescend to answer a single interrogation?"

Dan Thunden threw his white hair back with a head-snapping gesture. "What is yoah question?"

"How old are you?" Johnny asked, using small words for once.

"One hundred and thirty-one yeahs old," Dan Thunden said promptly.

Renny's jaw sagged. Long Tom and Johnny looked little less shocked.

"A dang lie!" Long Tom snapped. "Nobody could be as spry as you are at that age!"

Dan Thunden's white whiskers bristled indignantly and he seemed on the point of putting up a vociferous argument. Instead, he spun toward the door.

Doc Savage stood there, his great bronze frame almost filling the opening. Behind him were the homely Monk and sword cane-carrying Ham. The three of them had approached with great silence.

Thunden leveled a gun at the door, roared, "Yoah hands up, suh!"

But Doc was already hurtling forward.

THUNDEN'S gun convulsed. The shack quaked with powder roar!

Doc was moving with the full coordination of his tremendous muscles, and the bullet missed. A wall board split as the lead clouted it.

There was no time for a second shot. Thunden ducked wildly as Doc's great hands grasped for him. He got clear, dancing aside.

Johnny jumped for the white-haired man who said his age was a hundred and thirty-one.

Thunden threw a blue gun. It took Johnny in the middle. The bony geologist folded, face distorted, tongue protruding.

Monk came in from the rear with the speed of a great cat. Thunden hurled his second gun. Monk wailed and wrapped both hands over the top of his bullet of a head, where the weapon struck. He sank to the floor, his wail turning into a howl of rage and pain. All of him but his vocal apparatus seemed paralyzed.

The next few seconds held action as Doc's five men had never before witnessed. They had seen many fights, but never one in which their bronze chief had been pitted against a man anywhere near his own equal in agility.

Dan Thunden could not possibly possess the Herculean strength of the bronze giant, but the white-haired old fellow did move with an unearthly speed. Time after time, Doc seemed on the point of grasping Thunden, only to have the strange fellow get clear. They flashed to the ends of the room, two men of superhuman abilities.

Dan Thunden did not have an easy time of it, however. At first, when he had carelessly used his guns to lay out Monk and Johnny, he had seemed supremely confident of his own ability. A grin had been on his aged, but remarkably healthy looking face. But the grin faded. He began to look worried.

"You sho' are no ordinary man!" he gulped, and his expression was that of a man who had met something he did not believe existed.

Leaping desperately, he reached a window. Glass and aged wood exploded as he went through it head-first. Surprisingly enough, he managed to land on his feet outside—and started running.

The window was too small to pass Doc's big frame in a hurry, and he had to swing around and out through the door. That lost him time. Thunden had gained yards.

Renny and Doc's other men piled into the chase. Johnny, bringing up the rear, still had his arms across his middle and groaned with each jump.

It became evident that Dan Thunden was no match for Doc in a straight race. The bronze man overhauled the bearded fellow.

Thunden stopped, whirled. A gun—a tiny flat hide-away automatic—came from inside the waistband of his trousers.

"Down!" Doc rapped, and flattened with his men.

Thunden's bullet made an ugly hissing as it cut through the brush and salt water grass. Shot echoes slammed, then came jarring back in fainter echoes from the distant walls of Flushing warehouses.

"White whiskers seems to be a walkin' armory," Monk growled, and snapped the safety off on his machine pistol.

The superfirer hooted. Brush and grass toppled as if mowed. The homely chemist emptied an entire drum, then reared up to observe effects. He slapped down again in wild haste.

Dan Thunden had crawled through the salt grass and now fired from a spot fifty yards from where he had last been seen. Despite Monk's mad speed in flattening, he might well have been shot had it not been for bronze-haired Patricia Savage, who sent a bullet snapping near Thunden, startling the white-haired one into aiming badly.

Pat was in the sedan, parked a short distance up Fish Lane. She had remained in the car as a lookout.

Dan Thunden got away, reaching a paved street which abutted on the marsh ground and running up that until he had the good fortune to encounter a prowling taxi. He paused an instant before leaping into the cab to yell at his pursuers.

"If you don't believe I'm a hundred and thirty-one yeahs old, look up the records on the skippah of the *Sea Nymph,* a schoonah that sailed from New York in 1843!" he shouted.

Then, menacing the driver of the taxi with his gun, Thunden forced the cab to carry him away in great haste.

Farther up the street children were playing, and that prevented Doc and the others from using their superfirers, or Pat her single-action six-gun.

PAT, plugging fresh shells into her big revolver as Doc came up, grinned widely.

"Two fights and I've only been with you half an

hour!" she laughed. "Talk about leading violent lives!"

Big-fisted Renny overheard that and was puzzled. "*Two* fights?" he demanded.

Pat indicated the sedan with a slender, capable hand. The car windows had a frosty appearance and were pocked. Paint was knocked off the body.

Renny nodded soberly, comprehending. Windows and car body were of bulletproof construction. Indications were that the machine had recently been in the path of a barrage.

"Santini, Hallet and Leaking and their gang jumped us," Pat explained for the benefit of Renny, Long Tom and Johnny. "Stopped our car by blocking the street with a taxi. Then they ran out with guns and cut loose."

"What happened?" Renny boomed.

"I aged ten years wondering if the sedan was really bulletproof," Pat smiled. "And was it a good feeling when those bullets bounced off!"

"What about Santini's gang?"

"They ran," Pat advised. "They had things all set for a fast getaway. They were gone before we could get straightened out and follow them."

Renny's puritanical face grew long and gloomy, which meant, contrary enough, that he was delighted.

"You're in awful bad company, Pat," he said seriously.

"I love this company," Pat assured him.

An hour later, Doc Savage and his five men were going through ancient shipping records by way of complying with strange, white-haired Dan Thunden's suggestion that they check up on his age.

"Here it is," Doc advised, indicating yellowed papers.

The others gathered about and read. The schooner *Sea Nymph* had sailed from New York in 1843, according to the aged documents, and her skipper was a gentleman bearing the name of Dan Thunden, whose age at that time was exactly forty.

Gaunt Johnny fingered his monocle and did some mental arithmetic.

"Computation indicates Captain Dan Thunden of the *Sea Nymph* would be a hundred and thirty-one years of age if he had lived to this day," advised.

"Nuts," snorted the homely Monk.

"To whom are you attributing the qualities of a hard-shelled fruit?" Johnny asked in an injured tone.

"Not to you," Monk grunted. "But it's silly to think any guy a hundred and thirty-one years old could be as spry as that old white-whiskered gent."

Doc riffled through more of the ancient papers. He pointed.

"Look," he advised.

Again, the other read.

"Holy cow!" gulped Renny. "That voyage in 1843 was the *Sea Nymph's* last. She was lost at sea and never heard from again."

SHORTLY after the discovery that the *Sea Nymph* was listed as one of the mysteriously lost ships of the sea, Doc Savage spoke without consulting a timepiece.

"We have about thirty minutes to spare before heading for the airport to meet this Kel Avery who was ordered seized by Santini."

"Do you think they will go through with the attempted capture?" Pat asked curiously.

"Why not? They do not know we intercepted Santini's orders to Hallet and Leaking."

"Right," Pat admitted. "What about the half hour we have to spare?"

"We'll make a stab at learning what is behind this," Doc told her.

"How?"

"Recall the file of wealthy men in the offices of Fountain of Youth, Inc.?"

"You told me about it."

"I phoned one of the names in the file—a banker by the name of Thackeray Hutchinson," Doc explained. "He acted very secretive and hung up on me."

"Which means he knows something," Pat said promptly.

"Right."

"And we're going to ask him questions?"

"We are."

## Chapter VII
### MURDER

BANKER Thackeray Hutchinson's domicile was one befitting a man who was by way of being one of the nation's wealthiest and most unscrupulously greedy moneybags. It was a penthouse covering the entire roof of a costly building which Thackeray Hutchinson owned in the Wall Street sector.

"I never did like this Hutchinson octopus," Monk muttered as they unloaded before the building which supported the penthouse. "He should have been shot when he was born."

"He's an orphan robber," agreed pale Long Tom.

A private elevator gave admittance to the penthouse, and this was operated by a rather tough-looking fellow in a gaudy uniform.

"Mr. Hutchinson is not in," the operator advised harshly.

"We'll go up anyway," Monk growled.

The attendant started to object, but eyed the chemist's gorilla hulk and changed his mind. He ran them up in sour silence.

A butler put his nose in the air and also imparted that Hutchinson was not in.

"Don't lie to us!" Doc Savage said shortly.

The flunky stared coldly at the bronze man. Then his haughty aplomb collapsed. There was something about Doc's flake-gold eyes and the quiet power of his voice that did not promise easy going to those who tried to resist his will.

"In the library," the butler mumbled.

Banker Thackeray Hutchinson sprang wildly from his easy chair as they walked unceremoniously into his presence. He stared at Doc Savage and his expression was that of a rabbit hunter who has just met a bear.

The moneybags had the jowls of a bulldog, the eyes of a lizard and the body of a pelican, along with the pelican's neck. His head was utterly bald and an unpleasant white, as if the top of his skull were showing.

"Damn you, get out of here!" he yelled.

He wore a checkered suit with a ridiculously youthful cut, a suit such as a college freshman might wear until his classmates laughed him into leaving it at home. The effect was such that Ham, whose hobby was clothing, made a face as he glimpsed the loud suit.

"My name is Savage, Mr. Hutchinson," Doc began. "We have called upon you to—"

"I know you're Doc Savage, and a big shot with some fools!" the banker roared. "You may buffalo some people, but you won't get to first base with me! Get out!"

"We have called to learn what you know of Fountain of Youth, Inc.," Doc finished.

"Never heard of it!" the pelican man snarled.

"That is not true," Doc charged. "Your denial doesn't ring sound."

Hutchinson ground his teeth and leaped for a telephone. Monk moved with a lazy speed and got there first. The banker shrank away from the apish chemist.

"Help, police!" he screamed. "Help! Murder!"

"The police are here," Doc advised.

Hutchinson snarled, "Where?"

"We are the police. Myself and each of my men hold commissions on the New York police force."

The man whose manner of getting wealth had interested the Federal government retreated, scowling, trembling a little. He was the picture of a man in a panic.

Doc Savage studied the fellow. During Thackeray Hutchinson's trial in connection with the public utilities fiasco, there had been much in the newspapers and little of it complimentary. There was one angle worth remembering—this man had an awful fear of going to jail. It was rumored that he had spent over a million dollars in defeating the government charge.

"You are under arrest," Doc said abruptly.

Hutchinson blanched. "W-w-what?"

"Fountain of Youth, Inc., has made repeated attempts to kill me within the last two hours," Doc told him quietly. "You have been connected with the concern, and that means a trip to jail."

"Y-you're crazy!" the banker snarled.

"Accessory to murder, or attempted murder, is a criminal charge," Doc pointed out quietly. "Your money won't keep you out of prison."

Doc was bluffing, but the utter calmness of his voice gave Thackeray Hutchinson no hint of that. The threat of jail did what perhaps nothing else could have done. The pelican man collapsed in a chair.

"W-what do y-you want to k-know?" he mumbled. "I'll tell you."

AT one side of the room, dapper Ham twirled his sword cane and masked a smile. His law career had made Ham a master of scaring unwilling witnesses into divulging the truth, but even he could not have bested the job Doc had just done. The bronze man had hit on their victim's one fear—that of going to prison.

"I'm only a c-customer of Fountain of Youth, Inc.," Hutchinson stuttered in his haste to get the information out.

"A customer?" Doc prompted.

The banker wrung his hands. "This is horrible! If only Fountain of Youth had not gotten into trouble! They had the secret! The secret man has hunted for since he was able to think for himself! And now they've got in trouble and it'll be lost."

The hand wringing became more violent.

"I was to pay them a million dollars for the secret," the moneybags went on. "It was cheap at the price. A select list of other rich men was to receive the secret, too. We had been selected carefully because of our wealth and—er—er—other qualifications by Fountain of Youth. A million apiece, we were all to pay."

"Wait!" Doc put in. "This isn't making sense. What is this secret for which you and other wealthy men of your type were to pay a million each?"

Thackeray Hutchinson twisted his bald head to peer about uneasily.

"They've got a man here," he mumbled. "They said they had to be sure we did not tell the secret or plot against them to get the weeds."

"Fountain of Youth has a man here? One of Santini's gang?"

The bulldog-jowled capitalist shuddered. "Yes. One of Santini's men."

"Who is he?" Doc rapped.

Thackeray Hutchinson opened his mouth to reply. He shut it before words came out. He lifted half out of his chair. Gagging sounds escaped him as he tried to point at a door on the opposite side of the study.

The hard-looking elevator operator stood there, lifting a revolver.

"Spill your insides, will you?" he snarled.

His gun lipped flame; the recoil kicked his arm up. The room seemed to fly apart and come together again, so earsplitting was the report.

Thackeray Hutchinson sat down loosely in his easy chair. His eyes were closed tightly. There was a round blue hole in the middle of his forehead. Then his mouth fell open and let a scarlet flood spill down the vest of his loud suit.

Doc Savage scooped an ornamental vase off an end table. It was not an effective weapon, but the handiest one. He threw it.

The gunman tried to step aside. He was far too slow. The vase hit his gun arm. Enameled particles geysered. The man dropped his revolver, stooped to recover it, saw there was no time for that and leaped backward. He slammed the door.

"The elevator!" Doc rapped. "Watch it!"

Big-fisted Renny and homely Monk dived to obey.

The gunman got the key turned in the lock—they could hear it click.

Doc hit the panel. It was stout. The bronze man blocked out one metallic hand and struck. His knuckles drove completely through the wood, a feat that seemed more than bone and tendons could stand, yet, when he withdrew his fist after turning the key, there was no apparent damage.

Doc plunged down a passage. Yells and curses indicated the killer had been cut off from the elevators.

"He's makin' for the terrace!" came Renny's great rumble.

Doc crashed through double glass doors. The slayer was on the opposite side of the terrace, peering over the parapet. He looked around, grimaced, swore hoarsely, then swung over the edge and vanished.

Two long leaps took Doc to the edge. An ornamental fresco ran downward, the carvings of this forming fairly substantial handholds. The gunman was perhaps ten feet down.

Doc swung over and started after him. His movements were swift, making those of the man below seem slow by comparison.

The killer glanced up. Discovering Doc almost upon him, he yelled a meaningless threat. Then he tried to increase his own pace.

It was no spot for a race. The slayer missed his grip in his mad haste. He clawed the air furiously, but failed to recover, and his body tilted outward, arms windmilling.

At the beginning of his fall, he turned over so that he faced the street some forty floors below. The sight caused him to shriek long and horribly, and the sound grew rapidly fainter as his fall carried him away from Doc and the others.

On the street, pedestrians looked up, they ran away and made a place for the body to hit the sidewalk. The concrete cracked a little from the impact.

Doc climbed slowly back to the terrace.

Ham came out of the penthouse and said grimly, "Thackeray Hutchinson died like that!" and snapped his fingers to illustrate.

## Chapter VIII
### FAST STUFF

THE clock on the front of the main hangar was big enough that it could be seen from all parts of the flying field, but it was dusk now, and one had to be quite close to make out that the clock hands stood at eight.

Monk got out of Doc's streamlined car, saying in his small voice, "One thing is sure, and that is we haven't seen all the guys in this Fountain of Youth gang. So we gotta be careful." He jerked a thumb to take in the airport in general. "Some of them mugs might be around here anywhere, waitin' for Kel Avery's plane."

Somewhat of a crowd was about the airport waiting room with its long telescoping canopy that could be hauled out to planes on little wheels. The throng had a heterogeneous appearance. Some persons carried small books and others had cameras.

"Autograph hounds and photographers," rumbled big-fisted Renny.

"Which means a celebrity is arriving, doesn't it?" Patricia put in.

Doc said, "Pat!"

"Yes?"

"Can you change your appearance in a hurry?"

"If I had some dark glasses, I could. You can't imagine what a difference dark glasses make in a girl's looks."

Doc Savage dropped a hand into a door pocket and brought out a small leather case.

"Here they are. I do not think that Fountain of Youth crew got a good look at you this afternoon, and if you alter your appearance slightly, they might not recognize you."

"The idea is that nobody is to think I'm with you?" Pat queried.

"Exactly."

"All right." Pat tapped Ham on the arm. "Lend me that snappy topcoat you're wearing."

"Huh?" Ham was startled.

"It's cut like a ladies' garment. Come on, shed it!"

The homely Monk exploded stifled laughter and

Ham, ears getting red, slid out of his snappily tailored topcoat and passed it to the bronze-haired young woman.

"Keep your eyes open and be ready to grab any loose ends that we let slip, Pat," Doc directed.

"I will." Pat faded into the gloom among the other parked cars.

A few moments later, when they saw her again, she had donned the smoked spectacles, changed her hair, and had draped the topcoat over her shoulders.

"Smart kid!" Renny rumbled softly. "I'd hardly know her myself."

Monk, gurgling mirth, moaned ecstatically, "I always did know something was wrong with that topcoat, and now I see what it is. The thing was made for a woman."

Ham glared in the murk, fumbled his sword cane and snarled, "For two cents I'd make hash out of you!"

Doc put in, "Listen!"

Out of the southern twilight was coming the multiple drone of airplane engines.

"That'll be the ship carrying Kel Avery," decided the bronze man. "Let's go."

They got out of the streamlined car, six men so unusual as to attract more than one curious stare.

Doc kept in the background; he seldom wore a hat, but he wore one now, yanked low to help the murk hide his features. He did not want to attract the cameras or the autograph hunters.

Long Tom, so pale as to seem an ill man, stopped an airport attendant, asking, "Why the excitement?"

"Maureen Darleen, the movie actress, is coming in on this plane from Florida," the attendant replied.

WHILE the big passenger plane moaned closer, Long Tom sauntered over to Doc and spoke in a low voice.

"The photographers and autograph grabbers are here to meet Maureen Darleen, the picture queen," he imparted. "But if I remember my movies, this Darleen is not such a big shot. The best she's done is play opposite a well known actor or two. And that makes me wonder why all the fuss?"

"Haven't you read your papers lately?" Doc asked.

"Naw," Long Tom shrugged. "I been busy working on my electrical invention to utilize sonic waves to kill insects and crop pests."

"The papers yesterday and this morning were full of Maureen Darleen," Doc explained. "She was kidnaped in Florida yesterday, but escaped. Some of the newspapers hinted unkindly that it was a publicity stunt."

"Probably was," Long Tom grunted skeptically. "These movie people will do anything for publicity."

"They have to. If the public does not know their names; they have no box office pull, and big box office pull means big salary."

"You seem to be sticking up for this Maureen Darleen."

"I do not know her personally," Doc replied. "But I do know that she spends most of her salary to support a home for orphans in her hometown down in Georgia."

"That may be a publicity stunt, too."

"She does not advertise her connection with the home. Anyway, there are less expensive methods of grabbing publicity."

Long Tom patted his armpit where reposed a supermachine pistol.

"Some of these cameramen and autograph hunters may belong to the Fountain of Youth gang," he grunted.

Doc nodded. "I was thinking of that."

The big plane circled the field once, the motors decreased their clamor and the ship swung in, sinking. The pilot was good and touched his ponderous charge to the tarmac without a bounce; then, with whooping gusts from the propellers, drove the craft toward the canopy.

Field attendants yelled and grunted and shoved to keep the crowd out of range of the propellers, and other flunkies ran the telescoping awning out.

The plane engines stopped and the cabin door opened. The throng burst bounds and rushed for the door, cameramen yelling and jumping up in an endeavor to get pictures, the autograph fans shouting for Maureen Darleen's signature.

Doc Savage and his five men kept in a group, although they were jostled about. They lost sight of Patricia in her disguise of dark glasses and borrowed topcoat, as she was submerged in the excited movie fans.

Suddenly a voice yelled from the edge of the mêlée. It was a shrill voice, very loud, and the words were plainly distinguishable as they knifed through the bedlam.

"Here is Kel Avery!" it cried.

Instantly after that, a man shrieked. Blows smacked. Men cursed.

"Help! Help!" bawled a voice.

DOC SAVAGE pitched in the direction of the cries. His great frame went through the crowd like a torpedo through water. At his beck, his five men were a flying wedge.

"Help!" bawled the voice. "Leggo me!"

Doc sighted the fight. Several hard-faced, roughly clad men had seized a fat, stocky fellow and were hauling at him, beating and kicking.

"Stop that!" Doc rapped.

"Who the hell are you?" snarled a man, and swung with a clubbed revolver.

Doc was not where he had been when the blow descended, but a yard to one side. His fist lashed out; there was a wet smack. The man with the revolver threw up his arms and floundered hack, his lips a pulp and his teeth showing through splits where Doc's metallic knuckles had landed.

The others ran with the fat man. They did not get far. Doc was upon them, his five men close behind. They struck, grabbed, twisted.

Johnny, who looked so incredibly gaunt, grabbed a thug twice his own weight, enwrapping the fellow spider fashion. The victim shrieked terribly, proving that Johnny had a fighting ability that belied his professional appearance.

The brawl attracted a crowd. A newspaper photographer began to jump about in his excitement and fumble his flashlight apparatus.

"It's Doc Savage in action!" he howled. "T'hell with the movie dame! Get this!"

His flashlight gun made a *swhoosh!* and an eye-hurting splash of white light. Other cameramen joined the outskirts of the fray and their flashes winked blindingly.

A man wearing an aviator's helmet ran into the scrap, fists swinging, and was promptly knocked senseless, falling at the feet of a woman who began screaming hysterically.

Long Tom bored into the middle of a large man with a gun; his fists made a rapid drum roll, and the man collapsed, gurgling. Running for another foe, the electrical wizard went out of his way to bump a camera from a photographer's hands and step on it, ruining the exposed plates. Long Tom knew Doc's dislike for newspaper publicity, and the camera belonged to the newspaper which the photographer worked for, anyway.

Quite suddenly, the fight was over. Of the gang who had tried to seize the fat man, all were helpless, sprawled on the ground. There were exactly seven of them, and all had the earmarks of small-time criminals.

Doc helped the fat victim to his feet. "You're not hurt, Avery?"

"My name is not Avery!" shrieked the fat man. "I'm Joe Smith and I'm a reporter on the *Morning Comet!*"

Doc beckoned other newspaper men to come close. "This man says he's Joe Smith—"

"Sure, he's Joe Smith of the *Morning Comet*," said a journalist. "We all know him!"

Doc Savage's strange flake-gold eyes roved from Joe Smith to the overpowered assailants, and the bronze man's features were strangely fixed, more metallic than ever.

There sounded unexpectedly a weird, low, mellow trilling note, a fantastic sound which seemed to come from everywhere and yet from no definite source, and which ran up and down the musical scale, definitely rhythmatic, yet adhering to no specific tune. Even those bystanders who heard the exotic trilling and looked at the bronze man's lips, could not tell from whence it came. Yet Doc Savage authored the sound.

The trilling was a small, unconscious thing which Doc Savage did when under sudden stress, or when greatly surprised. Even he could not tell exactly how he made it, but the sound always had great significance. Just now it meant that he was shocked and utterly disgusted with himself.

At Doc's signal, the men who had attacked the reporter were hauled into the nearest hangar and the doors closed. The thugs were scared and bewildered and entirely willing to talk, hoping it would prevent them being charged with a worse crime than assault.

"A guy named Santini hired us to jump this bird Kel Avery when the plane came in, and beat him up," one of the men moaned. "Santini pointed out Kel Avery to us. We got fifty bucks apiece."

"It was Joe Smith, a reporter, you attacked and not Kel Avery," Doc said grimly.

"Santini said that guy was named Kel Avery, and for us to yell out his name," insisted the frightened yegg.

DOC SAVAGE turned the gang over to the airport officials and went outside to join his aides.

"We fell for a trick," he said grimly. "Santini hired these cheap crooks to attack a man in the crowd and get our attention."

"But why get our attention?" Ham demanded, puzzled.

Big-fisted Renny came up with the answer to that. The engineer was excited.

"Doc! Doc!" he ejaculated. "During the fight, another gang grabbed this Maureen Darleen and another woman and carried them off in a car—according to people I've talked to in the crowd. They slugged a bodyguard this Maureen Darleen had along."

A moment of silence followed the news—and Doc Savage's strange trilling sound seemed to echo, but it was very low and hardly perceptible to the ear.

"What beautiful dopes we turned out to be," Ham muttered. "That other fight was to get our attention while this gang grabbed Maureen Darleen."

"But I thought it was somebody named Kel Avery that they were after!" Renny rumbled.

"Where is this bodyguard of Maureen Darleen's?" Doc demanded.

"Over here." Renny led the way.

The bodyguard looked the part. He was an athletic giant almost as impressive in physique as Doc

Savage. The fellow's great muscles were more bulging even than Doc's, which meant he was a trifle muscle-bound. He had a square head, a corded neck and square, powerful fingers. Slung across his chest, in plain sight, was a harness for carrying two pistols in underarm holsters.

The man was sitting up, shaking his head slowly, when Doc approached him. He peered at the bronze man a bit vacantly, then felt of the holsters attached to his harness. They were empty.

Doc knelt, grasped the fellow's shoulders and shook him. "Are you Kel Avery?"

The overmuscled one shook his head from side to side. "Meester, my name, she is no Kel Avery. My name is Da Clima, yes."

His English was understandable enough, but the words were put together in the manner of one who had learned the tongue in later life. Such accent as he had was that of southern Europe.

"You are Maureen Darleen's bodyguard?" Doc questioned.

"Her guard, yes. Maybe *was* her guard." Da Clima sighed. "She, maybe it is, won't want a guard who as a guard is not so hot, no?"

"Do you know a Kel Avery?" Doc asked.

Da Clima squinted. Muscles as large as muskmelons bulged up under his coat as he lifted himself.

"Kel Avery is Maureen Darleen," he said. "You not know that, no?"

"Maureen Darleen and Kel Avery the same person?" Doc repeated, as if to make sure.

Da Clima nodded. "Kel Avery, or Kelmina Avery, she don't use that name, not so much. The name Avery, she not so good on the movie picture, no. Maureen Darleen much better, so the girl she use the name of Avery not so much."

"A lot of these movie actresses have stage names," Renny rumbled.

Monk came up, short legs taking great leaps.

"Pat ain't around here anywhere!" he snapped.

Doc gripped Renny's thick arm. "You said that gang made off with *two* women, didn't you?"

"Yes."

"Let's go!"

## Chapter IX
### KEL AVERY'S STORY

THE car bearing the kidnapers and their two women prisoners was a long blue phaeton. It had gone toward New York. These two bits of information were forthcoming from members of the crowd who had seen the snatching.

Da Clima piled into Doc's streamlined car with the rest.

"Da Clima, he go along," he growled. "We catch them and Da Clima, he do them like this!" His muscular hands made pantomime of breaking things.

"How about that, Doc?" Monk questioned.

"Let him come, of course. We want to ask him questions."

The big engine came to life under the tapered hood, but only sudden animation of ammeter and oil gauge showed that. The machine was fitted with an automatic shifting device, and Doc thrust the lever which meshed the gears, after which the shifting required no further attention.

Tires threw gravel all the way out of the flying field, shrieked on concrete as they swerved to the pavement, and then there was only the hiss of exhausts and the wail of air past the streamlined curves.

The speedometer arm jumped around to seventy. Doc touched a switch, and a siren started a banshee wail.

Doc spoke to Da Clima without taking his eyes off the scudding concrete.

"What do you know about this?" he demanded.

"Me, I not know the much," Da Clima disclaimed.

"Tell us what you do know."

"Yesterday, I read about it in the papers, the kidnap what is tried on Maureen Darleen," said Da Clima. "I am in this Florida then. Maybe you read about that, no? The kidnap what is try on Maureen Darleen—"

"Call her Miss Avery so there will be no confusion," Doc suggested. "Yes. We read about the attempted kidnaping."

"I go to her, to Mees Avery," Da Clima continued. "I am once the fighter, not so hot. Now, the nickel I pick up where I can. I fight. I shoot. I'm plenty the tough guy, me."

"Don't brag," Monk growled. "You're with guys who *are* tough, now."

"But you not so good in the head, no?" Da Clima queried. "You run to the wrong fight while them fellows, they get Maureen—Mees Avery. They make of you the sap, no?"

Monk scowled. "Say, you funny-talkin' bundle of beef, are you huntin' a scrap?"

"Stop it," Doc put in quietly. "Da Clima, you went to Miss Avery after you heard of the attempt to kidnap her and offered your services as a bodyguard—is that it?"

"That's her, the idea," Da Clima nodded. "I put up the talk and tell her that me, I am the one she need. So she hire me to watch out for her."

"A swell job you done," Monk snorted.

Da Clima started to answer, but caught sight of the speedometer and his eyes opened wide and black. He wet his lips uneasily and muttered, "Boy, we travel—no?"

The speedometer read eighty-five. Buildings went by like pickets and cars, frightened to the curb by the siren, were blurred.

"What else do you know?" Doc asked.

"Me, nothing," said Da Clima.

"Don't you know anything about Santini, Hallet, Leaking, or a white-bearded man named Dan Thunden, who claims he is a hundred and thirty-one years old, or a company which calls itself Fountain of Youth, Inc.?"

"Nope," said Da Clima. "Never heard of any of them, no."

"What an information mine he turned out to be!" Monk growled.

Da Clima scowled at the homely chemist and said, "Da Clima, he not like you, not much."

"Brother, the affection is returned," Monk rapped.

"Look!" pale Long Tom shrieked.

DOC SAVAGE had already applied the power brakes. The heavy streamlined car squatted a little, slithered, straightened, slithered again, then, as the bronze man alternately stamped and released the brake pedal, the machine spun with tires screaming and stopped with its radiator pointing back the way it had come.

Da Clima was pale, frightened by the wildness of their stop, and his hands were clenched, his breath coming and going rapidly.

Under the tread of the accelerator the big car lunged back upon their course, then slackened speed and swerved off the pavement, bounding over the packed shoulder, and stopped.

A woman was standing in the ditch beside the road, in water to her knees. She was disheveled, mud spattered, her frock was torn at the shoulder, as if she had pitched into the ditch from a rapidly-moving car. She came toward them, wiping mud off her face.

"Maureen—Mees Avery!" Da Clima cried in astonishment.

Kel Avery was a tall young woman, blonde, blue-eyed, and even though she was swathed in mud and roadside grime, it was not hard to see why, as Maureen Darleen, she was considered one of the up-and-coming young movie actresses.

She got in the car and said, "Back the way you were going, gentlemen! And step on it!"

Monk grinned as if he liked that and made room for her, while Doc jockeyed the car around skillfully. They resumed their cometlike progress, siren a-howl.

"Which one of you is Doc Savage?" Kel Avery asked.

Monk pointed at the front seat, but said nothing. Kel Avery took in the bronze man's remarkable head, his expanse of shoulders, the metallic texture of his skin.

"Oh," she said. "I didn't get a look at him, or I would have known."

"Ask her questions, Monk," Doc directed. "This driving takes a lot of attention. We're getting into the city limits."

On the floorboards, where he had been throughout, the pig Habeas Corpus sniffed of the movie actress' drenched, shapely ankles until Monk kicked him lightly in the ribs.

"They threw me out," said Kel Avery.

"After they went to all that trouble to seize you?" Monk asked incredulously.

"Oh, they thought I was my maid," explained the blonde actress. "The other girl made them think she was Kel Avery."

"What other girl?"

"The one who rushed to my side and acted as if she was one of my party, when the trouble started back at the airport. Say, that young lady would go great in the movies. She's got looks, and how she can act! She made them think she was Kel Avery, and when she got her chance, whispered to me to begin to scream and they might throw me out, and if they did, I should find Doc Savage and tell him my story. So I screamed and they did throw me out."

Doc tooled the plunging car past an intersection, then threw a question over his shoulder.

"What did this other girl look like?"

"She was beautiful, as I said," advised Kel Avery. "And she had bronze-colored hair-hair like your own, Mr. Savage."

"It was Pat!" Monk groaned.

THERE was unpleasant silence for a while—silence, if the whooping noise of the big car's progress could be excepted.

Doc Savage himself showed little expression, for his command of his facial muscles was complete, but his five men showed that the thought of Patricia Savage being in the hands of Santini's crew was anything but pleasant.

Da Clima held on, face white, and seemed to shrink each time the speeding car careened.

"I was coming to New York by plane to get your help, Mr. Savage," volunteered blonde Kel Avery.

"Did you tell that to anyone?" Doc questioned.

"Nobody. Why?"

"Because Santini and his outfit learned you were coming to me and tried to grab me and put me where you could not find me," Doc told her. "Or that's how it seems."

"Santini?" Kel Avery sounded puzzled.

"Ever hear of him?"

"No."

"Or of Fountain of Youth, Inc.?"

"No."

"What about Hallet or Leaking?"

"Never heard the names that I recall." The blonde's voice had a ring of genuineness.

"What about a white-haired man named Dan Thunden who says he is a hundred and thirty-one years old?"

"Oh!"

Doc lifted his eyes from the road and turned his head for a quick glance. The girl looked startled. "You have heard of Dan Thunden?" Doc asked.

"Yes," said Kel Avery. "He is my great-grandfather, according to the letter I got from him. My great-grandfather on my mother's side, his letter said."

"What else did his letter say?" Doc asked grimly.

"It said for me to take the package that was with the letter and guard it with my life, to be sure not to open it, and to come to Florida and I would be worth fifty million dollars within thirty days," the blonde said all in one breath.

"Holy cow!" Renny rumbled.

Doc inquired. "You obeyed instructions?"

"Oh, it sounds silly, but I did," Kel Avery sighed. "You see, the press agent of the movie company I work for thought it would be a great idea to get some newspaper space. The company even paid me a salary to go to Florida as instructed, and the press agent was going to meet me there. But before he came, I was kidnaped. That scared me. I came North."

"Why come North?"

The actress smiled. "To put the thing into your hands."

"Was that the press agent's idea?" Doc asked.

Kel Avery looked blank, then color crept up in her cheeks under the mud and she glared indignantly at the back of Doc's head.

"Those men threatened to kill me and I was scared!" she snapped. "They told me they would kill me unless I got the package. As a matter of fact, I didn't escape. They turned me loose to get the parcel. And the press agent does not know where I am. The press agent hadn't even gotten to Florida."

Doc was silent after the sharp answer, his metallic features expressionless. He made no movements, except such as were necessary in controlling the car.

A corner loomed ahead. Kel Avery screamed softly; Da Clima groaned and put big hands over his face; the car reeled, rubber shrieked, then they were around the corner, straightened out and going on safely.

"Where is the parcel now?" Doc asked, his great voice calm.

"In the plane on which I arrived, back at the airport," said Kel Avery. "You see, I sent it by air mail, knowing it would come on the same plane."

"Why that precaution?"

"I was afraid to carry it. Maybe I'm not very brave."

"You're brave enough," Doc assured her.

"This is what I call a deep, black mystery," Monk muttered.

Doc slowed the streamlined car abruptly, much to the relief of Da Clima, who swelled proportionately as the machine slackened speed, so that, when they were traveling forty, his chest was out, his chin up, his eyes bright and brave.

"It's no use," Doc said. "The car carrying Pat has given us the slip."

Bony Johnny absently fitted his monocle into his left eye, where it gave his optic a grotesque appearance, for the monocle was in reality a powerful magnifying glass which the gaunt geologist and archaeologist found occasion to use in the course of his work.

"This thing about Pat is appalling," he said. "Appalling!"

## Chapter X
## THE PACKAGE TRICK

MANY citizens of New York City knew of the headquarters which Doc Savage maintained on the eighty-sixth floor of Manhattan's most impressive skyscraper, for the newspapers had published that fact innumerable times. But not many citizens had seen the establishment. Had they done so, they would have been astounded.

The establishment consisted of an outer reception room and office which was sumptuously, but not gaudily furnished. Beyond this was a library which for completeness in its assortment of scientific books could be equaled perhaps by but one other library, its location unknown except to Doc Savage himself, being in a mysterious and remote spot which the bronze man termed his "Fortress of Solitude," and to which he retired at intervals to study, none knowing his whereabouts, not even his five trusted aides.

Connecting with the library was an experimental laboratory, this also having an equal only in the second laboratory which the bronze man maintained at his "Fortress of Solitude." The city laboratory held apparatus for almost every conceivable scientific experiment, as well as tools for the construction of the numerous devices for which Doc Savage found need.

Monk stood in the outer office, nudging Habeas Corpus gently in the ribs with a toe, and spoke his mind.

"That old yahoo, Dan Thunden, is sure a licksplitting freak," the homely chemist declared. "Imagine a gink a hundred and thirty-one years old being able to hop around like he can."

Only beautiful blonde Kel Avery was listening, but she was audience enough, since Monk would talk all day if it would keep him in the company of a girl as attractive as this one.

Doc was issuing commands, having just finished writing a number of names and addresses on slips of paper.

"Here are some of the wealthy men whose names were in that file which we found in the offices of Fountain of Youth, Inc.," the bronze man explained.

He distributed the slips to Long Tom, Renny, Ham and Johnny.

"Investigate," he directed. "Those names were in the file for some reason, just as was that banker, Thackeray Hutchinson."

Renny folded his paper slip with huge fingers. "Some of these birds should give us information," he said.

"Be careful," Doc admonished. "We do not want a repetition of what happened to Thackeray Hutchinson."

"That guy got what was coming to him," put in Monk, who had paused to overhear.

"What happened to him?" blonde Kel Avery asked curiously.

"He got shot between the eyes," Ham told her.

"Oh!" The young woman gasped and sank into a chair.

"This hairy ape"—Ham indicated Monk with his sword cane—"thinks it was all right for a man to get killed."

"Aw, he was an orphan robber," Monk said uncomfortably, knowing very well Ham had deliberately put him before the movie actress in a calloused light.

"What about Pat?" Renny rumbled anxiously.

"We haven't a lead to go on," Doc pointed out. "We'll have to see what turns up."

The four men departed with their paper slips, intent on running down some information about Fountain of Youth, Inc.

Big Da Clima went to the water cooler, drank deeply from the gurgling fountain, then came back and stood in front of Doc.

"Me, I think I go out, not for long," he said.

"Why?" Doc asked.

Da Clima shrugged muscle-bound shoulders, and said, "Business."

"Very well," Doc agreed.

Da Clima lumbered out toward the elevators.

Doc nodded at Monk. "Follow him."

Monk grinned and waved Habeas Corpus back.

"Boy, do I hope this Da Clima gives me some excuse to tie into him," leered the homely chemist. "I don't like him."

Monk went out.

KEL AVERY tried to wring muddy water out of her drying frock and asked, "You do not trust Da Clima?"

"Just a precaution," Doc told her quietly. "And it gives Monk something to do. He would feel neglected if he wasn't doing something."

"You have a remarkable group of men," said the young woman.

Doc bowed politely, suggested, "It is not advisable for you to leave here, since Santini and his crew must know about this headquarters. You can use the telephone and have fresh clothing sent up from a shop. There is an excellent one in the building."

"Thank you."

Doc Savage retired to the library where there was a second telephone—and while Kel Avery called the shop, the bronze man put in a call of his own to the post office officials. Much talk ensued, and he was transferred to several officials before he got full satisfaction.

He had to explain twice what he wanted, and he found it necessary to give the mail officials the number on a small card which he drew from a pocket.

The card which Doc used held the information that he was a fully commissioned postal investigator, and bore the postmaster general's signature. This was one of many honorary commissions which Doc held.

Doc went next to the laboratory, where he switched on a shortwave radio telephone transmitter-and-receiver. This communicated to other shortwave sets in the automobiles used by his aides in their work.

Doc called Johnny, Long Tom, Ham and Renny in rapid succession—but only Johnny answered. The others were evidently interviewing their rich men.

"You have my unadulterated attention, Doc," said big-worded Johnny.

"Listen," said Doc.

Then he spoke rapidly in the Mayan dialect which he used to communicate with his men when conveying secret and important orders.

"Supermalagorgeous," said Johnny when the conversation ended.

Doc went in and joined Kel Avery in the outer room.

"You have arranged for my air mail package to come here?" asked the movie actress.

"It will be here in not more than twenty minutes," Doc replied.

"You took quite a bit of time," the young woman pointed out. "Did you experience any trouble?"

The bronze man seemed on the point of informing her of something unusual about the call he had made to the mail officials, but before the words formed, the outer door opened and Da Clima came stamping in.

"Me, I get two new ones," said Da Clima, and threw back his coat, revealing in his shoulder harness a pair of heavy blue revolvers. "My other two ones, them feller at the airport they get," he added.

"Bought two new revolvers, eh?" Doc said slowly. "They are not easy to purchase here in New York."

"For the feller with the money, anything she easy," grinned Da Clima. "At a hock shop. I get them, and I no need the license for to carry, either."

Monk ambled in shortly, tossed a bundle of newspapers on the inlaid office table, said, "There they are, Doc," as if he had been sent out to get the papers instead of to follow Da Clima. Then he ambled into the laboratory.

Doc joined Monk as soon as he could do so without attracting Da Clima's suspicions.

"The mug went into a hock shop, stayed a while, then came back here," Monk grumbled. "He didn't do nothing else."

"Call the police and tell them to have that pawnbroker's license to do business taken away from him, for selling firearms to unlicensed persons," Doc directed.

Monk nodded. "Any word from Pat?"

"None."

DOC went back into the outer office while Monk used the inside phone to make his call about the pawnbroker who sold guns to unlicensed persons, and who was therefore undoubtedly a source of firearms to the underworld.

The clothing which Kel Avery had ordered came up, and a dressmaker accompanied the garments, ready to make any alterations which might be necessary.

Bedraggled and mud-caked, the light-haired young actress retired to the library, and was out again shortly, the frock having fitted her without changes.

"Now you look again like Maureen Darleen, the movie queen," Monk grinned. "Not that you looked bad before, though."

"Thank you," the young woman smiled, then studied Habeas Corpus. "A remarkable-looking pet pig you have."

"Habeas is quite a guy," Monk admitted. "Speak to the Hollywood heartthrob, Habeas."

"Monk, I think she's a queen," said Habeas.

Entrancing Kel Avery looked somewhat stunned, then realized Monk had used ventriloquism to make the homely pig apparently speak, and burst out laughing. But she sobered very suddenly.

"I'm worried about that other girl—Pat," she said uneasily. "What do you—think—they're doing to her?"

"Probably trying to buffalo her into telling them

where the box your great-granddaddy Dan Thunden sent you can be found," Monk guessed.

"I'll give up that mysterious box in an instant if it will get her freedom," Kel Avery said grimly.

"The mailmen with the box should be here shortly," Doc put in.

Kel Avery eyed the bronze man curiously, then said, "Just as Da Clima came in, you started to tell me something about the call which you made to the air mail officials about their sending my package here. What was it? Or have you changed your mind?"

Doc Savage smiled. "I haven't changed my mind," he said. Then, before continuing, went to the window and looked down from its tremendous height into the street. He was silent a moment as if in thought, then began, "What I was going to tell you—"

He fell silent, then pointed down through the window.

"An armored mail truck is pulling up in front," he said. "It must be bringing your package."

Kel Avery ran over to the window. "You told them to use an armored truck?" she asked.

"Of course."

Then Doc stiffened. The young woman glanced down and also became rigid, while Monk and Da Clima came over quickly, stared, then grew slack-jawed and attentive. The street below was brightly lighted.

"Oh, oh," breathed Kel Avery in a small, horrified voice.

A Uniformed postal carrier carrying a package, had gotten out of the truck and had started for the skyscraper entrance. But at the same time three men had stood erect in an open touring car which was parked nearby.

The men lifted their arms and threw what resembled glass bottles. The containers struck the sidewalk at the feet of the postal men and burst, making wet smears on the concrete. These wet splashes seemed to evaporate with startling suddenness. Bright street lights made this visible.

"Gas!" breathed Monk, the chemist.

The vapor, whatever its nature, was potent, for both postal men collapsed within a few moments. Another carrier, springing out of the truck with a revolver, apparently came under the spell of the gas, for he also went down.

One of the men sprang out of the touring car and ran forward.

"Santini's gang!" Monk groaned. "He's holding his breath. Doc, can't we do something?"

"Quiet!" Doc rapped.

The man far below reached the recumbent postal carriers, stooped and seized the package which one had been carrying. Then he galloped back to the touring car and dived inside. The machine was moving almost as he hit the cushions.

"There goes the package!" gritted Monk.

"Them damn feller, they sure the smart guys!" Da Clima growled, and swung for the door.

"Wait!" Doc barked.

There was a ring of authority to the bronze man's voice that brought the excited Da Clima up and caused him to return, his expression puzzled, to the window, where he peered downward again.

The touring car was rolling more swiftly down the street.

Monk wrenched up the window, roaring, "I can hit 'em with my superfirer pistol!"

"No," Doc told him.

Monk spun around. "Doc, have you gone nuts?" But before the bronze man could possibly make an answer, the homely chemist looked sheepish, then began to grin.

"Doc, you pulled a fast one," he accused. "What was it?"

"Have a look." Doc pointed.

Down in the street, a small undistinguished coupé was darting in and out through traffic in a manner that made it plain to the watchers above that it was following the touring car.

Those in the open car could hardly tell they were trailed, due to the intervening taxicabs and pleasure cars.

"Johnny's coupé!" Monk barked.

"Exactly."

"But how did he—"

"I got him on the shortwave radio at the time I called the postal officials," Doc explained. "Johnny was to follow the mail truck, and if anything came up, he was to use his own judgment."

"This may lead us to Pat," Monk grinned.

"Let us hope."

## Chapter XI
### THE SEIZURE

BUILT into the skyscraper which housed Doc Savage's headquarters, was a special high-speed elevator which gave access, not only to the ornate lobby downstairs, but to a basement garage where the bronze man kept his assortment of cars.

The presence of this garage was known but to few persons outside Doc's immediate circle of five aides.

Kel Avery was made a bit breathless by the terrific speed with which the elevator lowered them to the basement, while Da Clima, who seemed brave enough in the face of everything but speed, paled a little.

"The fast moving, you sure do a lot of heem, no?" he mumbled as they got out in the passage that led to the garage.

"There ain't no crook ever moved fast enough to keep ahead of Doc in the long run," Monk said. "They may outguess him once in a while, but the first thing you know—" Monk finished by making a gesture of catching something imaginary in the air.

Kel Avery put a hand on Doc's arm and asked, "It was about having Johnny trail the truck that you were going to tell me?"

Doc nodded.

She smiled. "I am glad of that, because if you had not told me, it would have shown you did not trust me."

Doc Savage selected a car which Santini or his followers would not be likely to recognize as they would if Doc used the streamlined machine. The machine he entered was a vehicle which resembled an ordinary delivery truck such as is used by small laundries or groceries.

Bulletproof glass and armor plate construction made this virtually a fast tank. The tires were filled with sponge rubber instead of air. The cab portion was fitted with comfortable seats which swiveled before concealed portholes, and there were racks holding superfirer pistols, body armor, gas masks, grenades, canisters of gas and even a small field gun that could be carried by two strong men and which fired a two-inch shell.

"This, she some bus," Da Clima said admiringly.

A sloping ramp let them through the street door, which opened automatically at their approach and closed behind them, actuated by a hidden mechanism.

Doc switched on the shortwave radio telephone and spoke into the mouthpiece.

"Johnny? Johnny?"

"Going north on Broadway," came Johnny's precise voice from the loudspeaker. "So far, there has been no difficulty."

"Have they seen you?" Doc asked.

"Emphatically a negative answered to that," said Johnny, who hated to use a little word where a big one would do.

"He means no," Monk advised Kel Avery.

The young woman was staring at Doc Savage as if fascinated, for sight of the bronze man's remarkable skyscraper establishment had brought home to her the fact that he was no ordinary individual.

"I begin to understand how you get the results which have made you famous," she murmured. "You do not depend alone on your own personal skill and that of your men. You use every scientific device possible in your work."

Doc said nothing, but gave his attention instead to the traffic. He disliked talking about himself.

"Deviating eastward over the bridge to Long Island," came Johnny's scholastic voice from radio.

Long Tom's tones came in over the air waves, following the professorial Johnny's information.

"What's goin' on here?" the electrical wizard demanded.

THE different radio sets used by Doc Savage and his men were all fixed on the same wavelength with crystal devices which prevented changes in frequency. Accordingly, conversation could be carried on much as if they were all hooked to a party telephone line.

Evidently Long Tom had just turned his set on and was puzzled at what he was hearing.

Doc told the electrical expert about the theft of the air mail parcel.

"Head for Long Island," the bronze man directed. "And tell me what information you received when you interviewed your rich man."

There was a pause while the distant Long Tom turned his car in the direction of Long Island, then he began speaking.

"My rich man had flown the coop," he advised.

"Unfortunate," Doc said. "What are the particulars?"

"He got a telephone call a little while before I arrived, according to a maid," Long Tom explained. "He acted excited, grabbed some money out of his private safe, snatched a few clothes and jammed them in a suitcase. He ran out of the door and that's the last they saw of him."

"Sounds as if he were tipped off that you were coming," Doc hazarded.

"You said it."

Shortly afterward, Renny and Ham both reported experiences similar to that of Long Tom. They had not found their men at home, and in both cases, the fellows had fled hurriedly only a few moments before their arrival.

Johnny interrupted to advise. "The men who appropriated that package are now traversing an unpopulated section of beach road."

"Careful," Doc warned him.

"You are cautioning me!" Johnny snorted.

There was silence, except for the noise of traffic and the muffled sounds made by the cars. Johnny reported his position more exactly, and Doc marked his whereabouts on a map of Long Island. The region into which Johnny was following his quarry was one of the most thinly inhabited sections of the Island.

Renny rumbled over the radio, "Doc, it's obvious Santini's gang warned the rich men to skip out, and they did it."

"What puzzles me is what persuaded them to skip so promptly," Ham interjected.

"They probably knew what happened to Thackeray Hutchinson," Doc stated. "The newspapers are on the street with news of his death by

now. Fear of a like fate is enough to urge those wealthy men to do what they were told."

"Santini is sure taking plenty of trouble to keep us from learning what this is all about," Renny boomed. "Brothers, it must be big, whatever is back of this."

A few minutes later, Johnny spoke. He forgot his big words. His voice was a rattle of haste.

"They've stopped their car and are getting out!" he exclaimed. Then he clipped off his exact location. "It's on an old road near the beach."

"It will take us fifteen or twenty minutes to get there," Doc advised. "You've been traveling faster than it seemed."

"I'm going to trail them," Johnny said.

"Do that. And watch your step."

JOHNNY switched off the radio transmitter with a bony forefinger. He had stopped the car after pulling into tall brush where the machine was fairly well hidden, and he did not want the radio speaker to attract attention.

Drawing his handkerchief from a pocket, the gaunt geologist wrapped it carefully around his monocle, then pocketed the padded glass where it was not likely to get broken. This was a habitual precaution with Johnny when he contemplated going into action.

The sand was so soft that it seemed alive under Johnny's feet as he moved forward. There was a brilliant moon which caused the scrawny beach shrubs to cast grotesque shadows. Somewhere a night bird piped, and waves on the beach sounded as if some unseen person was pouring buckets of water upon the sand.

Light from flashlights splattered ahead. Voices muttered; laughter cackled. That would be the quarry.

"The way them mail carriers caved!" a man laughed. "Sweet, I call it!"

"It won't be so sweet if they croak," growled another. "Uncle Sam is a tough monkey to have on your neck."

"Forget it!" he was told. "That gas just made 'em senseless for a while."

They went on and Johnny, hurrying, got close enough that he could hear the *mush-mush* of their feet in the soft sand. If they posted a lookout, he wanted to be close enough to hear the command.

Johnny was puzzled about their destination. This section of beach, low and unhealthy, was not even populated by summer cabins. Taken altogether, it was as remote a spot as could be found in the immediate vicinity of New York City.

"Who the hell's that?" challenged a harsh voice.

"Santa Claus," growled one of the trio who had robbed the mail carriers. "Who'd you think? Is his nibs here?"

"Santini is," said the one who had challenged, apparently, a sentry.

"He'll do."

Johnny, mentally thanking his lucky star that he had been close enough to catch the challenge, circled and evaded the watchman, then continued after the trio. They did not go much farther.

A haze of flickering red appeared, resolved into a camp fire which burned before a tumbledown shed that was open on one side.

Santini appeared in the fire glow, then Hallet and Leaking, the latter still perspiring despite the coolness of the night.

Johnny stared steadily at something in the murk beyond the fire. It stood in the edge of the water, a few yards offshore. Someone threw wood on the fire, and he made out the lines of the thing.

A plane! It was a big ship, massive of hull, with great wing spread and two canvas-swathed radial motors. An amphibian—for the thin geologist could make out the stream-lined humps which harbored the landing wheels, bow cranked up out of the water.

Santini mopped at a small cut on his chin and growled, "That damn Pat Savage is a cat. She kicked me in the face and almost got away!"

That snapped Johnny's attention off the giant seaplane. So they knew Pat was not Kel Avery! How had they learned that? But most important of all, Pat was here!

"We got it," vouchsafed one of the three newcomers.

*"Bueno!"* Santini pocketed the handkerchief with which he had been dabbing at his cut chin, adjusted his sharp mustache points, then extended a hand. "Give me!"

He was handed the parcel which had been taken from the mail men.

The breeze from the sea whipped in briskly, causing the moored seaplane to bob and fine sand to whisper against beach grass and shrubs.

"We will go inside where it is not windy," Santini decided.

The instant they were inside, Johnny started to advance. He wanted to observe the contents of that parcel.

But the bony geologist stopped as if his spine had frozen. And it did feel cold, too, from the chill metal object which had jabbed against the back of his neck.

"Unless you be proof against bullets, you'd bettah stand still," a remarkably youthful voice breathed in Johnny's ear.

## Chapter XII
### THE DISAPPOINTING PARCEL

JOHNNY stood as immobile as he could, for he had recognized the juvenile tone as belonging to white-bearded Dan Thunden, and common sense told him the cold thing against his neck was a gun snout. Hands slapped against his person and the superfirer pistol, his only weapon, was removed.

Johnny wore a bulletproof vest, a fact that Dan Thunden's search disclosed.

"I'll shoot you in the head," advised the boyish-voiced old man.

"So you're still working with them!" Johnny whispered back.

Dan Thunden cursed round, seafaring oaths under his breath.

"I'm wukkin' *on* them, not foah them," he gritted. "I laid aboard the lookout back yondah, and he won't set his sail foah some time to come."

"Then you and I had better work together," Johnny said hopefully, his large words forgotten in the urgency of the situation.

"Old Dan Thunden is wukkin' foah himself," Thunden whispered vehemently. "I didn't know who you was when I met you befoah, but now I know you are one of Doc Savage's outfit. Well, I don't want any paht of you."

"Listen," Johnny began. "What—"

"Belay yoah jaw an' walk up to that shanty," Dan Thunden grated. "We are gonna do some listening."

Johnny, feeling discretion the better part of foolhardiness, since the gun snout was a determined pressure against his neck, ambled forward and stopped against the shack wall. There were wide cracks between the boards which offered orifices for both eye and ear. Burning brightly on the open side of the ramshackle structure, the fire spilled light over the interior, and they could see plainly what went on within.

Johnny's first look gave him a shock. Patricia Savage was not in sight.

Several men besides Santini, Hallet and Leaking were in the shack, among them the killer of the banker, Thackeray Hutchinson, who had masqueraded as an elevator operator.

Santini kicked litter aside on the floor and made a clean place on which he placed the mail parcel.

"We've had fits over this," he said.

Fishing in a watch pocket beside the ribbon that crossed his chest so gaudily, he brought out a penknife with which to cut the tyings on the bundle.

After the string and outer wrapper of paper was removed, Santini lifted a folded square of heavy paper. He opened this. It crackled and fluttered in the breeze that eddied inside the shanty.

*"Veramente!"* Santini exploded. "Indeed! Dan Thunden, the old goat, even sent his great-granddaughter a map showing the island's whereabouts!"

"You are sure it is the island?" asked the man who had killed Thackeray Hutchinson.

"Yes. Here is the island," said Santini, and placed a finger on the map.

Johnny strained his eyes and made out the general location of the island—it was in the Caribbean, some considerable distance from Florida—then Dan Thunden gave his head a push to prevent him from seeing more. But Johnny had fixed in his memory the approximate location of the isle.

Inside the hut there was scuffling sound, a low, stifled cry.

"The damn girl!" snarled Leaking.

"We no longer need her," Santini said callously. "Shoot her!"

The man who had killed Thackeray Hutchinson leered, drew a revolver, spun the cylinder, then growled, "A knife won't make as much noise," and drew a long hunting knife from a sheath sewed to the inside of his vest.

Dan Thunden's gun nudged Johnny's neck.

"Walk," breathed the young-voiced old man. "Quick! Befoah they ha'm mah granddaughtah."

Johnny found himself urged around to the open front of the structure. Dan Thunden was going to use him as a shield—and the fact that he wore a bulletproof vest failed to ease Johnny's mind a great deal.

"I couldn't miss yoah-all from heah," Dan Thunden called from the open end of the hut.

NOT a man inside the ancient building stood still at the unexpected words, for it is human nature to start violently when surprised, an inheritance probably from tree-dwelling ancestors who found it necessary to leap for their lives at sounds of danger.

But only one man was foolish enough to try resistance.

The killer of Thackeray Hutchinson held his knife in hand. He whipped back his arm to throw the blade.

Dan Thunden's gun roared splittingly in Johnny's ear, and its muzzle flame seared his neck.

The knifeman let fall his blade, took two or three bobble-kneed steps, then put both hands over the spot where the top of his skull seemed to be torn off, and dived head-first to the sandy floor. He lay there, a red flood spilling out of the top of his head.

"He's dead," Dan Thunden advised the others meaningly.

Santini jutted his hands up and the others followed his example.

Then Johnny saw Pat Savage. She had been lying against the wall through the cracks of which they had peered, this accounting for the failure to discover her earlier. Ropes bound her arms and ankles and a strip torn from Ham's natty topcoat had been used to gag her.

Dan Thunden gave Johnny a shove. "Get ovah with them, wheah I can watch you!"

Picking up the map which Santini had dropped, the white-haired man hurled it out into the fire. Flames bundled it hungrily and it turned into a black crisp and a curl of yellow smoke.

"I should nevah have sent that to mah great-granddaughtah," Thunden growled. "But I didn't know but that we might find use foah it. I guess all concerned can find the island if need be." He paused to scowl at Johnny. "Except Doc Savage and his scuts, and we don't want them in on it."

With that, he continued unwrapping the package. A box of thin, light wood came into view. It resembled a large cigar box, except that there were no printing or labels on it.

Expression expectant, the young-old man flipped the lid back. He tensed, gulped something unintelligible under his breath. His long-fingered hand dipped into the contents—turning up flakes of greenish-gray leaves.

"This heah ain't it!" he howled suddenly. "This heah stuff is just plain sage!"

So shocked was white-haired Dan Thunden at the discovery that the box contained something other than he had expected, that his attention left his prisoners.

"Look out!" Johnny rapped.

He was too late. Santini leaped. His foot collided with Dan Thunden's gun arm. The weapon spun away.

"Presto!" Santini yelled. "Haste! Grab him!"

Men piled on Dan Thunden. They were met with a whirlwind of blows, a dazzling display of fighting skill. The old man was an amazing acrobat and a fighting cyclone.

Johnny joined the fray by clouting a jaw with a bony fist. He failed to drop his quarry, due to his own haste, and was clouted back for his pains.

A man jumped astride Johnny's bony back, locked legs around his middle and drubbed the back of Johnny's head and neck with hard fists. Johnny fell backward on the fellow. The man who had been hit on the jaw jumped on Johnny's stomach with both feet.

Pat Savage began to flip about, endeavoring to get rid of her bindings. Failing in that, she managed to trip a man who was running at Dan Thunden.

Thunden had felled three assailants with his bare fists. Then Santini danced around behind the old fellow and struck him a terrific blow alongside the ear. Thunden's knees hinged; his eyelids fluttered.

Santini's men took advantage of this weakness. They rushed, swarming over the white-haired man and bearing him down. In a moment he was beaten flat, gripped and held helpless.

Grinning, Santini got up, ran over and kicked

Johnny twice in the head, after which the bony geologist was easily subdued. Santini stepped back and adjusted his ornate mustache. The ribbon across his chest was loose and he carefully fitted it back in place.

"*Bueno!*" he exclaimed. Then his pleasure faded as his eye lighted on the box. He went over and scooped up some of the greenish contents, let the flakes sift through his fingers, then straightened.

"This is not the stuff!" he snarled.

Dan Thunden, straining at the men who held him, growled, "This heah gal must have made a change."

Santini swore.

Pat made unintelligible noises through her gag.

Dan Thunden glared at Pat. "What did you do with the package that I sent you?"

Santini started at that. Dan Thunden had addressed Pat as if she were his great-granddaughter, and this was a surprise to Santini, who had learned in some fashion that Pat was not Kel Avery.

Dan Thunden's mistake was no surprise to Johnny. Had blonde Kel Avery not said that she had never seen her great-grandfather? Old Dan Thunden did not know Kel Avery by sight, and naturally had mistaken Pat for Kel.

Santini took a full breath. It was plain that he was going to advise Dan Thunden of his mistake.

Johnny said loudly, "Miss Avery, don't tell them a thing! Whatever you do, don't tell them a thing!"

Instead of speaking, Santini blinked. His expression showed that he bore half a conviction that Pat was Kel Avery.

"*Mu-m-m-bur-r-r,*" said Pat through her gag.

"Untie her and see what she says!" ordered Santini.

A man started toward Pat, but stopped very suddenly, for Pat had whipped up a gun in her bound hands. It was the weapon which had been kicked from Dan Thunden's hand at the start of the fight, and which Pat had managed to reach without being noticed.

"*Mum-m-m-w-urr-r-a-h,*" said Pat.

It was not hard to understand what she meant, and hands went up.

"EXQUISITE!" breathed Johnny, and sprang to undo the gag and free her wrists.

Pat made hacking noises when the gag was out.

"I came to New York for excitement," she said. "Man, oh man, am I getting it!"

She stood erect, stamping her feet to restore cramped circulation, but keeping the gun level and determined.

"Why did you mail that package?" she asked Dan Thunden sharply.

The white-haired man shrugged. "I was hopin' you would see fit to become mah pahtnah."

"What?" Pat demanded incredulously.

"You see, I needed money," said Dan Thunden. "I was goin' to meet you in Florida and tell you the whole story." He paused to glare at Santini and the others. "But these gentlemen must have got the telegram you sent me tellin' me you would go to Florida. Or did you send such a message?"

"The message was sent," said Pat, evidently deciding she could get more out of him by pretending she was his great-granddaughter.

"I nevah got it," said Dan Thunden. "And that explains why I did not meet you in Florida. Did Santini send a man down theah to—"

Santini suddenly took a long chance. He stood near Dan Thunden at the moment. Leaping, he got behind the white-haired man and shoved with all of his strength.

Dan Thunden was hurled toward Pat. Taken by surprise, and not wishing to shoot the old man, Pat jumped aside. That gave Hallet and Leaking their chance, working with wits almost as deft as Santini's. They sprang quickly forward.

Pat shrilled angrily and fired, but her arm was knocked up and the bullet merely clouted rotten wood out of the ceiling. Santini ran in and got her gun.

Johnny struck Santini in the face. Whirling, Santini put the muzzle of the gun against Johnny's chest and pulled the trigger until the gun was empty.

The reports were deafening in the shack. Johnny was knocked back, spinning, by the force of the slugs. Coat fabric over his chest smoked and dripped sparks. He fell flat on his back and lay there, eyes widely open, all of his gaunt length immobile.

Dan Thunden, still stumbling from the shove which had propelled him at Pat, got his balance and whirled, but saw the odds were against him, for Santini's thugs already had their guns out.

Head down, Dan Thunden plunged outside. A Santini gunman shot at the white-whiskered form flying through the firelight, but Thunden only leaped higher into the air and went the faster, until he was lost in the darkness and the stunted brush of the beach.

Four men, struggling together, held Pat.

"What a life!" Santini gasped.

A MAN ran over to examine Johnny.

"Let him go," snapped Santini. "I shot him many times in the heart."

Leaking swabbed at perspiration running off his face in fast drops.

"Boss, I move we shake the dust of this place," he puffed. "Things are getting too tough. This skinny guy you shot is one of Doc Savage's outfit, and that means hell. This Doc Savage will move the earth to get the guys who rubbed out his pal."

"Only too true," put in Hallet nervously. "Kidnaping that bronze man was one thing. Killing one of his men is another. Savage is a wizard, and the United States is going to be too warm for us."

Pat said, "You birds are just getting wise to yourselves!"

A man slapped her over the mouth. She bit him. The man cursed, lifted a gun.

*"Non!"* yelled Santini. "She is the one who knows where the other box is!"

"But she ain't old Thunden's great-granddaughter!" objected Leaking.

"Maybe we make the mistake and she is Kel Avery," said Santini. "Did you not see the old goat accuse her of making away with the parcel?"

"Maybe," Leaking admitted. "But we got word—"

"Never mind the 'buts,'" Santini rapped.

After that, there was a brief pause during which no one seemed to know what to do next, and it was obvious everyone was thinking desperately.

**Men piled on Dan Thunden. They were met with a whirlwind of blows; a dazzling display of fighting skill.**

Santini's swarthy face lighted. His sharp mustache ends shot up in the air as he grinned. He swung a hand around his head and brought it down on a thigh with a great smack.

*"Bueno!"* he yelled. "Good! Excellent! Wonderful!"

"I hope it is," Leaking said pessimistically.

"It is," Santini laughed. "The one great idea, I have. We will take the plane and go to the island. Doing that, we will be away from this Doc Savage. We will get a supply of—" He stopped and eyed the surrounding night, and did not finish.

"What about the girl?" Leaking questioned.

"We take her along," Santini grinned. "We make her tell where that parcel go to. It may be we do not find the—" He paused again and scowled at the night. "—we do not find what we want on the island, then this box be very valuable indeed."

"Not a bad idea," Leaking admitted.

With that, Pat was hauled, kicking and striking, out to the beach and thrust into the giant seaplane.

"Boss," a man addressed Santini.

*"Si,"* snapped the chief. "What eating you?"

"When we reach this island and find the storeroom, do we get to use the stuff ourselves?" the man asked.

Santini hesitated, shrugged. "Of course. *Si, si.*"

The man who had asked the question expanded visibly and slapped his chest solidly, delightedly.

"I feel like a guy who had just been promised a million," he smirked.

The canvas jackets were wrenched off the motors; self-starters whirred, clanked, and the exhaust stacks spilled sparks, smoke and noise.

With everyone aboard, the plane wallowed away from the beach. Hammering motors put the big craft on step, and it took the air.

INSIDE the tumbledown beach shack, Johnny stirred slightly. He shut his eyes and moaned; several times he sought to arise, and at last succeeded. Propped up shakily, he tore open his coat, vest and shirt.

The bulletproof vest which he wore was of mail, not rigid armor plate. It was a vest designed by Doc Savage for himself and his men to wear continually, and therefore it was light, intended to save them only from an occasional bullet.

Impact of the revolver slugs at close range had stunned Johnny, rendering him helpless, and he had lain there, at no time unconscious, but unable to fight effectively and knowing it.

He had heard all that was said.

Getting up on his feet, he wavered outside, fell down, then got up and propped himself against the shack. There was a roaring in his ears and he coughed a crimson spray, but it was not until the roaring went away slowly that he realized it was the motors of Santini's enormous plane which he had been hearing, and that the craft had seemed to recede to the southward over the Atlantic Ocean.

Johnny peered around, unsteady on his feet, trying to find some trace of Dan Thunden. But there was none, and he was still peering fruitlessly when a fast car made noise on the beach road and headlights waved a white glare.

It was Doc Savage's armored delivery truck, and it stopped nearby. Doc and the others unloaded.

Monk ran up and stared curiously at Johnny.

"Do you know any cuss words?" Johnny asked thickly.

"Hell, yes," Monk said.

"Then cuss some for me," Johnny mumbled, and fell forward on his face.

### Chapter XIII
### FEAR CAY TRAIL

A THOUSAND big, noisy thunderbolts seemed to be making music for Johnny while he sat on a cloud in sepia blackness. The thunder music was steady, and not nice to listen to, nor to feel, either, because one of the cannonading thunderbolts occasionally flew off at a tangent and struck Johnny heavily in the chest, making him feel as if he wanted to open his eyes and jump, except that the cloud which held him up was so soft and comfortable.

Somebody said, "Close the windows. I think Johnny is coming out of it."

Johnny opened his eye—and what he saw showed him that he was not on a cloud, but on a comfortable berth in Doc Savage's largest speedplane.

Monk was closing the windows to shut out the motor noise, which was terrific, the silencers being cut off from the exhausts for greater power efficiency.

Around about were Kel Avery, burly Da Clima, Doc's five men and Doc himself. The plane hit an air bump, jumped a little, then settled level again. Cloud scud scraped past the windows.

"Where are we?" asked Johnny, and was surprised at the strength of his own voice.

"Over the Caribbean," Monk advised.

"What?"

"A good many miles off the southern tip of Florida," Monk elaborated.

"But the last I remember is folding up on that Long Island beach!" Johnny gulped. "How did you find out where Santini went?"

"You talked," Monk assured him. "Maybe you don't remember it. Doc shot some stuff into you to make you rest. You told us a complete story."

Johnny shut his eyes; opened them. "I recall now. It was like a dream. How badly am I hurt?"

"A few cracked ribs," said Monk. "You can navigate all right now, Doc says, unless you jump around too brisk."

"I'll be superamalgamated!" said Johnny.

"Which means he's all right," snorted Ham, who was on a berth opposite, sword cane across his knees. "A sick man couldn't think of such words."

Johnny sat up, found himself fairly steady, then asked, "How long have I been out of the picture?"

"You got slammed night before last," Monk explained.

The bony geologist asked hastily, "Have I missed anything?"

"Not a thing."

"What about the patriarch with the alabaster locks?"

"Dan Thunden?" Monk grunted. "Believe it or not, he hired one of the fastest planes in New York and lit out for this part of the world. A bird named Windy Allen owned the plane and flew it."

"How did you acquire that knowledge?"

"The pilot he hired, Windy Allen, was talkative and told around what a swell wad of coin he was to get for flying the old goat down to the Caribbean. Doc checked up the airports as a matter of routine, and got the dope there. That Windy Allen sure lived up to his name."

Johnny raised higher, leaned over and peered down through gossamer puddles of cloud which were almost blindingly white because of the sun shining upon them. Perhaps a mile below was a finely riffled expanse of ultramarine, a limitless vista of blue that slid away to the horizons in a panorama so vast that it was a bit breath-taking.

"The Caribbean," Johnny said.

"Right."

"Bring me a chart and I'll point out the exact spot that Santini indicated."

Long Tom had retired to the tiny, soundproofed cubicle which held the radio apparatus. He popped into view like a pale jack-in-a-box.

"I just got an S.O.S.!" he barked.

DOC SAVAGE swung back to his side. "Where is it coming from, Long Tom?"

"The bird isn't giving his position," advised the electrical expert. "From the sound of his fist, he's sending the letters as he picks them off a code chart."

The bronze man bent over the instruments and adjusted the dials. The signals from the loudspeaker were very weak, and he turned on more volume. Irregular, hesitant, the dots and dashes whined out of the ether.

"Whoever is sending does not know the code," Doc agreed. "We'll try the directional antenna."

Doc turned a larger knob, and this swung a directional loop aerial mounted in the plane fuselage to the rear of the cabin. Possibly thirty seconds were required to pick the point at which the erratic signals were the loudest.

"Either northwest or southeast of us," he decided.

Kel Avery wrinkled her brow, "But can't you tell nearer—"

"The directional loop only shows the plane of greatest intensity of radio signals," Doc explained. "The sending station is on a line drawn through our present position from the northwest to the southeast, but the only way we can tell the exact direction is to take another bearing when we have gone on a few miles."

Johnny came hobbling back, favoring his injured chest, holding a chart in both bony hands. He pointed.

"The place Santini indicated is southeast of here," he said.

"The radio S.O.S.!" Long Tom barked. "I wonder—" He did not finish.

The radio speaker continued to buzz three dots, three dashes, three dots in monotonous succession.

The signals seemed to grow weaker as the minutes passed.

Doc worked with dividers, rule and pencil on the chart, and some five minutes later, when the great plane had hurtled through almost twenty-five miles of sun-scorched sky, he took a second radio-compass bearing and drew a line. Where this intersected the first bearing, was the location of the wireless appeal for aid.

"Southeast," he announced, and promptly went forward to change the course of the plane.

Johnny had fallen to studying the chart. A puzzled expression overspread his long, studious face.

"I'll be supermalgamated!" he muttered.

"What's eating you?" Renny wanted to know.

"There is no island shown where Santini had his finger on the map," Johnny muttered.

Doc came back from the cockpit, having turned the flying over to the ingenious mechanical robot. Johnny met the bronze man with a look of bewilderment.

"The chart does not show an island, Doc," he advised.

The bronze man considered for a moment, then went on back to the radio cubicle. He switched on the transmitter and alternately sent and received for some time.

"There may be an island, after all," he said at last.

"Huh?" Renny grunted. "But the map—"

"I got in touch by radio with the hydrographic office of the Navy Department," Doc explained. "They looked over old charts of this region for us, and it seems some ancient maps did show the presence of an island."

"Did the island have a name?" Renny asked.

"Fear Cay," Doc said. "It was named that on the old maps."

RETURNED to the wavelength on which the S.O.S. call was being sent, the radio speaker continued to buzz dots and dashes. At no time, however, was anything received other than three dots, three dashes, three dots.

"Queer the guy don't give his position," Monk muttered. "Anybody with gumption would know enough to do that."

Long Tom, after listening intently, glanced around. "That sender cannot be far away," he said.

"How can you tell?" Kel Avery asked curiously.

Long Tom shrugged. "Oh, when you're close to a station, very close that is, there's a noticeable difference. You can almost hear the key close."

Ham laid his sword cane aside, got a pair of binoculars and began to use them through the scattered patches of cloud. A slight quantity of oil from the engines had smeared the windows and he slid one of the panes back in order that he might see better. The motor moan came in with whooping volume.

"Fear Cay!" Ham bawled suddenly.

Everyone in the plane crowded to cabin windows.

Pretty Kel Avery was breathless. She looked even more the cinema star now, for she wore about what a movie director would request his star to affect when making an adventure picture. Her boots, laced breeches and leather blouse were new, but serviceable.

Big, overmuscled Da Clima hulked in the background, his square face slightly purple, as if he were straining mentally, possibly trying to envision what not even Ham's powerful glasses could as yet reveal.

Fear Cay was still miles away. But it seemed to rush toward them, so terrific was the speed of the plane.

Doc went to the pilot's cockpit and tilted the plane downward.

The sea heaved up at them like a bloating green paunch and the cay, climbing out of the haze, took on definite contour.

"I say," Ham pointed out excitedly. "It doesn't look like a place where a boat could land!"

The lawyer was drawing attention to the coral reef around Fear Cay. Such reefs encircling islands of coral formation were a rule rather than an exception, but usually they had one or more openings which gave access to the lagoon within. But there were no apertures in the jagged band around this cay.

Looking down from the height of the plane, the reef resembled a necklace of ugly gray foam, for the waves broke over the coral fangs with smashing violence.

The island itself was low, a bog of mangrove swamp and jungle. Nowhere did it project more than a few yards above the sea.

"Couldn't be seen from a great distance," Renny boomed. "That helps explain why it isn't on the modern charts."

Long Tom jammed his head into the radio box, then hauled it out again.

"That S.O.S. is being sent from Fear Cay!" he barked.

Ham dropped the binoculars and scooped up his sword cane to point.

"Yes, and I think I see where it's being sent from," he shouted. "Look! That wrecked plane!"

THE reef around Fear Cay was a foaming ring of stone, but the isle itself had at most points a wide beach of silver-colored sand, lined with tall royal and coconut palms. The trees bobbed, their bundled fronds contorting, for there seemed to be considerable of a breeze.

The plane lay at the beach edge, half buried in a tangle of mangroves. Both slender wings were wiped off. The wind fluttered fabric around the edge of a great hole which gaped in the fuselage, and the single engine was detached and lay deeper in the mangroves, barely distinguishable.

Ham called, "Doc! See anyone?"

"No," said the bronze man.

"Are we going to land?"

"We are."

Doc banked the plane out over the reef where jade and emerald surf sloshed itself into an ivory suds, then swooped over the lagoon with its kaleidoscopic coloring. The hull touched so lightly that only the braking effect and the appearance of a long foam tail showed them they were down. Whooping motor gusts kicked them inshore.

The royal palms seemingly grew larger, standing up like pillars of silver from the gaudiness of oleanders, jessamine, poinsettia. Gulls and a fork-tailed frigate bird sailed inquiringly about the plane.

The breeze was blowing inshore, and the air above the beach was gray with fine driven coral sand. The palm fronds convulsed steadily, and palmetto leaves trembled to the wind.

Doc cut the motors. The plane was kicked around with its nose into the wind, then sailed backward until the reinforced hull grounded on the beach.

The men unloaded.

"Eyes open!" Doc warned.

They all ran toward the wrecked plane. The wind-blown coral grains gnawed at their naked skin like sleet, and the sun was brazen, merciless with its heat. They waded into palmettos, sank ankle-deep in soft ground, then worked through mangroves.

Doc stopped abruptly and pointed, saying nothing.

"Holy cow!" Renny gulped.

A long, grisly object lay under a bush. He was clad in khaki trousers, boots, a leather blouse, an aviator's helmet. It bore the shape of a man, vaguely, but where face and hands should have been there was only grisly, bare bone.

"A skeleton!" Renny rumbled. "But Doc, it takes years to turn a body into a skeleton! And those clothes are not even weather-beaten!"

Doc Savage advanced, while Monk caught Kel Avery's arm and guided her back so that she would not be unnecessarily upset.

The leather blouse of the thing on the ground was unbuttoned. Only rib bones were beneath. They were bare and white; almost polished.

"A freshly made skeleton," Long Tom decided

aloud. "Now, I ask you, brothers, what do you make of that?"

A brittle silence was his only answer. Doc picked up one of the boots, shook it—and bare white tibia, fibula and metatarsal bones rattled out.

"Whew!" Ham gulped, and his knuckles whitened on his sword cane.

"What d'you make of this?" Long Tom asked.

Doc Savage indicated the skull, after removing the helmet. "The top of the head is caved in, as if it might have been fractured when the plane crashed."

"I'll be superamalgamated!" Johnny murmured. "You maintain this is the pilot of the demolished aircraft?"

Doc did not answer, but arose and studied the tracks around the plane and the marks it had made when wrecked.

"The ship was trying to take off, probably just got into the air, and a number of bullets put the motor out of commission," he said. "The ship is full of bullet holes. Possibly it crashed trying to land!"

Doc came back and searched the leather jacket which had enclosed the bones. He found papers and letters which bore a name.

"This is Windy Allen, old Dan Thunden's flier," he announced.

THE bronze man gave attention to the wrecked plane. Inside, there was a radio transmitter and receiver. Doc removed the metal shields and held a palm on the vacuum tubes on the transmitter side.

"Hot," he said. "That means someone used them for sending, probably up until the time our plane was sighted."

"Who?" asked Renny.

The big-fisted engineer did not put the query with the manner of a man asking a question to which he does not expect an answer. Renny knew Doc's ability as a sign reader.

Doc circled slowly, the flake-gold pools of his eyes seeming a bit more agitated, more refulgent. There were tracks in the soft earth, prints which told the bronze man what had occurred.

He had seen the footprints of Santini, Leaking, Hallet, old Dan Thunden and the others on the south beach of Long Island. All of those prints were here about the wrecked plane.

"The ship seems to have been shot down by Santini and his crowd," Doc announced. "Thunden and his pilot were aboard. Dan Thunden escaped into the jungle, but the pilot got a fractured skull in the crash."

Renny indicated the skeleton. "But what made the pilot like—this? They couldn't have been here more than a few hours? What made him a skeleton so quickly?"

Doc Savage did not reply, and there was a somewhat breathless silence while the others waited hopefully. Then Renny shivered, knowing Doc was not going to commit himself.

"Who used the radio?" the big-fisted engineer persisted.

"Thunden," Doc said.

Renny boomed, "Then the whole crooked crew—Santini, Thunden and everybody—is on this island!"

"Exactly!" Doc said. "And that means it would not be a bad idea to locate Santini's plane."

"How?"

"From the air."

Renny nodded and looked about. Monk and Kel Avery were somewhere back toward the beach. Ham, Johnny, Long Tom and Da Clima had separated, evidently to look over the vicinity.

"We'd better call our gang together and get in the air," Renny decided.

They moved toward the beach, the whisper of wind-blown coral particles increasing, palm fronds a-rattle above, the small gale wailing faintly in the mangroves.

"I wonder if Pat is all right." Renny rumbled, and made flinty blocks out of his massive fists. "Say, if they've done anything to her —" His teeth ground audibly.

They gathered about the plane, prepared to wade out and clamber aboard.

"Look!" Doc said sharply, and pointed.

Down the beach some two hundred yards, a man had popped out of the mangroves. He was a wiry man with white beard that covered his chest like the front of a dress shirt, and a great mane of snowy hair.

"Dan Thunden!" Monk breathed.

Dan Thunden threw out his chest, fashioned a cup around his mouth with his hands and howled into the wind.

"Bomb in your plane!" he yelled.

HAD the bomb gone off at that point, astonishment could not have been more complete. Kel Avery and Doc's five men, all of whom had come running at the call, stood rigidly and stared at Dan Thunden.

Da Clima for once showed a nimble wit. He leaped toward the plane, big feet churning up water and sand. He dived through the cabin door. Doc Savage was on his heels. They raked the plane interior with anxious glances.

Doc worked aft, for there was the most likely hiding place. Da Clima went forward, musclebound shoulders hunched, eyes roving.

"The bomb, how she get in the plane?" he mumbled anxiously. "Every damn minute some of us feller, he watch the plane. Yes."

Doc pounced abruptly. He had discovered a cabin pocket which looked more plump than it had before. His hand delved in gingerly and brought out a bundle of six or eight sticks of dynamite to which was attached a trio of flashlight batteries wired together, a detonating coil, and an alarm clock with a crude set of contacts rigged on the minute hand and the clock face.

Da Clima lumbered up and looked.

"That, meester, she no so funny!" he gulped. "To go off in five minutes, the clock she is fixed, no?"

Doc clambered out of the plane with his explosive prize, carefully adjusted the clock hands to close the contact earlier, then flung the bomb far down the beach. It bounced, rolled close to a royal palm, lay there an instant, then detonated.

Coral sand climbed in a great mushroom. Tiny seashells were mixed with the sand and whistled about like buckshot. The silver bole of the royal palm split, fronds fell out of the top, then the palm upset slowly and majestically. Echoes coughed hollowly then subsided.

Even the whine of the breeze, the hissing of coral sand, seemed to subside. Dan Thunden still stood on the beach two hundred yards away.

Abruptly, down the beach in the opposite direction from there Dan Thunden stood, there was a commotion behind a gum bush. A man stepped out, stood staring at the plane, seeming surprised that it had not been blown into fragments.

The newcomer was Santini, and he was so far away that the red ribbon across his chest seemed small as a scarlet thread.

Doc Savage spoke rapidly in a low voice.

"Monk, Ham, Da Clima and Miss Avery—stay with the plane," he directed. "Johnny, you and Long Tom and Renny get hold of Dan Thunden if you can. He and Santini are fighting each other, and I'd like to know why Thunden won't throw in with us. He warned us and probably saved our plane from that bomb."

Renny rumbled, "What about you, Doc?"

"I'll try to do business with Santini," Doc said grimly.

## Chapter XIV
## THE ISLAND OF DEATH

SANTINI showed scant interest in doing business with the bronze man's party, however. The instant Doc started toward him, the mustached man dived a hand for the coat lapel under which his chest ribbon disappeared, and brought out his ornate automatic. Evidently he no longer carried it under the tails of his coat.

The gun whacked. Powder noise and its echoes cackled among the tall palms. The slug kicked up

sand, went on a hundred yards and kicked sand again.

Monk unlimbered a superfirer pistol and blasted away at Santini. But Santini had dived to cover.

In the opposite direction, Dan Thunden scampered to shelter, white beard flying.

Doc ran in pursuit of Santini. The three men he had designated to chase Thunden—Johnny, Long Tom and Renny—set out.

"Dang it, Doc, don't you want some help?" Monk yelled.

"If anything happens to that plane, we might spend the rest of our lives here!" Doc called, not turning. "You stick there!"

Santini did not shoot again. Tracks showed that he had set out directly across the island. The terrain was higher here, with a growth of crotons, calabash trees, custard apples and even guavas cactus. There was sand and enough grass that Doc could follow Santini's trail without great difficulty.

They crossed a low stretch where mangroves were a tangle, a festering morass populated by hump-backed spiders and land leeches. Then came high ground again and large gnarled silk cotton trees, and farther on, jungle with lianas and grotesque aerial roots entwining.

Santini was following a definite trail, one cleared through the jungle some months ago, judging by the shrubs which had grown up in the path. The swarthy man with the remarkable mustache was evidently running at a head-long pace, for Doc himself was going fast and had not yet sighted Santini.

From the air the island had seemed entirely of coral formation, but it now became apparent, as the terrain lifted sharply, that the central area was of more substantial construction.

The bronze man's casual glances discerned clay-slates, micaceous and talcose schists as well as crystalline and compact limestones, a formation which his knowledge of geology told him constituted what geologists call the Caribbean series.

Doc paused frequently and listened. He could judge Santini's progress now by the occasional outcries of tropical birds. These noises, raucous at best, might have sounded no different to an inexperienced ear, but the bronze man could detect those that were alarmed.

Abruptly, Doc turned aside. Santini had stopped.

A metallic phantom, making no appreciable stir in the jungle, Doc circled until he caught sight of Santini. The man had halted to use his eyes and ears. Santini seemed satisfied that he was not followed. The swell and collapse of his chest, as he sighed his relief, was visible.

Santini went on more slowly, breathing deeply to regain his wind, mopping perspiration.

The breeze made soft noise in the foliage. Gulls going past overhead sailed sidewise in the small gale. Thrushes and banana birds flew through the trees when disturbed, rather than above the foliage where the breeze was stronger.

Voices came from ahead. Doc quickened his pace, then halted to peer through a screen of vines.

Santini had met the lawyer, Hallet. The fat barrister seemed to be nervous, his birdlike mannerisms more pronounced. He had stripped to his undershirt and was fanning himself with a dry palm frond. Two heavy blue revolvers were belted about his middle, cowboy style, the belt loops stuffed with cartridges.

The pair consulted in voices so low that the words did not reach Doc. Then they went on, and the bronze man lost sight of them. He followed their trail.

It was not more than four or five minutes later when weird things began to happen.

A loud cry rasped out, guttural with an awful terror. It was Hallet's voice. And it ended in uncanny fashion, ended suddenly, as if the man who shrieked had been enveloped completely by the horror which had come upon him.

Macabre silence followed. Then birds flew up, calling harshly from all over the jungle, making a frightened bedlam.

DOC SAVAGE glided forward and soon caught sight of Santini.

The swarthy man with the waxed mustaches was backing across an expanse of rock, eyes fixed with hypnotic steadiness upon the stone a few yards distant.

The rock was smooth except for the undulations and tiny cracks made by the weather. There was nothing to show what fascinated Santini.

Doc Savage remained where he was, ears straining, and abruptly he caught a horrible moaning cry, muffled until he could not tell from where it came.

The cry affected Santini in grisly fashion, for he sprang backward as if the sound was that of some voracious beast, invisible in the scalding sunlight, but which was menacing him.

Santini veered to the left abruptly and ran across the expanse of weather-cracked stone. He vanished over a small ridge of rock.

Doc ran forward, swinging so as to pass near where Santini had been when he evidenced such terror. Nothing out of the ordinary came to the attention of the bronze man's eyes.

What had happened to Hallet was a profound mystery.

Doc topped the rocky ridge. He halted so suddenly that his feet skidded a little.

Santini had vanished!

Doc went forward a few yards, flake-gold eyes probing and alert. Then he circled, warily, lest there be a trap. It was too much to believe that Santini had sprinted far enough to get into the jungle beyond the rocky space.

Doc went completely around the rocky area, and nowhere did he find tracks left by the swarthy man who affected the waxed mustache and the scarlet chest ribbon.

Going back to the starting point, the bronze man began a painstaking process of following Santini's trail over the smooth, hard stone. To do this, he employed a small, powerful magnifying glass.

Santini had plunged through a small water puddle at one point, deposited by a recent rain. For the next few yards the trail was clear, wetly defined.

Doc ran ahead, following it. Suddenly, there was a low, dull clanking noise. Down went the slab of rock on which Doc stood!

There was no time to pitch clear. Doc plummeted downward. Eight or ten feet—he judged his fall to be. Great muscles enabled him to land lightly on hard rock.

Scufflings and scratchings came from one side. A terrific blow smashed down on his head. He sank as if struck by a gigantic hammer.

DOC SAVAGE was twisting aside instinctively as the blow landed, and the movement absorbed much of the violence. His head remained clear. On all fours he scuttled to the left, encountered a rough stone wall and stood erect.

Silence fell. Stone grated softly above, probably the stone trapdoor closing more tightly. It must have been made with diabolic exactness, for Doc's sharp gaze had failed to detect it. True, part of his failure to notice the trap could be blamed on Santini's wet tracks, for they had progressed boldly across the slab which had tilted.

The blackness was almost eye-hurting. Doc felt in a pocket, found a coin and tossed it. His opponent failed to fall for the trick. The metallic tinkle echoed and reechoed, indicating a large cavern with many passages.

Doc wore his vest of many padded pockets containing the mechanical devices which he used frequently. They were gems of scientific skill, these gadgets. They had saved his life on many occasions.

A tiny tubular container, hardly as large as a talcum can, came out of the vest. Doc opened it noiselessly, then made several passes through the air. A cloud of fine powder, quite invisible in the intense murk, was wafted in the direction in which he knew his foe to be.

Doc replaced the container, and more slowly, deliberately waiting for the powder to settle, he produced what an observer, had there been one who could see in the dark, would have mistaken for a flashlight. But this had a lens that was so purple as to be almost black.

Doc thumbed the button. The flashlight device was a tiny, powerful projector of ultraviolet rays, the light which is commonly called "black" because the retina of the human eye is not sensitive to them, the beams which cause certain substances, such as ordinary vaseline, to glow with weird colors.

A startling thing happened. The figure of Doc's foe stood out in the darkness, an eerie blue apparition. The floor on which he stood and the contour of a stone wall behind him, was also visible. This was due to the fact that the powder which the bronze man had thrown was one which glowed when exposed to the ultraviolet beams.

The enemy could not see his bronze quarry. He never knew Doc was close to him until metallic fingers closed about his throat, stifling an outcry.

Clutching, Doc got hold of a short rifle with which the man had clubbed that first blow. He wrenched and got the weapon. Then he crushed the fellow down to the floor.

The man struggled and kicked, tried to cry out, but his muscles might have been denuded of life for all the good it did him. Against the bronze giant who held him, the attacker was helpless.

Doc sought and found a certain spot on the back of the fellow's head, low down near its juncture with the top cervical, the chain of small bones which comprised the neck. He exerted pressure in a fashion taught him by his fabulous knowledge of surgery.

The victim promptly became rigid, paralyzed. He would remain helpless and speechless until Doc, or someone with equal skill and knowledge, worked on his neck again, after which he would have nothing more than a bad headache and a stiff neck to show for his experience.

Doc used a conventional flashlight.

The man was one of Santini's thugs. The fellow had been a member of the party which had endeavored to kill Doc and his companions in the car outside the office of Fountain of Youth, Inc., in New York City.

Roving his flash beam, Doc discerned a passage which led to the left and downward. The floor was sandy and showed numerous tracks. The bronze man advanced, following the tracks.

A TWIST at the head of the flashlight caused the beam to narrow until it was no larger than a cigarette, a long white string which roved ceaselessly. The flash was one which operated from a spring generator rather than a battery which might exhaust itself. The generator ran soundlessly.

Details of the cavern became apparent. The underground labyrinth was not the work of human hands, but of the elements. Softer stratas of stone had been worn or dissolved by subterranean waters. At spots there were chambers of considerable size. Again, it was necessary to stoop and even crawl.

But nature had received assistance at some points. On three different occasions Doc's light picked up spots where the passages had been widened by human hands to permit comfortable passage.

A strange odor, not exactly pleasant, soaked the stale air. Doc sampled the tang several times, once stopping for several moments to give his nostrils a chance. The smell was not animal, nor was it of putrefaction. It was vague, baffling.

Discovery of a light ahead caused Doc to forget the aroma for the time being. He doused his own illumination, then glided forward.

The other lights came from electric lanterns— several of them. Doc heard the thump of hammers on stone, and the scraping of shovels.

Santini and a number of his men were gathered in a long, low chamber. Evidently they had not heard Doc's encounter with their fellow at the entrance.

"Stop making noise!" Santini snarled. "*Fermate!* Stop!"

Men who had been tapping the stone walls and shoveling in the sand floor, ceased their efforts.

Santini took a long breath, shuddered and wiped his forehead with a silk handkerchief.

"*Che vergogna!*" he muttered. "What a shame! Our good friend Hallet has met with misfortune."

"Hell!" said a thick-necked fellow, and dropped his shovel. "You mean that Doc Savage got 'im?"

"Worse than that," replied Santini.

"Whatcha mean, worse?"

"There was a trapdoor in the rock of which we knew nothing," explained Santini. "Hallet walked in advance and fell through. He screamed, and I saw what happened to him before the trapdoor closed again." Santini paused to shudder. "*Si, signors*, I saw. It was ghastly! And after the trap closed, I could hear him moan!"

The man with the shovel cursed, then asked, "It was—"

"He is a skeleton by now," affirmed Santini.

DOC SAVAGE advanced a few paces more and stood well within the chamber, but to one side in another passage which led off to the north, or so it felt from the current of air against his neck. The air was strong with the unexplained odor.

The men with the lights and the tools were silent for a time. Evidently they all understood what had happened to Hallet, and were thinking it over. Several looked uneasy.

"It's that damned old Dan Thunden's work!" grated a man.

"Yeah," another agreed. "The old rip! He's sure caused us hell. It mighta been better if we hadn't tried to double-cross 'im in the first place. Givin' him his half split in the racket would've been better than goin' through what we're goin' through."

Santini sighed. "It is spilled milk. How were we to know that old Thunden would steal that package, containing all of the product that we had, and mail it to this relative of his, Kel Avery."

"Kel Avery," a third man grunted. "Damn it! I'm still wonderin' if the girl we've got is really Kel Avery, or that Doc Savage's cousin."

"We shall know the answer to that before long, I promise you," Santini declared.

The men stood in silence, as if not knowing what to do. Doc occupied the interval with thinking over what he had heard. Dan Thunden had once been a partner of Santini's, it seemed, and they had split after a quarrel over Thunden's receiving half the proceeds of whatever nefarious scheme they had underfoot.

"Why *did* old Thunden send the girl the package in the first place?" a man pondered aloud.

"It was undoubtedly his first step in an effort to persuade her to furnish financial backing for his project," said Santini.

"You mean that old white-whiskers intended marketing the stuff himself?"

"*Si,*" Santini nodded. "That is my guess."

"Did you destroy Savage's plane?"

Santini swore round oaths of south Europe. "*Non!* The bomb was in the plane—but Dan Thunden was watching, unknown to me. He jumped out and yelled a warning, and they got the bomb out in time."

The man with the shovel dug savagely into the sand. "But why'd Thunden do that? Is he workin' with Savage now?"

"*Non.*" Santini shook his head. "His is the game of a mastermind. He hopes for Savage and his men to vanquish us. Then he will step in and eliminate Savage."

"Give old Thunden credit," someone muttered. "He's got a brain."

"He oughta have," said another. "He's been around a hundred and thirty-one years. A guy that old oughta have some gray matter."

Again the conversation gave signs of getting nowhere, and Doc Savage decided to try an expedient which he had used on other occasions. The bronze man was a master of mimicry, of voice imitation.

The last man to speak had been on the outskirts of the group, in comparative darkness. Doc set himself to attempt a difficult feat, that of using his skill as a mimic and as a ventriloquist to make it seem that the man had asked a question. Doc wanted to find out just what had happened to Hallet.

Santini interrupted at the wrong instant, saying, "You had best resume the search. We must find Dan Thunden's supply of the material. The old devil has hidden it well."

"You think it's in this mess of caves?" asked someone.

"I'm not certain, but it is likely," Santini replied. "It was in these caves that Dan Thunden dwelled for the ninety-one years since his ship was wrecked here in 1843, and only he alone of the crew reached shore. It is reasonable to think that he would store it here."

"Right at that," somebody agreed.

Doc decided to try his ventriloquism trick.

"What gets me is just how those bodies are turned into skeletons so quickly," he said, assuming the voice of the man on the outskirts of the crowd. "Just how is it done?"

The bronze man got a bad break. From the direction of the entrance, feet pounded. Leaking appeared, a-drip with perspiration, excited.

"Doc Savage is in here!" he howled.

THE instant he heard that, Doc Savage moved silently along the wall, intending to get past Leaking unobserved, if he could.

"How do you know Savage is in here?" Santini roared.

"The guard at the door was laid out!" Leaking barked. "He's paralyzed, or somethin'. Only that bronze guy could've done it!"

Flashlights and electric lanterns which had not been in use by Santini's party, were now turned on. Their glow flooded the confines of the cavern— and outlined Doc's great bronze frame.

Leaking saw Doc. The fellow's pores seemed literally to squirt water as terror struck him.

"There he is!" he squawled.

Guns roared. Lead spaded at the hard stone, knocking off fragments, leaving metallic smears.

Only one avenue of flight was open. Doc took it. Back into the side passage he whipped.

Behind him weapons continued to thunder, the rap of pistols intermingling with the whoop of repeating shotguns. A machine gun let loose a staccato bedlam. Bullets squawled and ricocheted and seemed to pursue Doc like invisible bees.

Doc used his flashlight, for haste was more desirable than concealment. He rounded an angle in the underground channel, vaulted over a slab of stone which had fallen from the roof and slid down a steep slope.

Next came a large room, and beyond that a narrow passage again. Doc scuttled along this for a hundred feet. Then a door barred his way.

The door was of timbers, very solid, and nowhere could be discerned a fastener. Doc threw a shoulder against it. The panel held like Gibraltar, did not as much as squeak under his hammering bulk. He stood still, his flashlight roving the timbers.

A shouting, shooting tumult, the pursuit came closer. It looked very much as if Doc were trapped.

### Chapter XV
### THE NET TRAP

DOC SAVAGE kept his flashlight beam on the door. He had twisted the lens assembly again, making the beam wide and brilliant, and as he stared, he gave the spring wind of the generator another twist, an act which might possibly have been attributed to nervousness. But in no other way did he show that he was in peril of imminent death. His bronze features were composed, inscrutable.

He reached up abruptly and inserted his fingers in a narrow crack at the top of the door. Beyond, barely in reach of his fingertips, he found a small lever. He threw this, and the door came open.

Doc's eyes, sharp beyond the average under ordinary circumstances, had missed nothing in this moment of stress, for he had discerned faint smudges at the top of the door, a sufficient clue.

He pitched through the door and slammed it at his back.

Santini and his men reached the panel, cursing, firing their guns. The lead slugs dug dully at the hardwood, but did not come through.

Doc ran his flashlight beam about in search of fasteners, but they were concealed in the stone wall in such a fashion that he could not get to them without a lengthy search.

Fingers came through in search of the secret catch. Santini and his men obviously knew of it. Doc struck the fingers with a hardened, metal-like fist. A man screamed and the fingers were withdrawn, dripping crimson.

Somebody thrust a machine gun snout through the hole and began to spray bullets methodically. Doc grasped the gun muzzle, pulled, but the weapon was too large to come through. It continued firing, and the barrel soon became too hot to hold. Doc released it.

A second rapidfirer joined the first. Then someone began to fish for the catch with a bent ramrod. Doc clutched the ramrod and jerked it through, getting a scream from the fellow who had his finger hooked in the loop at the rod end.

*"Badate!"* yelled Santini. "Take care, *Signor!* We are getting nowhere this way!"

"I've got a grenade!" a man barked.

*"Come bello!"* Santini squawled, relapsing into his native tongue in his excitement. "How beautiful! *Datemi!* Give me!"

Doc retreated hastily from the door. The grenade would blow down the panel, and it was safer for him to attempt to find an exit.

He was a score of yards down the passage and rounding an angle when he heard the door grate open. They had discovered they could reach the catch, hence had not used the grenade.

Preceded by a storm of angry bullets, Santini and his gang charged in pursuit.

"We've got 'im now!" a man bawled.

"Fool!" grated Santini. "We do not know, but that there may be another exit from this passage."

"Haven't you explored all of this place?" someone demanded.

*"Non,"* said Santini. "On my first visit here, when we found the old man, Dan Thunden, living here, we did not pry into this place. It was not healthy."

Doc crossed a chamber, dived into another underground channel, and a moment later the voices of his pursuers were echoing behind him.

"Didn't old Dan Thunden trust you when you was here the first time?" a man grunted. "Looks like he'd have been so glad to see his first white man in over ninety years that he'd have fallen over himself to show you around!"

Santini said nothing to that except to snarl, *"Presto!* Make haste!"

And Doc Savage, with his pursuers close behind him, came to a sudden stop. His flake-gold eyes, aghast and faintly unbelieving, rested upon the macabre thing before him.

He had come upon a vision to impel horror in the most strong-willed of men.

COMPLETELY forgotten for the moment were the words which the bronze giant had overheard—words which had told him that Dan Thunden had been a castaway upon this island since the wrecking of the schooner of which the man was captain in 1843; and that the first visitors to the island had been Santini's party.

How Santini had arrived at the island remained to be seen, but it was probably by air, for the ugly reef completely around the island was an impassable barrier to any surface vessel.

Wrinkled trousers, a shirt open at the throat, costly shoes now mud-stained, lay on the floor before Doc's eyes. The garments were wrinkled—wrinkled, but not entirely collapsed, for there were bones inside. The skeleton of Hallet, the birdlike lawyer!

That the skeleton had belonged to Hallet was not

to be doubted, for Doc had seen the garments on the living man. The jungle muck on the shoes was still damp, and overhead was the mechanism of the trapdoor which had precipitated the shyster lawyer to his death.

Doc's eyes roved over the floor; his flash beam probed. But there was nothing to indicate the nature of the fantastic fate which had overtaken the bird-mannered barrister. The floor bore no stains, no prints.

There was a minor fracture on Hallet's skull, as if he might have fallen upon his head and been knocked unconscious, or perhaps mortally hurt. But what had turned him into a skeleton remained an unearthly mystery.

A yell pealed behind Doc. Flashlights splattered their beams upon him. Santini and his gang had arrived. A gun bellowed in the cavern, all but rupturing eardrums, and Doc felt the cold snap of the slug past his head.

The bronze man aimed his flashlight beam at the men and it raced an incandescent rod against their eyes. They cursed, blinded.

*"Fate presto!"* Santini yelled. "Make haste! Seize him!"

But Santini did not take the lead and his men showed no desire for a fight at close quarters. There was nothing to prevent them shooting, however. Their guns sounded as loud as cannons in the underground labyrinth.

One man was canny enough to throw up a hand and drag his black hair down over his eyes, serving to shut off some of the glare so that he could tell about where Doc's flashlight lens was. He emptied an automatic. Luck was with him.

A bullet collided with Doc's flash; glass geysered, and the white funnel of the beam collapsed magically.

*"Bueno!"* howled Santini. "Good!"

Doc whirled and glided down the passage. He was handicapped. He had no other light, except the one which utilized ultraviolet rays and the powder which glowed, and that was of no use just now.

Running was difficult, moreover, and slow, since each yard of progress had to be felt out, the subterranean way being full of stony outthrusts which snagged face and limbs at the most unexpected moments.

With his best speed and a reckless disregard of physical pain in smashing into jutting rocks, Doc barely managed to keep ahead of the baying pack at his rear. He covered what seemed to be at least a hundred yards. Side passages were everywhere. This portion of Fear Cay was virtually an underground honeycomb.

The bronze man halted suddenly, his ears alert. Ahead, there was sound.

He listened, and the skin at his nape felt an absurd tendency to crawl in spite of his power of control, for the sound from in front of him was weird, a noise which resembled nothing so much as a great pan of frying fat. It was louder at moments, a crackling and popping such as is heard when an egg is broken into a skillet of hot grease.

Santini and the others heard it, too. They stopped hastily. Strained silence held them for an instant.

"Hell's bells!" a man mumbled.

*"Ascoltate!"* breathed Santini. "Listen!"

"I'm draggin' it outa here!" another wailed in terror.

They fled in abject fear.

DOC SAVAGE stood and listened to the flight of the men who had been stricken with stark terror by the sound that was like grease in a pan on a hot stove. The strange noise came closer as the bronze man delayed, and he could tell that it was close to the cavern floor, as if it might be flowing in the fashion of liquid.

Out of his pocketed vest Doc brought the canister holding the powder. He flung some of the stuff in the direction of the sound. Then he used the ultraviolet projector.

What he saw made him feel as if cold fingers had grabbed at his nape and rimed up through his hair, standing it on end. There was no beast, no monster, nothing of physical size coming toward him.

The cave floor, however, seemed to be alive and undulating as if it were a river. Indeed, some fantastic fluid might have been flowing toward him. The powder, landing on top of such a sinister stream and floating there until it was made phosphorescent by the ultraviolet beams, would have caused such a phenomenon as he saw now. But it was very dark and the eerie sheen of the powder did not reveal details.

Doc backed away. The frying sound seemed to grow louder and the animation on the cavern floor more boisterous. It was as if the incredible menace was angered by his retreat.

The bronze man put on speed in his retreat. Santini and his gang had fled and were not menacing him, so there was no sense in risking his life just to learn the nature of the mystery on the cavern floor.

The crackling and popping was left behind. Whatever made it did not seem capable of traveling swiftly.

Doc found himself wandering through the tangle of underground tunnels. He still retained his sense of direction, but the course over which he had come was blocked by the mysterious horror which flowed on the cavern floor, so there was nothing to do but prowl cautiously in an effort to locate another exit.

Santini and his men were still in the subterranean passage. From time to time Doc heard echoing shouts, the words unintelligible. The sounds were ghostly in the inky darkness.

The bronze man searched through his pockets. And that was a sign that he was worried, for he knew very well that the pockets held no matches. True, there was a pair of tiny bottles holding chemicals which, when exposed to the air and mixed, would burn brilliantly and with great heat, but their light would last for only a moment. It would not be wise to waste them.

Unexpectedly, he saw light ahead, It was the unmistakable glow of the hot tropical sun. Doc ran forward.

There was a rectangular aperture overhead. Perfectly square, it had been evidently hewn out by human hands. A ladder led up to it, a stout ladder that was almost a staircase.

The bronze man was examining the ladder when an excited shout bawled out behind him.

"Here's the bronze guy!" the voice howled.

IT was one of Santini's men. His voice echoes bounced hollowly. Then Santini himself shouted from nearby.

"*Bueno!*" Santini barked. "Do not let him escape!"

Feet scuffled as men ran forward. A gun roared. The bullet chopped at the stone.

Doc leaped for the ladder. Three steps he mounted with dazzling speed, then four. But something happened. There was a grinding. The ladder dropped downward, carrying the bronze man with it.

Too late, Doc realized this was another of the traps which the fantastic underground realm held. There was no time to leap clear.

He fell fifteen or twenty feet, was torn off the ladder by the shock of landing, and slammed down on hard stone. Leaping up, not greatly damaged, he felt around him.

There was only smooth stone, circular, some eight feet in diameter, with no opening as far up as he could reach.

A man threw a flashlight beam into the rock pit from above, and Doc saw that his prison was a well-like cavity capped by a trap on which the ladder had rested. The man with the flash was Leaking.

Leaking mopped at his face, shifted his flashlight to his left hand and used the right to draw a revolver.

"Here's where I fix everything," he snarled, and leveled his weapon.

Santini lunged, knocking at the gun. It roared— and the bullet, deflected, flattened near Doc's feet.

"Wait, *Signor,*" Santini said grimly. "I have the big idea."

"Huh?" growled Leaking.

"We will make this bronze man do a job for us," chuckled Santini. "Ah—great, wonderful, majestic, superb! This idea of mine, she is the swell one."

"It'd better be good," Leaking muttered doubtfully.

## Chapter XVI
### THE TRAIL SINISTER

LEAKING'S gun, in firing the shot which Santini had knocked aside, had made a good deal of noise, and the sound had volleyed through the hole toward which Doc Savage had been climbing when the trick ladder collapsed. The report had carried some distance through the tropical sunlight.

The big-fisted engineer, Renny, heard it. He promptly halted. cupped big hands behind his ears and listened.

"Hey, gang, did you get that?" he rumbled.

"A percussion with the characteristics of a firearm," admitted the gaunt Johnny.

"Let's look into that," snapped Long Tom.

Renny dropped his oversized paws from his ears, started forward, then hesitated.

"Doc set us to hunting old Dan Thunden," he pointed out.

Long Tom shrugged his weak-looking shoulders and said sourly, "A fine lot of luck we've had! The old geezer gave us the slip like a ghost. We're wasting time prowling around here. Let's see what that shot was."

"A recommendation of acumen," said Johnny, and promptly threw his bony frame at the tangled jungle.

Johnny was the freshest of the three, for they had put forth no small effort in endeavoring to overhaul white-bearded Dan Thunden. The heat and the density of the vegetation was a combination to sap vitality. The huge Renny was perspiring and bedraggled, while Long Tom, although far from exhausted, seemed a bit paler than usual.

Johnny's fortitude was remarkable, considering the fact that another man would have been in a hospital from those cracked ribs.

In Johnny's incredibly thin frame there seemed to repose an unlimited resistance to fatigue. Johnny's outstanding physical quality, in fact, was his endurance. He seemed never to get tired.

They came out upon a comparatively level expanse of weathered stone.

"The shot came from about here," said Long Tom.

"I think it was farther on," Renny rumbled.

The electrical wizard shook his head in a violent negative. "It was muffled, as if fired in a hole or something. Let's look around and see if there's a pit or a cave in these rocks."

They advanced, eyes busy. Johnny, lifting his tower of bones on tiptoe, peered around and got himself located.

"I'll be superamalgamated!" he said quietly.

"Eh?" Long Tom queried.

"It was right around here that we last saw Dan Thunden," said Johnny. "The fellow traversed a convolutionary course prior to his evanescence."

"Eh?" said Long Tom. "I didn't get that last."

"He means that Thunden prowled around a lot before he vanished," explained Renny.

"You're going to choke on those words some day," Long Tom warned the bony Johnny.

They continued their search for the source of the shot. As a measure of safety, they carried their small super-machine pistols in their hands and made sure that spare magazine drums, fully loaded with the mercy bullets which produced quick unconsciousness, were handy in coat pockets.

Renny thumped something unintelligible, lifted his machine pistol and sent an ear-splitting bawl of sound over the cay.

Long Tom gulped, "What the—"

"Dan Thunden!" Renny rumbled. "Over there!"

He pointed—and his two companions, looking, saw a thatch of white hair, a snowy beard, an old-young face, vanish behind the thick bole of a coconut palm.

"HE flattened before I could line up that first burst of bullets," Renny growled.

The big-fisted engineer fired again. The machine pistol was charged every third cartridge with a tracer bullet, and a grayish thread seemed to stretch from the muzzle to the distant palm, where a shower of coconuts were kicked down.

Renny corrected his aim, but Dan Thunden had reached more substantial cover.

Forgotten was the investigation of the shot they had heard. The three men raced in pursuit of Dan Thunden.

They crashed headlong into brush, tore at lianas and entwining plants. Knee deep in slime where the ground was low, they kicked and wallowed, knocking off the big land leeches, avoiding the hideous looking spiders.

A cayman, an alligator not much longer than one of Johnny's bony arms, fled madly at the uproar.

For a time, they lost their quarry. Then they saw him peering at them from a tangle of mangroves, and they set out again.

But once more, Dan Thunden distanced them with an ease that was disgusting.

"He must know every inch of this island to get around like that," Renny grumbled.

"The fellow has the agility of an acrobat," complained Johnny.

Then they saw Thunden again. He was leaning from behind an upthrust of coral this time. He ran before they could fire.

Renny and his two companions, following, came near enough to the beach that they could hear the surf grumbling in sea coves of coral out on the reef.

Thunden had vanished once more, but only for a few moments for they saw him a third time, far down the beach, running easily.

"For a lad a hundred and thirty-one years old, he takes the cake," Long Tom snapped, and increased his speed.

Renny stopped, booming, "Wait!"

"What's the idea?" Long Tom pulled up.

"Yes, elucidate," Johnny invited.

"I just got wise to something," Renny rumbled. "Old snowy whiskers is pulling a fast one on us. He is showing himself deliberately, to lead us where he wants us to go."

Johnny absently drew his monocle out, unwrapped it from the protecting handkerchief, saw it was unbroken, then replaced it, seeming at no time to be aware of what he was doing.

"Eminently correct," he admitted. "We are being decoyed."

Long Tom plunged on, calling over his shoulder, "O.K.! Now that we know what he's doing, we'll keep our eyes open. But I'm in favor of giving him a chase."

The other two reached the same decision and ran after the electrical wizard. But they were more cautious now, at times barely trotting. That Dan Thunden was leading them to some spot which he wished them to visit was evident, for he was careful not to let them lose his trail.

"Strange way for him to act," grumbled Renny.

"No stranger than his warning us of that bomb in our plane," Long Tom countered.

Renny nodded. "I'd like to get my hands on him. He'd tell things."

"You said it," Long Tom agreed. "And the first thing he would explain would be just what turned that aviator into a skeleton."

The conversation ended sharply, for Dan Thunden had halted and was making strange gestures with his hands—one finger was to his lips; he patted the air with the other hand.

"Seems to be asking us to be careful," Renny decided aloud.

Dan Thunden now stepped off the beach into the jungle, and did not reappear.

Renny and the other two went forward cautiously, nearing a headland where the mangrove swamp jutted out. Beyond was a jungle-walled cove, with a beach of black manganese instead of white coral sand.

But they did not progress far. From the jungle a revolver bawled. The bullet squawked over their heads and chopped up water out near the reef.

The shot had come from the jungle.

THE three men pitched for the undergrowth, Johnny grimacing a little. The racing about, heedless of his fractured ribs, was beginning to have its effect.

They opened up with their superfirer pistols. The slugs mowed down leaves, splattered against hard palm boles and cut away vines.

A man howled in fright, and they could hear him running away through the tropical labyrinth.

"I recognize that voice," Johnny groaned. "It's one of Santini's gang!"

The agony in the gaunt geologist's voice caused Long Tom to eye him anxiously.

"The ribs?" he queried.

"No," said Johnny.

"That's a dang lie," Long Tom snapped. "You're about played out. Blast it, you oughta be in a hospital yet. Stay behind!"

Johnny obeyed that command as they rushed forward; but not from choice. He was simply too weak to hold up his end of the charge.

They sighted a man fleeing through the growth. He was making for the cove. Renny sighted deliberately. His superfirer moaned.

The runner threw up his arms, tossing a revolver high into the air. Then his head went down and he stumbled, turned a perfect somersault, after which he lay and squirmed with decreasing vigor until, by the time Doc Savage's three aides had reached him, the man was limp and unconscious from the effects of the mercy bullets.

The flesh was torn slightly across his shoulders, but he was not greatly damaged—unless infection set in from the wounds, which was unlikely, since the mercy bullets carried their own antiseptic agent, and even the tracer chemicals were of a type which did not produce infection.

"Let's see where he was goin'!" Renny boomed.

They plunged on, caught the blue wink of sun from water ahead, and came out on the cove beach. Gasoline smell met their nostrils.

"Holy cow!" Renny exploded.

The three of them pitched backward for the shelter of the jungle.

THE cove was a narrow, shallow indentation, and at one end the mangroves grew out into the water.

A plane—Santini's great seaplane—was beached near this point. Green boughs had been cut and spread over the cabin and wings of the plane; others, longer, cut and thrust into the soft black manganese sand around the ship. The result was a perfect job of camouflaging, which explained why they had not sighted the plane from the air.

Under the concealment of wideflung palm fronds near the plane there was a hut, also of green fronds, thatched so that its presence had escaped notice from above.

Three men stood near the hut. Each held a submachine gun. At sight of Doc's men, they began firing.

Renny's superfirer, bawling, sent back a hail of lead. One of the enemy trio went down. The other pair dived behind palm trunks.

The fight which followed was short. Santini's men were at a disadvantage, being outnumbered now, three to two. Nor were they as good marksmen as their foes. They had to plant bullets in vulnerable spots, and that was difficult because of the bulletproof vests which Doc's men wore.

The decisive factor in the fray, however, was the fact that the slightest wound from one of the mercy bullets would put the man who received it out of commission.

As the last of the pair fell from behind his palm tree, squirming with the delirium that preceded the quick stupor of the mercy chemical, Renny darted forward.

Johnny tried to follow, stumbled and went to his knees, grimacing. He tried to get up, but failed.

"I'll be superamalgamated," he gritted. "I seem to have—folded up!"

Big-fisted Renny went back, scooped the bony geologist up easily, and bore him along. They reached the plane under its covering of green limbs and Long Tom, tearing the boughs aside, burst in to inspect the ship.

His feet sloshed through the water; metallic thumps indicated he had stepped upon the floats; a clatter showed he was in the cabin. Then his voice came out hollowly.

"I'm a son of a gun!" he ejaculated.

"What is it?" Renny demanded.

"Come in here and look," the electrical wizard invited.

Renny, carrying the vociferously objecting Johnny, worked to the plane and found Long Tom pointing at the wings, more particularly at elongated punctures which gaped in the thin metal skin of the wings.

"I first noticed the fuel tanks showed empty on the gauges, then looked around for the reason," said Long Tom. "There's the reason."

Renny nodded soberly. The cuts in the wings must have been made by a small ax, or a knife wielded by a strong arm; and they had penetrated the fuel tanks.

**Renny's superfirer ... sent back a hail of lead.**

The strength of the gasoline odor moved Renny to glance down, and he saw in the black manganese sand the tiny pocks made by the dribbling fuel.

They stared at the evidence of vandalism in silence.

A jubilantly youthful voice said, "You gentlemen did a good job theah. But youah work is not done."

The three men knocked down a length of camouflage wall in getting outside. They stared in astonishment.

Dan Thunden stood some fifty yards distant, beside a ridge of ragged gray coral.

Renny snarled, lifted his superfirer.

"Wait!" howled Dan Thunden. "Youah boss, Doc Savage—Santini has gotten hold of him!"

Renny lowered his gun. "What?"

"You had bettah help Savage," called Thunden.

"Just tag along behind me and I'll show you what to do."

Renny yelled, "Wait!" but Thunden bobbed behind the coral ridge and vanished.

The three men started in pursuit, but wrenched up as they heard a stirring in the hut nearby. A feminine voice came out of the shack of green boughs.

"Do I get any attention around here, or not?" it asked.

## Chapter XVII
## TROUBLE UNDERGROUND

"PAT!" Renny howled—and all three men whirled back and dived into the crudely constructed hut.

Patricia Savage sat on the black sand inside, her face flushed and angry. A length of stout piano wire, evidently a spare piece from the plane repair kit, had been fastened securely around her slender waist and the other end spiked to a palm which formed the rear brace of the hut.

Renny lowered Johnny and pounced upon the piano wire. He wrenched at it, but it held. He began twisting it, kinking and unkinking in an endeavor to break it.

"You won't get anywhere that way," Pat advised. "I did that for hours."

Renny nodded and put his huge hands to work on the knots. They were tight, and had evidently been tied with pincers.

"You all right," Long Tom asked Pat.

They could see that she was.

"I'm madder than a tomcat caught in a rat trap," Pat imparted violently. "What was that I heard the old whiskered goat yelling about Doc?"

"Something about Santini having gotten Doc," Renny said grimly.

"Oh!" said Pat, and shuddered.

"I don't believe it," Renny informed her, after freeing one strand of the piano wire. "Doc has never yet been in a jam where he didn't have an ace up his sleeve."

"This Santini is the devil with a red ribbon across his chest," Pat murmured.

"Did they ever find out that you weren't Kel Avery?" Long Tom asked her.

Pat shook a negative with her bronze head. "I wouldn't be here if they had. Man, those fellows are bad! They'd have thrown me out of the plane if they had known who I was. They very near did it anyway."

"They kept you alive in hopes of making you tell them where the contents of that air mail parcel went to?" Long Tom questioned.

"That's why."

"Where did it go to?"

"Do you think I know?" Pat asked sarcastically.

"Ask that other girl—Kel Avery, or Maureen Darleen, or whatever she calls herself."

"You don't seem to like her."

"I don't like anybody who got me into what I've just gone through," said Pat.

Long Tom grinned. "I thought you wanted to be amused by a little excitement."

"This has gone past the amusement stage," Pat said, then grinned back at the electrical wizard. "But I don't mind, much."

Renny gave the piano wire a wrench. It came free and he straightened, advising, "There you are."

Pat jumped up and ran out of the hut. "Come on! Let's see if anything has really happened to Doc!"

Outside, they looked around hopefully. It was Johnny, his eye unaffected by the weakness that came from his shattered ribs, who leveled a pointing arm and declared, "There he is!"

White-haired Dan Thunden had waited. They could see him through the jungle, poised near a convenient palm bole that was bulletproof.

"Hey, you!—c'mere and tell us what this is all about!" Renny roared.

Dan Thunden's answer was a quick disappearance behind the palm.

"For two cents, I'd shoot him full of good hard lead bullets the next time he shows his nose," Long Tom snarled.

"I wouldn't," Pat advised.

"Why not?"

"He's on our side—until we clean up on Santini's outfit."

"Where'd you learn that?"

"From Santini's talk."

THEY set out after the elusive Dan Thunden, holding their anger in check, but vowing vengeance. It was humiliating to be pawns maneuvered about by the old fellow, but they were not so unwise as to fail to realize it was best that they follow him.

At such times as they lost the trail, Dan Thunden showed his white head and made a noise to put them right.

Toward the expanse of rock near the center of the cay, their course led—the same stony area where they had heard the shot which they had as yet no way of knowing had signaled Doc Savage's capture by Santini's crew.

"Did Santini's talk tell you anything else?" Renny asked Pat as they worked through the tangled undergrowth.

"Plenty!" Pat advised.

"What?"

"The most fantastic story you ever heard," Pat explained. "This Dan Thunden was shipwrecked here in 1843, more than ninety years ago, and was the only one from his ship to reach shore. He has lived here since."

"I've still got my doubts about that guy being a hundred and thirty-one years old," Long Tom put in.

"Santini does not seem to doubt it," Pat retorted. "And Santini is nobody's sucker."

"We'll let that ride, then," Renny grunted. "What else did you learn?"

"That Santini found this island by accident," said Pat. "He was flying from South America in a stolen plane. He had gotten into some trouble down there over killing a government official in Venezuela, and he was making for the United States, after leading everyone to believe he was flying south.

"He could not take the usual air routes, or fly over islands where there were settlements and radio, or where he was likely to sight ships. That explains why he happened to come over this out-of-the-way corner. He was having motor trouble and landed."

"Then what?"

"Then the mystery darkens," Pat replied. "They found Dan Thunden—and something else, something worth a great deal of money."

"What?"

"Search me."

Renny came to a full stop in order to eye Pat curiously.

"Do you mean to say you don't know yet what all this fighting is over?" he rumbled.

Pat wrinkled a nose at the big-fisted engineer. "Are you criticizing me?"

"No," said Renny. "But I had high hopes."

"So did I," Pat told him. "I tried to pump Santini, but got precisely nowhere. They were very glad to learn I did not know what was behind the trouble. And I had to be careful not to get them to believing I was not Kel Avery."

Johnny put in, rather weak-voiced: "Santini and his gang came to Fear Cay to get more of the stuff which was supposed to be in that air mail package, but wasn't, didn't they?"

"Right," Pat said, then looked anxiously at the bony geologist.

Johnny had neglected his pet luxury, his big words, and that showed he was suffering. Johnny managed a twisted grin of reassurance.

Pat continued: "Santini's crowd shot down Dan Thunden's plane when it arrived, and killed the pilot. Since then, they've been trying to catch Thunden to make him show them where the thing they're after is hidden."

"Santini—killed—the pilot?" Long Tom asked slowly.

Pat caught the strangeness in the electrical expert's tone said curiously, "Yes. Why?"

"The pilot was a—skeleton—when we found him," said Long Tom.

Pat shuddered. "And that reminds me of another thing. There's some horror on the island of which Santini and his men are in deadly terror. They would not tell me what it is."

RENNY tossed up a beam of an arm and advised, "There's that stretch of bare rock ahead where we heard the shot."

Dan Thunden vanished from sight of them a moment later, and they drew their superfirers and haunted the jungle shrubs as they crept ahead, aware that the strange old-young man's previous disappearance had marked the nearness of danger.

Pat studied the expanse of naked stone, then gasped, "Oh!" softly.

"Eh?" Long Tom eyed her.

"I heard Santini and his men talk about this place," said Pat. "It is honeycombed underground with caves. It was here that old Dan Thunden lived for more than ninety years. Santini and his gang thought the stuff—whatever it is that they are searching for—was hidden here."

There was silence while they peered through a bank of oleander and poinsettia in an effort to locate an opening. But there was no sign of an aperture. They advanced, Renny in the lead.

"Careful," Pat warned. "From Santini's talk, I think this place is a net of traps. Dan Thunden rigged them up as a diversion while he lived here."

"Some idea of a pastime!" Renny snorted.

They continued to go forward, eyes busy on the rocky surface underfoot. There were many cracks, numerous tiny pits, but none of them seemed to be a secret door.

Unexpectedly, Dan Thunden called to them from the jungle.

"Stamp on that square of reddish rock to youah right," he advised. "That'll open the trapdoah!"

Renny hesitated, then swung to the right. A few moments later he was inspecting the panel of faintly rose-colored stone. Then he put his hands in his pockets and teetered thoughtfully on his heels.

Removing the big hands from his pockets, he dropped to his knees and began to feel over the dull vermilion stone.

"The old goat said to stamp on it!" Long Tom snapped.

"Dry up," Renny said, trying to keep his rumbling voice down to a whisper. "I'm going to get even with white whiskers for his little tricks!"

Renny fumbled with the cracks around the stone for a time, then stood up. He stamped.

To Dan Thunden it undoubtedly appeared that Renny was slamming his heel down on the square of red stone, but he was actually kicking a few inches to one side. Renny turned.

"It don't work," he called.

"Try it again, suh!" yelled Dan Thunden.

Renny stamped—again missing the square panel.

"Something has gone wrong!" he shouted. "We'll get over to the other side of the place while you come and open it."

With that, he guided Johnny, Long Tom and Pat away. They stopped some hundred and fifty yards from the stone, turned and saw Dan Thunden scuttling for the rock.

The old man reached the panel and delivered a resounding blow with a heel. The panel promptly flew open, lid fashion.

Dan Thunden howled, "I told you to stamp—"

Then he sank down prone on the stone and seemed to go to sleep.

RENNY and his three companions, reaching the white-haired man, found him snoring loudly, unmoving. The square of red stone was still open. A black cavity was below.

Pat looked puzzled for a moment, then smiled understanding.

"Doc's anaesthetic bulbs!" she exclaimed.

"Good guess," Renny grinned. He indicated the edges of the secret door, where tiny particles of thin glass could be distinguished. "I put some of the bulbs around the slab, and they broke when the lid opened. The gas inside of them produces quick unconsciousness."

Pat drew back instinctively.

"The gas loses its strength in less than a minute," Renny advised her. "It won't overcome us now."

Long Tom, who looked like a physical weakling, stooped and picked up Dan Thunden's frame with manifest ease.

"The old goat wasn't so wise after all," he grinned. "Boy, when he wakes up will his face be red!"

There was a stir in the black void below the secret door. A man cursed, then queried, "What's goin' on out there?"

It was one of Santini's men; he must have heard the noise as the hidden panel opened, and come to investigate. He was canny; they could tell by his voice that he was well back in the subterranean depths, protected from a bullet.

Renny tried a trick, knowing that his voice would sound unnatural to the man below and hoping the fellow would fail to identify it.

"We've got old Dan Thunden," Renny said. "Come up and have a look."

"Yeah," growled the man beneath. "Who're you?"

That stumped Renny; but Pat came to the rescue.

"Tell him Snicker," she breathed. "That's the name of one of the three who were watching me."

"Snicker!" Renny called.

The man in the cavern was silent, still suspicious, and finally said, "C'mon down here where I can get a look at you. I gotta be sure it's you, Snicker."

Renny's long, puritanical face was very sober for an instant, because he knew the Santini gangster would become alarmed before long. Then the gloomy-looking engineer dipped a huge hand into his coat and brought out some of the tiny glass globes which held more of the anaesthetic gas that had vanquished Dan Thunden.

Taking careful aim, Renny lobbed three of the bulbs in quick succession. Hitting and breaking, they made squishing sounds. The gas was colorless, odorless, and victims were always unaware of the effects until it was too late to do anything.

There was a sound as of a bundle of old clothes being dropped, and they knew the man below had collapsed.

AFTER descending a series of steps cut in the native stone, they found their victim—a broad and squat man with a crooked nose and a pitted face—snoring lazily behind an outthrust in the cave wall. They relieved the fellow of a submachine gun and a canvas knapsack containing extra ammunition drums.

Johnny, who had been receiving Renny's assistance in traveling, asked, "What impends now?"

Long Tom, who did not smoke, but who carried a cigarette lighter in lieu of matches, thumbed the tiny flame alight and squinted in the fitful glow which was cast over their surroundings. He noted particularly the rugged nature of the cavern floor.

"This is no place for you, Johnny," he breathed. "The going will be too rough for those ribs of yours."

The thin geologist sighed. "That is regrettably true."

"So you better stick here on guard. You can watch Dan Thunden and this other guy."

"They will be unconscious for at least an hour," Johnny pointed out. Then he groaned slightly and sat down. "But I'll stay here."

"Sure you won't pass out?" Renny asked.

"Positive," Johnny insisted.

They left him there, a form as thin as death itself, crouched above the two men who slept so weirdly. His bony fingers held a superfirer pistol, and handy in his right coat pocket were several of the anaesthetic bulbs.

A man who knew how, could use those bulbs without a mask, simply by holding his breath for the space of almost a minute, during which time the vapor would have its effect on an enemy who breathed it, then dissipate itself. The stuff worked only when taken into the lungs.

Pat whispered, "Careful! Remember, there's something on this cay that can turn a man into a skeleton. Whatever the thing is, Santini and his men are in deadly fear of it."

"We've seen a sample of its work," Long Tom replied quietly, thinking of the skeleton of the aviator which they had found on the beach.

They endeavored to make as little noise as possible. Between the three of them only Renny had a flashlight, one of the instruments which got its current from a self-contained spring generator. The beam of this was played about cautiously.

Once they heard a faint, strange noise from some side avenue of nocturnal murk. Listening, they were puzzled.

"Sounded like fat frying," Long Tom mumbled.

When the sound did not come closer, but continued low and barely audible, as if coming from behind a closed door, they went on.

To avoid becoming lost, they daubed spots of a chemical mixture at intervals. This stuff would glow when exposed to ultraviolet light, and Long Tom, the electrical genius, carried a projector of the "black light" similar to the one which Doc kept on his person. Thus their back trail would be marked plainly if needful.

They were crawling along a sand-floored tunnel, when Renny's huge hand stopped them.

"Get that!" breathed the engineer.

THERE were voices ahead, hollow, the words not understandable. They advanced—and a glow of light appeared. Men stood in a circle around a great metallic figure which lay on the sandy floor of a chamber.

"Doc!" Renny gulped. "They did get him after all!"

Doc Savage was bound with a stout rope woven from plant fibre. Literally hundreds of turns encircled his mighty frame. He resembled a mummy.

Santini and a part of his gang made up the circle of men. They seemed still to fear the bronze giant, securely though he was bound, for they did not venture close. And they were careful to keep their flashlight beams off the bronze man's eyes. There was something about those flake-gold orbs, a hypnotic quality that chilled.

Santini said, "You're probably wondering why we did not shoot you when we had the chance, *Signor* Savage."

Doc said nothing.

Santini scowled. "You were kept alive to do a bit of work for us. *Si!* And if you do it well, we will permit you to live."

Long Tom's machine pistol clicked softly as he threw the safety.

Renny, gripping the electrical expert's arm, breathed, "Let's listen to this first."

They could hear Santini perfectly.

"There is something on this island which is worth many millions of dollars, *Signor* Savage," Santini continued. "It grows here. But we do not know what it looks like when it grows. We only know what it resembles after it is dried and treated. This material is hidden somewhere, and only old Dan Thunden knows of the hiding place.

"When we visited this island the first time, we learned of this thing and arranged with Dan Thunden to sell it to wealthy men who could afford to pay us millions for it. We went to New York and made contact with a number of wealthy men."

"The names in the file at the office of Fountain of Youth, Inc.," Doc suggested, and his powerful voice showed no strain.

"Exactly, *Signor* Savage," Santini agreed. "They were very anxious to buy what we had to sell, and pay a handsome price. It was then that we decided to get rid of Dan Thunden. That might have been a mistake. He found out our intentions and seized a box containing our entire supply of this fabulously valuable substance.

"The old man had very little money, and he hit upon the idea of persuading a relative who had much money—Kel Avery—to finance him in selling the stuff. He sent the box to Kel Avery and arranged a rendezvous in Florida, which we were fortunate enough to apprehend his mail and prevent him keeping.

"We tried to kidnap the girl and get the box, but failed, and she became alarmed and decided to call on you for aid. We tried to seize you before she got to you, and there our troubles really started."

"Why the review?" Doc demanded sharply.

Santini smirked. "Merely a foundation for telling you that we want your aid. We will trade the safety of yourself and your party for your help."

"How can I help you?" Doc asked.

"I know something of your ability," Santini said. "You will notice that we keep our flashlights off your eyes. That is because we happen to know you are a skilled hypnotist. You can hypnotize Dan Thunden and make him tell where this—shall we call it a treasure—is hidden."

"You haven't got Dan Thunden," Doc said dryly.

"We will get him," Santini snapped. "Now!"

The man whirled with his flashlight and started for the exit.

So unexpected was the move that Renny, Long Tom and Pat were caught unprepared. Santini's flashlight illuminated them.

"HOLY cow!" Renny boomed. "We've gotta make a fight of it!"

His superfirer blared. Simultaneously, he pitched into the cavern. Long Tom trod his heels.

**HAM**

**MONK**

## MONK, HAM AND THEIR PRIVATE WAR

They always squabble, these two. To listen to them when they are together, a stranger would think them on the point of slaughtering each other. One would well believe, from the sharp-tongued Ham's talk, that nothing would give him more pleasure than to run the keen sword cane which he carries through Monk's anthropoid form.

Monk and Ham's squabble dates back to the Great War, to an incident which gave Ham his nickname. As a joke, Ham taught Monk some French words which were highly insulting, telling Monk they were the proper things with which to curry the favor of French generals.

Monk tried the words out on a French general, and that worthy promptly had Monk clapped in the guardhouse for several days.

But within the week after Monk's release, Ham was hailed upon a charge of stealing hams from the supplies. Somebody had taken the hams, and Ham's—he was Brig. Gen. Theodore Marley Brooks then—billfold, with his private papers inside, was found upon the scene. A search of Ham's quarters turned up the missing pork.

Ham's agile tongue finally got himself out of the scrape, but not before the whole army knew about it, and had a good laugh.

Somebody stole the hams and planted the evidence. Just who it was, Ham had his suspicions. But he had never been able to prove it, and that still irked him, for the nickname of "Ham" had stuck, and he did not care for the cognomen.

Monk had always been entirely too innocent about those stolen hams.

---

Santini's gang, taken by surprise, reacted variously. One cried out in fright. Another dropped his flashlight. Others drew guns. One fell from Renny's blast of mercy bullets.

It was Santini himself who showed the most presence of mind. He sprang backward and vanished into the gloomy rear of the underground room. It seemed that he had a definite destination.

Long Tom and Renny were both shooting now. They concentrated on the flashlights, the blinding beams of which were a menace. With explosions of glass, bowls from the men who held them, the flashes went out. More men dropped. Confusion grew.

"We've got 'em goin'!" Renny roared, and charged.

Long Tom and Pat followed. Pat carried the submachine gun which they had taken from the man at the entrance, but she did not use it, knowing that it was the way of Doc and his men never to take human life.

Then something happened. There was a rattling at the sides of the room. The sand seemed to come alive, exploding upward.

A net appeared, a mesh woven of stout fibre. It had been buried under the sand, and was being pulled by ropes attached to the sides and hidden in recesses in the walls. The motive force was evidently a great weight sliding in a pit, for they could hear the rumble and jar of its descent.

Renny and the other two were jerked from their feet. The net mesh was large enough to pass their feet and their arms through, and they hung there like fish caught by the gills.

The net trap was cleverly constructed. It hauled them over and slammed them against one wall, holding them there with an inexorable strength.

Renny snarled, and tore at the net. His huge hands did manage to snap two of the strands. He shot down a man who ran toward him.

Then Santini's gang was upon them. Santini appeared from where he had retreated to actuate the trap, howling, *"Non! Non!* There is no need to kill them now!"

Clubbing guns reduced the prisoners to senselessness.

"Go see if they left a watcher at the entrance!" Santini gritted.

## Chapter XVIII
### LOTS OF LUCK—ALL BAD

WILLIAM HARPER LITTLEJOHN was sitting on the top step of the secret entrance when he heard men running through the caverns beneath him, coming closer. Johnny was perspiring and pale, absently fingering his monocle magnifier. He was suffering from his injured chest.

He stood erect hastily. An instant later, he knew it was Santini's men who approached. He grasped some of the anaesthetic bulbs, took his time, then threw them into the blackness below.

Startled curses indicated he had downed at least one man. There was a confab. He could not catch the words. Someone tried to shoot him, but had no luck. Johnny returned a blast from his superfirer for effect.

Had there been only the one exit, Johnny might have held Santini and his men prisoners below for an indefinite period—but there were other openings.

A hundred yards distant, a section of stone flew up. Two men popped out with sawed-off shotguns.

Johnny did the only thing possible—he got up and ran. Grasping Dan Thunden's inert frame, he attempted to carry the white-haired old-young man along.

In Dan Thunden reposed the secret of Fear Cay, and Johnny wanted mightily to get at the bottom of that mystery.

Santini himself put in an appearance and yelled, *"Non! Non!* Do not shoot Thunden!"

Johnny tightened his grip on Thunden, realizing that the presence of the white-headed man meant safety. But the burden slowed his pace amazingly. He staggered. Twice he went entirely down.

It dawned on Johnny that he was never going to escape with his prisoner. So, reluctantly, he dropped the form of Thunden, then sprinted into the jungle. He reached the dense growth, palms and gum trees sheltering him from a storm of lead.

Head down, Johnny ran with a long-legged stride. He was headed for the spot where Doc's plane had landed, and he kept going in that direction. At his back, pursuit was steady, but the enemy did not gain.

Johnny was reeling and nearly out when he came upon Monk and Ham.

The apish Monk was bristling, eager for a fight, his pet pig, Habeas, trailing him. Ham had his sword cane in one hand, his superfirer in the other.

"We heard the shootin'!" Monk grunted. "What's goin' on?"

Johnny waved a bony hand to indicate pursuit, then sank down weakly on the most comfortable-looking spot, an expanse of rank green plants. He sat there while Monk and Ham dashed forward.

"Where's Kel Avery and Da Clima?" he called in a feeble voice.

"Back at the plane," Ham called without stopping.

An instant later there was a bawling of machine pistols, the slamming reports of repeating shotguns and the cackle of automatics. Lead made eerie noises in the jungle. Leaves were cut free and drifted with the breeze. Occasional coconuts dropped noisily. Frightened birds made a great uproar until they had all fled the scene of hostilities.

For perhaps five minutes, the guerrilla warfare continued intermittently. Then Ham and Monk came creeping back through the jungle. They had resumed their perpetual quarrel.

"If you'd throw that sticker away and learn to shoot, we'd have better luck," Monk growled, eyeing Ham's sword cane.

"How could I find anybody to shoot at when you charged around like an elephant and showed them where we were?" Ham snapped. "Nature had sure run out of brains when she got around to equipping you!"

This was a slight exaggeration, considering Monk's reputation as one of the greatest of living chemists.

They reached Johnny, and Monk advised, "There was just a lot of lead-throwing and noise. I don't think anybody was hit. And they beat it. Now, tell us what's happened."

Johnny did not reply. He was on all fours, eyes close to the ground, and he did not look up. He seemed in the grip of some spell.

"What's been going on?" Monk asked Johnny again.

The bony archaeologist and geologist did not lift his eyes. He seemed frozen in his crouching position.

"Hey!" Monk barked anxiously. "What ails you?"

Johnny lifted an arm, beckoned.

"Look at this," he requested, and indicated one of the plants in the bed of which he had been seated.

Monk came over and stared.

"Just a funny-lookin' weed," he snorted.

JOHNNY looked pained, and pointed at the growth of plants.

"Weed!" he sniffed. "Neither of you ever saw flora of that type before."

"So what?" Monk queried.

"Examine the confines of this area of vegetation," Johnny invited.

Monk and Ham complied with that request, and the result was a surprising discovery. The plants which had intrigued Johnny grew in even rows, as if cultivated.

"Somebody's garden patch," Monk grunted.

"This is very strange," Johnny murmured.

"Not half as strange as some other things," Monk said. "For instance, what is it that is making people into skeletons around here? And what is Santini after? C'mon. Let's go back to the plane."

Before leaving the spot where he was seated, Johnny carefully plucked a few shoots of the plants which had so intrigued him and tucked the sprigs inside his hat band where they would not be crumpled.

By the time the men had reached the plane, Johnny had completed a rapid outline of what had occurred. Monk and Ham grinned widely over the news that Dan Thunden had been seized, but scowled darkly at word of the final outcome.

They stood on the white coral beach where the sand stung their faces, and looked about. There was no one in sight.

"Thought you said Da Clima and Kel Avery were here," Johnny suggested.

Monk, his expression suddenly anxious, lifted his voice, "Miss Avery!"

Silence followed.

"Blazes!" Ham muttered, and nervously sheathed and unsheathed his sword cane.

Monk called again. Once more there was no answer.

"Something's happened!" he rapped. "Da Clima and Kel Avery had orders to stick right here!"

A moment later, Habeas Corpus began squealing and grunting off to one side. The three men dived for the spot, Ham using his sword cane to knock aside the jungle vegetation, Monk and Johnny with their machine pistols ready.

"I'll be superamalgamated!" Johnny mumbled, and all three stared at what Habeas had found.

BIG DA CLIMA was piled slackly on his stomach in the leafage, his legs crossed in a grotesque fashion, one arm twisted under his chest, the other flung up and over his head as if to protect it.

His head was askew, the face up, and a crimson rivulet had crawled down out of his hair, trickled on down his face and over neck, to redden his shirt collar.

"Look for Kel!" Ham barked, and sank down to see how badly Da Clima was hurt.

Monk dashed about; Johnny tottered. Both waved their rapidfirer pistols, anxious to find a target, and both had rage-tensed faces. But neither found a sign of the enemy.

When they went back, Ham looked up from his task of kneading Da Clima's wrists, got their disgusted head shakes, then said, "He's coming out of it. There's hardly any bump at all on his head."

Da Clima sat up at last. His manner was remindful of the first time they had seen him back at the New York airport. He blinked, swayed his head from side to side and looked stupid.

"Where's Kel Avery?" Ham snapped.

"Da Clima, how he know?" the overmuscled man mumbled.

"What happened to you?"

Da Clima did not seem quite positive on the subject.

"For you feller, I stand around and listen, yes," he said vaguely. "Then all of a sudden the top of my head, she go *bang!* like the firecracker on the Fourth of July."

"Then what?"

"How do I know?" Da Clima scowled. "The world, she kind of stop for to go around, then."

"Somebody sneaked up behind and kissed your bean with a gun barrel or something, eh?" Monk growled.

"Maybe," Da Clima admitted. "I no see the soul, not a soul."

The big man stood up, glared at his knees which seemed inclined to buckle, then hammered himself upon the chest—weakly at first and erratically, almost missing with his own fist, then more accurately and soundly, so that his great torso gave off hollow boomings.

"Show me the damn feller who is do this to Da Clima!" he roared. "I tear from him the arm and leg, yes!"

"You sure do talk, big boy," Monk growled. "But in action you ain't been so hot."

Da Clima glowered. "What you mean by that? The insult, no?"

Ham put in placatingly, "Don't mind the missing link, Da Clima. He fell out of the nest when he was little."

Da Clima laughed harshly and frowned at Monk. "I might have known this feller he born in a nest in the tree, like the monkey."

Johnny snapped, "Stop it! This is no time for personalities! What are we going to do?"

"Take the plane and try to spot Santini's men," Ham suggested. "Maybe we can locate them before they get Kel Avery to their headquarters."

They ran for the plane, clambered into the cabin, and Monk took the control bucket. He threw starter switches. Nothing happened. They clambered out and investigated.

"Santini's men took the carburetors off the motors!" Ham groaned.

THEY unloaded, held a brief conference, and it was decided to head for the rocky area afoot. Just what they would do when they reached the scene of the underground caverns they were not sure, but each man made a pack of equipment which he thought might be necessary.

Johnny described the location of the expanse of stone, and they concluded the place could be reached more quickly by taking the slightly circuitous route around the beach. They could travel more swiftly, especially Johnny, who was not equal to much more jungle.

"Boy, you're gonna suffer for that crack about me fallin' out of the nest," Monk promised Ham in an undertone as they trotted along the white coral sand.

Ham started some caustic retort, held it back and pointed. "What is that?"

All four men followed his indicating arm. Bits of timber, aged and weather-beaten, projected above the sand close to the jungle.

"An old wreck," Monk snorted, and would have gone on.

"Wait!" Johnny said sharply.

The skeleton-thin geologist and archaeologist went forward, eyed such of the timbers as were above the sand, then kicked about, uncovering others.

It was the frame of a ship—not a large Vessel. The wood had once been carved in elaborate fashion.

"What're we killin' time here for?" Monk demanded impatiently.

Johnny eyed him. "Did you ever see a Roman galley?"

"Blazes, no!" Monk growled. "I'm not two thousand years old."

"This," Johnny indicated the wreckage dramatically, "was once a Roman galley. I am sure of it."

The emphasis which the gaunt scientist put on the declaration was enough to impress the others. They knew from past experience that Johnny was not addicted to excitement without just cause.

"A Roman galley," Monk said slowly. "But how did it get here on this side of the Atlantic?"

"Drifted, perhaps."

"Nix. Ocean currents are wrong for that."

"Then possibly it had sails which were set, and the wind blew it across," said Johnny. "The thing is not impossible. It could have happened. This island is on the outskirts of the Caribbean, and a craft blown across the Atlantic might conceivably have landed here, or been wrecked, as this one was undoubtedly."

Monk nodded. "I still don't see why all the excitement?"

Johnny touched his hat band where the sprigs of weed reposed.

"I have an astounding theory," he said. "But we will go into it later."

"Yes," said Ham. "We've got Kel Avery and the rest to worry about now."

Soon they turned into the jungle. They went as quietly as possible, but banana birds and noisy parakeets were stirred up, while gulls and frigate birds sailed inquiringly overhead.

"Gonna be hard to get close without bein' heard," Monk opined.

The expanse of smooth stone opened before their eyes. The sun was nearing the horizon, but still hot, and the rock was like so much molten substance poured out, still white with its own heat.

Crouched behind a gnarled silk-cotton tree at the edge of the stony area, they used their eyes and small pocket telescopes, but discerned no sign of life. More important, there was no trace of the secret entrances. The flinty surface looked one solid mass.

"Can you find any of the trapdoors?" Ham asked Johnny.

Johnny grimaced doubtfully. "I don't know. I shall try."

They advanced, weapons ready, pausing frequently to sink down and jam ears to the hot stone to listen for sounds from below. The heat waves danced and all but scorched their skins. They were already red with sunburn, their northern tan being little protection against this tropical inferno. But they heard nothing.

Suddenly Da Clima, off to one side, dropped to all fours and pawed at a crack.

"Me, I find the hole!" he gulped.

DA CLIMA wrenched, pounded with the heel of a hand—and so suddenly that they all sprang backward, a lid of stone flew up, exposing a dark gullet that led downward.

Monk extended a hand. "Shake," he smiled.

Da Clima glared at the hairy paw. "What for?"

"I'll take it all back," Monk informed him. "You have finally performed a useful service."

"Ahr-r-r," growled Da Clima, and scrambled down into the black cavity which he had uncovered.

The others unlimbered flashlights which they had brought from the plane, and followed the over-muscled Da Clima. Roughly hewn rock enclosed them so closely that Monk's massive shoulders rubbed and at times he had difficulty in passing. Da Clima's bulk was only slightly less.

The way widened for a time, then narrowed again. They passed a side tunnel. A stout hardwood log, which they tested carefully, bridged a crack that cleft beneath them.

Monk dropped a tiny pebble, counted almost to twenty before it hit water.

"Nice place, this," Monk whispered.

"Pipe down," Ham suggested.

Monk picked up Habeas, who was following them, and carried the big-eared pig tucked under an arm. Habeas was making no sound now. Not for nothing had Monk spent innumerable hours in training the shoat.

Da Clima, first into the depths, was still in the lead, and as they came to a point where it was necessary to get down on all fours and crawl, he went ahead.

*"Ugh!"* Da Clima exploded unexpectedly.

The next instant, his gun emitted a blast that all but ruptured their eardrums. Then the muscular giant scuttled forward, reached a sizable chamber, and reared erect. He plunged on.

"A man, he see me!" he howled. "That guy Santini, I think it was!"

Men shouted ahead. They caught Santini's foreign accent. A gun lashed red flame. They fired back. Their shots were not answered.

"Gonna be tough from now on," Monk growled.

They stood there in darkness, their flashlights extinguished.

"I," said Ham, "have an idea."

THE dapper lawyer could be heard fumbling at the pack which held the stuff they had brought from the plane.

"What is this idea?" Monk whispered.

"We'll use the light-spot cartridges on those birds," Ham said grimly. "That should give them something to think about."

"Boy, you *are* bright," Monk admitted, and dug into his own pack.

Light-spot cartridges was the designation given by Doc Savage's men to a special shell which the bronze man had designed for the superfirer. Doc had created many unusual bullet types for the

remarkable guns, from tracers and mercy slugs to explosives of such power that a single one could knock down a small house.

The light-spot pellets were among the most unique. They were charged with a mixture of ther-mite and magnesium, the exact ingredients known only to the bronze man, and burned with a brilliant white light wherever they struck.

Certain of the ammo drums were charged alter-nately with five light-spot slugs and five mercy bullets, an effective combination. The new drums were fitted and the guns latched into single-fire position.

"Let's go!" Monk growled.

They charged forward. One of Santini's men fired at them.

"Let 'em have the spots!" Monk rapped.

A volley of metallic clicks followed. Utter silence ensued.

"Blazes!" groaned Monk.

"Something's wrong!" Ham grated. "These ammo drums are duds!"

Monk snarled unintelligibly. "I know! When those birds got to the plane, they doctored the bullets—"

He got no further. Santini must have heard their voices.

"Rush them!" he howled.

Feet slammed. A gun glared red lightning. Monk thumbed on his flashlight, then tossed it to the floor where it would furnish illumination for the fight.

The next instant, Santini's men were upon them. There was no shooting now. The Santini gang seemed confident. They swung clubbed guns, fists, kicked and clawed.

A dozen seconds of desperate conflict told Monk and the others that they were outnumbered. They tried to retreat.

Da Clima got the retreat idea first. He popped into the cramped tunnel through which they had just crawled. In some fashion, he seemed to stick there. He began to bawl in terror.

Monk pinched Da Clima, shoved him, but the big fellow did not budge, although Monk's pinches must have been very painful.

"Danged if this mess of meat ain't a jinx!" Monk roared, and gave Da Clima another terrific pinch.

Three Santini followers sprang upon Monk, and three guns bludgeoned together for his head. For Monk, it seemed as if all of the lights went out sud-denly and his surroundings became very still.

## Chapter XIX
## THE WEEDS

MONK'S eyes opened a little, rolled until they were all whites, then slowly assumed normalcy, and he looked at Doc Savage.

The bronze man was some ten feet distant, tied around and around, mummy fashion, with turns of fibre rope. His head and his hands alone projected from his tyings, and cloth had been lashed over his hands so that he could not use his fingers.

Monk tried to move, groaned, "Blast it, I'm paralyzed!" then realized he was tied in much the same fashion as Doc.

"They don't take many chances, do they?" he mumbled.

"Are you all right?" Doc asked.

"His skull is thick," Ham's voice said from somewhere.

Squinting about, Monk saw that Ham lay nearby, bound like himself. Johnny, Long Tom and Renny formed a row along the sandy floor.

Da Clima scowled at Monk and strained against his ropes. He lay just at the edge of the area lighted by an electric lantern.

Pat Savage and Kel Avery were opposite, both tied, and white-bearded Dan Thunden was between them. Thunden seemed to be slumbering yet from the effects of the anaesthetic gas.

They were in a ragged stone chamber. Santini and his men stood about, looking elated.

"It is the big reunion, eh, *signors?*" Santini inquired.

"In your hat," Monk grunted.

Santini laughed jubilantly, came over and stood playfully on Monk's chest, bouncing up and down a little.

Monk rolled abruptly, throwing Santini, and Santini, regaining his feet, kicked Monk in the side with great violence, swearing the while in his native tongue.

Monk showed his teeth and grunted loudly at each impact, like an animal in distress.

"This is the joyful occasion for me," said Santini.

Then he went to Renny and began to kick and abuse him as he had Monk. He treated Long Tom in like fashion, and was standing on Da Clima's massive torso when Dan Thunden rolled over and groaned.

Dropping his diversion, Santini sprang forward and pointed at the white-bearded old-young man.

"This is what I wait for!" he snapped. "Take him somewhere and make him answer our questions!"

Two men picked up Dan Thunden, head and heels.

"Do not go near that door with the secret lock," Santini warned, apparently as an afterthought. "We do not want our friends here to turn into skeletons. Not yet, *signors.*"

The two who carried Dan Thunden started out with their burden, but before they had gone far, Doc Savage spoke. His words were in the guttural, not unmusical tongue of ancient Maya, the language which only the bronze man and his five aides spoke and understood, excepting those in the lost Central American valley to whom the language was native.

"Talk to me in this language," Doc directed in Mayan. "Make them think we're cooking up something."

Santini glared as he heard the unintelligible words, then snarled, *"Non! Non!* Speak so that I understand!"

"Go chase yourself," Monk advised him in Mayan. "Say, Doc, what's the idea of this jabbering? It'll only start him kicking our ribs again."

"I want them to separate us," Doc said in Mayan, "if I can get by myself, I have a scheme to try."

Monk asked in Mayan, "What is it?"

He never got his answer. Santini, sputtering his rage, took the bait.

"Take this bronze man to another room," he ordered. "Two of you watch him! Shoot him at the least suspicion!"

Doc was promptly hauled out.

Monk muttered in Mayan, "I don't see what Doc can do. They've searched him, and he's tied up like nobody's business."

"Losing faith in Doc?" Ham asked sourly.

Monk sighed and lay back. "Brother, he's the only hope we've got."

DOC SAVAGE was carried into a circular recess in the stone, a place from which there was only one egress, and deposited on the sandy floor. The two who had carried him straightened up, puffing, perspiration like a shiny grease on their foreheads.

"The guy weighs a ton," one captor grunted.

"Pipe down!" the other muttered, and planted an electric hand lantern so that its beam bore upon the bronze man.

"That's the idea," said the first. "We've gotta watch 'im."

But Doc Savage did not want them scrutinizing him too closely, and he discouraged their attention by the simple expedient of staring at them intently, lids widened so that the full power of his flake-gold eyes had effect.

"Cut it out!" snarled one of the two captors.

Doc seemed not to hear, and a moment later, the hand lanterns were shifted so that the bronze man did not lie in direct brilliance, nor yet in complete gloom, but in a half light where he could not move appreciably without being observed.

"The guy can hypnotize a feller with them eyes," the more burly of the pair mumbled. "That's what Santini said, anyhow. I ain't takin' no chances myself."

There was no apparent possibility of Doc Savage

gaining his freedom, so securely was he bound. The bronze man's five aides knew something of his remarkable ability, had seen him accomplish the seeming impossible in the past, and even they had been skeptical about his chances. Mixed with the skepticism had been hope, though, for Doc had a way of making the incredible seem simple.

Santini's men had wrenched the heels off Doc's shoes to make sure no gadget was hidden there. The nails which had held the heels projected. The shoes were fitted with modern zipper fasteners instead of time-honored laces.

Moving an imperceptible bit at a time, Doc hooked a heel nail in one zipper ring and stripped it down. He did the same with the other shoe.

From somewhere down the passage that led from the room, Santini's voice ordered, "Come here, you two!"

"You mean us?" called a guard.

"Si, si, you!" snapped Santini's voice.

"But we're watching—"

"Canes!" snarled the voice. "Dogs! He will not escape in the minute I need you!"

The two watchmen walked out of the stone cubicle.

Doc Savage kicked off his shoes. His great frame seemed to turn to rubber, for he doubled backward in the fashion of a skilled contortionist, and his toes found the knots that secured his rope bindings. There were no feet in his socks, merely spatlike straps under the instep, leaving his toes uncovered.

The bronze man's toes took on the prehensile deftness of fingers. In fractional seconds, the knots were untied. He twisted about, working with fabulous speed, but making little noise. He came to his feet.

Down the stone passage, the two guards were peering about in puzzled fashion, for they had not found Santini at the point from which the man's voice had apparently come.

"Boss!" one growled. "Where the deuce did you go?"

There sounded two dull thumps. Both men dropped senseless. Neither was ever exactly sure what had happened, for they did not see or hear the metallic nemesis who loomed abruptly behind them and struck with both fists simultaneously.

Nor did either guard realize at the moment that they were the victims of a skill at voice mimicry and ventriloquism.

Santini had not called. Doc had done that.

DOC went forward and looked into the room which held his five aides, along with Pat, Kel Avery and Da Clima. A number of Santini's men were there, alert and watchful. An attempt to free the captives was sure to mean a fight, noise, an alarm.

From a nearby cavern emanated gruff words, interspersed with angry explosives. That would be Santini questioning old Dan Thunden. Doc made for the sounds.

In addition to Santini, four men were with Thunden. Four ropes had been tied to the white-haired man's wrists and ankles and a man held the end of each rope, pulling backward with all of his strength.

Thunden's fingertips were gory horrors. Santini held a pair of small pliers. Even as Doc sighted the group, the pincers were employed to yank another nail off one of Thunden's fingers.

Thunden moaned, writhed. Crimson crawled from lips into which he sank his own teeth.

"That is all of the fingernails, Signor Thunden," Santini said callously. "It seems that we will have to pull out an eye next. I will do it slowly, so that you can see with the other eye the knife as it cuts the muscles to free the orb from your head."

The recitation of grim details seemed to accomplish what the previous torture had not done.

"What do you want to know?" he groaned.

"I suppose you have no idea?" Santini sneered.

Doc advanced a little to be in a position to better catch the words. His feet, still bare, contacted something. He stooped and felt with sensitive fingers.

It was the packs which his aides, Monk, Ham, Johnny and Da Clima, had brought from the plane. The knapsacks made a little mound. Doc stepped around them and went on a few feet, then stopped.

Dan Thunden said, "The stoahroom, suh, is just inside the wooden doah."

Santini swore. "You mean that we have to take a chance with those—with those—"

"With my little friends, yes," Dan Thunden growled. "And I do hope you have an accident."

"How do we get in there?" Santini demanded.

"Can you walk on stilts?"

"Non!"

"I don't give a hoot how you get in!" Dan Thunden snapped. "I have told you wheah the stoahroom is."

"Just how is it opened?" Santini asked.

"Theah is a black ledge in the rock," said the white haired man. "You jam youah weight against that."

Doc Savage waited to hear no more, but glided backward. He paused to run deft fingers over the packs lying on the floor, and thus managed to locate the one which Monk had borne.

Monk's pack was distinctive because it held a thing without which Monk seldom ventured into action—the apish chemist's amazing portable laboratory which contained chemicals and apparatus for almost every purpose, all nested in a marvelously compact space.

With Monk's pack, Doc raced along the passages.

THE bronze man reached the massive wooden door without incident. He listened, an ear against it. There was no trace of the sound that was like fat frying. His fingers found the secret catch and the timbered panel swung back, grating softly.

Doc's movements in the passage beyond were silent. Monk's pack held a spare flashlight, and he used this. The black ledge which Dan Thunden had mentioned was easily distinguished.

Doc started to plant weight against the dark stone, then hesitated. He drew back and searched for something with which to exert force without getting too near. He was thinking of those many traps which old Dan Thunden had rigged in this strange subterranean place.

Footsteps sounded beyond the door. They were rapid, running. Doc drifted silently into a patch of gloom. A flashlight swayed close.

Leaking appeared, dripping perspiration, his upper lip held between his teeth. There was a desperate expression on his unlovely face, a quivering eagerness in his plump hulk.

Leaking's look showed Doc exactly what was up. Leaking had heard Dan Thunden's words and was bound to inspect the storeroom ahead of Santini. Such action could only mean treachery.

Leaking must intend to double-cross his boss.

The flashlight which the perspiring man carried picked up the black ledge. Leaking's time was evidently short, for he threw his weight against the black ledge. Nothing happened.

The man stood back. In his excitement, he had failed to attach significance to finding the heavy wooden door open. Once more, he plunged against the strip of dark stone.

Mechanism grated. Steel flashed. There was a hollow *glug!*

Leaking reeled, swayed. He seemed to come apart in the middle and fall in a flood of scarlet.

The upper part of his torso fell forward and blocked the slender panel of stone which had opened.

Doc advanced swiftly, not looking at Leaking's body, and examined the unholy mechanism inside the door. It was of hardwood, cleverly made, actuated by a lever on which a heavy weight bore.

Attached to the device was a great, razor-sharp cleaver, roughly fashioned from some iron part of a sailing ship. This was rigged so as to slash outward when pressure was placed upon the black stone.

It was this cleaver which had chopped Leaking in two halves.

Doc Savage still carried Monk's pack. He opened it, using his flashlight. The bronze man knew where every phial of chemical reposed. He drew out bottles, then walked into the storeroom, eyes alert for other grisly traps.

THE storeroom was not large, and the walls were inset with crude shelves. On these reposed jars of baked earthenware.

Doc opened the handiest, dipped in fingers and brought up some of the contents.

The bronze man did not seem surprised at what he saw—leaves, a bilious green in color, dried and carefully packed. The sprigs did not have the color and shape of tea, nor yet of sage.

A botanist would have been intrigued by the leaves, for they were of a type difficult to catalogue. But Doc Savage, who was ordinarily interested by anything new and strange, gave them little attention. He let them fall back, and opened several more of the most convenient containers.

Over the leaves in each jar, he sprinkled a bit of the chemical which he had taken from Monk's portable laboratory.

His departure was as ghostly as his coming, and executed none too soon, for steps could be heard as a number of men came near. They appeared, Santini and some of his followers.

They did not glimpse Doc, for he had concealed himself where they would walk past, leaving him behind them. At sight of the open door, Santini snarled profanely and sprang forward. He discovered Leaking's decapitated form.

*"Che!"* he gulped. "What—what is this—"

Then he burst into a roar of ugly mirth which bent him over and caused him to slap his beribboned chest to regain his breath.

"Leaking is try to pull the crooked deal on us, *si,*" he chortled. "And old Dan Thunden is try the same thing. Leaking is fall into Thunden's trap. *Come bello!* How beautiful!"

They advanced into the storeroom and clutched up the handiest jars, which were those that Doc Savage had opened and sprinkled with chemical.

"At last we have the material," Santini murmured, and waved an arm to take in the other jars. "There is enough of it here to make us all rich men."

A man eyed Santini eagerly. "Boss?"

*"Si."*

"You're going to keep your promise, ain't you?" asked the man. "You said, back on Long Island that night, that we would all be given the weed when we found the storeroom."

Santini hesitated, then nodded. "It is true. Later, you can all—"

The men were bright-eyed with eagerness. There was a near madness in their manner, a strange spell woven by sight of the unusual weed in the jars.

"Now," muttered the spokesman. "Let's sample the stuff. It's supposed to make a guy feel better right off, ain't it?"

Santini nodded. "It is."

"What's the word? Do we sample it now, or not?"

"It must be mixed with water," said Santini. "We will try it at once. All of us."

"That's the idea!" The speaker was almost blubbering his joy, and the others were like him, excited to the point of incoherence.

"The real Fountain of Youth," one gulped.

"You said it," agreed another. "The stuff that makes you live forever!"

## Chapter XX
## THE FOUNTAIN OF YOUTH

SANTINI and his men appeared shortly afterward at the long cavern which held the prisoners, carrying the jars of the weed.

The captives stared at them and seemed puzzled—with one exception.

Johnny, the bony geologist and archaeologist, who also knew a great deal about botany, was the only one of the prisoners who looked as if he had an inkling of what it was all about. But he said nothing for the moment.

"We have found it!" Santini shouted. *"Buena! We shall all live forever, my men, and we will sell enough of the stuff to make us all millionaires!"

Santini retired to a nearby room which had, it seemed, been Dan Thunden's living quarters in the past, and where could be found utensils for mixing the strange leaves, as well as a spring of fresh water.

In the excitement of the moment, the guards forgot their charges. There was little chance of the captives escaping unaided, however.

Laughing, excited, the men crowded to the point where the mixing was in progress, and the room where Renny and the others lay was left unwatched.

"I don't get this a-tall," Monk muttered. "Did you hear what they said? The crazy dopes seem to think they've found something that will give them everlasting life."

Ham made a sudden tongue click of surprise. "I get it now! Fountain of Youth, Inc.! Remember the Fountain of Youth that history says Ponce De Leon hunted for? It was supposed to be somewhere in Florida."

"You've gone as crazy as they have!" Monk snapped.

"The Fountain of Youth could be on this cay," Ham insisted. "Maybe, long ago, the reef was passable and canoes came here. The Fountain of Youth might not be a fountain at all, but that funny-look-

ing weed Santini had. Maybe that plant does bring everlasting life."

"Nuts!" said Monk. "I won't swallow no such scatterbrained ideas. Not much!"

"Stay stupid, then," Ham retorted. "Or have you a better explanation?"

Johnny had been holding his tongue with an apparent effort, and now he spoke.

"Ham is eminently correct," he said.

Monk managed to roll over where he could eye Johnny. "Yeah?"

"Remember the wreckage which we found that bore a pronounced resemblance to structural segments from an ancient Roman galley?" Johnny queried.

"Has that got something to do with this?" Monk asked.

"It has, emphatically," said the big-worded geologist. "That wrecked galley was the clue that made me think of a legend from history which explains the presence of this weed that brings everlasting life—supposedly."

Monk sniffed, "I still maintain that's hooey! There isn't no—"

"Ever hear of Cirene?" Johnny interrupted.

"Cirene?"

"C-i-r-e-n-e." Johnny spelled it out.

Monk assumed a pained expression, his habitual look when thinking. "Was that a city that grew up about the time of old Egypt and Carthage?"

"Right," Johnny nodded vehemently. "Cirene stood on a plateau, and its source of wealth was a fabulous medicinal herb known as silphium. Even the coins of Cirene bore a design of the ruler watching his subjects weigh this remarkable plant.

"Legend gives this herb great powers, claiming it cured every ailment; wounds—even disease. From all over the ancient world ships came for this herb, and it became extremely high-priced.

"The Romans came and put a tax on silphium, an enormous tax. The people of Cirene were enraged and, hating the Romans tremendously, they set about destroying the herb to rid themselves of the high taxes. In time, silphium became extinct.

"Men have searched for some sprigs of it, even a single plant, since that age. Only a year or two ago, there was a newspaper story about an Italian doctor who thought he had discovered silphium again in Cirenaica."

"I don't believe it," Monk grunted.

"It's in the history books, dammit!" rapped Johnny. "Now, it is foolish to think the people of ancient Cirene would destroy a plant so valuable. Perhaps they loaded some on a galley and sent it out for an island or another part of the coast, and the galley got lost and eventually wound up here on Fear Cay."

In his vehemence, Johnny had departed from his big words, and his recitation was the more emphatic.

The others were silent after he finished.

Two of Santini's men came in. Without a word, they picked up big Da Clima and carried him out.

Renny shuddered, rumbled, "They've started their killing!"

"Poor Da Clima," Pat said sorrowfully.

A voice of quiet power came from the murk nearby. "Do not worry too much about Da Clima," it said.

"Doc!" Renny breathed.

The bronze man appeared, admonishing silence, and began untying them.

"I was waiting for them to take Da Clima away," he advised.

Monk grunted, "You figured they'd take him! Why?"

"He is one of them."

Monk's jaw fell down on his barrel of a chest. "Da Clima is working with Santini?"

"He is."

"How long have you known that, Doc?" the homely chemist breathed wonderingly.

"Since Santini was tipped so mysteriously that the air mail package was coming to my office in New York," Doc said. "Only Da Clima had an opportunity to pass that information along."

KEL AVERY, still looking very much the motion picture actress in spite of all that she had been through, overheard Doc's information and seemed deeply shocked.

"When Da Clima came to me in Florida and offered his services as a bodyguard, Santini had sent him!" she gasped.

Doc nodded. He had Renny, Johnny and Monk free of their bonds. He went to work on Pat's ropes. Their situation was dangerous. At any instant, some of Santini's men might return.

"Doc, was I right about that silphium from Cirene theory?" Johnny questioned.

"You were," Doc replied. "I saw the weed, and it is unquestionably the highly medicinal species of silphium."

Johnny glanced triumphantly at the doubter, Monk. But Monk appeared not to have heard, being engaged in making fierce faces and rubbing his huge arms to unlimber muscles.

"Wait'll I get that egg Da Clima!" he gritted. "I knew he was a phony all along. He was responsible for us bein' caught. Pretended to get himself wedged in a hole and blocked our retreat."

All were on their feet now. Doc opened a knapsack and passed out the superfirers which had been taken from his men, and which he had found in the course of his prowling through the stone labyrinth.

Receiving the guns reminded Monk of something else.

"Some of our ammo drums were duds," he growled. "I'll bet Da Clima was responsible for that."

They grouped closely and started an advance. They were, they knew from words they had previously overheard their captors drop, in a dead end of the caverns. To escape, it would be necessary to pass Santini and his men, either by violence, or by stealth.

"There's just one thing that ain't cleared up," Monk said softly. "What's turnin' men into skeletons on this island?"

"Quiet," Doc breathed. "That will have to wait."

"So you know what it is?"

"I saw the things—after a fashion," Doc replied, and did not elaborate that his glimpse had been by use of the powder which glowed under ultraviolet light.

Misfortune walked with them, it developed, for Santini and three of his men appeared, laughing, swabbing at their lips, evidence that they had quaffed of the silphium brew.

Santini emitted a startled bawl. His hands, clawing for his inlaid gun, tore the bright ribbon loose from his chest. He shot as he leaped backward. His bullet, fired hastily, hit no one. Those with him sought cover, one lifting a submachine gun.

Storming lead from the rapidfirer drove Doc and the others to cover. They crouched behind stone bulwarks, and it could not but dawn on them that their position was as dangerous as at any time hitherto.

"Blazes!" Monk mumbled. "Got any of those anaesthetic bulbs, Doc?"

"I could not find them," the bronze man advised. "Santini did not put them with the rest of our weapons."

Santini began yelling again. "*Fate presto!* Make haste! Bring me the bundle containing those glass balls which we took from these *porcos!*"

"Hey, boss, you can hold your breath until the gas loses its punch," said a member of the gang. "Da Clima, here, says to do so."

"We will throw them one at a time," snapped Santini. "Thus we will keep the cloud of gas fresh. They cannot hold their breath forever."

"That, she is the big idea of mine, yes," Da Clima's big voice chimed in. "Da Clima got the good head, no?"

Tense uneasiness gripped Doc's party as they heard the words, for they knew that their enemies had hit on a most effective way of capturing them.

"That damn Da Clima hatched that one," Monk grated. "If I could have one wish before I kick off, it'd be to get that bird in my hands."

"For once, I can agree with you," Ham growled.

Renny boomed, "Doc, I'm in favor of rushing 'em. Let's go out with fireworks!"

"Wait," Doc advised.

"Blazes! Do you think there's another way out?"

"No. We won't even waste time hunting for one."

"Then—"

"Just wait," Doc advised. "Let's see what happens."

DURING the next few moments it seemed that the future held nothing but trouble. Santini and his men fired occasionally to prevent a charge. They were only waiting for the thin-walled glass balls which contained Doc's unusual anaesthetic gas.

Then Santini, in a strained, uneasy voice, said, "Do you feel—queer—*signors*?"

A man cursed. Another groaned.

"That damned weed—" someone began, and did not finish, but fell to coughing and gagging. These sounds of agony decreased in strength, terminating in a thump which might have been a man falling.

Doc and his party waited. Pat stood near enough to Doc that the bronze man could hear her even breathing. Somewhere in the distant reaches of the cavern there was a piping, forlorn squeal.

"Habeas," said Monk. "I'm glad he's all right."

"Come," said Doc, and stepped out boldly.

Monk clutched anxiously for the bronze giant, thinking he was taking unnecessary chances in thrusting himself into the zone of fire. But nothing happened. Gingerly, half expectant of a bullet, Monk followed Doc's example. They were not fired upon, although they stood boldly outlined in the glare from the flashlights of Santini's gang.

"Holy cow!" Renny rumbled, and leaped forward.

They found Santini sprawled upon the stone floor, limp, but still breathing, and the other members of the gang were nearby, all immobile on the sandy floor. Not one of the crew was conscious.

"I've seen lots of unexpected things happen," Monk muttered wonderingly, "but this one comes nearer to magic than the rest. How do you explain it?"

"The silphium tea that they drank," Doc told him.

"Huh? Is the stuff poison?"

"Not that I know of," Doc elaborated. "You see, Monk, I put some powerful narcotic from your chemical laboratory into the handiest containers of the silphium."

"You drugged 'em!" Monk exploded.

"Indirectly," Doc agreed. "Yes."

Kel Avery emitted a sudden piercing shriek. They whirled upon her, startled. She threw back her head and began to laugh, wildly, madly, while tears ran from her eyes. She trembled and beat her hands together.

"She's hysterical, now that it's all over," Monk mumbled, and went over to quiet the young actress as best he could.

"Let's get out of here," suggested Ham.

In single file, the most convenient way of traversing the tortuous passages of the underground network, they worked forward.

"We've still got to find the parts they took off our plane," Long Tom reminded.

"Sure," Renny agreed. "But even if we don't find them, we can repair the fuel tanks in Santini's plane and shift the gas from our ship. Reckon old Dan Thunden punctured Santini's tanks."

Monk stopped suddenly. "Dan Thunden! What became of him? I forgot all about the old goat."

The answer to Monk's query came from no member of the party, but from the stone of Fear Cay itself. The entire cay seemed to jump violently. There was a roar that left their heads aching. A torrent of air, sand and small stone gushed upon them, bowling Long Tom and Johnny off their feet.

"That came from one of the entrances!" Doc rapped.

They ran forward, but did not go far before a whoop of hateful laughter yanked them up. The sound came from a passage to the left, and it was Dan Thunden's old-young voice.

"I've got Santini's grenades," the strange character shrilled. "You just heard me close one entrance, and I'll get the othahs when I open the place up again, theah won't be nothin' of you but bones!"

## Chapter XXI
## THE CRAWLING TERROR

IT was difficult to locate the enraged voice in the hollowly-resounding passages. Doc led the rush for the spot from which it seemed to emanate.

"He was tied up the last I saw of him," the bronze man offered quietly. "He must have gotten loose. He is tremendously strong."

"A living example of how effective this Fountain of Youth is," Ham agreed.

Dan Thunden evidently had a gun—for it roared in the cavern.

Monk grunted loudly and fell down, but heaved up again, grimly silent.

"Are you hurt badly?" Doc demanded.

"My leg," said Monk. "I can still navigate."

Dan Thunden became terrified at their advance and fled. Knowing every cranny of the caverns as he did, he traveled so swiftly that they barely managed to keep within earshot of his footsteps.

"Where's he headin' for?" Renny pondered aloud.

"There's a heavy wooden door which shuts off a part of the cavern," Doc explained. "He seems to be making for that."

"What's behind the door?"

"The things which made that skeleton we found on the beach, and turned Hallet into one like it," Doc replied.

They found the bones of unfortunate Hallet shortly afterward. They were scattered, for some of Santini's gang had evidently given them a kick in passing.

Johnny was weak, and being helped along by Renny. Pat kept close to Doc's side, along with Kel Avery, whose hysteria had subsided magically at the return of danger.

"That old man is dangerous," Pat warned. "If we don't head him off, he'll entomb us in here and turn his pets, or whatever is behind that door, loose on us."

They soon caught sight of Dan Thunden. He had opened the massive door with the secret fastener, and was just passing through. His form towered fully eight feet off the floor.

"He's on stilts!" Long Tom barked. "What d'you think of that!"

"I think he's thinking fast," Doc said grimly. "And we haven't much time. Get that door shut. Let him go, if necessary."

But Thunden had other plans for the door. He spun, facing the glare of their flashlights, and thrust a hand into a coat pocket. Bringing out a small object of metal, he threw it.

A hand grenade! The thing arched toward them. But not far! Doc's hands, as usual, were empty of guns. The only thing he held was a flashlight. He threw that.

Flashlight and grenade met in the air, a little nearer them than Dan Thunden, and almost in the big door. There was a white flash, a roar, and the inevitable rush of air.

Johnny and Renny both upset, as did Pat and Kel Avery. Doc himself was staggered. The door split and the massive timbers made a great noise falling to the floor.

Dan Thunden on his tall stilts was overbalanced. He toppled, tried to balance himself against one stone wall, and in doing so, bore his entire weight on one stilt. The stilt snapped off.

The old man fell squarely on his white-thatched head.

A weird thing happened to the floor about him. Seemingly, it came to life and began to undulate and crowd toward where Thunden lay. In fractional seconds, the rusty-looking floor spread over the prone form, covering it, until Thunden's body resembled only a rugged hump of reddish-black sand. There was a great frying noise.

"Too late to help him!" Doc rapped. "Let's get out of here."

They ran back the way they had been coming, fleeing from the horror on the cavern floor. Not until they had gone scores of yards did they discover that the concussion of the exploding grenades had in spots jarred great rock fragments from the ceiling.

Farther on, the way was entirely blocked.

"Blazes!" Monk muttered, resting his injured leg. "How are we gonna get to Santini's outfit?"

They were not to get to Santini, it developed, for they could not find an opening large enough to crawl through—and behind them grew the sound that was like the gentle popping of hot grease into which an egg had been broken.

They gave up the effort to reach Santini, found an exit, and climbed out into the sunlight.

JOHNNY was the last to leave the cavern. He sat on the lip of the hole through which the others had scrambled, squinting his eyes in the hot evening sunlight, listening to the frying sound below.

"What was that thing we saw?" Kel Avery asked thickly.

"You mean the things that got your great—"

"Yes, the things that covered my great-grandfather, Dan Thunden," said the actress.

*"Carnivorous formicoidea,"* Johnny told her.

Monk glared at him and snapped, "I ain't in a good humor! Use little words for once, will you!"

"Ants," said Johnny. "Flesh-eating ants. Isn't that right Doc?"

The bronze man nodded. "They used one part of the cavern for their colony. That is undoubtedly why Dan Thunden shut it off with that door."

Monk leaned back and sighed, "So it was that simple! And I had visioned a new menace that was threatening mankind."

The voracious ants, literally millions of them, were not a menace to be taken lightly, they discovered in the days following. It was necessary to be always on guard against the carnivorous insects, for they traveled in armies and their bites induced a poison, if suffered in sufficient number, that would render a victim helpless. Woe to the man whom the insects came upon when asleep.

The ants were not, Doc explained repeatedly, of a species new to science.

Their stay at the island was to dig out the entombed Santini and his men. But they found only bones. There had been cracks large enough to admit the voracious ants.

The store of silphium was intact, and Doc, searching, located growing plants on the cay. These were carefully dug up, packed, and made ready for transportation to the United States.

Monk tried out some of the silphium tea on his wounded leg, and the results were remarkable. The puncture began to heal almost at once.

"Boy, we've got something," Monk insisted. "We've cornered the Fountain of Youth!"

Doc did not disillusion him at that moment. The bronze man suspected that old Dan Thunden's longevity was due to perfect health—that, of course, the result of drinking silphium tea—and the fact that Thunden, an exile on the island, had been kept away from the distractions and dissipations of civilization which might undermine health.

That the silphium was only a valuable medicinal herb proved correct, for it was an amazingly efficient antiseptic and tonic, a disease preventative. But they did not learn that until months later, after a number of scientists and doctors had made careful experiments.

In the meantime, things were to happen which caused them to forget all about silphuim, or the Fountain of Youth weed, as they dropped into calling it. Forgotten, also, was the trouble they had met at the hands of Santini and his gang. There came upon them a peril infinitely greater—a menace, not to themselves alone, but to thousands of others.

A naval destroyer in the Brooklyn Navy Yard was about to sail. Suddenly, workmen in the yard threw off their overalls, revealing strange uniforms of silver, uniforms of no known country. They seized the destroyer, and as they sailed her out of the harbor, opened fire upon a certain skyscraper, destroying it. The stolen destroyer went on to sea and was never heard from again.

Who were these men in silver? Why was the skyscraper destroyed, with the death of hundreds of innocent persons? That was what Doc Savage and his crew found themselves striving to learn.

*Death in Silver* was to pitch them into danger such as they had never before encountered, was to throw them against a master of terror beside whom Santini would have been an amateur.

All of that was in the foreground, unsuspected, as Doc and his party got their plane ready to leave Fear Cay. They had found the missing motor parts.

"I just thought of one thing that ain't been cleared up yet," Monk said in sudden excitement as they were loading up.

"What?" Doc questioned.

"The package of silphium that Kel Avery sent by air mail from Florida," explained Monk.

"That is in New York," Doc told him.

"Huh?"

"Remember when I talked to the air mail officials?" Doc countered.

"Sure. But nobody heard you, except the mail people."

"I told them to open the package, take out the real contents, and substitute something which looked similar," Doc said. "They did."

Pat looked at the bronze man and asked, "Do you ever overlook *anything?*"

THE END

# FEAR CAY ON THE AIR by Will Murray

*Here comes...*
*Monk Mayfair, the ape-like chemist.*
*"Blazes!"*
*Ham Brooks, the sword-wielding lawyer.*
*"Take that!"*
*Renny Renwick, the two-fisted engineer.*
*"Holy cow!"*
*Long Tom Roberts, the adventurous electrical*
*genius.*
*"Pipe down, you guys!"*
*Johnny Littlejohn, the fighting archeologist.*
*"I'll be superamalgamated!"*
*And their leader, the greatest adventure hero of*
*the 1930s. The Man of Bronze ... Doc Savage!*
*The Variety Arts Radio Theater, by special*
*arrangement with Condé Nast Publications, presents*
*...The Adventures of Doc Savage! A new series of*
*radio adventures based on the novels by Lester Dent.*
*Today, "Kidnapped." Chapter One of the*
*fantastic story of ...*
*"Fear Key."*

Doc Savage is not usually associated with Old-Time Radio drama the way his older brother, The Shadow, is. The Shadow dominated that medium from 1930 to 1954, becoming a literal symbol of that era of broadcasting.

Yet over the span of 50 years, three distinctly different Doc Savage radio shows were produced.

Lester Dent was behind the first one. He wanted to adapt his own novels chronologically in half-hour serial format, but was forced to compromise. As a result, a series of 15-minute programs originated on the Don Lee California network early in 1934, and was syndicated nationally that fall. Dent scripted the stories, all of which were original adventures and self-contained. Only 26 episodes were broadcast of this obscure early adaptation. No transcriptions are known to survive, and to this day the true identity of the Doc Savage radio cast remains unknown even to broadcast historians.

A decade later, in 1943, New York's WMCA produced *Doc Savage, Man of Bronze.* Based on Street & Smith's *Doc Savage* comic book, it starred Bernard Lenrow as Doc and Earl George as Monk Mulligan (!). Eleanor Audrey played Doc's secretary, Myrtle Rose. A wild reimagining of the pulp Man of Bronze, this Doc Savage battled criminals with a magic ruby

hood he received in Tibet. When he called upon the sacred ruby's power, it literally extinguished evil with its mystic power. Edward Gruskin scripted this incarnation, basing such episodes as "The Skull Man" and "The Living Evil" on his own Doc comic book scripts.

The most recent Doc Savage program remains the most faithful. It aired over National Public Radio in the Autumn of 1985. Unlike its predecessors, which featured original self-contained stories, *The Adventures of Doc Savage* serialized two complete Doc novels in an attempt to recapture the spirit and sensibilities of Lester Dent's exciting works.

Selected to kick off the 13-week series was *Fear Cay* (slightly retitled "Fear Key"), which introduced Doc and his men—and of course Pat Savage—to a new audience.

Roger Rittner of the Los Angeles-based Variety Arts Radio Theatre—and a lifelong Doc Savage fan—was inspired to adapt Doc to radio when he learned that Lester Dent had scripted an earlier program. He wondered if the surviving scripts could be rerecorded with a new cast.

"We're always looking for projects to do for National Public Radio," Rittner said in 1985. "We'd done our *Darkness* macabre and our

THE GREATEST ADVENTURE HERO OF THE 1930s COMES TO RADIO!

Listen for

**THE ADVENTURES OF**

**DOC SAVAGE**

COMING THIS FALL          TO NATIONAL PUBLIC RADIO

Funding provided by
THE TRANSAMERICA LIFE COMPANIES
and local Transamerica Occidental
Life Insurance representatives

Additional support by
EFX SYSTEMS
and
The Corporation for
Public Broadcasting

PRODUCED BY
THE VARIETY ARTS
RADIO THEATRE

**Daniel Chodos provided the voice of Doc Savage in the NPR series.**

*Midnight* mystery series, so I thought doing something that had actually been done before, as well as doing a new version, would be right up our alley. Because that's what we do anyway. We recreate radio the way it sounded back then, except with modern methods for a modern audience."

Discovering that Dent's 1934 scripts were only 15 minutes long, and therefore too short for a contemporary time slot block, Rittner reluctantly abandoned the Dent scripts as his raw material.

"So we just decided why not go back to the source, and serialize the original books," he explained. "As it happened, I had just finished rereading *Fear Cay* for about the fifth time, and it felt right for the kind of shows we do. I thought the story was very strong. And it lent itself to the way we do shows, which is to play them absolutely straight, not camp them up, have fun with them, and produce shows that are a lot of fun to listen to."

Rittner also chose *Fear Cay* because it afforded him an opportunity to include Pat Savage. *The Thousand-Headed Man* was selected for the second serial. An atmospheric lost-city tale to contrast with the high-velocity action of 'Fear Key,' it was one of Dent's favorite Doc Savage adventures. Back in the mid-1930s, it had been slated to kick off a series of Doc films starring TV's "Rifleman," Chuck Connors, that ran afoul of rights issues.

Although the scripts were composed in 1982, production stalled due to an NPR budget crunch. Rittner sought outside funding elsewhere. Underwriting for the retro-experimental show did not come through for more than three years, when The Trans-America Life Companies agreed to fund the project.

"At that point, I went looking among all the people who worked for us at one time or another to cast the show," Rittner recalled. "And we did some disk recordings on different combinations of voices for Doc and his five aides, which worked out quite well. And the rest is history."

Daniel Chodos was cast as Doc Savage. Robert Towers played Monk, Art Dutch voiced Ham, Bill Ratner was Renny, Kimit Muston essayed Johnny, and Scott McKenna had the role of Long Tom Roberts. Pat Savage was voiced by Robin Riker, who had starred in the cult film *Alligator,* and more recently had a recurring role on *Boston Legal.*

"It's a great role," Riker recalled. "This is really a ball. I love doing this radio stuff. And I tell you, Pat is just the best character to do. When you think about it, it's kind of the epitome of the 80s woman—to be adventurous, sexy but strong with the men, and able to know where they stand. I thought of her as what they called, in the 30s and the 40s, a great sport who loved adventure, and doesn't like to sit by and observe. When something happens, she wants to be part of making things right—or righting a wrong. I couldn't stand these films where a woman stands on the sidelines and

**Robin Riker voices Pat Savage.**

The cast of NPR's "Fear Cay" included (from left) Art Dutch as Ham, Robin Riker as Pat Savage, Bill Ratner as Renny, Daniel Chodos as Doc Savage, Robert Towers as Monk, Kimit Muston as Johnny and Scott McKenna as Long Tom.

goes 'Eek!' I never could. Pick up a chair! Hit the person. You can participate here, and maybe make a difference."

Other cast members included Glen Shadix, who played Dan Thunden, Bob Farley doubling as Hallet and DaClima, William Irwin as Shorty, Douglas Coler as Leaking, and Marcia Kramer in the role of Kel Avery. The announcer and narrator was Bobb Lynes.

In addition to scripting "Fear Key," Rittner produced and directed the entire season of *The Adventures of Doc Savage.*

"I tend to write best for radio, of all the things that I write," Rittner revealed. "I'm a good dialogue writer, which of course falls into radio very well. Particularly in directing but also in writing, I tried to make this series sound the way 1940s movie serials looked. I don't want to say there's no depth to them, because I think there's a great deal of depth to them, but our emphasis was always on action. Not letting too long a period go by when something doesn't happen. Oddly enough, Dent's writing style fell just perfectly into a half-hour format. Each half hour as it went through the books, seemed to build nicely. There was a little bit of exposition at points that built up to a nice climax at the end of each chapter. Without too much screwing around, I think we adapted *Fear Cay* fairly religiously in terms of the plot and the characters."

Rittner had other inspirations as well. "I happen to be a fan of 1940s action movie serials. Right before we started 'Fear Key,' I sat down and watched *Captain Marvel* all the way through—all 12 chapters. In a sense, I used the structure of those—particularly those fight scenes—for the fight scenes in 'Fear Key.' A fight scene too short isn't satisfying. A fight scene too long gets boring. So you have to find just that right length for a fight to go where you establish the fact that it's happened. but psychologically, you don't start boring people."

Rittner did not ignore Old-Time Radio drama inspirations. "If I had to pick an old radio model for *Fear Cay,* I guess it would probably be *Terry and the Pirates.*"

Ironically—since Rittner had no knowledge of it at the time—Lester Dent had attempted to market a Doc Savage radio serial modeled after that same program in 1939, but without success. Dent had chosen to adapt *The Polar Treasure.*

*The Adventures of Doc Savage* was recorded at EFX Systems' studios in Burbank, California, over the summer of 1985. It premiered in late September,

**The cast and crew of NPR's 1985 *Doc Savage* series**

airing first on NPR station KBBI in Homer, Alaska, then nationwide in virtually all 50 states in the 8 p.m. Monday night time slot as part of the NPR Playhouse umbrella series.

In seven installments, "Fear Key" ran three and a half hours. Ironically, this was exactly the format Lester Dent had attempted to get off the ground 50 years previously. But Dent in his wildest imaginings, never envisioned a radio broadcast that would be transmitted by satellite feed to participating radio stations.

A mixture of vintage and modern electronic sound-effects technology was also employed to bring the series to life.

"I always like to put one stereo effect in the beginning of every show I do," Rittner related. "A good example is the opening chapter of 'Fear Key.' We blocked it in the studio. The policeman who's talking to Doc Savage walks across. And you can hear him do that. That's about the extent to which we go for effecty things. We do that just to give those people who are looking for an effect, we satisfy them. So then we can sit back and concentrate on the story.

"The Doc Savage stories are filled with gimmicks and gadgets that you can't find on a sound effects record, like the supermachine pistols and the carnivorous ants in 'Fear Key.' They are really effecty effects. It's something you go out of your way to create, which we did. Our sound effects guy came up with a supermachine pistol effect that I thought was just terrific. It sounded exactly like what we wanted it to sound like."

"I had no idea what it was supposed to sound like," sound-effects artist David Surtees explained. "Except it was deep-throated. It was just one of the tom-toms from my drum set, with a heavy piece of paper laid on the head. And then a towel over that.

The paper gave me more of a crisp noise. Then I muffled it on top of that to try to hide the drum sound. And just did a single-stroke roll."

"When it came to the ants, obviously that's not on a sound-effect record anywhere," Rittner continues. "Oddly enough, Dent keys all of those effects in the books he writes. At one point, Long Tom suggests that the ants sound like bacon frying. Well, that's exactly what I used. I went to a track of bacon frying. I sweetened it a little. And I actually added a musical track behind it so that along with this augmented bacon-frying sound, you get a high-pitched violin, which lends an eerie quality to it."

The most challenging aspect was recreating Doc's signature trilling sound, as Rittner explained to host Bobb Lynes over KCRW's *Old-Time Radio Show*:

"The hardest was Doc's trilling. Now anyone who's familiar with the books knows that Doc Savage has a kind of an unconscious habit of trilling whenever he finds something totally inexplicable, or is curious. And we really didn't know what to do with that because it is described in a number of different ways throughout the books. Some say it sounds like a jungle bird. Some of the books describe it as being almost a high-pitched whine. In some of the books it's a ventriloquial sound. And I must hand it to Danny Chodos for making a valiant effort to actually do it live. But we realized that it was just something supernatural that couldn't be done by anything vocal. So we finally went for a track out of one of our libraries. It probably is the one thing we are not the happiest about in the whole series. We didn't get exactly what we wanted. We got a number of things we thought were really good, but they were so disruptive of the flow of the show that we just didn't put them in."

Normally, radio actors are given roles and allowed to interpret them within the parameters of their character. Not with Doc Savage and his mighty crew.

"In this case of course we had a lead character whose voice is better described than in any other book or medium," Rittner observed. "There must be three paragraphs in every book of what Doc sounds like. And we knew from the very beginning that we weren't going to please everybody. In fact, we might not please anybody. Given that everybody is going to have their own conception of what Doc sounds like, I merely told Danny that I wanted a very powerful, mature, commanding voice. He has a very expressive voice to begin with, and he came through fine. All the other characters have basically pre-set voices also, so we cast to fit those. But in terms of the other characters like Leaking, Santini, Kel Avery and Pat even to some extent, I just put people in the roles that I knew had the kind of voice that I saw for it originally. Then I just let them do what they wanted to."

Michael McConnohie played Santini in 'Fear Key. "I had a lot of trouble with him," he confessed. "Italian is not easy to do. And contrasting what I could come up with in terms of the character vocally, with how he was described in the script, was really bizarre. It was hard to give him the strength that was apparent in the words. And still get a sense of this foppish sort of dandy. In that regard, I had to pretty much forget what the visual is supposed to be, and go with the presence and the strength I could give him otherwise. Not too maniacal—although he got a little crazy there toward the end."

McConnohie looked to *Saturday Night Live* for outside inspiration. "Father Guido Sarducci," he deadpanned. "Finest guy, Don Novello. The most lasting Italian dialect of our age. Everybody knows Father Guido. Actually, it was not a bad accent either. Dan Chodos, who plays Doc Savage, is essentially a dialectician, and a vocal coach by profession. He gave me pointers as well. Overall, I'm more proud of Santini than a lot of other things I've done because it was an effort for me. It was. And I was rather pleased with how it came out. I exceeded my own expectations, which is pretty neat."

The same might be said for the man who made it all happen.

"It's been a fun project, particularly for me because I'm a great fan of all aspects of this show," Roger Rittner admitted. "I like pulp novels. I like Doc Savage in particular. Our entire organization is supportive of radio drama, not only preserving what's gone on before, but creating new drama."

Although one was discussed, a second series of *The Adventures of Doc Savage* never materialized. Had the show gone forward, it would have adapted *Resurrection Day* (with Pat Savage written into the story as Dent originally planned to do) and Will Murray's *Python Isle,* which had not yet been published.

*Will Murray scripted "The Thousand-Headed Man" serial for National Public Radio, and seven Doc Savage novels published by Bantam Books.* •

*Doc Savage* sound effects artists Jerry Williams and Davis Surtees

**Lester Dent** (1904-1959) could be called the father of the superhero. Writing under the house name "Kenneth Robeson," Dent was the principal writer of *Doc Savage,* producing more than 150 of the Man of Bronze's thrilling pulp adventures.

A lonely childhood as a rancher's son paved the way for his future success as a professional storyteller. "I had no playmates," Dent recalled. "I lived a completely distorted youth. My only playmate was my imagination, and that period of intense imaginative creation which kids generally get over at the age of five or six, I carried till I was twelve or thirteen. My imaginary voyages and accomplishments were extremely real."

Dent began his professional writing career while working as an Associated Press telegrapher in Tulsa, Oklahoma. Learning that one of his coworkers had sold a story to the pulps, Dent decided to try his hand at similarly lucrative moonlighting. He pounded out thirteen unsold stories during the slow night shift before making his first sale to Street & Smith's *Top-Notch* in 1929. The following year, he received a telegram from the Dell Publishing Company offering him moving expenses and a $500-a-month drawing account if he'd relocate to New York and write exclusively for the publishing house.

Dent soon left Dell to pursue a freelance career, and in 1932 won the contract to write the lead novels in Street & Smith's new *Doc Savage Magazine.* From 1933-1949, Dent produced Doc Savage thrillers while continuing his busy freelance writing career and eventually adding Airviews, an aerial photography business.

Dent was also a significant contributor to the legendary *Black Mask* during its golden age, for which he created Miami waterfront detective Oscar Sail. A real-life adventurer, world traveler and member of the Explorers Club, Dent wrote in a variety of genres for magazines ranging from pulps like *Argosy, Adventure* and *Ten Detective Aces* to prestigious slick magazines including *The Saturday Evening Post* and *Collier's.* His mystery novels include *Dead at the Take-off* and *Lady Afraid.* In the pioneering days of radio drama, Dent scripted *Scotland Yard* and the 1934 *Doc Savage* series. •